PRAISE FOR

An Arsonist's Guide to Writers' Homes in New England

"Wildly, unpredictably funny. . . . Although it is his fourth book, it feels like the bright debut of an ingeniously arch humorist, one whose hallmark is a calm approach to insanely improbable behavior. . . . The parodies here are priceless." —*The New York Times*

"Funny, profound. . . . Clarke's novel is an agile melding of faux-memoir and mystery. Spot-on timing gives it snap, and a rich sense of perversity . . . lends texture. It's a seductive book with a payoff on every page." —*People* magazine, Critic's Choice, four stars

"Clarke's novel sizzles. This straight-faced, postmodern comedy scorches all things literary, from those moldy author museums to the excruciating question-and-answer sessions that follow public readings. . . . They're all singed under Clarke's crisp wit." —*The Washington Post Book World*

"[An] absurd, if weirdly compelling faux 'memoir,' which takes aim at the danger of stories—at least false ones. . . . Gets at some unexpectedly poignant emotional truths." —*USA Today*

"*An Arsonist's Guide* contains sentences and images that could stand beside the works of the former owners of the literary residences put to flame." —*The New York Times Book Review*

"Absurdly hilarious. . . . Searingly funny." —*Entertainment Weekly*

"Enormously funny. . . . A cautionary tale about the strength of stories to burn a path of destruction." —*The Chicago Sun-Times*

"Darkly comic. . . . Bittersweet and ultimately sorrowful, Clarke's book suggests that we're all subject to the whims of the stories we tell ourselves." —*Los Angeles Times*

"This is a sad, funny, absurd, and incredibly moving novel. Its comic mournfulness, its rigorous, break-neck narrative, delight. Bless Brock Clarke and his spookily human arsonist. They've given us a wonderful book about life, literature, and the anxieties of their influence."

—Sam Lipsyte, author of *Home Land*

"Clarke turns up the heat on New England's classic novelists—and their homes. . . . Moving and memorable." —*The Charlotte Observer*

"Clarke has the ability to crack us up with his clever insight into human nature and suburban angst, but there is also a depth to his characters that helps raise the story above straight satire." —MSNBC.com

"Every bit as quirky and engaging as its title. . . . Evokes John Irving, with a dollop of Tom Wolfe tossed in for good measure. . . . Pulisfer's disarming charm and witty insight carry the day."

—*St. Louis Post-Dispatch*

"While I was reading this dark, funny, tragic novel, I would look at the people around me and feel sorry for them because they weren't occupying the same world I was; they weren't living, as I was, inside the compelling, off-kilter atmosphere of Brock Clarke's pages. This is the best book I've read in a long time."

—Carolyn Parkhurst, author of *The Dogs of Babel*

"Both philosophical and deeply funny. . . . Resembles Richard Ford crossed with Borges: a thoughtful, playful exploration of everyday life, as well as a metafictional examination of the purpose stories serve in our lives." —*Time Out New York*

"Sam's disasters are good news for readers . . . particularly if they like their comic novels with a sharp edge, witty commentary and hilarious allusions." —*The Miami Herald*

"[A] wacky and wildly imaginative novel. . . . It's nearly impossible not to care about and laugh with Sam. He's a misunderstood outcast, a knight errant on a quest to clear his name. But in this hilarious and original novel he does much more: He appeals to the fool in everyone and comforts us in knowing that we're not alone." —*Chicago Tribune*

"Part mystery, part comedy, part insightful memoir, *Arsonist* defies the conventional formula in producing a wildly entertaining novel."

—*Daily Candy*

"Brock Clarke flames entire genres of fiction in this clever and often hilarious tale." —*Paste*

"[A] brilliant novel." —*People*, Style Watch issue

"Sam Pulsifer is now one of the great naïfs of American literature. . . . [This] rollicking, hilariously and subtly heartbreaking novel . . . is at the same time a wrenching examination of what happens when you pry up the floorboards, flake off the stucco, open up the books and see what's really going on between husband and wife, parents and children, friends and lovers." —*The San Diego Union-Tribune*

"An incisive satire that takes on everything from authors to reading groups and Harry Potter." —*Milwaukee Journal Sentinel*

"A witty, intensely clever piece of writing that scrutinizes our relationship with stories and storytelling. . . . Clarke composes with panache, packing his pages with offbeat humor, vibrant characters, and tender scenes." —*Utne Reader*

"Rousing. . . . The antic goings-on and over-the-top characters are so entertaining." —*Minneapolis Star Tribune*

"Brock Clarke is our generation's Richard Ford . . . [and] Sam Pulsifer is an Everyman suburban nomad, a literary misadventurer who is as insightful and doomed as he is heartbreakingly hilarious. . . . I love this book." —Heidi Julavits, author of *The Uses of Enchantment*

"A loopily shambolic narrative as captivating as its feckless firebug narrator. . . . The perfect end-of-summer book, funny and sharp and smart enough to ease the transition from beach to boardroom. Just don't leave it near a pack of matches." —*Village Voice*

"It's a blast—its story line rollicking and often absurd, its themes satisfyingly hefty." —*Time Out Chicago*

"Like TV analysts who deconstruct Tiger Woods' swing, it's not easy to do justice to writers like Brock Clarke. But I know just enough to recommend *An Arsonist's Guide to Writers' Homes in New England* to anyone, and especially to anyone who wants to read the best, newest manifestation of great American writing." —*Pittsburgh Post-Gazette*

"A multilayered, flame-filled adventure about literature, lies, love and life. . . . Sam is equal parts fall guy and tour guide in this bighearted and wily jolt to the American literary legacy." —*Publishers Weekly,* starred review

"A subversively compelling, multilayered novel about the profound impact of literature. . . . Rendered masterfully by Clarke, Sam's narrative tone is so engagingly guileless that the reader can't help but empathize with him, even as his life begins to fall apart within the causal connections of these fires. . . . A serious novel that is often very funny and will be a page-turning pleasure for anyone who loves literature." —*Kirkus Reviews,* starred review

AN
ARSONIST'S GUIDE
TO WRITERS' HOMES
IN NEW ENGLAND

An
Arsonist's Guide
to Writers' Homes
in New England

A NOVEL BY

BROCK CLARKE

Algonquin Books of Chapel Hill | 2008

Published by
Algonquin Books of Chapel Hill
Post Office Box 2225
Chapel Hill, North Carolina 27515-2225

a division of
Workman Publishing
225 Varick Street
New York, New York 10014

Although this novel is written as if it were a memoir, none of the events
depicted in it are remotely true. The home of the poet Emily Dickinson still stands elegantly in
place on a lovely street in Amherst, Massachusetts. Also still standing are the homes of Edith
Wharton, Mark Twain, Robert Frost, and assorted other
literary greats mentioned herein. As for the characters and their actions, they
either are products of the author's imagination or are used fictitiously.

LIBRARY OF CONGRESS
CATALOGING-IN-PUBLICATION DATA
Clarke, Brock.
An arsonist's guide to writers' homes in New England:
a novel / by Brock Clarke. — 1st ed.
p. cm.
ISBN-13: 978-1-56512-551-3 (HC)
1. Dickinson, Emily, 1830 – 1886 — Homes and haunts — Massa-
chusetts — Amherst — Fiction.   2. New England — Fiction.   I.
Title.
PS3603.L37A89 2007
813'.6 — dc22   2006100732

ISBN-13: 978-1-56512-614-5 (PB)

10 9 8 7 6 5 4 3

At the end of an hour we saw a far-away town sleeping in a valley by a winding river; and beyond it on a hill, a vast gray fortress, with towers and turrets, the first I had ever seen out of a picture.

"Bridgeport?" said I, pointing.

"Camelot," said he.

— Mark Twain, *A Connecticut Yankee in King Arthur's Court*

The memoirs written by the members of the Autobiographical Association . . . already had a number of factors in common. One of them was nostalgia, another was paranoia, a third was a transparent craving on the part of the authors to appear likeable. I think they probably lived out their lives on the principle that what they were, and did, and wanted, should above all look pretty. Typing out and making sense out of these compositions was an agony to my spirit until I hit on the method of making them expertly worse; and everyone concerned was delighted with the result.

— Muriel Spark, *Loitering with Intent*

AN
ARSONIST'S GUIDE TO
WRITERS' HOMES IN
NEW ENGLAND

Part One

1

I, Sam Pulsifer, am the man who accidentally burned down the Emily Dickinson House in Amherst, Massachusetts, and who in the process killed two people, for which I spent ten years in prison and, as letters from scholars of American literature tell me, for which I will continue to pay a high price long into the not-so-sweet hereafter. This story is locally well known, and so I won't go into it here. It's probably enough to say that in the Massachusetts Mt. Rushmore of big, gruesome tragedy, there are the Kennedys, and Lizzie Borden and her ax, and the burning witches at Salem, and then there's me.

So anyway, I served my time, and since the sentencing judge took mercy on me, I served my time at the minimum-security prison up at Holyoke. At Holyoke there were bond analysts and lawyers and day traders and city managers and school administrators, all of them caught with their hands in the till and nothing at all like me, an eighteen-year-old accidental arsonist and murderer with blood and soot on his hands and a heavy heart and plenty to learn and no high school diploma. I flung in and tried. I took a biweekly self-improvement seminar called the College of Me, in which I learned the life-changing virtues of patience, hard work, and positive attitude, and in which I earned my GED. I also hung around this group of high-stepping bond analysts from Boston who were in the clink for insider trading. While they were inside, the bond analysts had set out to write their fond, freewheeling memoirs about their high crimes and misdemeanors and all the cashish — that's the way they talked — they had made while screwing old people out of their retirement funds and kids out of their college savings. These guys seemed to know everything, the whole vocabulary of worldly gain and progress, so I paid extra attention during their memoir-brainstorming sessions, listened closely to their debates over how much the reading public did or did not need to know about their tortured childhoods in order to understand why they needed to make so much money in the manner in which they made it. I took notes as they divided the world between those who had stuff taken from them and those who took, those who did bad things in a good way — gracefully, effortlessly — and those bumblers who bumbled their way through life.

"Bumblers," I said.

"Yes," they said, or one of them did. "Those who bumble."

"Give me an example," I said, and they stared at me with those blue-steel stares they were born with and didn't need to learn at Choate or Andover, and they stared those stares until I realized that I was an ex-ample, and so this is what I learned from them: that I was a bumbler, I resigned myself to the fact and had no illusions about striving to be something else — a bond analyst or a memoirist, for instance — and just got on with it. Life, that is.

I learned something from everyone, is the point, even while I was fending off the requisite cell-block buggerer, a gentle but crooked cor-porate accountant at Arthur Andersen who was just finding his true sexual self and who told me in a cracked, aching voice that he wanted me — wanted me, that is, until I told him I was a virgin, which I was, and which, for some reason, made him not want me anymore, which meant that people did not want to sleep with twenty-eight-year-old male virgins, which I thought was useful to know.

Finally, I learned to play basketball from this black guy named Terrell, which was one of the big joys of my life in prison and which ended badly. Terrell, who had written checks to himself when he was the Worcester city treasurer, was in prison for the last three of my ten years, and whenever he would beat me in one-on-one (this wasn't often, even when I was first learning to play, because although he was very strong, Terrell was also shorter than I was and about as sleek as a fire hydrant; plus, he was twice my age and his knees were completely shot and would crack like dry wood when he ran) — whenever he would beat me, Terrell would yell out, "I'm a grown-ass man." That sounded good, and so after our last game, which I won easily, I also yelled out, "I'm a grown-ass man." Terrell thought I was mocking him, so he started hitting me around the head, and since I get passive in the face of true anger, I just stood there and took Terrell's abuse and didn't try to defend myself. As the guards dragged him to solitary, he promised that he would beat on me a little more once he got out, which he shouldn't have, because, of course, the guards then gave him more solitary than they might have otherwise. By the time Terrell got out, I'd already been released from prison and was home, living with my parents.

That didn't work out too well, living with my parents. For one, my burning down the Emily Dickinson House caused them some real heartbreak, because my mother was a high school English teacher, my father an editor for the university press in town, and beautiful words really mattered to them; they didn't care anything for movies or TV, but you could always count on a good poem to make them cry or sigh meaningfully. For another, their neighbors in Amherst weren't exactly happy that I'd burned down the town's most famous house and killed two of its citizens in the bargain, so they took it out on my parents. People never had trouble finding our old, creaking house on Chicopee Street: it was always the one with the driveway that had been spray-painted MURDERER! (which I understand) or FASCIST! (which I don't), or with some quote from Dickinson herself that seemed to promise vengeance, but you could never tell exactly what the vengeance might be, because there were a lot of words and the spray-painter always got sloppy and illegible from fatigue or maybe overemotion. It only got worse when I went home after prison. There was some picketing by the local arts council and some unwelcome, unflattering news coverage, and neighborhood kids who cared nothing about Emily Dickinson or her house started egging the place and draping our noble birches with toilet paper, and for a while there it was like Halloween every day. Then things really got serious and someone slashed every tire on my parents' Volvo, and once, in a fit of anger or grief, someone hurled a Birkenstock through one of our bay windows. It was a man's right shoe, size twelve.

All of this happened within the first month of my return home. At the end of the month, my parents suggested I move out. I remember it was August, because the three of us were sitting on our front porch and the neighbors' flags were out, caught between the Fourth of July and Labor Day and in full flutter, and the light was spectral through the maple and birch leaves and it was all very pretty. You can imagine how much my parents' request that I leave home wounded me, even though the College of Me said that life after prison wouldn't be easy and that I shouldn't fool myself into thinking otherwise.

"But where should I go?" I asked them.

"You could go anywhere," my mother said. Back then I thought she was the harder parent of the two and had had high hopes for me, so the disappointment weighed on her more heavily. I remember that my mother was a dry well at my trial when the jury brought back the verdict, although my father had wept loudly and wetly, and he was starting to cry now, too. I hated to see them like this: one cold, the other weepy. There was a time when I was six and they taught me to skate on a pond at the Amherst public golf course. The ice was so thick and clean and glimmery that the fish and errant golf balls were happy to be frozen in it. The sun was streaking the falling snow, making it less cold. When I finally made it around the perimeter of the pond without falling, my mother and father gave me a long ovation; they were a united front of tickled, proud parenthood. Those times were gone: gone, gone, forever gone.

"Maybe you could go to college, Sam," my father said after he'd gotten ahold of himself.

"That's a good idea," my mother said. "We'd be happy to pay for it."

"OK," I said, because I was looking at them closely, really scrutinizing them for the first time since I'd been home from prison, and I could see what I'd done to them. Before I burned down the Emily Dickinson House, they seemed to be normal, healthy, somewhat happy Americans who took vacations and gardened and who'd weathered a rough patch or two (when I was a boy, my father left us for three years, and after he left us, my mother started telling me tall tales about the Emily Dickinson House, and all of this is part of the larger story I will get to and couldn't avoid even if I wanted). Now they looked like skeletons dressed in corduroy and loafers. Their eyes were sunken and wanting to permanently retreat all the way back into their skulls. A few minutes earlier, I'd been telling them about my virginity and the lecherous Arthur Andersen accountant. My parents, as far as I knew back then, were both modest Yankees who didn't like to hear about anyone's private business, but the College of Me insisted that it was healthy and necessary to tell the people we love everything. Now I was regretting it. Why do we hurt our parents the way we do? There's no way to make sense of it except as practice for then hurting our children the way we do.

"OK," I said again. "I'll go to college." And then: "I love you both."

"Oh, us too," my father said, and then started weeping again.

"We certainly do," my mother said. And then to my father: "Bradley, quit crying."

Later that night, after my mother had gone to sleep, my father came into my room without knocking, stood over my bed, then leaned down — either to say something to me or to see if I was asleep. I wasn't asleep: I was thinking hopeful thoughts about my future, of how I would go to college and make a clean, honest, painless life for myself, and how proud my parents would be once I'd made it. My father, bent over at the waist the way he was, looked like a crane there to either lift me up with its hook or wreck me with its heavy ball.

"Come downstairs," my father whispered, his face close to mine in the darkness. "I want to show you something."

I got out of bed, followed him downstairs. My father walked into his study, which was — like most of the rooms in the house — lined floor to ceiling with overflowing bookshelves. He sat in a chair, opened the end table drawer next to him, pulled out a Converse shoe box, the sort of box in which you kept your old photos or Christmas cards, and handed it to me. I took the lid off the box and saw that there were envelopes inside, envelopes slit open with a letter opener. The envelopes were addressed to me, all of them. The letters were still inside the envelopes, so I took them out and read them.

There were at least a hundred letters. Some of them, as I mentioned, were from scholars of American literature, damning me to hell, et cetera. There is something underwhelming about scholarly hate mail — the sad literary allusions, the refusal to use contractions — and so I didn't pay much attention to those letters at all. I'd also received several letters from your ordinary arson enthusiasts, which were minor variations on the "Burn, baby, burn" theme. These particular letters didn't affect me much, either. The fact that the world was full of kooks wasn't any bigger news than the fact that the world was full of bores.

But there were other letters. They were from all over New England and beyond: from Portland, Bristol, Boston, Burlington, Derry, Chicopee, Hartford, Providence, Pittsfield — from towns and cities in New York and Pennsylvania, too. They were all from people who lived near the homes of writers and who wanted me to burn those houses down. A man in New London, Connecticut, wanted me to burn Eugene O'Neill's home because of what an awful drunk O'Neill was and what a bad example he set for the schoolchildren visiting his home, who needed, after all, more positive role models in the here and now. A woman in Lenox, Massachusetts, wanted me to torch Edith Wharton's house because visitors to Wharton's house parked in front of the woman's mailbox and because Wharton was always, in her opinion, something of a whiner and a phony. A dairy farmer in Cooperstown, New York, wanted me to pour gasoline down the chimney of the James Fenimore Cooper House because the dairy farmer couldn't stand the thought of someone being from such a rich family when his family was so awfully poor. "I've had it harder than Cooper ever did," the man wrote. "That family's got money up to *here* and they charge ten dollars' admission to their home and people *pay* it. Won't you please burn that son-of-a-bitching house right to the ground for us? We'll pay, too; I'll sell some of our herd if I have to. I look forward to your response."

There were more letters, and they all wanted the same thing. All of them wanted me to burn down the houses of a variety of dead writers — Mark Twain, Louisa May Alcott, Robert Lowell, Nathaniel Hawthorne. Some of the correspondents wanted me to burn down the homes of writers I'd never even heard of. All of the letter writers were willing to wait for me to get out of prison. And all of them were willing to pay me.

"Wow," I said to my father when I was done reading. He hadn't said anything in a while. It was interesting: when my mother was around, my father always appeared weak minded and softhearted — a slight, unnecessary, and mostly foolish human being. But now, in that room, with those letters, he seemed to me wise — silent and massive like a Buddha in wire-rimmed glasses. I felt the enormity of the situation, in my throat and face and elsewhere. "Why didn't you tell me about these letters while I was in prison?"

He looked at me but didn't say anything. This was a test of sorts, because this, of course, is what the wise do: they test the unwise to make them less so.

"You wanted to protect me," I said, and he nodded. It heartened me to know I could give him the right answer, and so I persisted. "You wanted to protect me from these people who thought I was an arsonist."

My father couldn't leave this one alone. He went into a violent struggle with his better judgment, wrestling with his mouth as he started and stopped himself from speaking a dozen times. It was like watching Atlas gear up to hoist that big boulder we now live on. Finally my father got it out and said sadly, so sadly, "Sam, you *are* an arsonist."

Oh, how that hurt! But it was true, and I needed to hear it, needed my father to tell it to me, just as we all need our fathers to tell us the truth, as someday I'll tell it to my children, too. And someday my children will do to me what I did to my father: they will deny it, the truth.

"You're wrong," I said. "I'm a college student." I put the top back on the box of letters, handed it back to him, and left before he could say anything else. When I got back in bed, I made myself promise never to think of the letters again. *Forget about them,* I commanded myself. I thought I could do it, too. After all, wasn't this what college was all about? Emptying your mind of the things you didn't want to remember and filling your mind up with new things before the old, unwanted things could find their way back in?

I left for college two weeks later; it was ten years before I saw my parents again, ten years before I reread those letters, ten years before I met some of the people who'd written the letters, ten years before I found out things about my parents that I'd never suspected and never wanted to know, ten years before I went back to prison, ten years before any of what happened, happened.

But I'm getting ahead of myself. College: Since it was late in the application season, I went to the only school that accepted me — Our Lady of the Lake in Springfield, about twenty miles south of Amherst. It was a Catholic college that had just started accepting men because apparently there weren't enough Catholic women left in the Western world who wanted to pay a lot of money to get an education with no men around except for Jesus and his priests, and even the priests who supposedly ran it didn't want to teach there. A few nuns with nothing else to do other than deliver communion at the early, unpopular masses taught a couple of classes — World Religions 101 and 102 — and the rest were taught by normal, irreligious teachers who couldn't get jobs anywhere else.

My first major was English, because I knew what a disappointment and sorrow I'd been to my parents and I wanted them to be proud of me despite everything that had happened. Besides, my mother had read to me all the time when I was young, and then when I was older she'd made me read all the important books and give detailed reports about why the books were so awfully important, and so I figured, at least, that I had the proper training and background to succeed. Plus, there were the bond analysts, with their memoirs and their stories; they didn't get tired of talking about themselves one bit. *Whom else would we talk about?* seemed to be their attitude, and maybe they were onto something. Maybe, I thought, by reading these other stories, I could understand something about my own.

It didn't work out. These things never do. You can't ever repeat the past, and the books I once believed to be so important and wise now seemed ordinary in the extreme, and I couldn't concentrate on them. Instead of thinking about how great Gatsby was or wasn't, I mezzed out on the grilled cheese bits that were lodged in Dr. Melton's goatee. And then there was the time when we were reading Dickinson's poetry and the teacher said that she would have taken the class to the Dickinson House for a tour except that it had been burned down years before, and as she tried to remember the name of the arsonist, I realized that I didn't want to tell my story — I knew it all too well. So in order to interrupt and escape the uncomfortable line of inquiry and the recrimination that was sure to follow, I faked a coughing fit and ran to the bathroom and didn't come back to that class for the rest of the semester, and the only reason I got a D and not an F in that class was the same reason I got a D and not an F in my other English classes: the school didn't want anyone to flunk out, because they needed everybody's full tuition. The school really was in horrible shape. There were piles of fallen plaster in the hallways. The drop ceilings were buckling. Even the crucifixes on the classroom walls were in need of repair.

So the bad grades were one reason I quit English, but there was another reason, a bigger reason: I couldn't shake the feeling that there was something else I should be doing, something I hadn't tried or considered, something new and better. There I'd be, sitting in Medieval Literature, supposedly learning to speak the Old English that Beowulf and Grendel spoke, and all I could hear was this voice in my head saying, *There must be something else.* Asking, *What else? What else?* This was a surprise, since I wasn't much of a striver and had never asked that question — *What else?* — out loud in my life. But there was the voice in my head, asking it for me.

Briefly: I quit English and literature and the people who wrote it — for good, I thought — and became a packaging-science major. This was a good move for three reasons. One, packaging scientists were less likely to know that I'd burned down the Emily Dickinson House, or even know who Emily Dickinson was, or even care. Two, I had a knack for remembering what kind of packing material was best for which fragile object, and I immediately understood why it was better that personal-size bags of chips be torn vertically, while family-size bags be torn horizontally, and where the tabs should be located to allow each sort of tearing. I never got anything lower than a B+ in packaging science and managed to do four years of coursework in two years, and immediately after college I got the job for which I was trained, in product development and testing at Pioneer Packaging in Agawam, just outside Springfield.

So those were two good things about switching over to packaging science. The third thing was that I met my wife.

Her name was (and is) Anne Marie, and I met her in our senior seminar in packaging science, the class where you finally stake your claim and choose your path, et cetera. Anne Marie was pretty, extraordinarily good looking, really, and tall, with long, long legs that looked about ready to run away from her torso, and lovely, curly black hair always fastened and arranged and piled high on the top of her head, and a smart smile that was so beautiful you didn't mind the way it made you feel so stupid. What else? In moments that required contemplation, Anne Marie smoked the kind of very thin, sleek cigarettes that, in my experience as a watcher of women, only very thin, sleek women are inclined to smoke. All in all, she looked like an Italian goddess, which was about right, since her last name was Mirabelli and her ancestors were from Bologna.

About my looks: I was tall and skinny as a kid, but with a big head. I looked like a vertical matchstick. I lifted weights in prison to some effect, including pulling muscles I didn't know I had, and this was another thing I bumbled. My face is the most prominent thing about me: it's red, and sometimes it looks healthy and windburned and full of what you might call life, and sometimes it just looks enflamed. If I were embarrassed, on a dark night you could find your way by the glow of my face. But the College of Me warned against being too hard on oneself, and so it should be said that I'm probably, everything accounted for, ordinary-handsome. My teeth are only slightly crooked, and most of them are white. I have almost all my hair, which is curly and brown. My chest was concave when I was a child, but if you look closely, this is true of most children, and the weight lifting I did in prison helped with that, and while I don't actually have a barrel chest, I might have a half barrel. My legs aren't nearly as scrawny as they used to be, and have muscles and definition now. My nose would be Roman if my head were smaller. Even though I'm close to legally blind, I don't have to obscure my piercing blue eyes with glasses, because I wear contact lenses. They're the sort of eyes that can see right into your soul, if I'm wearing the lenses. But still, I wasn't what you'd call good looking. Plus, I was a virgin, don't forget that, and all of this is why I'd never spoken to Anne Marie, even though we'd been in five classes together: Anne Marie was clearly much too beautiful for me to speak to.

"That's silly," she said when I told her this after we were married. "I wasn't too beautiful for you to speak to. I never thought so, not ever."

"If you didn't think you were too good looking," I asked her, "then why didn't *you* come up and talk to *me* in the first place?"

"That's a good question," she said, and I never did get the answer.

But back to our senior seminar, where we were to choose our paths, and Anne Marie's path was lids — those plastic travel lids you put on your coffee and soda cups. This was in the spring of our senior year, and Anne Marie had the misfortune of giving her presentation right after James Nagali, the only other male student at Our Lady of the Lake, who gave a masterly speech on new soap-dispensing technologies. James was from Ivory Coast, and immediately after graduation he went to work for Ivory soap, but I don't think there's any connection.

Our teacher for the seminar was Professor Eisner, a mostly bald man who looked like a walking advertisement for forehead and who, it was rumored, had screwed up a supposedly revolutionary sanitary napkin packaging design that had cost Procter and Gamble a million dollars or two — which was why, the rumor went, he had ended up teaching us. Professor Eisner gushed over James's presentation, but not over Anne Marie's. He pointed out certain structural flaws in her lid designs; he asked her rhetorically if she knew what it felt like to have hot coffee pour not into your mouth but onto your chin and down your neck; he asked Anne Marie if she had learned nothing in her four years as an Our Lady of the Lake packaging-science major; he asked her if she had any contingency plans for when the offers from all the prestigious firms didn't come rolling in. "Because roll in they certainly will not," he said.

It's true that Anne Marie wasn't exactly a born packaging scientist, and it's also true that her lids, had they ever been manufactured (they weren't), would have burned a few faces and spawned a few lawsuits. But still, I didn't like the way Eisner was talking to her. I looked over at Anne Marie, and while she didn't look a bit upset, not anywhere near tears — she was a tough one, and still is — Anne Marie *was* playing with her gold crucifix necklace in an agitated manner, and I felt I had to say something in her defense.

"Hey, Professor Eisner," I said. "Ease up a little. Be nice." It's true I didn't exactly scream this at the top of my lungs, and it's also possible that Professor Eisner might not have heard me at all, because he moved right on to the next presentation, but the important thing was that Anne Marie heard.

"Thank you," Anne Marie said to me after class.

"For what?" I asked, although I knew, because, of course, I'd said what I'd said so she'd thank me, because there's not a pure motive in me or in anyone else, I don't think.

"For standing up for me."

"You're welcome," I said. "Would you like to have dinner?"

"With you?" she asked.

This was just the way she talked — bluntly and always in pursuit of the simple truth — and it didn't suggest anything negative about her true feelings for me. As proof, we did have dinner, at this German place in Springfield called the Student Prince. She was the rare thin Italian girl who liked German food; you couldn't talk her out of the Munich sausage platter, and this was just one of the reasons I fell in love with her. And then a month later we slept together, in my apartment, which happened to be directly above the Student Prince. There must be something of my modest parents in me, because I won't say anything about the sex except that I enjoyed it. But I will say that I missed my virginity, maybe because I'd had it for so long, and right afterward — my face so hot and red it felt like something nuclear — I said to Anne Marie, "I was a virgin."

"Oh, sweetie," she said, "I wasn't." She put her hand on my blazing cheek, and you could see the sweet sadness in her eyes, the pity for the thirty-year-old virgin I'd just been. I'd never seen a person's heart so over-large and weak with real emotion, and so I asked, "Will you marry me?"

"Yes," Anne Marie said. There may have been pity behind her saying yes, but there was love, too: in my experience, you can't expect love to be unaffected by pity, nor would you want it to be.

Moving quickly now: We graduated. A few months later we were married, with the wedding at St. Mary's, the reception at the Red Rose in the South End. Anne Marie's family paid for it and was in attendance (more on them eventually), but my parents were not, mostly because I didn't tell them about it. When Anne Marie asked, "Why aren't you inviting your parents to our wedding?" I told her, "Because they died."

"How?" she wanted to know. "When?"

"Their house burned down," I said, "and they died in the fire," which just goes to show that every human being has a limited number of ideas, and which, as you'll see, ended up being pretty close to the truth. Anyway, my answer seemed to satisfy Anne Marie. But the truth was more complicated. The truth was, I could hear that voice in my head asking *What else? What else?* and I couldn't be sure if it was my voice or my parents'.

Anne Marie and I took our honeymoon in Quebec City, and since it was December and cold, we skated, which reminded me of my parents' applauding my skating on the golf course pond, so many years ago, and of how nice that was. It should also have reminded me of how badly my parents and I ended up, but I was me, and Anne Marie was Anne Marie, and we weren't my parents, and this wasn't any pond but the mighty Saint-Laurent (St. Lawrence) River, which was frozen over for the first time in who knows how long and everyone was speaking French and things were different enough to make me think that history does not necessarily repeat itself and that a man's character and not his gene pool is his fate. We talked it over that night in our room at the Château Frontenac and Anne Marie was game, and so we decided to make a baby.

We made one; it was a girl. We named her Katherine, after no one in particular. By the time she was born, I was already turning heads at Pioneer Packaging, helping to make antifreeze containers that were more translucent than previously thought possible. Katherine was a good baby: she cried, but only to let you know she hadn't stopped breathing, and it never bothered us much, and it didn't bother the people downstairs at the Student Prince, either. They would often bring up plates of cold schnitzel for her to gum when she was teething. During our first Christmas we strung blinking lights around our windows, and on Christmas Eve, Mr. and Mrs. Goerman, who'd owned the Student Prince for fifty years, brought up platters of creamed whitefish and several bottles of Rhine whine and we toasted the birthday of the baby Jesus, and all in all, this might have been our happiest time.

Then, two years later, we had another child, a boy named Christian, after Anne Marie's father, and suddenly the apartment we loved got too small, and suddenly the smells from down in the restaurant became too strong and we started eating potato pancakes in our dreams. One day Anne Marie came up to me looking like a less happy, more tired version of the woman I'd married just three years earlier and Christian was shrieking in the background like a winged dinosaur fighting extinction, and she said, "We need a bigger place."

She was right: we did. But where? We liked Springfield just fine, but the Puerto Ricans had moved in and Anne Marie's parents and the other Italians had moved out, to West Springfield and Ludlow and so on, and while we didn't want to live where they lived, we didn't want to live in Springfield, either — not because of the Puerto Ricans who would be our neighbors, but because of what the Mirabellis would say about them when they came to visit. This was one of the things the College of Me preached — avoid heartache, even at the expense of principle — and it was one of the few things it got right.

So Springfield was out, but we had to go somewhere. One day Anne Marie said, "I hear Amherst is nice. What about Amherst?"

It should be said here that I hadn't told Anne Marie about my past, and right then I wanted to, badly: I wanted to tell Anne Marie everything — about the Emily Dickinson House and how I'd burned it, accidentally, and the people I'd killed — and by the way, it wasn't the first time I'd wanted to tell her such a thing. I should have told her right away, I know this now and I knew it then, but new love is so fragile and

I thought I would wait until it got stronger. But then time and more time went by, and now my original crime was compounded by the crime of not telling her about it for so many years and things were too complicated and I couldn't tell her the truth.

So I said yes. Amherst. Why not? We put the kids in the minivan and headed up to Amherst. On the drive up I convinced myself of things, crazy things. I told myself that we'd get to the town and find an old, lovely New England house in old, lovely New England Amherst, move in, then present my house, my wife, my kids, my job, myself, to my parents, who would have by this point begun to miss me. *I've changed,* I would say. And they would say, *Us, too. Welcome home.* Because the heart wants what the heart wants, and the heart was telling me, *Don't be ridiculous, they've forgiven you, all of them.* Saying, *It's time, it's time, it's time.*

It wasn't time. This was on a Friday. Amherst was exactly as I'd remembered it: the leafy, prosperous streets, which were filled with so many Volvo station wagons it was like mushrooms in a cave; the two-hundred-year-old houses with their genteelly overgrown lawns, their tiger lilies and blue mums and birch trees and historical markers; the white college boys with dreadlocks playing their complicated Frisbee games on the sweeping town green; the white clapboard Congregational churches and the granite Episcopal churches and the soaring spires of the college everywhere visible over the high tree line; the well-scrubbed college girls barely dressed in workout clothes; and the boat-shoed and loafered professors drinking their coffee on the sort of wrought iron outdoor patio furniture that looks too delicate to sit on even if you were as wafer thin as most of the college girls were. All of this was familiar to me, but it didn't make me feel happy, didn't make me feel at home. I felt like a cousin once removed, which meant, I guess, that you weren't really a cousin at all: you were estranged from blood relation in some permanent way, and my remove from Amherst was that I had burned down the most significant of its significant, beautiful, aged houses, had killed two of its loafered citizens. A cousin once removed was not a cousin; a criminal citizen was not a citizen.

This was a big disappointment, the biggest, because I'd taken up packaging science, and I'd forgotten my literature, forgotten that you can't go home again, and so I thought that Amherst — the town where I'd grown up, the town where both my parents had grown up, the town where both their families had lived for two hundred years — would still be my hometown. How could it not? Was I not the town's own humbled prodigal son? Did not every town need someone like me, someone — as the song says — who was lost but now was found? But from the driver's seat of our minivan, I had the definite feeling that Amherst would never be my town again, that the town itself wouldn't stand for it, that they didn't need a prodigal son, that a prodigal son was exactly what they *didn't* need. We drove past my old high school: there were bars on the windows where there hadn't been before I went to prison, armed uniformed guards out front where before there'd been old-lady hall monitors with whistles, and I imagined that the bars and the guards were there to protect the students from me and not some teenage crazy in a trench coat stuffed with homemade ordnance. I could hear the principal during assembly that morning: *We were not vigilant and he burned down the Emily Dickinson House and killed two people in the bargain. But we are ready for him now.* I imagined that after school the students and their parents, and for that matter the whole town, would — à la *Frankenstein* — take up their torches and pitchforks and drive me out of town and leave me — lurching, grunting, monstrous with my scarred and stitched body and the bolt through my head — wandering, lost in the strange, cruel world, never to be heard from again.

"What do you think?" Anne Marie asked me, her face happy and expectant, about the opposite of how mine surely looked.

"Pitchforks!" I said. "Torches! Monster!"

"What?" she asked. "What's that?"

"Nothing," I said, and I kept driving, in a kind of trance, so that Anne

Marie's cries of "Wait!" and "Where are you going?" and "We haven't
looked at any houses yet — hold on!" were something out of the faint,
distant past and I had trouble hearing them. Yes, I kept driving, right
past Chicopee Street, where my parents lived, and then out of town, and
for five more years I was pretty glad I had. Soon we were on Route 116
and out of Amherst proper, and this, too, was familiar — the small brick
ranch houses that housed the Asian grad students at the state university,
and the student laundromats and the family-owned greengrocers and
the tiny, poorly stocked nonchain video stores in which you couldn't
ever find the movies you wanted. But soon things began to change. First,
there came the river of superstores: the super garden-supply stores and
super toy stores and super children's clothing stores and super building-
supply stores and super furniture galleries and super supermarkets
and so on. The buildings that housed these superstores were as cheap
looking as they were big, just oversize tin pole barns with parking lots
so huge that the entire town of Amherst could have fit comfortably inside. Amherst didn't seem big enough to justify all these superstores
and their parking lots; it was like building a *sub* without first building
the *urb*.

But these stores were just an introduction to what had *really* changed:
what had really changed were the subdivisions beyond the stores, the
subdivisions where ten years before there had been only broadleaf tobacco and corn fields, subdivisions with signs at the gated entrances
that said MONACO ESTATES and STONEHAVEN, and with streets named
Princess Grace Way and Sheep Meadow Circle. I drove around these
subdivisions, looking for a FOR SALE sign and not finding one until we
turned into a subdivision named Camelot — so said the wooden sign
carved into the shape of a castle.

Camelot was beautiful. There were no trees anywhere — it was as
though Camelot had been nuked or had been the brainchild of the log-
ging industry maybe — and each house was exactly the same except that
some had powder blue vinyl siding and others had desert tan. There

were elaborate wooden playgrounds in the backyards and mini – satellite dishes on every roof, and each driveway was a smooth carpet of black-top and there wasn't a sidewalk crack to trip over because there were no sidewalks, and each house had a garage that was so oversized it could have been its own house. There was the constant, soothing hum of lawn maintenance coming from somewhere, everywhere, even though the grass seed in front of most houses hadn't matured yet and I couldn't spot a lawn mower anywhere, and the sprinkler systems were all acti-vated even though it was late September and too late for grass watering, the spray arcing and dancing in the streetlights, of which there looked to be about 150, all of them on even though it was the middle of the afternoon.

"Wow," I said.

"Wow what?" Anne Marie said. "Are you talking about *that*?" She pointed at a tan house that was exactly like the others except that there was that FOR SALE sign on the lawn. Anne Marie and I got out of the van; the kids were sitting in their seats, screaming about something, everything, but the windows were rolled up and their screaming noises were as soft and welcome as rain on the roof.

"What are you thinking?" Anne Marie said finally. There was a weary, sighing quality to her voice, which I took for simple human fatigue, but which might have been resignation. I wish I'd paid more attention to Anne Marie back then, but I didn't. Oh, why didn't I? Why don't we listen to the people we love? Is it because we have only so much listening in us, and so many very important things to tell ourselves?

"Sam, what are you thinking?" Anne Marie asked again, because I hadn't answered her, because I was still thinking about Camelot and the house.

"Hello, life," I said back.

"Are you crying?" she asked me.

"Yes," I said. I was crying, because I was so happy, because this was my new home, and because it was clean and perfect and I couldn't imagine anyone knowing me here, anyone wanting to know me. My neighbors, were they ever to introduce themselves, and upon hearing that I was an arsonist and a murderer, would start talking about the virtues of Bermuda grass as opposed to Kentucky blue. I could not be normal in Amherst, but I could be normal in Camelot. I felt so happy, so grateful. I wanted to thank somebody. If there were any neighbors visible, I would have thanked them. But there weren't any neighbors visible; they were all inside, minding their own business, and that was one of the things for which I was grateful.

"Thank you so much," I said to Anne Marie.

"I guess you're welcome," she said, without having to ask what I was thanking her for, because that's what our love was. We called the real estate agent and bought the house and said good-bye to the apartment over the Student Prince (it wouldn't be a permanent good-bye, although I didn't realize that at the time) and moved to Camelot, and for five years we lived there and I commuted my half-hour commute and the kids grew up a little and Anne Marie got a part-time supervisory job at the super housing-supply store, and for five years there was no story to tell and we were happy enough, as happy as anyone can expect to be. True, it took Anne Marie some time to find happiness: she cried the first year when she discovered that the fireplace was ornamental and always would be; she cried the second year when she found she could put her index finger through the surprisingly thin plaster walls without really trying so very hard and she did this repeatedly in her dismay, and the house probably still has the many finger holes to prove it; she cried the third year when our neighbors still didn't know her name and she didn't know theirs, either. This time she really cried and couldn't stop, and I had to send the kids to stay with Anne Marie's parents while she worked it out. But even Anne Marie seemed happy enough after a while, and if prison was my first not entirely unpleasant exile from the world, then this was my second, and not once was I recognized as the man who burned down the Emily Dickinson House, et cetera, and not once did

I hear that voice, the voice inside me that asked, *What else? What else?* Not once, that is, until the man whose parents I accidentally killed in the Emily Dickinson House fire appeared at my front door one day, and then the voice returned and then I moved back in with my parents and reread those letters, and then the bond analysts showed up and started giving me a God-and-country hard time, and then people (not me! not me!) started setting fire to writers' homes all over New England, and that's when all the trouble started.

2

First, there was the man, the son whose mother (she was one of the Emily Dickinson House tour guides) and father happened, unknown to me, to be sharing a private, after-hours moment on Emily Dickinson's bed when I accidentally burned the house down and killed them those many years before. He showed up in early November, on a Saturday, which was about right, since nothing ever happened in Camelot during the week. During the week, everyone worked and went to bed early and got up early and you couldn't clip your toenails on your front porch for fear of bothering someone with the noise.

Weekends were different, our chance to prove that we could pour gas out of a spout and into a hole and pull a cord and make noise and then cut some grass. I'd just finished cutting mine. There wasn't much to say about it. It was short, and I'd cut it with a mower, the kind of mower all my neighbors used: one of those self-powered, space-age things where you stood on a platform and steered with levers at the handles. The mower moved so fast that it seemed to hover and basically did all the work for you. But still, I managed to work up a sweat while riding it, which caused me to take off my shirt, which got me in some trouble with my neighbors, my male neighbors (no women mowed lawns in Camelot; in this we were like the Muslims), who all wore big, padded recording-studio-type headphones while they mowed, and also huge, floppy hats and safety goggles and heavy-duty gardening gloves and long-sleeved oxford shirts and paint-spattered khaki pants tucked into the top of work boots. Except for tiny swatches of upper cheek and neck, there was no skin visible on them at all. My barechestedness ran counter to some unwritten subdivision behavioral code and had earned me some hard, disgusted stares from my neighbors. Every Saturday I reminded myself to remain fully clothed, but once I started sweating I could never remember to keep my shirt on and in this way fell into my own little unintentional piece of rebellion. I was like the patriot who kept forgetting *not* to dump the king's tea into the harbor. This is not to say that because I sweated and took off my shirt and unintentionally rebelled, I was better than my neighbors. I wasn't. I can't remember any of their names, but they were all good people. I hope they're well.

I was sitting on my front porch, which was really just a concrete slab that we called a porch because we liked to sit on it. I'd just turned off my mower, the roar of it still in my ears, and so I didn't hear the son of my accidental victims drive up, park his Jeep on the street, then walk up the driveway, didn't know he was there at all until he was right in front of me. His name was Thomas, Thomas Coleman, although I didn't know this yet. I was looking down in thought when he came up to where I was sitting, and so I saw his feet before I saw the rest of him. He was wearing hiking boots, the waterproof kind.

"Are you Sam Pulsifer?" he said. At the sound of the voice, a stillborn lump caught in my throat, because I thought I knew who this voice and those feet belonged to. I was sure it was a reporter. I hadn't spoken to one in years, but I remembered the way they talked, always leading you away from your version of the truth and toward theirs; I remembered their tiny spiral-bound notebooks and the way they looked so eager to ask you their questions, to which they already knew the answers, and so disappointed in the way you answered them.

"Yes, I'm Sam," I said, then raised my eyes to look at the reporter and found that he wasn't one, which I could tell at first glance. For one thing, no visible notebook. For another, no pen or pencil. And unlike the reporters I remembered, now that he'd asked his question and I'd answered it, he didn't seem inclined to ask another one but instead just stood there and looked at me. I let him, and looked back, too. He was not so tall, but he was skinny, real skinny; I could tell this even under all his clothes. He was wearing lined jeans (I could see the red flannel peeking out from under the cuffs and over the hiking boots) and a flannel shirt over which he wore a corduroy shirt over which he wore a fleece vest, even though it was freakishly warm out for November, and if I'd known the guy better I would have told him that if he ate more he wouldn't have to wear so many clothes. I was a walking, shirtless advertisement for that truth. And then there was his face, which was gaunt, and pale, so pale, and pockmarked, too; if my face was the flaming sun, then his was the cratered moon.

"I'm Thomas Coleman," he said.

"OK, nice to meet you," I said, and stuck out my hand, which Thomas didn't take. His jaw started pumping a little bit, as if working up some saliva to spit on the hand I offered to him, and so I took it back.

"You don't recognize my name, do you?" he said, and he was right in that. There was nothing, no bells or whistles; right then my memory was a happy, empty, echoing place.

"Well, I do recognize the name Thomas," I said, trying to be polite. "But then again, it's a pretty common name." Which it was, and I meant this seriously, but he took it as sarcasm. I could tell by the way his jaw started working double time. He was an angry man, all right, and maybe that's why he was so skinny: chewing so hard on his anger that he didn't have the time or the energy or the appetite to chew on anything else.

"Thomas Coleman," he finally said. "My parents were Linda and David Coleman. You killed them in the Emily Dickinson House fire."

"Oh!" I said, since I didn't know what else to say, and then, because this suddenly seemed like a more formal occasion, I put my shirt on. Once I was fully clothed, and out of nervousness, I went into a flurry of greeting: I shook his hand — I went out and grabbed it this time, there was no stopping me — slapped his back, asked, "How are you? So good to see you. How've you been?" and so on. All of this may seem horribly inappropriate, but what *should* I have done? There is no etiquette book for this sort of thing; I was writing it as I stood there. Besides, Thomas didn't seem to think that I'd been so inappropriate — maybe after you've accidentally killed someone's parents, every other offense is minor by comparison. His face even seemed to get a little color when I asked him if he wanted a drink — beer, juice, I told Thomas he could have whatever he wanted — although it may have been the glow off my own face illuminating his pockmarks. I really was giving off some heat and light; I probably could have powered the whole subdivision if there'd been a blackout.

"Do you recognize my name now?" he asked. "Do you recognize my parents' names?"

"Sort of," I said, even though I didn't, not really, and even at the trial I tried hard not to know their names, as my future seemed a lot more likely a prospect if I forgot the details of my past. "I don't really remember the whole thing all that well," I told him, which as I've mentioned is a talent of mine and was true besides. Even now, with Thomas in front of me, the fire and the smoke and his parents' burning bodies were so far away they seemed like someone else's problem, which is awfully mean to say and in that way perfectly consistent with most true things.

"*Sort of?*" he repeated. A little more color crept into Thomas's face when he said this, and I could already see I was doing his health some good, and if this kept up I might even get him to eat something. "*Sort of?* Don't you feel even a little bit bad about killing my parents?"

"It was an accident," I said. Thomas drew himself up at this and made a face, and in his defense I could see how he didn't believe me: because if you said over and over again about the fire you'd set and the people you'd killed, "It was an accident," it sounded as though you were whining, and if it sounded as though you were whining, it also sounded as though it wasn't an accident, and then it didn't matter whether it really *was* an accident or not. If you said about something terrible you'd done,

"It was an accident," you sounded like a coward and a liar, both. I sympathized with Thomas completely. But still, the truth is the truth is the truth. "It was an accident," I said again, again.

"There's no such thing as an accident," Thomas said.

"Wow, it's funny you say that," I told him. Anne Marie had said the same thing many a time: in our life together I'd ruined more than one surprise party and leaned over backward and broken more than a few of our neighbors' cherished heirloom chairs and told far too many ethnic jokes in the company of someone of that same ethnicity, and after each of these unconscious, unpremeditated bumblings, Anne Marie accused me of doing it intentionally. "This wasn't an accident," she'd say. "You did it on purpose." And I always told her, "I didn't! I don't!" And she'd say, "There is no such thing as an accident." And I'd say, "There is, there is!" But maybe there wasn't. I could see what she was talking about, and Thomas, too.

"I miss my parents so much," Thomas said. "It's been twenty years since you killed them, and I still miss them so fucking much."

"Oh, I know you do," I told him. I was feeling empathy for him deep down in my gut, and his missing his parents made me miss mine, too, and in a way we were both orphans and in the same boat. "Hey, listen," I said, "are you sure you don't want a drink or something?" Because I was still thirsty from the lawn mowing, and besides, I was really starting to feel close to him and in his debt for doing what I'd done to his parents and his life, and would have gotten him anything he wanted.

"No," he said. And then: "Do you know what they did to me in school?"

"Wait a minute," I said. "Who? When did this happen? What school?" Because I need to know the specifics of a story if I'm going to care, I mean really care, about it. As a child I could never feel much for the three little pigs and their houses because I didn't know whether the houses — straw, brick, or otherwise — were in a town or a city or a village, or whether that municipality had a name, and without one I just couldn't bring myself to care.

"This was at Williston Country Day," Thomas said, "right after you killed my parents." He said this slowly, as if I were somewhat slow myself and so I would get it all down and understand, which I appreciated. "The other kids, students, friends even, they made fun of my parents."

"You're kidding me," I said. "That's awful, Thomas. Those were no friends."

"They were. They made fun of the way my parents died, you know, in bed." He stumbled over these last words and was obviously still in a lot of pain and haunted by it, the poor guy.

"For a long time," he went on, "I was ashamed of them, hated them because of what they were doing when you killed them."

"That's understandable."

"There was a girl in my class whose parents died in a car wreck," he said. "They were both decapitated. I was jealous of her. For a long time, I wished my parents had died like that."

"Totally understandable," I said.

"For a long time," he said, sucking in a big, wet breath, "I wanted to kill myself."

"Don't say that, Thomas, don't even think it," I said. Again, I would have done anything for the guy. If he'd brought out the razor blades to slit his wrists, I would have ripped my shirt into bandages; if he'd had pills and swallowed them, I would have pumped his stomach, even without the proper know-how or medical equipment. I wanted to save him just like I wanted to save myself, I suppose. In this way I was like the mirror who wanted to save the guy looking into it and thus save the mirror image, too. It was a complicated emotional response, all right, and I'm not sure I understood it myself, which was how I knew it was complicated.

"And when I didn't want to kill myself," Thomas said, looking at me from underneath his eyebrows, which were blond and thin, like his hair, "I wanted to kill you."

"Well," I said, because I didn't have a response to this except to say that I was glad he hadn't. Killed me, that is.

"Don't worry," he said, although he said this in a deep, dark tone of voice that belied his skinniness and suggested that maybe I *should* worry. "My shrink talked me out of killing you."

"You have a shrink?"

"I've had a bunch." Thomas said this as if he were weary of his sadness, as if grief were a Halloween costume he still had on after the holiday and wanted to take off but couldn't, and suddenly I had a very clear vision of his life, which I had helped make for him just as surely as I had helped make my own. I could see him going from shrink to shrink, and except for those shrinks and his grief and his awful past, he was all alone in the world. I doubted he had his own wife and kids waiting for him at home, and then I thought of Anne Marie and the kids, out there on their normal Saturday errands and then picking apples at a self-pick apple orchard, or petting domesticated wild animals at a petting zoo, or being read to at some library's reading hour, and it occurred to me that the world didn't need to be so big for just the four of us. I missed them badly and would have gotten in my minivan — we had two of them — and joined them at the petting zoo, for instance, except the minivan was low on gas and I didn't know where the petting zoo was.

"Anyway," Thomas said, shaking his head as if just waking up and trying to clear his head of a dream, "that's why I'm here. My shrink said I should find you and ask you to apologize. For killing my parents."

"Oh, I do, I do apologize," I said. "I'm so sorry." And I really was sorry and at the same time so happy that there was something I could do for Thomas after all these years. It is a rare thing, to be allowed to apologize for something so horrible and final. It was like Abel coming back from the dead and giving his brother Cain the chance to apologize for killing him. "Oh, I'm so sorry for killing your parents," I said, and I was so full of penitence that I got down on my knees in a begging position. "I truly am sorry — it was an awful thing and changed too many lives and I wish it had never happened."

Thomas had his head down as I gave him my apology. After I was done, he kept it down as if waiting for more or contemplating what he had already been given. Finally he raised his head and gave me a look that was grim and I knew meant trouble. "So that was your apology?" he asked. "That's it?"

"Yes," I said, and then I said, "Sorry," for good measure.

"That was an awful apology," Thomas said. His eyes looked about ready to pop out of his head and he clenched his fists: he was really steaming, there was no doubt about it. Thomas looked exactly like those people you see on TV, those people whose loved ones have been killed and who then get to speak to their killers in court, and who say the things to the killers that they think they need and want to say in order to get on with the rest of their lives and achieve some piece of mind, et cetera, only to find out that the words don't mean anything and aren't even theirs, really, and so end up feeling more desperate and grief stricken and angry after they've spoken than they had before. Thomas looked an awful lot like that. "You're not sorry at all," he said.

"I am, I am," I said, and I was but didn't know what else I could do to convince him, because that's the trouble with being sorry: it's much easier to convince people you really aren't than you really are.

"You dick," he said.

"Hey, now," I said. "No need for that."

"You fucking dick," Thomas said. He moved forward a little, and for a second I thought he was going to jump me, but he didn't, maybe because he saw or smelled the dried sweat from my lawn mowing, or maybe because I was bigger than he was and had about fifty pounds on him. Thomas didn't know that he probably *could* have roughed me up, and without getting even a little bit dirty: I could feel the old passivity coming on, could hear my heart beating, *Hit me, hit me, I deserve it and won't fight back, so hit me.* But Thomas couldn't hear my heart, which is just one of the reasons I am happy to have one. Instead he took a step

back, and his face took a step back, too, and began to look contemplative
but still furious.

"I wonder how many of your neighbors know that you're a murderer
and an arsonist," he said. "I wonder if your friends know. Your co-
workers."

"Well . . . ," I said.

"I bet you haven't even told your family," he said, and when he said
this, the world suddenly became blurry and squiggly lined as though I
were seeing it through extreme heat, and now I couldn't recognize it, the
world, and be sure that it was still mine.

"I know you're not sorry about killing my parents," Thomas said.
"But you will be."

And then he left: he turned, walked down my driveway, got into the
black Jeep parked at the curb, and drove away. After he'd left, my heart
slowed down a bit and my head cleared and I could hear the low roar
of my neighbors' mowers. I knew that no one had seen Thomas, or if
they had, the neighbors wouldn't have thought anything strange about
his visit or even paid attention to it. The week before, my across-the-
cul-de-sac neighbor's estranged wife started banging on his door at
three in the morning, screaming and threatening to cut off his vital
parts with her grandfather's Civil War saber, and he called the police
on her and all in all they made a racket, but it was a distant, vague-
sounding racket and we just thought someone had left their TV on too
loud, until we read about it in the paper the next day. Our unspoken
motto in Camelot was "Live and let live," as long as you lived with your
shirt on. Now that Thomas was gone it looked and sounded like a normal Saturday in Camelot. It was as though none of what had happened,
had happened.

But it had. The past comes back once and then it keeps coming back
and coming back, not just one part of the past but all of it, the forgotten
crowd of your life breaks out of the gallery and comes rushing at you,

and there is no sense in hiding from the crowd, it will find you; it's your crowd, you're the only one it's looking for.

Anne Marie and the kids wouldn't be back until three o'clock. It was two now. That would give me enough time to take a long walk and try to work up the nerve to tell my family the truth about my past. I knew that was what I finally had to do: tell the truth. And how did I know that?

3

Because of my mother: she could tell a story, and the stories she told, once my father left us, were always about the Emily Dickinson House. For instance, there was the story she told me when I was eight, a story about a boy and a girl, always nice enough, never too much older or younger than I was. They held hands and raced on foot and yelled sarcastic, innuendo-ridden taunts at each other, things that they'd heard or seen at the movies or on television or from their friends, who'd heard them in the same places and who'd changed them and made them their own.

They were good kids, this boy and girl: they went over to each other's houses after school, on weekends and national holidays; they gave each other cards on birthdays and talked on the phone for hours. And one day when they walked past the Emily Dickinson House, the back door was open, which was unusual, and so they decided to check it out. As they crossed the threshold, as my mother told it, the door slammed behind them and the big house hummed like the warming up of an oversize garbage disposal. There were screams, faint but distinct, and when my mother finished the story I would let out a long, sour breath and whine, "But it's so unfair." And my mother would nod and say, "Emily Dickinson's House is like the last hole of a miniature golf course. Like the ball on that final hole, the children go in and then the game waits for someone else." Which was an unfortunate analogy, because my mother and I did a lot of miniature golfing together at this time.

So my mother had her story (a story that never made either of us very happy, by the way), but now I was going to have mine, and it would be true. I would tell Anne Marie and the kids the truth about me and the Emily Dickinson House and how I'd burned it to the ground and killed those poor Colemans. I had lied for too long. Now that Thomas Coleman had shown up and threatened to spill the beans, I knew I should tell my family the truth while the truth might still do me a little bit of good and while I was somewhat in control of it. And maybe the truth would make me happy. This was what the bond analysts had told one another during their memoir-brainstorming sessions: "Just tell the truth, dude" (this was the way they talked: like surfers outfitted by Brooks Brothers). "You'll feel better afterward." It seemed a simple matter of cause and effect, which was the kind of thing I, as a packaging scientist, could understand and appreciate. But it would be tough, I knew that. On my walk out of Camelot, across Route 116, and around and around the parking lot of the gardening-supply superstore (I would have walked on the sidewalks along 116 or in Camelot, except there weren't any), I was picturing my little bambinos' faces as I tried to explain that Daddy was a murderer and an arsonist, not to mention a long-term liar, and that weakened my resolve a little. But that was OK, because I knew I was right to do what I was going to do, and I had surplus resolve and could stand to lose some of it.

And then I walked back into Camelot, into my driveway, and lost some more of the resolve. Anne Marie's minivan was parked there. Like Camelot and the house and the children and Anne Marie herself, the van was well maintained and I loved it and them so much, could feel my love growing and growing, could feel my heart wanting to get bigger and bigger until it was so full of love that it would explode all over the place and make a mess and I would die and not care. I went around the house and through the back door and into the kitchen, the floor covered with gleaming adobe tile. I had no idea what *adobe tile* meant, exactly, except that I thought it had to do with Indians and clay and earth, and none of that seemed to have anything to do with what was on my kitchen floor. That floor and its name were mysterious and inexplicable, like love itself, and my heart continued to grow, testing the limits of its chambers. I bent to kiss the floor, put my lips right on the cool, cool tile. *You are mine.* That was my very thought, to the tile. *You are mine, and I love you.* But would the tile still love me back after I told it the truth about my past? I could feel the tile shrink from my lips at the very thought. Would my family not do the same? How could they not? Oh, I was afraid, not of one thing, but of everything, even though I'd been full of courage and determination not a minute earlier. I was even afraid of the adobe tile, wanted to get away from it as fast as possible before it rejected me completely. I wiped my lip prints off the tile and got up from my hands and knees just as my daughter, Katherine, walked into the kitchen.

Katherine was eight now, tall and bony, the kind of girl her mother had been — the kind of girl who in adolescence lived in overalls as she made her trip from tomboyishness to beauty. She'd learned from some television show or her friends to greet people not in the conventional fashion but by saying, "Hey-low," and she said it now, to me, in the kitchen, and I wanted to say back, *Oh, dear heart, my first born, I have to tell you something, and you might hate me for it, but even if you do, will you at least promise to never say "Hey-low" again?* Instead, I asked, "Where's your mother?"

"She's upstairs, working out." It was that time of day. Anne Marie would be upstairs in our bedroom, in her exercise outfit, all spandex and white strips of flesh and hair piled high and beaded sweat on her upper lip, watching television and pedaling the hell out of her stationary bike. At times I wondered how much longer it would stay stationary if she kept pedaling it that hard. My heart took a sad tumble at the thought of telling her about my true self; and then, since I'm not afraid of the big questions, I wondered if she would have been happier with someone else, someone who wasn't a bumbler like me. There had been no shortage of bumbling in our time together. For instance, there was the time when we had dinner with a guy I worked with and his wife, and we got around to talking about Jews, or the Jewish religion at least, and Anne Marie asked the woman (she was an American) if she was Jewish, and she wasn't, and then I said to the guy I worked with, "I know *you're* not." I said this because he was German, actually from Germany—his name was Hans—the implication being that since he was a German he must be a Nazi. Anne Marie pointed this out later on. As I told her, this wasn't my intention, but our guests may have taken it that way: they left in a big hurry, even before dessert was served. After they left, Anne Marie got exasperated with me—exasperation, that testy cousin of resignation, which is what Anne Marie seemed to feel about me most of the time. I apologized to her. But in my defense, guess what: I found out later that the guy wasn't. Jewish, that is.

But I suppose that wasn't the point. Was Anne Marie happy? Had I ever made her happy? Or did I only make her busy: running the kids here and there, going to work, doing the things that needed to be done around the house that I didn't do—which (except for the lawn and some bedtime TV watching with the kids) was pretty much everything—and cleaning up my accidents, so many of them that she didn't believe they were accidents anymore? I was one of the things that kept her busy, all right, me and her stationary bike. Did she recently seem less miserable and weepy than she'd been because she was happy or busy? Did I make her happy, or just busy? Or was there a difference?

"Earth to Dad," Katherine said. She was tall enough to reach up and knock on my head, as if checking to see if I were home, and she did just that, striking me on the forehead, but softly, so that it barely hurt and only for a second. "Are you still there?"

"Yes," I said. "What's your brother doing?"

"He's watching TV in his room."

I could picture Christian watching television (all of us had televisions in our bedrooms, plus one downstairs, plus one in the finished basement—we were like mission control with our many monitors). When Christian rode his scooter, he made happy sounds the way he had when he was a baby, noises that sounded like "Whee." When he watched television he looked confused and angry at what he was seeing, like a dumb bully. I wished he were riding his scooter, even in the house, which we don't normally allow, so I could picture him doing that instead of looking dumb and brutish in front of the television. I also wished I could give Christian and Katherine something to remember me by; this was a parental wish, I recognized it. For instance, my mother, during my father's absence, gave me the stories about the Emily Dickinson House so that I'd have something besides a runaway father. And I still have them; I've kept them all this time, in my head, because they were good stories.

My mother always talked about the Emily Dickinson House in terms of last gasps, of children vanished and sadly forgotten, of the last drop, drop, drop of bodies, big and small, new and used, down a lonely and unforgiving chasm. When I was nine years old, for example, she told me increasingly long and horrific stories about strangers, out-of-towners: men with shady pasts, faded jeans, outstanding warrants, and Marlboro whispers. They arrived as hitchhikers or bus riders, looking for a place to sleep, a place to work, not voting, not paying taxes. For them, the Emily Dickinson House didn't loom or threaten but existed only for their temporary use: another big old house with easy locks, daytime-only occupancy, and a dust problem. Their forced entries were casual, experienced, which made their disappearances (according to my mother's stories, you could barely hear their howls over the creaking of that venerable hell house) even more awful: because these men had known bad things out there in the world and had survived them, but they couldn't survive the house. That's how bad and interesting the house was, and it was right down the street, too. And there was my father, who did not smoke and wore khaki pants and not blue jeans and had never known trouble before: he wouldn't even make it *back* to Amherst and the Emily Dickinson House; he'd be swallowed up by the world before he made it home. When I say I was afraid for these outlaw men of my mother's stories, I was really afraid for my father, who I believed was out there alone in the bad, bad world. My father was what my mother's Emily Dickinson House stories were about, really, which is why I thought about them, and it (the Emily Dickinson House) and my mother and my father, so much way back then, and why I still did, and do.

But enough. There were many, many more stories, and they were my mother's gift to me, and look where that gift got me — that's the point. I didn't want to leave my kids anything like that; but neither, I was realizing, did I want to give them the truth, which was dangerous and might end up hurting all of us and helping no one. While I was thinking of something safer to give them, Katherine opened the refrigerator, reached in, took out a tall Styrofoam cup, and began sucking loudly on the straw coming out of its lid.

"What are you drinking?"

"A smoothie," she said.

"Is that like a milkshake?"

"No," she said.

"What makes a smoothie different from a milkshake?" I asked.

Katherine thought about this for a moment, and then said, "It's smoother."

"Good," I said, and meant it. I had come home intending to give my family the truth. But instead I had given my daughter a nice, factual conversation about smoothies, something not to remember me by, and maybe this is the most we can do for our children after all: give them nothing to remember us by. "Good," I said again.

"What's good?" Anne Marie said, coming into the kitchen from behind me. I turned to face her. Her hair was wet; she'd obviously just taken a shower. It was funny: she never blow-dried her hair, even though it was rope thick and long enough for Rapunzel to be jealous of — even so, she never owned a hair dryer, and still her hair managed to dry. I often imagined, in my spare moments, that her hair had its own heating coils, firing from within, and just looking at her I felt my own heating coils firing from within, the flames coming up through my legs and private parts and chest and into my face. I had to resist the urge to tackle her right there, out of love and desire. I had done this once, in the Pioneer Valley Mall, in a shoe store, where Anne Marie was trying on a pair of black knee-high boots, turning this way and that like the model she easily could have been, and my need for her was so big that there seemed no way to do justice to its enormity except to tackle her. So I did, scattering boxes and display tables and other customers. After we'd cleaned up the mess and apologized to the manager and bought the boots, Anne Marie had made me promise never, ever to do it again. So instead I said, "Smoothies."

"Smoothies what?"

"Katherine is drinking one. We were just talking about how a smoothie isn't a milkshake." Anne Marie looked at me quizzically, as if I were speaking one of the many foreign languages I'd never learned to speak. So I clarified. "They're different."

"How was your day?" Anne Marie asked. "Anything special happen?"

This was the moment, of course, for me to tell her the truth. It was there in front of me, like another family member in the room. I thought of the bond analysts, could see the pages of their memoirs flapping like gums, telling me: *Tell the truth, tell the truth; you will feel better, dude.* I could do it, could I not? I would tell Anne Marie about the Emily Dickinson House fire and the Colemans and my time in prison; I would tell her about my parents and how I'd hurt them so, and how they sent me off to college because of it; I would tell her about how Thomas Coleman had just come to see me. I would tell Anne Marie that I'd lied to her out of love and fear of losing her, and now I was telling her the truth out of the same fear, and that if she'd please, please forgive me, I'd never tell her another lie again.

So what did I actually tell Anne Marie? I told another lie. Because this is what you do when you're a liar: you tell a lie, and then another one, and after a while you hope that the lies end up being less painful than the truth, or at least that is the lie you tell yourself.

"Nothing special," I said. And then, before she could ask me another question to which I'd also have to lie, I told her something true: "I love you so much, Anne Marie. You know that, right?"

She smiled at me, put her hand on my cheek, which was her favorite fond gesture, and said, "I do know that. I do."

"I'm starving," I said. "Let's make dinner." We did: Katherine shredded the lettuce, washed it under the faucet, then put it in the salad spinner, which she spun violently, switching hands when one got tired; I set the table, putting the utensils where I thought they should go; Anne Marie made the actual meal, which I don't remember specifically but I'm sure consisted of most of the important food groups. Christian came down, still logy from his TV watching, and managed to do his part, too, which was to sit in his chair and stay out of everyone's way.

While we made dinner, the kitchen was filled with the usual chatter: Anne Marie talked about the book club she'd just joined, Katherine the soccer team she was the star of, Christian the cartoon he'd just watched and partially understood. Me, I didn't talk much, mostly because there was that voice — *What else? What else?* — booming in my head, the voice I hadn't heard in so many years. I was distracted by it, didn't understand what it was doing there. I had what I wanted, it was with me, in the room, including the room itself. Was it possible that we hear that voice not when we want something else but when we're in danger of losing the things we already have? The voice was so loud that I smacked myself on the side of the head to get rid of it, which Christian saw and imitated, and then, because he'd hit himself too hard, started crying and I had to comfort him, which at least helped me forget about the voice for a second.

Finally we all sat down. After the day I'd had, it seemed to me something like a miracle that we were all eating at the same table, the way a family is supposed to. A miracle is something to be commemorated in prayer, they taught us that in college, except I didn't know any prayers, had forgotten the few the nuns made us memorize. So I simply said, "I am the luckiest father and husband in the world." I was, too; I had been lucky for ten years, and I was lucky for four more days, and then my luck ran out and I did something I shouldn't have.

4

I went out of town on business. My bosses sent me to Cincinnati, where I was to pitch a revolutionary kind of sausage casing to the people at Kahn's. All told, I was gone for less than thirty-six hours and everything went well (the casing pretty much spoke for itself and did all the work). The only hitch was that after I'd flown into the airport, gotten my van out of long-term parking, and driven to Amherst, I stopped to get gas only two miles from my house and managed to lock my keys in the van while doing so. I didn't want to pay someone at the gas station to jimmy the lock, so I called Anne Marie to ask her to drive over a spare key.

Anne Marie answered the phone. It was Wednesday afternoon, four o'clock or thereabouts. She smokes a cigarette in the morning, another before dinner, and a third last thing at night, and she must have just smoked one, because her voice came at me like a distant train, a lovely, throaty rumble bearing down on me through the receiver, and it made me happy and hopeful just hearing her say, "Hello?"

"Hey, Anne Marie, honey," I said, "it's me, Sam."

"Sam," she said, "are you having an affair?"

That question stabbed me and changed my mood immediately. Oh, happiness can turn to despair so quickly it's a miracle we don't pull a muscle or wrench a neck with the suddenness. I was about to say, *No, of course not, don't even think it,* when it occurred to me that by not ever telling Anne Marie what I'd done to the Emily Dickinson House or Thomas Coleman and his parents, I was having an affair of sorts, an affair with all the betrayal and the guilt if not the woman and the sex. Yes, I was in bad shape, my mind a clogged drain, and so it's possible that I didn't respond to Anne Marie for a few seconds or even half a minute, and finally she cried out, "You *are* having an affair, you are, it's true!"

"It is," I said, and this was more bumbling on my part. I meant my response as a question, but maybe it sounded otherwise, like a statement, a confession, because Anne Marie started crying harder.

"No, no," I said, snapping to a little. "Of course I'm not having an affair. Why would you think that?"

"Well, for one," she said, "you went out of town on business."

"Yes," I said, "that's true, I did. I told you that. You *knew* that."

"Sam," she said, in that righteous, cocksure tone we use when we've known someone too well for too long, "I thought about it while you were gone. You've not once been out of town on business in your life."

This wasn't true, exactly. My first year at Pioneer Packaging, I was sent to do a product demonstration, and the thing I was sent to demonstrate was that unbreakable mayonnaise jar. I demonstrated the hell out of it and wouldn't rest until I'd dropped it from places low and high, bounced it off concrete and blacktop. Before I knew it, I'd taken up the better part of the day, and the potential clients were a little tired around the eyes and they didn't buy the product, either. From then on the higher-ups at Pioneer Packaging always sent other people out into the world to meet clients and attend conventions, while I stayed around the plant. So as with the adultery, Anne Marie was wrong in letter but right in spirit, and the more I thought about it, the more this true story of mine sounded like a lie. But still I persisted.

"But it's true, it's true," I said, and started telling her about the sausage casing I'd designed, how it preserved the integrity of the meat in a way that no other casing ever had, but Anne Marie interrupted and said, "You're lying. I don't believe you."

"Anne Marie," I said, "honey, you've got it all wrong. All of this is just a big mistake. I love you so much."

"You just shut up," she said. "He told me you'd say that."

"Wait," I said. "Who did? Who said I'd say what?"

"The man whose wife you're sleeping with. He told me that you'd say it was all a big mistake. That's the other reason I know you're having an affair. Because he told me so."

"Who is this guy?" I said, grateful that I had another lying man to focus on. "What's his name?"

"I'm not going to dignify that with a response. You *know* who he is."

"I don't, I don't," I said. "What's his name? Please tell me. *Please.*"

And maybe I sounded sincere; I mean, I was sincere, but maybe I actually sounded that way, too. You can never tell how you sound over the phone, that evil piece of machinery, and I would stop using one, we all would, if only there weren't these great distances we need to put between us and the people we need to talk to. Still, it's possible that I truly sounded sincere. Or maybe Anne Marie was holding out hope that I wasn't the cheater and liar she now believed me to be. Because she told me his name, as if maybe I didn't know. Which, it turns out, I did.

"Thomas," she said, and her voice sounded kinder, softer, more hopeful than before. "Thomas Coleman."

"Oh no. Shit," I said. This, of course, was the wrong thing to say and did nothing at all to convince Anne Marie of my innocence.

"That's what I thought," she said, her voice hard again, the way it gets after you've cried and then discovered you've been crying for a good reason.

"He's lying," I told her. "Don't believe a word that guy says."

"He said you'd say that, and so he asked me to ask you why he would lie."

Oh, that hurt! Thomas had outsmarted me, and it felt bad. It's a painful thing, finding out that you're dumber than someone else. But then again, there is always someone smarter than you; you'd think we'd die from the constant pain of our mental inferiority, except that most of the time we're too stupid to feel it. Yes, Thomas Coleman was smarter than I was, I knew it, and now my wife knew it, too.

"That's what I thought," Anne Marie said again. "He also said that you'd say the whole thing with his wife was an accident, that you'd never meant for it to happen."

"That sounds like me," I admitted. You had to hand it to Thomas: he really knew me, inside and out, and how to use that knowledge against me. I had no idea why he'd told Anne Marie I was cheating on her, rather than telling her the truth about my burning down the Emily Dickinson House and killing his poor mom and dad, but no doubt there was a reason, a good one, and he was smart enough to know it and I wasn't. How did he get so terribly smart, so determined? Maybe it was the pain I'd caused that made him that way, and if that were true, then I'd sort of had a hand in it, in making him as smart and devious as he was. I was really starting to dislike the guy. But I also felt a little proud, like Dr. Frankenstein must have felt when his monster turned on him, because, after all, it was Dr. Frankenstein who had made the monster strong and cunning enough to turn on him.

"You know what else he said?" Anne Marie asked.

"Tell me," I said. I didn't want to know, of course, but she was going to tell me anyway, so why not invite in the inevitable, which is why, in the movies, vampires have to be asked inside by their victims and always are.

"He said that we didn't belong together anyway, and good riddance. He said I was much too beautiful to be with a man like you."

"Hey, Anne Marie, I've said the same thing. Many, many times." And I had. But it was different with Thomas saying it. When I said Anne Marie was too beautiful for me, it was as if only I knew and saw the truth. Now that Thomas had said it, though, I could see us as everyone else no doubt did: we were the couple that no one could figure out. *What does she see in him?* That was the unanswerable question.

"Listen," I said. "I know you don't believe me. But don't trust this guy Thomas; he's bad news."

"You'd know," she said.

"I would?"

"Bad news knows bad news," she said. I could hear her light up another cigarette, which meant that she was on track to smoke more than her daily three. She didn't like to smoke around the kids, and so I thought maybe I could talk to them while she finished her smoke. I'd lost her; it felt that way already. But I hadn't lost the kids yet, I didn't think. Apparently this is what you do when you lose someone you love: you scramble to make sure you don't lose everyone you love.

"Hey," I said, "are the kids around?"

"Yes."

"Can I talk to them?"

"No," she said.

After that, silence opened up between us, big and yawning and much wider than the actual two miles between the gas station from which I was calling and our home to the west. The gap was so big that it felt as though there were nothing I could do to close it, nothing at all. It was the worst feeling in the world. Think of when California finally breaks off from the rest of country, and the people in Nevada watching it happen from their new coastline. That's what I felt like.

So what did I do? Did I finally, out of desperation, do what the bond analysts told one another to do? Did I tell Anne Marie the truth? I didn't. It would have been like reaching inside of me and yanking out one of my organs — my liver, my spleen, or one of their vital neighbors — and I just couldn't bring myself to do it. But I could tell Anne Marie what she *thought* was the truth. This is what I decided, right there on the phone: that I would tell Anne Marie I'd had an affair with Thomas Coleman's wife. After all, wasn't it better to be a philanderer than an arsonist and a murderer? Wasn't I catching a bit of a break here, that my wife was convinced I was a philanderer and not something much worse? Wasn't it better — if your wife thought you were a philanderer and wouldn't be convinced otherwise — just to go ahead and admit to her truth, so that you could then apologize and beg her forgiveness, and then she could get on with the business of forgiving you and things could get back to normal? This was my thinking when I admitted to Anne Marie, "OK, yes, I cheated on you. I am so sorry. Please let me come home and we'll talk this over."

I could hear Anne Marie suck in a breath, one, two, three times, as if she were inhaling the words *love, honor,* and *cherish* before exhaling loudly into the receiver, releasing those words into the mysterious fiber optics between us.

"Good-bye," she said. "Don't call back. I'm serious. Don't come home, either." She paused dramatically again, sucked in one more breath, and then said, "You've really fucked things up this time, Sam."

"Wait . . . ," I said, but she didn't and hung up.

I stood there in the gas station. It was a big one, right off the highway, with too many pumps. Suddenly the place seemed full of families, parents and their children, and there were a few extended families, too, grandparents with weak bladders who'd requested the pit stop, all of them so grateful to have a brood of their own. I hated them, the way you hate the morning after a night of not sleeping, when it comes up both blurry and sharp at the same time. It made me want to howl — howl about the world that wasn't mine anymore and how I hated it, howl about the truth and how I wasn't brave enough to tell it — and so I did exactly that: I howled right there in the gas station and was given a wide berth by the other gas pumpers.

But the howl had a fortuitous effect: it summoned the gas station attendant. I stopped howling long enough to tell him about locking the keys in my van, and he unlocked the door with his ingenious thin slice of metal. I paid him, climbed in, started the van, and then sat there. I had a full tank of gas and nowhere to go. Nowhere to go! I started howling again, except the windows were rolled up and so it was as though I were howling in my own crypt, with the engine running. Oh, that was loneliness! I empathized with Thomas Coleman right then, even though he'd made a ruin of my life. Because the loneliness I felt was the loneliness of someone all alone, the loneliness of an orphan.

Except I wasn't one. That thought stopped my howling, because after all, I had a father, a mother, too, and as far as I knew they were alive, which was a plus. So I would go to them, even if they didn't want me. Besides, I had nowhere else to go.

5

That's how I came to be driving on Amherst's streets for the first time in five years, even though I lived only two miles from the center of town. I'd learned that I could drive the spur around town on the way to work, and Katherine's school, which was called Amherst Elementary, was actually a new, sprawling red brick building outside of Amherst, and all the necessary superstores we shopped at weren't in Amherst, either; they were on Route 116, which is to say they weren't really anywhere. This is how it is these days: you can live in a place without having to actually have a life there.

And there was that voice, back as loud as ever, asking, *What else? What else?* The van was awfully quiet and lonely without the kids making noise and Anne Marie telling them not to, and so to fill the loneliness I listened to the voice carefully, maybe too carefully, and didn't pay enough attention to my driving, and that's how I ended up ramming into a K-Car in front of me. Luckily, it was a gentle ramming: the old lady driving the car wasn't hurt and neither was her car, really, and after some initial confusion she seemed to remember that the bumper had been loose and hanging off the frame *before* I'd rammed it. I *had*, however, knocked over a few bags of vegetables and fruit in the backseat, and so I crawled into her car and tried to put the produce back in the bags. The bags were broken, though, and the produce ended up rolling all over the backseat and floor. Still, the old lady was very sweet about it, and even though I was pretty sure I remembered her from my younger days, she didn't recognize me as the boy I'd been, the boy who burned down, et cetera, which I thought was promising indeed. We exchanged information — which by law we were required to do — and then parted ways. All in all, it was a very pleasant, civilized accident I got into on the way to my parents' house. As the old lady pulled away, I had a vision of the fruit and vegetables happily rolling around her backseat, and I remembered that my father was a big fan of fresh produce and had once even started up a garden, which didn't work out the way he'd planned.

And so, a few facts about my father and then his failed garden. My father was an editor for the medium-size university press in town. He mostly edited books on American history, but his subspecialty was the relationship between popular music and American culture. In addition to his books, my father also covered the area's annual squeeze-box festival for the local newspaper.

"Sam," he once asked me, "do you know why the accordion is so important? Do you?"

I was seven at this point. I didn't know anything about anything and told my father as much.

"Because it is part of the history of music and immigration," he said. "The Acadians played it, and when they moved from Canada to Louisiana, they brought their squeeze-boxes with them. The accordion is their instrument. It is their gift to the world."

"It hurts my ears," I told him.

This simple, seemingly innocent comment pretty much ruined my poor dad. He couldn't stand knowing that his son did not admire his occupation. I was seven, let me remind you, and knew nothing about the relationship between a man's lifework and his sense of self-worth, and my father should have ignored me. But he didn't: instead, my father left the editing and musicology business and searched around for something else to do, something I might respect him for. Somehow he decided that I would respect him if he became a farmer. Amherst is not exactly the country, but my father turned our half-acre backyard plot into a minibreadbasket anyway. For six months — May to October — my father grew beets, zucchini, tomatoes, pumpkins, garlic. Our backyard was teeming. But we never ate any of it, because my father wouldn't let us. He said we couldn't "reap the harvest" until the time was right.

"When will the time be right?" I wanted to know.

When I asked this, my father looked at me in complete surprise, as if he were hoping all along that *I* would tell *him* when he should pick his vegetables. I was eight by this time, but even I could tell that my father didn't know what he was doing, and also that he was in some real emotional trouble. Or maybe he didn't want to harvest his crops because he was afraid that the vegetables would somehow be *wrong*. Anyway, that night my father told my mother (and later she told me) that he needed to go out in the world and find something worth doing, something that would make us — her and me — proud of him.

My mother apparently told my father in response that if he sliced himself open, stuffed himself with his accordions, concertinas, and rotting vegetables, and then hung himself on a pole in the middle of his miserable little garden, then he would probably make one impotent, homely-looking scarecrow.

My father left the next day and didn't come back until three years later and then was rehired by the university press when he did. But right after he left, my mother starting telling me stories about the Emily Dickinson House and the terrible mysteries therein, and if those stories were supposed to lead me, eventually, to break into the Emily Dickinson House in the middle of the night and accidentally burn it down and kill Thomas Coleman's parents in the process — if my mother's stories were supposed to do all this *and* send me to prison and thus take away ten years of my life — then they did what they were supposed to.

I got angrier and angrier in the car, just thinking about all this bad family history, and by the time I got to my parents' house, I was ready to take my anger out on someone or something. So I took it out on the front door. I banged on the door and banged and banged until my fist hurt. No one answered, so I yelled out, "It's me! Sam! I'm home!" Still no one answered, and my anger turned to dread, that sort of dread you feel when you go home and wonder whether everything has changed or nothing has.

Then I opened the door—it wasn't locked—and found that everything had changed: it looked nothing like the house I remembered. The house I remembered had the neat sort of disorder peculiar to the well-read and overeducated: in the house I remembered, there were books and magazines everywhere, but everything else—dishes, glasses, clothes—was in its proper place. This house, on the other hand, looked as though it had been strip-mined by Vikings. There were empty bottles—gin bottles, beer bottles, red wine bottles—scattered everywhere. There were even empty peach schnapps and wine cooler and white zinfandel bottles here and there—in between couch cushions, in the fireplace, on top of the microwave—which made me wonder if my parents had been drinking in the house with high school girls or sorority sisters. My parents had once been big believers in natural woodwork—the wainscoting, banisters, overwide windowsills—but now the wood looked pale and sickly, as though it were turning into linoleum. There were ashtrays on nearly every surface—the kind of shallow, thin metallic ashtrays that you could only get by stealing them from diners and restaurants—but since all the ashtrays were overflowing, some of the bottles had cigarette butts soaking in the remaining drops of booze. There were stacks of dishes in the sink and piles of pots and pans on the stovetop, and none of them had been washed; the food had been caked and dried on them for so long that the spaghetti sauce and the flecks of vegetable and meat matter looked as natural a part of the pots and pans as the handles and the lids. The pantry shelves were totally empty except for those things—confectioners' sugar, toothpicks, tiny marshmallows—that you couldn't ever get rid of, plus boxes and boxes of these candy-bar-looking things. They were called Luna bars, and I assumed they were some sort of health food for women because the boxes featured highly stylized drawings of women jogging around the moon. The only items in the refrigerator were a half-empty two-liter bottle of tonic water and a jar of light mayonnaise that had probably been there for several presidential terms. The whole house smelled like a perfumed dog, even though my parents had never, to my knowledge, owned a dog, and my mother, to my knowledge, had never worn perfume. There was an exercise bike stationed in front of an enormously big and impossibly thin TV, which was perched on the middle shelf of an otherwise empty bookcase — empty of books, and empty even of other shelves. That was the biggest change: in the house I remembered, there were books everywhere, but now I couldn't find a one, not even a *TV Guide*. I had even begun to wonder whether I was actually in the right house when I heard a noise — a grunt or a squeak — coming from the guest room. I followed the sound. That's when I saw my father.

He was an invalid and in bad shape; this was obvious at first glance. His face was shrunken and drawn back, and he had a plaid wool blanket on his lap. When he saw me, my father made a kind of wounded-animal noise that I took to mean one-third surprise, one-third *Welcome home,* one-third *Please don't look at me, I'm hideous,* and the blanket slid off his lap and onto the floor, kicking up a good amount of dust that floated there in the sunlight like something beautiful and precious and then sank to the wide-planked pine floor.

I returned the blanket to his lap and asked, "Oh, Dad, what happened to you?" even though it was obvious what had happened to him: he'd had a stroke. There is no mistaking a stroke victim, even if you haven't seen one before, which I hadn't. I didn't know what else to say, so I repeated, "Oh, Dad." He seemed to appreciate my awkward position, because he made the wounded-animal noise again, but this time it was much more soothing, and I was calmed by it.

"Don't say another word," I told him. "Relax. Let me do the talking and get you up to speed." I told him about college and my switch from English to packaging science, and I told him about Anne Marie and

Katherine and Christian and about my job at Pioneer Packaging and our house in Camelot and how much I missed him and Mom. I didn't tell him, though, about the voice that asked, *What else?* or Thomas Coleman or Anne Marie's kicking me out, because I figured he already had enough to worry about. But even so, this story must have over-whelmed him a little in its detail and scope, because by the time it was done he seemed to be asleep. I shook my father by the arm, gently at first, but then harder and harder until he woke up with an alarmed snort. From then on I asked only short, factual questions, like "Where's Mom?" to which he responded in a two-syllable grunt that I took to mean, *She's out.*

We sat there for a while in silence. It got darker and I turned on the light. I didn't feel the need to talk, maybe because whatever I might have said wouldn't have been as smart as the silence. My father had a holy-man quality to him: he struck me as having the sort of deep wisdom cripples seem to get with their crippling, and I was prepared to sit there and soak up whatever knowledge he might emanate. It was nice. But the place really was a mess. Even my father's bedroom was littered with beer cans and empty wine bottles, and there were even a few boxes of wine, the sort that comes with its own spigot. I was certain they were my mother's because she would always have a drink with dinner and my father never did. Besides, I couldn't imagine him drinking anything now without a straw and I didn't see any of them scattered around.

And on the topic of my mother, where in the hell was she? Where did she get off, leaving my crippled father alone in his condition and not even cleaning the house before she left it? Did her crippled husband not deserve a little more dignity, a little less filth? The more I ruminated on it, the more I realized how typical this was of my mother. She, as men-tioned, was always the hard-hearted one, and even when my father left us for those three years, she didn't shed a tear. My mother wasn't exactly the welcome wagon when my father came back, either, and my old man really wore himself out trying to get back in her good graces. Thinking about it now, I decided there was a direct connection between his stroke and that difficult time, too. And then there were those Emily Dickinson House stories she used to tell me, the ones that ruined so many lives, and I was really getting worked up about her, my callous mother, who had now apparently abandoned my father in his time of need. Where did she get off? I might have said this out loud, because my father nearly raised his eyebrows at me and for a second I thought he was going to chastise me for being rude to my mother, but instead he said, "Man."

"Man what?" I said.

"Grown," my father said, or that's what I thought he said, and then he raised his finger as if to point at me. Or that's what I thought he was doing. The finger made it only about an inch off his lap and then fell back again. Of course, this could all have been a big misunderstanding. But then again, maybe misunderstanding is what makes it possible to be in a family in the first place. After all, when I was eight I understood my father all too clearly: he was scared, and so he left us. My mother was lonely and angry at his leaving, and so she told me those stories about the Emily Dickinson House. I understood that, too. Maybe we had understood too much about one another; maybe if we'd misunderstood one another, then we'd have been more of a family. Maybe if we'd been more of a family, I would have seen my father in the last ten years and he wouldn't have to marvel at how much I'd grown. Maybe, maybe, maybe.

"I *am* a grown man," I said to my father. And then, remembering Terrell in prison, I clarified: "I'm a grown-*ass* man."

My father stared at me for a good half minute until his blanket slipped from his lap again. He leaned over slightly in his chair to catch the blanket before it hit the floor, and that movement, that one little thing, caused me to remember what for so many years I'd been trying not to: that moment when my father had bent over, opened the end table drawer next to him, pulled out a Converse shoe box, and shown me those letters asking me to burn down those writers' houses. There was the end table, still in the same place; there was the drawer, inside the end table. Was the shoe box still in the drawer? Were the letters still in the shoe box? I hadn't thought of those letters for years, but now they were in my head again and they were alive, making noise, joining the chorus of my neighbors' lawn mowers, the Emily Dickinson House fire, and other sounds of the past. And among those sounds was my father's voice, telling me those many years earlier, "Sam, you *are* an arsonist," which was why I blurted out now, so many years later and out of the blue, "You're wrong."

"Wrong," my father repeated, doing his best to keep up.

"Yes, wrong," I said. "I work at Pioneer Packaging. I make containers, good ones."

My father pursed his lips and made a derisive raspberry sound; a glob of spittle landed on his chin and I tried very hard not to wipe it off for him.

"I know it doesn't sound like much," I said. And it didn't, not even when I told my father, in some detail, about the tennis ball can I'd just designed, a can that was vacuum sealed by soft plastic and not by the sharp metal top that you always sliced your finger on. He made another raspberry sound and there was more spit on his chin.

"No ... greatness ... in ... tennis ... ball ... cans," he said over the course of what might have been half an hour. Greatness! Me! What son doesn't want to hear his father say he could be great, if that's what he was saying? What son doesn't dream of such a thing? What wouldn't a son do or give to hear these words come out of his father's mouth, especially a son like me at a time like this, when I was so down and most needed a kind word or two from my dad? It was as though I'd taken the words I most needed to hear, placed them in my father's mouth, and watched them come out again, slowly and haltingly and coated with saliva.

"Are you really saying I'm great?" I asked him.

"No," he said, clearly, very clearly. And then, "Could ... be."

"Could be if what!"

"You . . . could . . . help . . . people," he said.

This helping-people business was an attractive idea, I'll admit, because up to now I'd done not much more than be, and when I wasn't just being, I'd caused some pain, too. There was the Emily Dickinson House, of course, and the pain that everyone knows all about by now. Then there was Thomas Coleman, still in his agony after all these years — I couldn't forget about him, especially since he seemed determined to ruin my life as I had his. And then Anne Marie, whom I had hurt so badly and had practiced hurting for years. There was the time, for instance, at our next-door neighbors' daylight-savings party when I found Sheryl (I have no memory of her last name, and if my memory is to be trusted, she might not even have one) weeping in the butler's pantry because (as I found out) her husband had just left her for another woman, and now she was staring down the barrel of those dark, late afternoons all by herself and she didn't know how she was going to manage. I hugged her — it seemed the right, bighearted thing to do — and in breaking the hug I kissed her, too. It was a comforting, "there, there" sort of kiss, but I confess that in getting to her cheek I might have touched her lips, briefly. This felt wrong, very wrong, and so to lighten my heart and conscience, I went and found Anne Marie at the party, interrupted her conversation, and told her — in front of a half dozen or so people — that I'd kissed Sheryl, and that it was an accident and well intentioned, but that I thought I should tell her about it because of the guilt I felt because of the way our lips brushed and maybe even briefly lingered — even though it was an accident and well intentioned — and I could hear soft, embarrassed noises coming from some of the guests who were listening. Immediately I knew I'd done something wrong, because of the noises and also because of the pain I saw on Anne Marie's face just before she turned away from me and returned to her conversation. That same pain was in her voice, on the telephone, when she called me a cheater and told me not to come home. I had made Anne Marie's pain, just as surely as I'd made that mayonnaise jar that wasn't quite plastic and wasn't quite glass, either, but in any case was unbreakable. It was solid, the jar, not unlike the pain. Yes, it would be nice to help someone and not hurt them.

"But wait," I said, coming back to my true self in a rush. "I can't help people. I'm a bumbler." My father didn't seem to understand this — his eyes went even glassier — and so I said, being helpful, "I bumble."

"Bumbling," my father said, "not . . . a . . . permanent . . . condition."

"Of course you'd say that," I told him. Because I was thinking of the garden my father had bumbled and how he'd left us for three years to try to prove he wasn't one. A bumbler, that is.

And where did my father go during those three years? He went everywhere, did everything, and then sent us postcards to let us know exactly where he'd been and what he'd done.

First my father went to South Carolina, because he'd never been in South Carolina before and his own inner voice said that he had to — had to! — visit all fifty states over the course of his lifetime. He also attended a game at every major league ballpark. He traveled to Yosemite and Badlands and Sequoia and every other national park of note. He went to the site of every Civil War battle that was supposed to be pivotal and especially bloody. He made a point of listening for the whispering ghosts of our dead boys at Gettysburg and Antietam and Vicksburg but could hear only a creaky voice squawking from rental cassette guides in the other cars as they crept at a reverential speed along the battlefields and cemeteries. My father scrutinized his Rand McNally *Road Atlas* and then made a point of driving every famous roadway made obsolete by the federal superhighway system and mourned daily on National Public Radio. He rented a canoe and paddled fifteen miles on the Erie Canal. He walked the Appalachian Trail from Georgia to Pennsylvania before packing it in after being menaced by two hunters sitting in a deer stand just south of Carlisle. He went out of his way to have a drink in every bar in North America in which Hemingway was rumored to have imbibed. He drove up Mt. Washington in New Hampshire and then bought a bumper sticker as testimony. He kept track of every march commemorating every civil rights atrocity and victory and then made sure he attended the march, no matter how much of a hardship it was to do so. My father went to the site of an oil spill off the coast of Washington and bought a vial of oil and a poster of a baby seal mired in the slick and looking wistful and tragic. He went to Wounded Knee and to his great surprise found himself conflicted about the lessons to be learned there. He visited the book depository and the grassy knoll in Dallas and bought what was supposed to be an authorized copy of the Zapruder film, although he had no notion of who had authorized it. Zapruder himself, my father supposed, or maybe a close relative.

But my father was no dilettante, or didn't want to be thought one, and had to make a living somehow. Besides, it was his uncertainty about his purpose here on this planet that took him from us in the first place. Sure, he was a book editor by training, but he could pretend to be other things and then tell us about them in the postcards. He pretended to be a large animal veterinarian in Enid, Oklahoma, and found the job less onerous and foul than you might think. He pretended to be an air traffic controller in Newark and was admired by his co-workers for his cool-headedness and his new variations on old raunchy jokes. He pretended to be a music instructor in Mississippi and led the Dream of Pines High School Marching Band to the state championship. He excavated dinosaur bones in South Dakota as a member of the state university's Archaeology Department. He was an emergency room surgeon, conducted minor surgeries in four Rocky Mountain states, and didn't botch a single stitch. He was a funeral director in Delray Beach, Florida, and found the corpses inoffensive but their survivors unbearable. He was a pediatrician in Ypsilanti, Michigan, and found that this job was more dangerous and less rewarding than being a large animal veterinarian in Enid, Oklahoma. He was a charter fishing-boat captain in Rumson, New Jersey, and named his boat the *Angry Clam*. To my father's surprise, his customers cared nothing about catching fish and everything about buying a T-shirt silk-screened with the boat's namesake — a scowling littleneck clam with a cigar hanging out of its mouth — for sixteen dollars a pop. He was a real estate agent in Normal, Illinois, and found married couples highly erotic when they whispered in bathrooms and hallways about what they could and could not afford. He was a Palatine priest in Platteville, Wisconsin, and found he could take confessions for hours and not hear a single sinner confess to anything but habitual self-abuse. He was a stock car driver based in Fayetteville, North Carolina, and found it even more boring and pointless a pursuit than he'd ever imagined it would be.

When I was a boy, I would read those postcards and know exactly why my father was doing what he was doing: he was taking a stab at greatness, that is, if greatness is simply another word for doing something different from what you were already doing — or maybe greatness is the thing we want to have so that other people will want to have us, or maybe greatness is merely the grail for our unhappy, striving selves, the thing we think we need but don't and can't get anyway. In any case, I knew that greatness was the thing my father had left us to find.

And then he came back. Maybe *What else? What else?* had been the question before my father left us, and maybe he thought by leaving us he'd answer the question or at least stop hearing it, and maybe he never stopped hearing it; maybe none of us ever do. I can't say for sure: neither of my parents mentioned why he came home, and I never asked, and together, through our silence, we conspired to make it one of those family secrets that had to remain secret if we were to remain a family. My mother had told me, after my father came back, that my father was "sensitive" about what he'd done while he was gone and that I should never mention the postcards to him. She never told me why my father should be so "sensitive" about the postcards, and again, I never asked. I put the postcards in an envelope and stowed them way toward the back of my highest closet shelf and never mentioned them again. But no matter what his reasons, my father came home and got his job back at the university press, and we forgave him, or at least I did. Because he was my father, and I'd missed him.

"I've missed you," I said.

"Mother," he said.

"What about her?"

"Yes, Bradley," said a voice from behind me. "What about me?"

It was my mother, of course, I knew this without turning around, and so I didn't, at first. I sat there with my back to her, imagining all the things I'd say to my mother, all the well-deserved grief I'd give her about my poor, crippled dad and the filthy house she'd left him in and the stories she'd told me when I was a boy and what a ruin they'd made of me and my life and so on. When I turned around to face her, I would be eloquent and fierce, I knew that much. Maybe it was remembering the arson letters and their possible proximity that made me feel this bold — the letters and my father's talk of my could-be greatness. Maybe it was because I'd seen this mother-son moment so often in the books my mother had made me read, and so I knew how it was supposed to go. Whatever the reason, I felt powerful and righteous, like an avenging angel or something. And what do you do when you become an avenging angel? You turn around and tell your mother about it.

So I turned around to tell my mother about it. There she was, standing in the doorway. I couldn't get a good look at her — maybe because it was late and my contacts were dry and cloudy, and because the hall light behind my mother made her seem hazy and mysterious and bathed in white, like the Lady of the Lake, whom my mother had also made me read about those many years before. I couldn't see her clearly, is the point, and so I couldn't see the expression on my mother's face when she said, "Your wife kicked you out of the house, didn't she?"

One of the things that mothers are good for, of course, is cutting to the heart of the matter, and in cutting to the heart of the matter, my mother had also sliced off some of my good feeling. Whether I was an avenging angel or not, my wife still thought I was a cheater and a liar and still hated me, I still couldn't see my kids, and I still couldn't go home to Camelot. Anne Marie had kicked me out, maybe for good. That was the truth, and my mother saw it, and suddenly I was tired, so tired.

"I'm so tired, Mom," I said.

"OK," she said. My mother turned and walked out of the doorway and into the hall, and I followed her, wordlessly, through the blackened rooms, up the stairs, to my old bedroom. Because this is another thing mothers are good for: they know how to get at the truth, and then, when that truth makes you too tired to hear any more of it, they know when to guide you through the darkness and put you to bed. My mother opened the door to my bedroom, turned to me, put her hand on my cheek, and said, "Get some sleep, Sam." I was so grateful for that, so very grateful, and to express my gratitude I did exactly what my mother told me to do. I slept.

Part Two

6

Now that I've returned home, to the very bedroom where my mother told me all those stories about the Emily Dickinson House — the stories that, as you know, caused me to inadvertently burn the house to the ground — perhaps it's time to clear up some misunderstood or misreported facts about that famous fire.

I did not, as the prosecutor argued at my trial, "case the joint" earlier on the day of the fire. I merely took the Emily Dickinson House tour, the official two-dollar tour, along with a group of students and their teacher from some school called Dickinson College ("No relation," the teacher joked, and oh, everyone laughed and laughed). The teacher tossed a pen from one hand to the other as she walked. The students all wore ski jackets. If I was guilty of "casing the joint," then so were they.

I was not, as the *Hampden County Eagle* suggested, a southerner who hated Yankees. True, before the tour began, I did sign the guest book "Sidney," from Baton Rouge, Louisiana, but only as a joke and to sound mysterious. As Mrs. Coleman might have been able to tell you if I hadn't killed her in the fire, I regretted the joke immediately because she read what I had signed and said, "Nice to meet you, Sidney," and I didn't speak for the entire tour for fear of not sounding southern.

It was certainly not the case that, as one of the Dickinson College students testified in court, I was agitated and not a little maniacal during the tour. I was a kid, a normal kid, normal as kids get and as normal as I am now. It's probably so, however, that I was a little *restless*. I was restless because, after my mother's stories, I expected there to be something exceptional and sinister and mysterious about the house. There wasn't. We were shown a glass case displaying one of Dickinson's letters; we were shown her bedspread, which was red with white daisies; we were shown her furniture, which, Mrs. Coleman explained, was not actually her furniture but rather a faithful reproduction of what her furniture would have looked like. Oh, it was dull! Nothing like my mother's stories. So I was probably restless — I remember yawning overloudly in boredom once and everyone looking at me — and that's probably why I broke into the house later on that night: to see what I could see when the tour guide and the students and their teacher weren't around.

It was not true, again as the prosecutor argued, that I killed the Colemans "in cold blood." I didn't even know they were in the house. I've said this many times, although it seems to satisfy no one nor make them happy, which is the truth all over, which makes you wonder why everyone wants to hear it so badly.

It was not true, as rumor had it around my high school (I went back to the high school while I was out on bail, which was where I heard the rumor), that the whole thing had been some sort of sex club gone horribly wrong. It is correct that I'd *thought* of inviting this girl China, whom I knew well enough and wanted badly, in the way boys are supposed to want girls with exotic names and their own cars, which China also had. And it's true that, as far as China was concerned, I had sex on the mind, prominently, in the very front of the lobe. But I didn't invite her to break into the Emily Dickinson House with me that night. I knew better. I did! Do you think I wanted to have sex with someone in that house after the stories my mother had told me? Especially the story about the time two kids from the high school (again a boy and a girl — "mere babes," my mother called them) bought a six-pack of Knickerbocker beer and decided to break into the Emily Dickinson House.

These were the same young children grown up, still nice but not quite as nice as they might have been. My mother stressed that these kids thought too much about what they were doing and what they'd like to do. Their fall lay in the calculation, and I took the lesson to be "Don't calculate," and to this very day I try not to. They walked and made out at the same time, a difficult trick, to be sure. The boy carried the six-pack in a plastic bag with handles; he had condoms in his wallet and a mini-crowbar in his jacket pocket. He was secure in his physical ability and in his equipment and calculated that if he couldn't blow the door down, he'd pry the lock. The door usually gave way easily, though; it was an old door, slightly rotten, and swung open right when you kicked it the first time, as I know very well to be true.

My mother told me this story when I was fourteen, after my father came back, and after my father came back my mother's stories both hardened and became easier, less tense but more gruesome, as was the case with the story about the kids with the six-pack and the condoms. Oh, it was a mess. They walked into the house and started going at it, and soon enough, bits of bone, flesh, tendon, began flecking the walls, crawling under dressers, hopping into the mail slot and sticking there: a cruel change-of-address notification. Imitation gold rings, baseball caps, hair bands, condoms, and full beers were found conspicuously in view, leftovers, the breathing out after a long swallow. A reminder of the evil of illicit sex and its punishment. It was a scene, all right, a regular bloodbath those kids got themselves into, and it seemed obvious to me that if I were ever to have sex, it would never, ever be in the Emily Dickinson House.

So no sex, and no sex club. Of course, I can't say how far Mr. Coleman got with Mrs. Coleman that night. After the fire was through with them, they were just so much bone and connective tissue. That much I know.

And it was not true that I was, as my first-grade teacher testified, a "little firebug." Not true! As proof, she told, in court, about the time on the playground when I was six, when she found me burning an anthill with a magnifying glass, or trying to (there were clouds that day, too many of them). Let me tell you, I was not the only kid in Miss Frye's class that tried to torch an anthill and learn a little something about solar power in the bargain. And let me tell you, what happened in first grade had no bearing whatsoever on what happened in and to the Emily Dickinson House. I had forgotten all about the anthill, in fact, and wasn't thinking of fire at all that night when I broke into the Emily Dickinson House. I was thinking of my mother's stories — like the one in which Emily Dickinson's corpse was hidden in one of the house's many secret compartments and came to life (or at least became ambulatory) only when there was a full moon. There was a full moon that night, and out of nervousness I was smoking a cigarette — which was a new habit, a short-lived one, too — when I heard a noise. Who knows what it was? It could have been the house creaking or a tree moving in the wind. It could have been the Colemans, enjoying their last private moment on earth together. Or it could have been Emily Dickinson, as glassy eyed as your best movie zombie, breaking out of her secret compartment and heading full steam in my warm-blooded direction. Whatever, I dropped my cigarette at the noise and hightailed it out of the house and so didn't notice that my dropped cigarette had lit a heavy living room drape on fire, which set the living room rug on fire, and so on. So. Accidental fire starter? Yes. Firebug? No.

But you know what *is* true? My mother's stories were good, or must have been. The judge pointed this out at my trial, the sentencing part, when my defense attorney was again explaining why I was in the Emily Dickinson House in the first place, and I was explaining again about my mother's stories. The judge interrupted and said, "Those must have been some good stories."

"I guess they were," I said.

"But then again," the judge said — and he was really editorializing here, but I guess his robes and his elevated seat and his handsome wooden gavel gave him the right — "if a good story leads you to do bad things, can it be a good story after all?"

"Come again?" I said. "I'm not following."

"I'm afraid I'm not, either, Your Honor," my lawyer said.

"I agree," said the prosecutor, who was exactly the same as my lawyer except that he wore a cheaper suit and was touchier because of it.

"Bear with me," the judge said. "It's an interesting question, is it not? Can a story be good only if it produces an effect? If the effect is a bad one, but intended, has the story done its job? Is it then a good story? If the story produces an effect other than the intended one, is it then a bad story? Can a story be said to produce an effect at all? Should we expect it to? Can we blame the story for anything? Can a story actually *do* anything at all?" Here he looked at me learnedly, over his glasses, and you knew right then that he'd always longed to be a college English professor instead of a judge and that he subscribed to all the right literary periodicals and magazines. "For instance, Mr. Pulsifer, can a story actually be blamed for arson and murder?"

"Huh," I said, then acted as if I were thinking about the question, which I should have been; instead I turned and looked at my mother, who was sitting behind me in the courtroom. There might as well have been a neon sign on her forehead that flashed the words DEFIANCE, OUTRAGE, REGRET, much like our driveway would flash the words MURDERER and FASCIST in the years to come.

"Huh," I said again.

"You'll have plenty of time to think about the question in prison, Mr. Pulsifer," the judge said to me. "Make sure you do."

"I will," I said. Because it was an interesting question, to the judge.

But I hadn't thought about the question, and I wasn't really thinking about it in the morning, either, when I woke up in my old bedroom for the first time in ten years. I wasn't thinking about any of the things I should have: my wife, my kids, Thomas Coleman, or his dead parents. No, I was thinking about those letters, couldn't stop thinking about them — maybe because I'd stopped myself from thinking about them for so long. Or maybe I was thinking about the letters because it's easier and safer to think about the things we shouldn't than the things we should. The voice asking, *What else? What else?* knew that truth, too. There I was, lying in my childhood bed, and when the voice asked me, *What else?* it didn't mean, *What about your wife, your kids? What about going home and telling them the truth?* It meant, *What about the letters? Where are the letters?* Yes, that voice was a coward, just like me.

I put on my pants and shirt from the day before, then crept down the stairs and into my father's room. The lights were off in the room, the bed was made, my father wasn't anywhere to be seen or heard. I opened the end table drawer, and there it was, the shoe box, and inside it were the letters, just as I remembered. It wasn't so much a dramatic moment as it was comfortable, reassuring: the house and my father had changed, but at least the *letters* were in the same place. They were more tattered, smudged, and *used* than I remembered, and I could picture my father, sitting in his chair, reading the letters and reading them again and again and thinking of me, somewhere out in the world. It was a touching father-son moment in my head. Then I heard a noise — a sputter of a cough — coming from the living room, and I took it as a warning of sorts. So I put the letters back in the box, put the box back in the drawer, closed the drawer, and followed the noise.

The living room was a good deal more together than when I'd seen it the day before. There were no booze bottles to be seen, no rings on the tables where they had been, no trace of them at all, as if they'd been called home by the mother ship. There was only one ashtray, a glass one, on the living room coffee table, with no ashes in it. The exercise bike was still in the living room, but off to the side and not smack in front of the TV the way it had been. As for the TV, it wasn't on, but my father was sitting in front of it on the couch.

"Dad," I said. "Good morning."

My father turned to face me. He had twelve extra hours of gray, patchy beard grown on him since I'd seen him last, and his eyes were filmy and half-closed, or half-open, depending on how you wanted to look at it. Dad had one leg crossed over the other, which I thought was quite an accomplishment for someone as stroked out as he was. And he was drinking a forty-ounce beer, a Knickerbocker in the can. I looked at my watch. I'd slept late. It was two in the afternoon, still a little early for drinking a beer that big, especially since I didn't remember my father drinking before, ever. But then again, my old dad had been through a lot, and who was I to tell him from where he should get his pleasure and whether it was too early in the day to get it. After all, he'd managed to cross his legs, the brave guy, and maybe the beer was in celebration of that huge accomplishment.

"Good afternoon," my mother said, coming in from offstage, as she had the previous night. I turned to face her. She also had a big beer in her hand, and unlike the night before, today I could see her clearly, could see clearly that she had changed since I'd seen her last. For one, she was pretty. I remembered her face being severe and impressive; it could scare you into admiring it, but it wasn't what you'd call pretty. She had always been one of those harsh, clear-eyed New England beauties whose scarily blue peepers always seemed to be looking through the disappointment that was you and back to her own clear-eyed Puritan kin. But now there was a softness to her face, not as though she'd gained weight, but as though she and her face had called some sort of truce and were at ease: her blue eyes seemed at home over her nose, which hung like an awning over her mouth, which was smiling at me. My mother's name is Elizabeth, and she had always seemed like an Elizabeth; but now she seemed like a Beth. As Elizabeth, she had always seemed to be what she was — a stern high school English teacher — but as Beth, she seemed something kinder and gentler. A nurse, maybe, an especially pretty one.

"You look like Nurse Beth," I told her.

"Ha," she said, girlishly tucking her hair — it was black as it had always been, and long, too — behind her ears. My mother went over to my father, took the empty beer can out of his hand, opened a new one, and placed it in the gnarled cup holder of his right hand. He said something garbled and multisyllabic, which I took to mean, *Thank you.*

"Should you be giving him another beer?" I asked. My mother didn't respond in facial expression or word, and so I added, "Because of his stroke."

"Did you hear that, Bradley?" my mother said to my father, her smile getting even softer, full of some private pleasure. "I shouldn't get you another beer because you've had a stroke."

My father didn't say anything back, but he shot her a look and she met it, the look, halfway, and it remained there in the room, like another son, another human being with some mysterious, shifting relationship to the two adult human beings that had made it. Because maybe this is what it means to be a son. No matter how old you are, you are always a step behind the two people who made you, the two people who always know something that you need to know, too — like, for instance, how my mother had known that Anne Marie had kicked me out of the house, or even that there was an Anne Marie, or a house.

"Last night you said that my wife had kicked me out of the house," I said. "How did you know that?"

"What?" my mother said loudly, because my father had begun drinking the beer, slurping it heroically and at top volume, and I had to shout the question — "How did you know that my wife had kicked me out?" — so she could hear it over the soggy racket of my father's imbibing.

"Oh, Sam," my mother said, "it's an old story."

"An old story," I repeated, thinking *now* of what the judge had said to me at my sentencing about good stories and bad stories, and for the first time in years I recognized that stories were everywhere and all-important. There were all those letters stashed away in the shoe box, all those people who wanted me to burn down those writers' homes because of the stories the writers had told; there was the story that Thomas Coleman told Anne Marie that made her kick me out; there were stories that the bond analysts had told about themselves in their memoirs, if they'd even written them (one had, sort of, but I didn't know that yet); and there were my mother's stories, which everyone knows all about, and suddenly I knew the answer to the judge's question, or at least half the answer. Of course a story could produce a direct effect. Why would anyone tell one if it didn't?

But what was the direct effect? That, I didn't know, didn't know the stories — new or old — well enough to know what effect they might have. But my mother did, that was clear, and I hated her for it, hated her on top of already hating her for what her stories had done to me, hated her for knowing something that I didn't and for making me feel powerless because of it, and maybe this is also what it means to be a child: always needing your parents and hating them for it, but still needing them, and maybe needing to hate them, too, and probably *that* was an old story as well.

"An old story," I said again, and then in a rush reminded my mother about the judge, what he'd said so many years before about stories and what they could and could not do, and how I still didn't know and needed to: because if my wife's kicking me out was an old story, then her taking me back (or not, or not!) was also an old story, and I needed to know it. Would my mother help me? "It's important," I said. "Please." I was even prepared to grovel and cry a little, too, and then also prepared to hate her for making me grovel and cry.

"You're talking to the wrong woman," my mother said. "I'm through with books. I'm through with stories of any kind."

"You are?" I said. This was big news, all right. I couldn't imagine my mother without her stories, stories that had meant so much to her that she'd had to force them on me. It was like imagining a musketeer without his sword or musket or the other musketeers — just one unarmed Frenchman, alone with his fancy mustache and his feathered hat and his foppishness. Then I looked around and noticed what I'd already noticed the day before: there were no books anywhere. "What happened to your books?" I asked her.

"I got rid of them," she said.

"Why?"

"Why?" she said. Here her voice got sharp, her face got sharp, too, and I could see my new mother, Beth, revert to the old mother, Elizabeth; it was like watching the presidential faces on Mt. Rushmore morph back into the big rock they once were. "Do you want to know why?"

"I do," I said, because I did.

My mother looked at me for a long time, and as she did, her face got kindly again. You could see pity, love, and pain filling her up, rising from her toes, through the hollow tubes of her legs and torso and leveling off in her eyes, where I could see them, the emotions, sloshing around in her pupils. My mother raised her right arm slightly, as if to touch my cheek, and I needed her then more than ever, but this need was closer to love than to hate. I wanted to say, *Oh, touch my cheek, Mother. You told me those stories and ruined my life, and I ruined yours, too, but if you touch my cheek . . .*

I didn't get to finish the thought, and my mother didn't touch my cheek, either. Instead she grabbed the (empty) can of beer out of my father's hand and went into the kitchen. Then it was just me and my father again, just two men in a room struggling to understand the woman who had just left them alone with each other. This would clearly be a never-ending battle. I could see the two of us sitting in that room until kingdom come, trying — and failing — to understand the women we loved. The past washed over me right then, as you can't ever stop it from doing, and there was Anne Marie, in my heart, my eyes and ears and brain, wondering what I was doing there with my parents when I should be at home, begging Anne Marie to let me come back to it, and her, and them, and us.

"Should I just go home, Dad?"

"Home?" he asked, confused, as if to say, I think, *Home? Why, you're already in it.*

"My other home, I mean. Shouldn't I just go back to Anne Marie and the kids?" I asked. "Wouldn't it be better that way? Wouldn't things have been better for all of us if you hadn't taken three years to come home?"

"Wait . . . wait," my father said.

"For what?"

"Time," he said.

"How much time?" I asked. "I don't think I can wait three years. Do I have to wait three years like you did with me and Mom?"

Speaking of my mother, there she was again, in the living room, holding a triangle of big beers in both hands. She placed one can in my father's ready claw and he immediately began drinking from it, violently, as if trying to suck up some of the aluminum from the can along with the beer. Then my mother tried to give me a beer, and I held up my hands in protest and said, "Oh no, not me."

About me as a drinker: I wasn't much of one and had a short, bad history of doing it. The few times I'd tried drinking—in high school, at subdivision barbecues—I either became too much like myself or not enough, but either way it was always calamity on top of calamity and I found myself saying way too much about too little and doing the wrong things in the wrong places. Once, at my boss's Christmas party (it was vodka I was drinking, more than two glasses, and so too much of it), I passed out for a minute—passed out but still, like a zombie, remained fully ambulatory and mostly functional—and when I came to, I found myself in my boss's kitchen, the refrigerator door open and me next to it at the counter, spreading mayonnaise onto two slices of wheat bread and licking the knife after each pass before I stuck it back in the jar. I heard someone cough or gag, looked up, and saw the kitchen's population—there was a big crowd in there, including my boss, Mr. Janzen, a tall, stern man who had a big nose that he couldn't help, physically speaking, looking down at you with—staring at me, all of their mouths open and slack, obviously wondering what I thought I was doing, exactly, and all I could think to say was, "Sandwich." Which is what I said. And then, to prove my point, whatever the point was, I ate it. The sandwich, that is.

"I don't really drink," I told my mother.

"You do now," she said, with such certainty that I believed her. I took the can and we all drank our big beers, one after the other, and I discovered that my mother was right: I did drink, and I learned that when you drank, things happened, nearly by themselves. It got dark, and someone turned on the light; it got too quiet and someone turned on the television; the television got too noisy and someone turned it off; we got hungry and someone produced food — pretzels, chips, popcorn, *something* we ate right out of the bag. Things happened, and questions were asked, too, that might not have been asked without the beer. I asked my mother, "You got rid of your books because of me, because of what I did and what happened to me, didn't you?" and she said, "Ha!" And then I asked, "Are you still an English teacher?" and she said, "Once an English teacher, always an English teacher." And then I asked, "How can you teach English if you're through with books?" and she said, "It's perhaps easier that way." And then I asked, "Were those stories you told me, those books you made me read, supposed to make me happy?" and she said, "I don't know *what* they were supposed to do." And then I asked, "Why did you tell me those stories, then? And why did you make me read if the reading wasn't supposed to make me happy?" And she said, "Why don't you ask me questions I can answer?" And then I said, "Dad is a tough old guy, isn't he?" and she said, "No, he's not." And then I asked, "Will you ever forgive him for leaving us?" and she said, "All is forgiven," and raised her beer, and for a second I thought she was going to dump it on my father's head in a kind of baptismal forgiveness. But she didn't, and I asked, "Can people know each other too long, too well?" and she said, "Yes, they can." And then I asked, "What happens to love?" and she said, "Ask your father." And I said, "Dad, what happens to love?" and he said something that sounded like, "Urt." And then my mother asked me, "You have a job, correct? Are you going to work tomorrow?" And I said, "I think I'll quit," and I did so, right there, called up Pioneer Packaging and told the answering machine that I was quitting. And while I was at it, I also mentioned a number of things I hated about them and the job they'd given me, things that were totally untrue and that I wouldn't be able to take back later on and that I would have regretted immediately if I hadn't had so much beer in me in the first place. In this way I discovered something else drinking made possible: it made self-destruction seem attractive and let you say things you didn't mean and you might regret, but it also made you too drunk to regret them. When I hung up on my career in packaging forever, my mother said, "Are you going to stay here for a while?" and I said, "Do you want me to?" And she said, "I've missed you, Sam. I'm so sorry about everything," which I took to mean, *Yes, I do want you to stay awhile.* And I said, "Who needs another beer?" We all did, and then we all did again, and again, until I forgot that I'd been kicked out of my house, just like my father seemed to forget he was incapacitated: the more beer he drank, the more mobile he seemed to be, and by his sixth beer he was walking around and could get to the refrigerator and back under his own power, even, and his slurring wasn't quite so dramatic when he asked if anyone needed another drink, which we all did. We drank together, as a family, until there was nothing left to drink and nothing else to do but pass out, right there on the couch. Not once while I was drinking did I think about Anne Marie and the kids, just a few miles away, and this was another thing I learned that night: drinking helps you forget the things you need to forget, at least for a little while, until you pass out and then wake up two hours later and vomit all over yourself and then the hallway and then the bathroom.

Because drinking was another thing I'd bumbled and wasn't much good at. All the beer flooded out of me, and all my failures flooded back in, as if in retaliation for my thinking I could forget them: those letters, my wife, my kids, my job, my parents, Thomas Coleman, his parents, their deaths, my life! They were all speaking to me, their voices shouting over the sounds of my retching, a regular chorus of recrimination bouncing off the porcelain and tile. And then there was another voice, a voice that had a hand, a gentle hand on my back, and was saying, "It's OK, it's OK."

"It is?" I asked.

"You'll feel better in the morning," she said.

It was my mother. And because it was my mother, I felt I could say anything and not be too ashamed of it, and so I said, "Oh, Mom, I'm scared I've lost them forever. I miss them so much."

"I know you do," she said.

"Is that an old story, too?"

"Yes," my mother said. "The oldest."

"Stories," I said. "It feels like I don't know anything about them. Please teach me something about these stories."

"I already tried to," she said, and then she led me to bed, which is where I made up my mind: I would have to learn something about stories, and fast. My mother wouldn't teach me; that much was clear. My old dad was too far gone to do me much good; that was clear, too. I would have to go somewhere else to learn, and I thought I knew where.

7

I would go to a bookstore. I couldn't go to a library, I knew that, because libraries demand quiet and decorum and I wasn't exactly wired for that: as a child I'd been shushed to death too many times by too many bony librarians in their cardigan sweaters, and I wasn't going back, the way the intelligent bull never goes back to the china shop after that disastrous first or second or third time. But I didn't recall bookstores' requiring any such absolute delicacy, although it's true that I hadn't been to one in twenty years.

But first I had to do something about my hangover. The story of one's first significant hangover is overlong and familiar and I won't add to it here except to say that it felt as though someone had taken their diseased head and switched it with my healthy one. I got out of bed, hopped in the shower, which didn't make my hangover go away but did wet it down some. Someone — my mother, I assumed and still do — had taken my suitcase (the one I'd taken with me to Cincinnati) out of my van and put it in my room. I unpacked the suitcase, got dressed, and went downstairs. The house was empty — you can always tell when a house is empty, especially if you yell out several times, "Hello! Mom? Dad? Anyone here?" and then check each and every room for signs of life. They were both gone, all right. I had once again woken up late: it was just past noon. My mother had gone to work, no doubt, but where was my father? Had the university press kept him on out of pity so that he'd still feel somewhat normal? Oh, I missed Pioneer Packaging right then, missed the feeling of normality it gave me. Because isn't this what work is good for? Not so much a way to make your money, but a way you can feel normal, even (especially) when you know you are not? I had those hungover, jobless blues, all right, and maybe my father knew I would, because on the kitchen table there was a tall glass full of something dark, murky, and potent and next to it a note, in his handwriting, hand-writing that was a little shaky but definitely still his — I recognized it from those many postcards he'd sent me — that said, "Drink me." Like Alice, I did. For a second I felt much worse, and then the second after that I felt much better. Whatever the cure for drinking was, it was much like drinking itself, which I suddenly felt ready to do more of, right after I went to the Book Warehouse.

The Book Warehouse: I'd driven past it many times. It was maybe a mile from my house, right on Route 116. I knew that Anne Marie and the kids went there all the time: for story hour, story circle, story time, story share, and other story-related activities, all, apparently, with their own separate purpose and function. But I'd never been there, and how was that possible? This was the question I asked myself as I pulled into the enormous parking lot, next to a series of other enormous park-ing lots serving adjacent superstores. How had I, who'd lived near this place for years and years and whose life had been ruled by stories and books — how had I not once entered its doors? I was like the ancient fisherman who'd never been swimming and who, on the verge of tak-ing his invigorating first dip, wondered what had taken him so awfully long.

The Book Warehouse was big. That was the first thing I noticed. Plus bright. The bookstores my mother had taken me to when I was young smelled like the back of a damp storage closet and were dim and narrow and filled with towering, overflowing bookshelves that leaned over the aisles and obscured the flickering overhead lights. The Book Warehouse was nothing like that. No, when you walked into the Book Warehouse it was like walking into an operating room, with cheerful music piped in and purple banners hanging from the ceiling that told you to READ!!! Except there weren't any books, not that I could see, because when you entered the store, you walked right into a café. There isn't much to say about the café itself. I don't remember what it looked like, really, or whether they served food there, and if they did, whether there was any-one there to serve it to you. It was the sort of place where you entered and seemed to pass out for a second and suddenly you came to and were holding a cup of coffee. It was West African native dark bean coffee. I don't know what that meant, exactly, but the coffee was excellent and came in an attractive ceramic mug with good heft and balance to it. I remember that much.

It was three in the afternoon at this point, and the café was empty except for a group of women, mostly, sitting around in a circle in their comfortable chairs sipping their coffee with their books on their laps. These women looked like our female neighbors in Camelot, with their severe, sensible haircuts and expensive casual clothes that were baggy enough to hide how thin they either were or weren't and shoes that were somewhere between clogs and running sneakers and that in any case had very good traction. I'd never really thought about this kind of female Camelotian, pro or con, but Anne Marie hated these women before she started to become one of them. And because I was married to Anne Marie and was on her side, I'd hated them, too, although without much feeling or reason. After all, were they so different from me? What was wrong with them? Was that same thing wrong with me? How could the books help make us all better? I decided to sit down, inconspicu-ously eavesdrop on their conversation about the book spread-eagled in each of their laps, and find out.

They weren't talking about the book, not exactly; that's the first thing I found out. Instead, they were talking about how they felt. When I sat down, one woman with a flowing tan barn coat and dark circles under her eyes was talking about how a character in the book reminded her of her daughter.

"Oh, it was heartbreaking," the woman said. "It made me cry." Speaking of that, she started crying right then, and since crying is as contagious as laughter or the worst kinds of disease, I nearly started crying, too. But I got hold of myself and managed to choke back my tears, and finally the woman did, too — her sobs became whimpers that became sniffles that became brave, quivering sighs. She wiped her eyes with the backs of her hands, wiped the hands on her barn coat, and again said, "It made me cry. I loved it. That's all I have to say."

"Wait a minute — hold on," I said. I had all these questions already. What exactly in the book reminded the woman of her daughter? And why did this make her cry? Did she, the woman in the barn coat, cry in great, shameless, heaving sobs in public places, or quietly, behind a closed bathroom door with the water running so that no one could hear her? I remembered my mother assigning me books and asking me, after I'd read them, to tell her about them. Details, she always wanted details and more details, and apparently I was my mother's son, more than I wanted to be, because now I wanted details, too. But I'd said too much already, this was obvious: the other women, mostly, were glaring at me as if I'd murdered both the woman and her daughter with my outburst, and the woman herself looked as though she were on the verge of another crying jag. "Sorry," I said, then sank back into my chair and pledged to listen quietly, very quietly, and with my mind as wide open as possible.

So I listened and learned some things. Another woman wearing a matching sky blue velour sweat suit insisted that anger could be a good thing, a positive thing (she did not say what, if anything, this had to do with the book); a man (he was the only other man there; I thought this near-total absence of men meaningful, even though I couldn't be certain of what it might mean) in his fifties, wearing a shiny warm-up jacket scarred with multiple zippers and Velcro patches, said that he read the book in one sitting and then immediately went and hugged his father's gravestone. The man explained that he had hated his father for years for reasons he couldn't quite remember, and that he had also hated his father for dying on him before they could talk about the hate and the mysterious reasons behind it. "I felt lost, so lost," the man said, "and it was my father's fault." In his resentment the man had let his father's gravestone fall into something of a ruin. The man said that he hugged the gravestone for a long, long time, just so that his father would know that he loved him and that all was forgiven. "I got all dirty from hugging the gravestone," the man said, "but I don't care. It felt good to get dirty."

"Bring on the *dirt*," one of the women said. She was a white woman wearing wide-wale corduroys and penny loafers and she had the most severe of all the severely blunt, sensible haircuts, but she said, "Bring on the *dirt*," in a vaguely black-gospel fashion. This clearly gave the lone black woman in the group some pause. The black woman cleared her throat and got up to get some more coffee and left her book on her chair unattended. I made sure no one was looking, then picked up the book. On the front cover was a drawing of a coffee cup, the coffee steaming from inside. The title of the book was *Listen*. On the back cover was a picture of the author, a benign-looking, bearded man with a long-billed fishing cap, sitting in an Adirondack chair, drinking a cup of coffee. On the inside back cover was a list of topics for discussion, and the number one topic for discussion was "How does this book make you feel about the Human Condition?"

It made me feel good, all right, about the Human Condition and about the women (mostly), too. I hadn't read the book, of course, but as far as I could tell, neither had anyone else, and besides, that wasn't what it was there for: the book was there to give the women (mostly) a reason to confess to the feelings they'd already had before reading the book, which as far as I could tell they hadn't actually read. The confessions made everyone feel better, I could tell, because the café was now filled with their bright, non-book-related chatter. The book had made them happy! This was a revelation to me because I remembered how unhappy reading books had made me back when I read them — they were full of things I didn't entirely understand and never would, and they made my head hurt. Books had made my parents unhappy, too, even though they professed to love them. My mother, for instance, taught *The Scarlet Letter* every year, and every year after she read and taught it, she looked miserable and depressed and *angry* about Hester Prynne and her *A* and her Dimmesdale, as though she would like to take the book and beat herself over the head with it and then go out and find the Human Condition and beat *it* over the head, too. The look on my mother's face had told me that she was certain that the Human Condition would have been grateful for the beating. *Put me out of my misery,* would have been the Human Condition's sentiment, according to my mother.

But that happened only if you *read* the book, or if you read certain kinds of books. The women (mostly) had put aside the book and were now talking about ordinary, worldly things — money, clothes, food — and they seemed happier now that they'd confessed and unburdened themselves. It wasn't just that they were happier, either: they seemed *lighter,* and if it weren't for gravity I was sure they'd have been floating up somewhere near the ceiling with their cups of coffee. Their voices were optimistic and clear and not at all afraid or weepy anymore; they were the kind of voices that made you forget that there was pain and longing and fear and dishonesty in the world, and for the moment I forgot all those things existed for me, too.

There was only one more matter I needed to clarify. I walked up to the woman who'd said, "Bring on the *dirt,*" pointed at her copy of *Listen,* and asked her, "Is this book true?"

"It's a memoir," she said.

"OK," I said, not really sure whether that meant yes, it was true, or no, it wasn't. The bond analysts had been working on their memoirs in prison, but I hadn't been sure whether they were true or not, and for that matter the bond analysts never seemed too clear on the distinction, either, and had spent many hours engaged in debates over the relationship between creative license and the literal truth. I knew better than to press the issue further, because when I'd done so with the bond analysts, when I asked them whether they were telling the whole truth in their memoirs or not, they laughed at me as though the question was just another addition to the house of my bumbling. So instead I asked the woman if she liked the memoir.

"Oh yes," she said.

"Why?"

"It's so useful," she said without hesitation.

"That's all I needed to hear," I told her, because now I knew the answer to the judge's question: books were useful, they could produce a direct effect — of course they could. Why else would people read them if they could not? But if that were the case, then why did my mother get rid of her books? Was it that some books were useful and some were not and weren't doing anyone any good and so why not get rid of them? Clearly my mother had read the wrong books. But I would not make that same mistake.

I took my leave of the women (mostly) and the café and began wandering through the bookstore proper, making my way to the memoir section. It didn't take too long. The memoir section, it turned out, was the biggest section by far in the whole bookstore and was, in its own way, like the Soviet Union of literature, having mostly gobbled up the smaller, obsolete states of fiction and poetry. On the way there, I passed through the fiction section. I felt sorry for it immediately: it was so small, so neglected and poorly shelved, and I nearly bought a novel out of pity, but the only thing that caught my eye was something titled *The Ordinary White Boy*. I plucked it off the shelf. After all, I'd been an ordinary white boy once, before the killing and burning, and maybe I could be one again someday, and maybe this book could help me do it, even if it was a novel and not useful, generically speaking. On the back it said that the author was a newspaper reporter from upstate New York. I opened the novel, which began, "I was working as a newspaper reporter in upstate New York," and then I closed the book and put it back on the fiction shelf, which maybe wasn't all that different from the memoir shelf after all, and I decided never again to feel sorry for the fiction section, the way you stopped feeling sorry for Lithuania once it rolled over so easily and started speaking Russian so soon after being annexed.

Anyway, I moved on to the memoir section. After browsing for a while, I knew why it had to be so big: who knew there was so much truth to be told, so much advice to give, so many lessons to teach and learn? Who knew that there were so many people with so many necessary things to say about themselves? I flipped through the sexual abuse memoirs, sexual conquest memoirs, sexual inadequacy memoirs, alternative sexual memoirs. I perused travel memoirs, ghostwritten professional athlete memoirs, remorseful hedonist rock star memoirs, twelve-step memoirs, memoirs about reading (*A Reading Life: Book by Book*). There were five memoirs by one author, a woman who had written a memoir about her troubled relationship with her famous fiction-writer father; a memoir about her troubled relationship with her mother; a memoir about her troubled relationship with her children; a memoir about her troubled relationship with the bottle; and finally a memoir about her more loving relationship with herself. There were several memoirs about the difficulty of writing memoirs, and even a handful of how-to-write-a-memoir memoirs: *A Memoirist's Guide to Writing Your Memoir* and the like. All of this made me feel better about myself, and I was grateful to the books for teaching me — without my even having to read them — that there were people in the world more desperate, more self-absorbed, more boring than I was.

And then I found the memoir I was looking for, without even knowing that I was looking for it or that it even existed: *A Guide to Who I Am and Who I Pretended to Be,* written by Morgan Taylor, one of the bond analysts.

Except according to the book he was now an *ex*–bond analyst. That was the first thing I found out about his life after prison (I sat right down on the floor and started reading the book, as though catching up with a long-lost friend): Morgan didn't go back to being a bond analyst. "That life was dead to me now," he claimed in his memoir, without saying why it was dead or how it was ever especially alive in the first place. But in any case, instead of resuming his career as a bond analyst, he became what he called a "searcher." The first thing he did after he got out of prison was to go to South Carolina because he'd never been in South Carolina before and his inner voice said that he had to — had to! — visit all fifty states over the course of his lifetime. He also attended a game at every major league ballpark. He traveled to Yosemite and Badlands and Sequoia and every other national park of note . . .

"Wait a minute — hold on," I said to the book, and to Morgan, too, wherever he was. Because I recognized the story: it was my father's. He'd told me those things on his postcards, during those three years he'd left my mom and me, and I, in turn, had told the story of my father's travels to the bond analysts in prison. They were especially interested in the story — I remembered that now, too.

Was I angry? Of course I was. Is this what memoirists did? Steal someone else's true story and pass it off as their own? I was tempted to put the book right back on the shelf and not buy it, except that I wanted to see whether Morgan had gotten my father's story right and also whether I was in the memoir or not. I wasn't on the acknowledgments page, that's for sure: I checked, right there in the store, before I moved on to the cash register.

AFTER I BOUGHT Morgan Taylor's fake memoir and left the Book Warehouse, I did exactly what my father said I shouldn't: I didn't wait. Instead I drove out to Camelot. Because this is another thing your average American man in crisis does: he tries to go home, forgetting, momentarily, that he is the reason he left home in the first place, that the home is not his anymore, and that the crisis is him.

It was after four by this point, but beyond daylight savings and so already dark and getting suddenly cold and weirdly cheerful and Yuletide-like. Camelot was festive in a way it had never seemed when I lived there, with its streetlights and floodlights, and in a few houses you could tell the ventless gas fireplaces by their steady, nonsmoky, nonflickering blaze. I knew our own ventless gas fireplace wouldn't be in use — Anne Marie was a big believer in wood fire, and no other kind would do — but the lights were on downstairs, in the living room and dining room and kitchen. I parked across the street so that I could see through our living room's enormous bay windows, turned off my headlights, and watched as each member of my family passed the window in turn, as if modeling for me. There was Katherine, carrying that gigantic ringed binder full of the homework that came so easily for her that she would already have finished it; there was Christian, holding his plaster hammer above his head as if preparing to strike a blow for the working man; there was Anne Marie, gesturing wildly about something, her free hand flapping around her head as if defending herself against bees, sometimes smiling, sometimes scowling, the whole time talking to someone else in the room, I couldn't tell who. It wasn't the kids, because I could see them sitting at the table now, and Anne Marie's back was to them. She was speaking either to herself or to *someone else*. But who? I couldn't tell, because there was me, Sam, sitting in my van and not in the house, looking at the three of them (plus this invisible guest), feeling so far away from them, longing for them and afraid to knock on the door and find out that they weren't longing for me. Yes, I was outside looking in, all right, which was not unlike being a reader (this was my very thought), and maybe this was another reason why my mother gave up reading: she was sick of being outside the house. Maybe she wanted to be inside, with my addled father, drinking beer until there was no beer left to drink and nothing to forget that hadn't already been forgotten. Suddenly I wanted that, too, so, so badly, and so I drove out of Camelot, back to my one family, my one family that I didn't have to long for, my one family with whom I could drink myself to sleep and forget about the other one.

8

In many of my mother's books, the troubled narrator has a telling dream at a crucial moment, and so I wasn't at all surprised that night when I had one. A telling dream, that is.

In my dream I was standing in a cupola, four stories in the air, on the very top of a sprawling, gray-shingled mansion. The mansion backed up to the ocean, and there was a storm. The white-lipped, whip-backed waves crashed against the boats, which were coming unmoored in the surf, their lines snapping off like overextended rubber bands. The water was a bruise; the sky, an even darker, more violent blue. Up in the cupola, my back was to the water, facing inland toward a compound of five slightly smaller shingled mansions, and I was holding a red plastic gasoline can by its handle, daintily, like a purse. The smaller mansions were all on fire: there was more flame than wood, more smoke than structure. But there were people still inside the buildings, and they were leaning out windows, clinging to trellises. Each one was holding books; they were all burdened by books. Some of them were throwing the books out the windows; some were lowering overflowing sacks of books down the trellises toward men waiting on the ground below. There was one woman on top of a roof. She was wearing a gauzy, nearly transparent nightgown. Her hair was on fire: the flames ringed her skull like a crown, dripped down her long, curly locks like wax. I couldn't see her face, but it was obvious, in the logic of the dream, that she was beautiful and necessary. She was leaning against the chimney, beating

her head with one of the books as if to put out the fire. The book was
a hardcover, though, and the woman quickly knocked herself unconscious. Slumped against the chimney the way she was, I could see that
the woman had no underwear on: her black pubic hair looked like a
tattoo against her pearl white stomach and thighs. One of the men on
the ground saw this, too. He became distracted, understandably, and
while gazing at the unconscious woman's exposed nether regions, he,
too, was knocked unconscious by a falling sack of books. Another man
knelt to attend to his fallen comrade, then looked up and pointed to the
woman on the roof. Her nightgown was flickering and hissing in the
fire; the book, still in her right hand, caught fire and exploded. A severe,
sharp cry came from the men on the ground, from the men and women
in the windows and on the trellises. It appeared to be the first book lost
in the fire. A great despair washed over them all. The men and women
abandoned hope, hurled themselves out the windows and off the trellises. The men on the ground below did not attempt to avoid the falling
bodies and were crushed.

It was quite a dream, all right, and not at all the kind I usually had.
I usually had the kind in which familiar people showed up in unlikely
places, like the one in which I found my boss sitting at my kitchen table,
drinking coffee, which I found interesting — my boss had never been
in my house and didn't even drink coffee — but no one else did, and
when I relayed these dreams to my family, their eyes glazed over as if
they were having a dream of their own. No, this dream was different,
and I wished my family were around so I could tell them about it and
prove what sort of fantastic dream life old Sam Pulsifer was capable of
having — although I'd have to edit out the pubic-hair part for the kids.
Or maybe I wouldn't have told them after all, because the dream didn't
make me feel so hot: my head hurt and I was breathing hard. After a
dream like that, you're grateful that it was just a dream, that no matter how bad your actual life, it couldn't be worse than your dream life.
That's how I felt until I went downstairs (the house was empty again,

my hangover more familiar and less terrible, the hangover potion on the table again less urgently needed, though I drank it anyway), opened the *Springfield Republican,* and discovered that someone had set fire to the Edward Bellamy House in Chicopee, Massachusetts, not twenty minutes from where I sat, reading about it.

At first I didn't remember that Bellamy was a writer, and, by extension, that his house was a writer's house. The headline read LOCAL LAND-MARK RECEIVES MINOR FIRE DAMAGE, as though the minor fire damage had come in the mail. Only after reading a little bit did I discover that Bellamy had been a writer and that his most famous book was *Looking Backward.* Only *then* did the author's name and his book sneak through the fog of my hangover and appear in my memory bank. I put down the paper, walked to my father's room, opened the end table drawer, rifled through the box of letters, and finally found it: a letter from Mr. Harvey Frazier of Chicopee, Massachusetts, asking me to burn down the Edward Bellamy House. The letter had been mailed only fifteen years ago (so said the postmark on the envelope), but it was so crinkled and smudged and creased that it looked like an ancient artifact. I put the letter in my shirt pocket, put the shoe box back in its not-so-secret hiding place, then went back to the newspaper article: it said that the fire damage was minor and that the fire department said the cause of the fire was "suspicious." I knew what that meant: they'd called my fire "suspicious," too, even after they already knew I was the one who'd accidentally set it.

A confession: my mother never let me read detective novels when I was a child, not even *child* detective novels. Once, when my mother caught me reading an Encyclopedia Brown book (it was, I believe, about the neighbor's cat and who had caused it to go missing), she confiscated it and said, "If you want to read a mystery, read this." She handed me Mark Twain's *Pudd'nhead Wilson,* which, as far as I could tell, was not a mystery but instead a book about black people who weren't, and white people who weren't, either, and an outcast New York fingerprinter

and some Europeans and Virginians in Missouri, and the only mystery
as far as I was concerned was how these non-Missourians got to the
state in the first place, and why they then stayed there for as long as
they did.

My point: if I'd ever read a real detective novel, about a real mystery,
then maybe I'd have known what to do next. Instead I muddled through
the best I could. I seemed to remember hearing, or maybe seeing on TV,
that detectives drank impressively, even (especially) while on the case.
So I had a drink, the last beer in the fridge, left over from the previous
night's family binge. While drinking, I thought about who might possibly have set fire to the Bellamy House. Thomas Coleman was the first
person I thought of, obviously. I knew he was going to make more and
greater trouble for me, and maybe this was it. He would burn down
the Bellamy House and somehow blame it on me. But then again, how
would he even know someone wanted me to burn down the Bellamy
House in the first place? After all, the letter was here, in my shirt pocket;
I patted it to make sure.

But if not Thomas Coleman, then who? Could it have been Mr. Harvey
Frazier himself? After all, he'd been waiting such a long time, and maybe
he felt he couldn't wait anymore. Or maybe it was someone else entirely,
someone I obviously hadn't yet thought of. I didn't know, but I decided
to visit Mr. Harvey Frazier and find out. How I would find out, I had no
idea. Again, if I'd read the right books, I might have known how to be a
proper detective. And if I hadn't quit my job at Pioneer Packaging and
had something else to do, then maybe I would have been too busy to
try to be one. And if I hadn't been all alone, if there had been someone
else in the house, then maybe they would have warned me: maybe they
would have told me not to go near the Edward Bellamy House, just to
stay put and not go *anywhere*.

But then again, maybe that's who a detective is: someone with nothing else to do but act like a detective and with no one around to tell him
not to.

MR. HARVEY FRAZIER of Chicopee, Massachusetts, was awfully cagey for an old guy and pretended not to recognize me or my name at first. And he was *old*, at least eighty, and spooky, too, because he opened his door just as I was ready to knock on it, as if he were expecting me *right at that moment*. Even though I was startled, I managed to say, "Sir, it's me, Sam Pulsifer," then unclenched my knocking fist and extended my hand for Mr. Frazier to shake. He didn't shake it; instead he said, "I was about to walk," and then he did, right past me and down the street. He was difficult to read, all right, and suddenly I wanted not only to know whether he'd set the fire or not, but also to know *him*, to really *know* why he wanted what he wanted, to know him in a way I hadn't known anyone else — not my parents or Anne Marie or the kids — and you could say I was making up for lost time and missed opportunities as I chased after Mr. Frazier.

He was fast, too. For an old guy. Or maybe the speed was part of his anger at me for not responding to his letter for so long. I jogged until I caught up with him, and then said, "A walk, huh?" and when he didn't take this conversational bait, I asked, "Where to?"

"Store," he said. He spoke with that serious, terse Yankee accent that always makes me feel I've done something wrong, and when he said "store," he sounded so ancient and formal that I imagined he was walking to an old-fashioned family-owned store, where he was going to buy something obsolete, like dry goods, whatever dry goods might be, or maybe tobacco, maybe some good-smelling pipe tobacco. But no, scratch that; Mr. Frazier didn't smoke and never had, I was guessing, not even before it was known to cause cancer, because tobacco was expensive or at least an expense and Mr. Frazier was a tight-ass. I knew this because Mr. Frazier was wearing brown wool pants and a brown cardigan sweater and a houndstooth sport coat that were worn down to the last thin layer of fabric. He probably hadn't bought new clothes in thirty years, and he'd probably bought the clothes he had on at a department store whose name he wouldn't be able to remember, nor its location, although no doubt it was in a downtown somewhere, and no doubt it had gone out of business by now. Mr. Frazier would think the idea of new clothes silly. Absolutely ridiculous. Especially if you bought clothes made out of good, durable wool, which his had probably been before he'd worn them all to hell, which was how I knew he was a tight-ass. I mean no disrespect when I say this. I was merely trying to get into his head, trying to get a bead on his whole psychology.

"What are you getting at the store?"

"Newspaper," he said, and I noticed that he didn't use articles, either, and I added that to his psychological profile. A few blocks ahead of us I could see a big chain supermarket, a Super Stop and Shop, and not a "store" at all. If this was where we were headed, I would add *delusional* to his profile while I had it out and was working on it.

Another thing about Mr. Frazier's getup: it was excessively heavy for the very warm Indian summer November day that it was, and it was also an excessively formal getup for a daily trip to the supermarket or store or wherever it was we were headed. Or maybe it was just our immediate surroundings that made it seem so. Because the neighborhood was really gone, and Mr. Frazier was the best-looking thing in it. There was garbage everywhere — bottles, egg cartons, diapers — and almost no cans to put it in. On the sidewalk someone had written in pink chalk, "Shamequa eat pussy." It was too bad because the neighborhood had once been very pretty, you could tell. The big white houses had probably been Victorian at one point, but they had been added onto so often that they now defied architectural classification. Yes, I bet the houses had once been owned by families, good, respectable families, and they'd probably all dressed like Mr. Frazier, and the families had made sure that the houses had straight ridgepoles and well-pointed chimneys and elm trees and squirrels, and they, the families, could do this because they had jobs at Pratt and Whitney making airplanes or at the Indian motorcycle plant making Indian motorcycles or at Monarch making insurance premiums. But at some point between the wars, people started losing their jobs. It's an old story. They lost their jobs and then couldn't afford to keep their ridgepoles straight or their chimneys erect or their homes single-family, and the elm trees began dying and so did the people, or they moved and *then* died, and the houses were aluminum-sided and divided into apartments — the multiple mailboxes, the tangled and bunched telephone and power lines, and the rusted cars parked curbside told me so. The neighborhood wasn't Mr. Frazier's anymore, it didn't need him, and how could this not make him good and mad?

Just then we passed our first two human beings: two boys sitting on the front steps of one of those multifamily homes. They were shirtless and wore shorts that were not properly shorts, because they came down well past the knee. The boys were emaciated and their chests were as concave as mine had once been, and both of them had their nipples pierced with silver hoops. I wondered if air had escaped from the boys' chests with the piercing.

"Good afternoon," Mr. Frazier said as he passed them.

"Fucked *up*," one of the boys said. When he said the word "fucked," he didn't exactly enunciate the *c* and the *k* but slurred the word straight into the final *d*. The other boy didn't say anything but just laughed and shook his head.

I wanted to say something to the boys, something like, *Hey, what's that? What did you say?* or maybe, *Why don't you show some respect, punk?* But I was following Mr. Frazier's lead and he kept walking and so did I. He had to know, of course, that the boys were talking to him, but he probably didn't know to what exactly they were referring, and neither did I. *Something* was fucked up, that much was clear, and it wasn't Mr. Frazier, no matter what the boys said. If anything was fucked up, it was the boys. Maybe they weren't really boys at all: maybe they were grown men dressing like boys and acting like boys and not working adult jobs and not supporting their families, if they had families, and swearing like black people were supposed to swear, even though the boys looked white. The word *wigger* came to mind — it was a word I'd once heard

on television—but I quickly got rid of it and didn't mention the word to
Mr. Frazier. No, Mr. Frazier did not want any new words in his mouth
or head; I knew this without having to ask. There were enough words
in the world already, and too many of them were curse words, and too
many young people cursed in such a way that you could not discern the
object of the swearing and in such a way that made you think that this
was simply the way they talked—to one another, to strangers—and
it made it difficult to tell whether the swearing was friendly or threatening, whether the swearing was black swearing or white swearing,
whether there was a difference, whether it mattered to the person who
was being cursed, if he was actually being cursed. I imagined poor Mr.
Frazier all alone in his house at night, his lights off and him standing at
the front windows, not being able to sleep, just looking at the neighborhood, which is even darker than his house and so, so strange to him.
Somewhere out there, Shamequa is eating pussy and then testifying to
that fact on the sidewalk with her pink chalk, and the trash is rolling
through the streets like tumbleweed, and the words "fucked up, fucked
up, fucked up" are blowing in the wind, and you can't get away from
them or know if they refer to you or to someone else. It was fucked up,
all right. For Mr. Frazier, not knowing whether he was being cursed at
or not must have seemed liked the most fucked up thing of all.

By the time we got to the store—it was a Super Stop and Shop all
right, but I was on Mr. Frazier's side now, and so it was a store—I was
in something like agreement with the boys: it was *fucked up*, "it" being
the store itself, which was more parking lot than building. And it was
fucked up that those boys could speak to Mr. Frazier, that sweet guy, the
way they had and suffer no consequences. Mr. Frazier *had* to be angry,
at least angry enough to burn down a house or to want someone else to
burn it down. But why the Edward Bellamy House? That's what I didn't
understand.

"Hey, what do you say, Mr. Frazier?" I said to him. "I have a couple
questions for you."

Mr. Frazier didn't respond. He bought his paper from the machine outside the store (who knows why? Maybe as long as he didn't enter the building, he could in good conscience continue calling it a store), then turned and began walking back home. He was really setting a good pace, and I broke a sweat trying to catch up with him. Soon after I did, we passed by those boys again, still sitting on the steps, as if waiting for us. You don't often get a second chance in this world to say what you wanted to say, or ask what you wanted to ask. So I stopped in front of them and grabbed a fistful of Mr. Frazier's jacket to get him to stop, too. Mr. Frazier didn't turn to face the boys but, like a spooked horse, looked at them sideways. I turned to face them, though, and I could feel my face get fiery red and I hoped that it shone on the boys like a beacon of sorts.

"Earlier," I said to the boys, "you said something to Mr. Frazier here."

"True," one of the boys said. They both looked exactly the same, with their faint mustaches, their flat alabaster stomachs, their nipple rings glinting and glistening in the sun.

"Well," I said, "I'd like you to apologize to him. I think he deserves an apology."

One of the boys shook his head, and said, "Fucked up." He said this without malice or slyness or any emotion at all. It was delivered as a statement of fact.

"*Hey!*" I said, because I couldn't take it anymore. Mr. Frazier had so much life left in him, but even if he hadn't, even when old people were taking up space and air, they'd lived through a lot and you had to give them some credit and respect. I moved toward the boys in what I hoped was a menacing fashion. When I did so, they stood up — also menacingly — and I noticed that their white socks were pulled up very high, probably to their knees (I couldn't tell exactly, because of the length of their shorts). Why pull your socks so high? There was only one reason I could think of: these were the kind of guys who might have knives in their socks, except the socks were so high they could probably have hidden a short sword in there. Me, I had no weapons anywhere. Plus, my socks were the ankle-high kind and couldn't possibly harbor anything dangerous. I backed away from the boys, palms facing out, and as I backpedaled I whispered to Mr. Frazier, "Let's get out of here."

But Mr. Frazier ignored me. He turned his head slowly and slightly to look at the boys. Even that head-turning gesture was impressive. I wondered if it occurred to the boys how inferior they were to him. It was like watching a world-weary colossus swiveling to ask the puny villagers why they were pelting him with rocks. "To what are you referring?" Mr. Frazier said to the boy who'd spoken earlier.

"It's hot and you wearing some *sleigh-riding* clothes, dude," the boy said, and then fanned himself with his left hand to remind us all of the heat.

"Fucked up," the other boy said.

"I see," Mr. Frazier said, and resumed his walking, beating the now rolled-up newspaper against his leg, keeping time with his outrage, which must have been huge. I fixed the boys with one last meaningful stare and then, before I could see how they'd respond, turned and ran until I caught up with Mr. Frazier.

His clothes: they were what was fucked up, and all of a sudden Mr. Frazier was hot, very hot, his face nearly as red as mine ever got. He stopped beating his leg with the paper and began using it as a fan. The fanning would do no good; I knew this from experience because we both had powerful heating mechanisms inside us, big furnaces of shame and rage somewhere down there around our hearts and livers and other inner organs, and you can't cool the inside from outside. Mr. Frazier learned this truth quickly. There was an overflowing trash can on the corner and Mr. Frazier tossed the newspaper on top of the heap and crossed against the light, daring traffic to hit him, us. But there was no traffic and we reached the other side unscathed.

He kept walking, beating his leg with his hand (I bet he already missed his newspaper). I didn't say a word; I felt bad for the old guy. He was in worse shape than before I'd arrived, I could see that, and as if to illustrate the point, he sat down right on the curb. I sat down next to him, glad for the rest. Like me, Mr. Frazier was breathing heavily, and again I feared for his heart and what I had done to it. Yes, I felt bad for him, and for myself, too, which has to be the truest kind of empathy. I wanted to help him but didn't know how. Was it possible that I was incapable of helping someone? It didn't seem fair. Was it possible that there was no such thing as fair? These were my questions, and I was about to think of others when I looked up and noticed that we were sitting in front of the Edward Bellamy House. There was a big, handsome brown wooden sign on the house that said so. I could read it clearly from our spot on the curb.

"Hey," I said, "there it is." And in my excitement, I pulled Mr. Frazier to his feet. It wasn't difficult: there wasn't much weight to him beyond his clothes. I pulled him up and dragged him across the sidewalk and to the house. I don't know how I missed it in the first place. Next to Mr. Frazier it was the best-looking thing in the neighborhood, even though someone had tried to torch it: it was gray with green trim and a neatly mowed lawn and electric candles glowing in the windows and a picket fence outside and even an antique black iron boot scraper next to the front door. It was pretty. It was very, very pretty. You wouldn't have noticed anything was wrong with it except that it was ringed by yellow police tape, and there were some faint black singe marks near the foundation. It was like looking at a beautiful woman who'd just gotten a bad haircut. After all the ugliness we'd seen in the neighborhood, its beauty was a fresh, cool breeze on a hot day, and I still couldn't figure out why Mr. Frazier would want to burn it down. Why not burn the boys' house down if they were bugging him so? To burn this handsome old house was screwy and made no sense.

"Why?" I asked him. "Why would you want to burn that beautiful house down?" As I asked the question, I realized the answer was right in his letter, which I'd skimmed, but only far enough to know *what* Mr.

Frazier wanted me to burn and not *why*. So I pulled the letter out of my jacket pocket. But before it was all the way out, Mr. Frazier snatched it away from me. I didn't even see his hand come between mine and the letter. His reflexes were that incredible. He was quite an old guy.

But he wasn't much of a reader, at least not without his glasses. It must have taken him half an hour to get through that letter, which he held right up to his face.

"Mr. Frazier," I said, "why don't you let me read that for you? It'll go faster."

He ignored me and was right to do so. Because I was wrong about his eyesight; or maybe I was right, but it had nothing to do with the glacial pace of his reading. It was obvious that Mr. Frazier simply loved what he was doing. He was like my mother in this respect. He really knew how to read and get something out of it, too, and while he was reading, his face started going through phases, like the moon. He made reading seem like something noble and worth doing — life-altering, even. I again cursed myself for giving up reading so many years ago and vowed to continue reading Morgan Taylor's fraudulent memoir just as soon as Mr. Frazier finished with the letter.

Finally he did. I knew this because even though it appeared he was still reading — his face was still very close to the letter — I heard this sound, this familiar, repetitive, guttural sound, and when I looked closely I saw that Mr. Frazier was crying, and his tears were getting all over the letter.

"Please, Mr. Frazier," I said, "don't do that, don't — hey, why are you crying?"

"I miss you," he said in between heaving sobs.

And oh, that was terrible, much worse than the crying! Except that I couldn't figure out whom he was missing. It wasn't me, I knew that. For one, I was right there, next to him; for another, he wasn't looking at me. First Mr. Frazier stared at the letter; then he raised his head and seemed to look at an American flag sticking out of the porch flagpole stand. "I miss you," he said again, in the direction of the flag this time. So I walked over, yanked the flag out of its stand, and handed it to Mr. Frazier. But that flag didn't seem to be the thing he was missing: he immediately dropped it on the sidewalk and started crying again, really crying. I thought for sure his heart was going to give out this time, just fall out of his chest and right onto the sidewalk.

"Oh, I'm all alone, all alone," Mr. Frazier said. Then it was my heart I thought was going to give out. And then it was me who started crying: we were a duo of weepers, all right; we probably scared away the neighborhood cats.

"I'm all alone," he said again.

"I know," I said. "I'm all alone, too." Because no one was more expert in loneliness than yours truly: there is nothing more lonely than being an eighteen-year-old accidental arsonist and murderer and convict and virgin. So I told him that story, which of course he already knew in part. And because I had so much more story to tell and so many words with which to tell it, I went on a philosophical jag and told him that we spend most of our lives running away from loneliness, only to turn around and go and search it out, and as proof, I mentioned how I'd lied to my family for years because I was afraid to be alone, and then lied again on top of the lying, and in doing so I'd pretty much guaranteed that I *would* be alone. Yes, even though I didn't know what the letter said, I knew what Mr. Frazier was talking about and why he would want to burn down the Edward Bellamy House and make a good, roaring fire out of the thing. I had seen and heard the reasons myself: the boys had told Mr. Frazier that he didn't look like them, or, I guessed, like anyone else in the neighborhood, told him in so many obscene words that he didn't belong anymore, that he was all alone. This was where the fire came in, because after all, you couldn't feel lonely sitting — toes wiggling — in front of a fire. This was a known fact: even if you were all alone in the world, as long as there was a fire (and the Bellamy House was the biggest, most beautiful house in the neighborhood, and so logically it would also make the biggest, most beautiful fire), you could stare into it and feel its heat and it would remind you of another, happier time, a time long ago when the world belonged to you, when you understood it, when you could live in it for just a few damn *minutes* and not feel so lonely and scared and angry. "You're not alone, Harvey," I told him. "You're just not."

What was Mr. Frazier's response to this? He said (he was stone faced and dry eyed at this point), "Did you just call me Harvey?"

I thought he was objecting to my informality, and so I said, "Yes, sir, I'm sorry, Mr. Frazier."

"Harvey was my brother," he said. "My name is Charles."

At first I thought Mr. Frazier was lying, that he'd made up a brother out of thin air and as a proxy for his own wishes. As a kid I'd used this brother trick many a time myself, like when I accidentally threw a baseball through someone's window, or accidentally ate someone else's lunch in the cafeteria, or accidentally backed into someone's car in the high school parking lot after the junior prom, and I would have used it after accidentally burning down the Emily Dickinson House if I'd been thinking on my feet. But I realized Mr. Frazier wasn't making up his brother; making up a brother is easy, but it's much more difficult to cry convincingly about how much you miss the made-up brother when he's gone.

"OK," I said. "But why exactly did your brother want me to burn down the Edward Bellamy House?"

"Because he was . . . " And here he paused as if trying to understand his brother's reasons. "Because he was odd," Mr. Frazier finally said. "He had problems."

"I bet he was a reader, your brother, like you," I said.

"Yes," Mr. Frazier said. "He read too much. That was one of Harvey's problems. The world wasn't enough like the books. It was always disappointing him. But at least he had the position at the Bellamy House . . ."

"Let me guess," I said, awed by the serendipity of it all. "He was a tour guide."

Mr. Frazier nodded. "He was a tour guide until the state had budget problems and they cut his position."

"And that really disappointed him," I guessed.

"Correct."

"And so he wanted me to burn down the Edward Bellamy House because he got fired."

"I suppose so."

"And now he's dead," I said, wanting to get all the straight answers while Mr. Frazier was in the mood to field the questions. "He's dead and you miss him."

For a minute I thought Mr. Frazier was going to start crying again, but he didn't. He looked at me a long time: once again his face started shifting, from anger to grief to resignation to nostalgia — he went all the way through the range of human emotions. He might even have smirked a little, no small accomplishment for the grave old Yankee he was. Finally Mr. Frazier said wistfully, "Yes, I do."

"And so you finally couldn't wait for me anymore, and you took it upon yourself to set fire to the Bellamy House." It just came out of my mouth like that, as if I knew the truth and was only waiting for Mr. Frazier to congratulate me for knowing it.

Except he didn't. "No, no," Mr. Frazier said. He seemed genuinely surprised that I'd think such a thing. He even brushed off the front of his sport coat with the back of both hands, as though my accusation were lint.

"Well, who did, then?"

"I thought it was you," he said.

I assured him it wasn't me, it wasn't me, and he assured me again that it wasn't him, and we went around and around like this until we'd convinced each other of our innocence (was this a bad quality in a

detective, I wondered, to be so easily convinced of a suspect's innocence?) and there was nothing more to say. I said my good-bye, shook
his hand, and headed toward the van. Then I remembered I had one
more question. When I turned around, Mr. Frazier was already on his
porch — I saw now that his house was just three houses away from the
Edward Bellamy House — and I asked him, "Hey, what's that famous
book that Edward Bellamy wrote, again?"

At that Mr. Frazier really perked up; you could almost smell the book
learning come out of him, out of his pores. "He wrote the novel *Looking
Backward*. Among other, lesser works."

"*Looking Backward*," I repeated. "What was it about?"

"A utopia," he said before closing the door to his house behind him.
He'd taken his brother's letter with him, I realized after the door was
closed, but I decided to let Mr. Frazier keep it. Maybe he would cherish
it, the way my father obviously cherished all those letters to me. Maybe
Mr. Frazier would hold his brother's letter close to him and feel less
lonely. In any case, I just let him keep it. This turned out, much later, to
be something of a mistake on my part, but how was I to know that at
the time? How are we supposed to recognize our mistakes before they
become mistakes? Where is the book that can teach us *that*?

WHEN I GOT HOME it was just after five. I found my father in the living
room, sitting on the exercise bike. He was dressed in gray gym shorts
and a faded red tank top, and if he'd been wearing a headband, he'd have
looked a lot like that fitness instructor who was so obviously gay that
you thought he probably wasn't. My father wasn't pedaling the bike — he
was just sitting there with his feet on the pedals — but I thought it was
a huge accomplishment that he'd even managed to mount the thing in
the first place. He'd even broken a little sweat. My father was drinking
one of his forty-ounce Knickerbockers (someone must have gone to the
store, unless he had a private stash); propped up in front of him, on the

exercise bike's magazine stand, was Morgan Taylor's book. My father was flipping through the book, skipping forward one hundred pages and then back fifty, as though he'd never read a book before and wasn't sure how it was supposed to go. I couldn't tell how much of the book my father had actually read, but I *could* tell he was reading: the good half of his mouth was moving along with the words, the words Morgan had stolen from him.

"Oh, hey, I'm really sorry about that, Dad," I said. He looked up when I spoke, and dropped the book off the stand and onto the floor, which was just about what that book deserved. I picked the book up, walked over to the hall, and threw it into the open front-hall closet, just to show what I thought of the book. "That guy had no right."

"No . . . right," my father repeated: repetition, I'd learned by now, was his version of normal communication, the way jokes are for some people and sign language is for others.

"It's my fault, really," I said. "I'm the one who told him those stories about you."

"About . . . me?"

"About where you went, what you did when you left us."

"You . . . did?" my father asked. Only then, as though he was on tape delay, did his eyes slowly move through the air, following the book's trajectory. His eyes rested for a minute on the hall closet, as if trying to picture the book there among the winter coats and file cabinets and partnerless shoes he knew to be inside. "No . . . right," he said again. My father looked at me in displeasure, then took an especially angry pull on his beer.

"I know," I said, bowing my head. "I'm so sorry."

We sat there for a while in silence, me ashamed, my father angry, waiting for our third to come and break the impasse. Because this is what it also means to be in a family: to have two of its members break the family and then wait around for a third to make it whole again.

Finally, after fifteen minutes or so (my father had a cooler of beer near the base of the exercise bike and drank two beers, but he didn't offer me one and I didn't blame him), my mother showed up. She wasn't wearing exercise clothes: she was wearing green corduroy pants and a white shirt that somebody, for some reason, might call a blouse and not a shirt, and brown leather boots. She looked classy, regal, like a man without being at all manlike, like Katharine Hepburn but without the shakes or the Spencer Tracy. She looked young, too, not at all like the fifty-nine-year-old woman I knew her to be. Her face was flushed — healthy and outdoorsy in a way that made you think of a commercial for the most expensive, physician-endorsed kind of lip balm. My mother was carrying a twelve-pack of Knickerbocker: she freed one of the cans from the cardboard, threw it to me, and said, "I don't care why you're so gloomy, but stop." Then she turned to my father and said, "You, too."

"OK," I said, and my father grunted something that also sounded affirmative. I cracked the beer, took a long drink of it, and asked, "Hey, what did you do today?" Because it occurred to me that this is what family members ask one another after a long day, and it also occurred to me that I had no idea what my mother had done the previous three days I'd been home, either.

My mother was taking a slug of her beer when I asked this, and it was weird: there was a slight pause in her drinking, a hitch in her gulp, a slight but noticeable arrest in her imbibing, before she continued her drinking, finishing the whole beer in one long swallow, as a matter of fact. "Work," she said, and then, without looking at me, she tossed another full can of beer at me, even though I was only half-done with the first one.

"What about you, Dad?" I asked. "What did *you* do today?"

It was more difficult to read my father's reaction, since he had so few of them and they were so spastic and incomprehensible to begin with. But I did notice this: my father glanced pleadingly at the television, as though asking it for help. Then he looked at his cooler, which was apparently empty, and to the cooler he said finally, "Work." As if in reward for his giving the right answer, my mother tossed my father a beer, the way a trainer throws a seal a fish. My father amazingly caught it, too, although in doing so, he nearly capsized the bike, and I had to run over and catch him and it before they crashed to the floor.

"What about you, Sam," my mother asked. "What did *you* do today?"

I didn't know at the time whether my parents were lying or not, but I did know that it *appeared* as though they were, and I decided then and there as a poorly read and unschooled detective learning on the fly that the key to telling lies is to act the opposite of those who might be liars. I looked my mother square in the eye and said, "Nothing," and then looked my father in the eye and said, "Nothing," even though he hadn't asked the question, which I'll admit probably hurt my credibility some. But while I was looking them in the eye, I was also wondering if they'd read the morning paper (I'd left it on the dining room table, but it wasn't there now), if they knew about the Bellamy House fire, if my father knew that I'd been looking through those letters and had even taken (and now lost) one, if my mother even knew about the letters at all. Who knew what — that was the operative question for all of us.

"Well," my mother said, "we went to work and you did nothing. Another normal day."

"Just like it used to be," I said, thinking about when I was a kid and they would go to work, or said they did, and I did nothing, or said I did. We all drank to that, as was not true when I was a child, and drank some more, and they seemed to forget about the whole thing. My parents were very wise in their forgetting, of course, amnesia being, like a fixed mortgage, the thing that keeps your house your house. But I wasn't wise. I didn't forget. I got drunker and drunker, but still, the whole time I was thinking about my parents' normal days and whether they were anything like my normal day, and I was still thinking about this as I went upstairs. I took off my watch before climbing into bed. It's the expensive, indestructible sort of watch that tells you things — the barometric pressure, wind speed, and high tide in the second-largest city in Sri Lanka, for instance — that you don't necessarily need to know, but two of the useful things it does tell you are the time and the day of the week. And right then, my watch was telling me the time was 11:21 p.m. and the day of the week was Saturday. It was Saturday. "It is Saturday," I said out loud, making it official. My parents had gone to work on a Saturday, or said they had. For my father this wasn't so strange: apparently you could edit or not edit books on whatever day you wanted, and he'd always kept irregular work hours and days. But what sort of teacher goes to work on a Saturday? The question exhausted me, and I fell asleep before I could begin to answer it. I had already looked into the Edward Bellamy House fire and now I was going to have to look into this, too. As everyone knows, once you start looking into one thing, you can't help but start looking into others.

9

And once you start looking into others, then apparently you can't stop others from looking into you. I learned this truth the next day when I woke up and found Thomas Coleman leaning over my bed, his face far too close to my own, as if trying to make sure I was breathing.

"What do you think you're doing?" he asked.

"What?" I said, and then, "Hey!" and so on as I scrambled out of my bed, threw on some clothes (like the first time I'd met Thomas, I was half-dressed and thought that maybe our second meeting would go better if I were fully clothed), went to the bathroom, brushed my teeth, and walked downstairs, Thomas following me everywhere I went until I settled at the dining room table, where my hangover potion and "Drink me" note were waiting. I sat down and did what the note told me to. Thomas was still standing; he looked more substantial than he had the first time I saw him, which had been less than a week earlier. It seemed as though he'd put on some weight; even his hair looked a little thicker and had a little wave to it now, and there was a little color to his face, and all in all he looked like a matinee idol almost all the way recovered from cancer and chemo.

"What do you think you're doing?" Thomas asked me again.

I didn't respond, this being one of the all-time most difficult questions to answer, especially if you're not doing anything or think you're not doing anything.

"You quit your job," Thomas said, barely holding on to his patience. I could almost see it against the back of his bared teeth, struggling mightily to escape.

"That's true," I said.

"I called up Pioneer Packaging Friday to tell them that you'd burned down the Emily Dickinson House and killed my parents, and did they know they had a murderer and an arsonist working for them, and before I could get it all out, they told me you'd already quit." Here he paused, as if letting me catch up to his swift train of thought, which I appreciated. "What do you think you're doing?" he asked for the third time.

"I was drunk!" I told him, realizing for the first time that one of the things drink could transform was one's bumbling. Sober, one's bumbling was a kissing cousin to failure; but drunk, one's bumbling could be triumphant. "I quit my job because I was drunk!" I told him. "And you were right: they didn't know I was a murderer and an arsonist. But I quit before you could tell them! And I didn't even do it on purpose!"

This deflated Thomas. He sighed and sat down across from me; some of the color left his face. Disappointment took its rightful place in him, evicting strength and optimism. I felt a little sad for Thomas until I remembered why we were having this conversation in my parents' house and not my own, and what he'd told Anne Marie.

"Why did you lie about me having an affair?" I said. "Why did you tell Anne Marie I was having an affair with your wife?"

The question cheered Thomas up some. His eyes grew far away and dreamy and this disturbed me more than anything he'd done or said thus far. "She's kind of beautiful, you know," he said. "I can't figure out why you would ever cheat on her."

"I *didn't* cheat on her," I said, and nearly reached over the table to shake him out of his fiction and into our truth. He must have sensed this, because he stood up from his chair and backed a few feet away from the table. "I burned down that house and killed your parents," I yelled. "Why didn't you tell her *that*?"

"Why do you think?" Thomas asked. I could see that he was trying to be a detective, too — that is, if being a detective means making someone answer questions that you should be able to answer yourself but can't. This didn't make me feel any better. Did he really not know why he'd told Anne Marie one thing and not another? Did he not know what he was doing here? Was he an amateur life wrecker after all, and if so, would he do more damage as an amateur than he would if he were an expert? There was no way to ask these questions, of course, and expect an answer, and so instead I asked, "Why did you set fire to the Edward Bellamy House?"

"What?" he said. "Who?" Thomas looked genuinely baffled: his eyes retreated a little deeper into their sockets, leaving little lines in their wake, and his mouth puckered as though bewilderment were something sour. Then curiously, his face relaxed: a little, flickering smile illuminated his lips. Thomas cocked his head in the general direction of my dad's room and said, "Is your father home?"

"No," I said. "He's at work." And then, "Wait, do you know my father?"

"So long, Sam," he said, and then turned heel and walked out the front door. I sat there for too long, making sure I fixed the details in my head before I lost them for good. Thomas had mentioned my father. But so what: after all, he knew where to find me, and so he also knew that I had a father, as so many people did and as Thomas did not. But there was that cock of the head. Was that coincidental? Was it just a tic? Or did he cock his head in the direction of my father's room, knowing that it was in fact my father's room? And if so, how did he know *that*?

I got out of my chair and ran to the front door, trying to catch Thomas before he left my life for who knows how long this time. And I might have caught him, too, if the bond analysts hadn't been there, on my porch, blocking my way.

I CALL THEM THE bond analysts, but of course they had names. There was Morgan, as you know, and there were also two Ryans, one Tigue, and one Geoff, whom everyone called G-off. G-off was the only one whom I could keep straight, because he had dark, curly hair and looked slightly— by comparison and for lack of a better word—*ethnic*. The rest I could never tell apart, and looking at them now, I still couldn't. It wasn't especially cold out, but they were wearing duck boots and khaki pants and ribbed turtleneck sweaters, and each of them—other than G-off—had his hair combed to the side in a youthful, private-school fashion. They were all shifting uncomfortably from foot to foot, as if they'd have liked nothing better than to have something elevated—the bumper of a classic car, maybe, or a picket fence, or a day boat's prow railing—to prop their legs upon. Except for G-off, they kept flicking their hair out of their faces with a twitch of their necks. Since prison (and until the day before in the Book Warehouse), I hadn't thought about them much, which of course is a talent of mine, and it seemed as if time hadn't thought about them much, either: they looked exactly the same as they had ten years earlier. As for me, my belly was a little softer and bigger than it had been, and so, with my half-barrel chest and in right profile, I probably looked like a misshapen version of the letter *B*, and while I had kept most of the hair on my head, I had also added some elsewhere. The point is, the bond analysts had not aged and I had, and this was another thing I'd bumbled.

"Hello, Sam," one of them said—it might have been Morgan. I say that because he'd always been sort of their leader, and on the porch the other four had fallen into a ragged flying V behind him, which I thought was kind of them, to distinguish Morgan as the important one in that way. Other things should organize themselves in the same way. Life, for instance. "Long time no see."

"I don't want to hear it," I said. With Thomas and his surprise visit, it had taken me a few minutes to locate my anger, but with the bond analysts and *their* surprise visit, I'd fallen right into it. I figured that if I kept getting surprise visits, I'd start getting angry beforehand, that the anger would in fact announce the arrival of the surprise visitor and not follow it. "You had no right."

"What?" one of them said — maybe it was Tigue. "What did we do?"

"What did we do?" G-off said, and I remembered that one of their talents was to parrot one another to reinforce a point.

"You took my father's story and passed it off as your own," I said, and then pointed accusingly at what I hoped was Morgan. It was: he put his head down for a moment in shame, and while he did I got a good look at his part, which was straight and deep, like a canal cutting through the landmass of his hair.

"OK," he said, raising his head. "I'll admit it: that was wrong of me."

"Very wrong," G-off said.

"But I paid for it," Morgan said.

"What do you mean?" I asked.

"As you know, I wrote the memoir and stole your father's story," Morgan said. "As you also might know, I was on parole when I wrote the book. Well, my parole officer read the book when it came out."

"*Lots* of people read it," Tigue said.

"It did quite well," G-off said. "It even went into paperback."

"Not all books do, you know," Tigue said.

"Anyway," Morgan said, "when the parole officer read the book, he thought I'd violated my parole by leaving the state. He wanted to put me back in prison. So I had to tell him that I'd made the whole thing up, that I hadn't even left Massachusetts and I'd never done those things or gone to those places and that it wasn't my story to begin with."

"Then word got out," Tigue said.

"The publisher found out and was pissed," G-off said. "He demanded the advance back, plus all royalties."

"I had to take out a loan to pay back the money," Morgan said. "I even had to move back in with my parents for a while."

"Hey, just like me," I said, meaning for our common experience to cheer him up. Which, of course, it didn't.

"It was humiliating," Morgan said.

"But I don't understand," I admitted. "I don't understand why you had to steal the story in the first place. Why didn't you go out and do something on your own and *then* write a book about it?" I'd been in the Book Warehouse, after all, and knew that it could be done. As far as I could tell from the memoir section, if you were a memoirist, you did something — *anything* — only so that you could write a book about it afterward.

"That's why we're here, Sam," Morgan said. "We came here for a reason."

"A specific reason," Tigue said. The two Ryans hadn't spoken yet. In the movies these guys would have been the muscle, except they were too trim and they kept their hands in their pockets instead of menacingly smacking their fists into their palms.

"What's that?" I asked.

"Tell him about Africa," Tigue said.

"Shut up," Morgan said, and I had the definite impression that he would have smacked Tigue upside the head if they'd been a little closer in the V. But Morgan didn't smack Tigue upside the head. He drew himself taller, as if to make a rehearsed speech. "In the past," he said, "men like us, men of a certain means and of a certain age, if we'd gotten bored or dissatisfied or restless, if we needed to get our blood pumping, take a big, life-affirming risk and so on, we would have gone to Africa, on safari. We would have hired native guides. We would have hunted lions or gazelles; we would have come back with some animal horns or tusks of some kind. We might even have written a book about it after we'd returned. We can't do that anymore."

"Why not?" I asked.

"They're protected," Morgan said. "Lions, rhinos, okapi — you can't touch them anymore."

"The veldt is closed, man," G-off said.

"We've even tried bungee jumping," Tigue said. "We thought it might be risky enough."

"You tie a big rubber band around your legs," Morgan said. "You jump. You hang there and wait until someone cuts you down. That's it."

"That's it," Tigue repeated.

"It's humiliating," G-off said, "hanging there like that."

"Hey, listen," I said. "Do you want to come inside, have a drink or something?" I was starting to get nervous, the six of us standing on the porch the way we were. In Camelot no one would have paid any attention, but my parents' neighborhood was different, and there were always people out in their front yards, mulching their mums and tiger lilies, and listening to National Public Radio on their transistor radios while they mulched, and looking around to make sure everyone was listening to the same station. I didn't want to draw any attention to myself; I didn't even want them to know that the guy who'd burned down the you-know-what had moved back into the neighborhood.

"Forget the drinks," Morgan said. "We want you to tell us how to burn down houses like the one you burned down. And after we do, we can write a book about it."

"*An Arsonist's Guide to Writers' Homes in New England*," G-off said. "We've already come up with the title."

"Why do you even need to be an arsonist to write the book?" I asked. "You could always just pretend to have burned down the houses and write the book anyway."

"Ouch," Morgan said. "I deserved that."

"Come on," Tigue said. "Be a pal."

"That has to be some rush," G-off said. "The fire, the smoke, the heat." G-off looked at his hands as if they might tell him what to say next. "The fire," he said again.

"You always seemed so happy," Morgan said. "Happy in a simple way, like a child, only bigger."

"Your jolly red face," Tigue said.

"Elemental," Morgan said. "Primal. Just like the fire you set. Please, we just need a little instruction."

"A little push," G-off said. "Your expertise and know how."

"But I told you all about it in prison," I said.

"Yeah, yeah," Morgan said. "But then there's that fire you set yesterday."

"Two days ago," G-off said.

"The Belmont House," Morgan said.

"The Bellamy House," G-off corrected.

"Shut up," Morgan said. And then, to me: "The Bellamy House."

"Guys . . . ," I said.

"Sam, buddy, we're in a rut, a big, scary one," Morgan said. "We're scared. There, I said it."

I believed him. They were in serious need, I could tell, because the two mute Ryans actually parted their lips as if preparing to speak. I even felt sorry for them, which was a switch because in prison I always admired them. Now they seemed pathetic and desperate, and I couldn't be mad at them, not even Morgan. No, I couldn't stay angry with them, but I knew they'd be angry with me once I told them what I was going to tell them.

"I'm sorry, guys," I said, "but it wasn't me who set fire to the Bellamy House."

"Oh, come on," Morgan said. "Who else would do it?"

"That's a good question," I admitted. "But whoever it was, it wasn't me."

"Sam —," Morgan began, but I cut him off.

"I can't help you," I said.

I didn't even listen to what came next, the chorus of threats and pleading and further, more detailed threats — I knew it all too well from Thomas Coleman's visit to Camelot, knew exactly what the bond analysts would say and how they would say it, and so I stood there and let the white noise of their recriminations wash over me until the bond analysts exhausted themselves, broke the flying V, walked back down the front steps, and piled into a Saab, the humpbacked kind. "You'll be sorry you didn't help us, Sam," Morgan yelled, and he was right: in just a few days I would be very sorry that I hadn't helped them. As though to emphasize the point, Morgan again yelled, "You'll be sorry," then jammed the car into gear and drove off.

I looked at my watch. It was only eleven in the morning. There was the big, yawning day still in front of me, plenty of time for somebody else to appear out of my past. There seemed to me to be two choices: sit around the house and wait for another unwelcome surprise visitor, or leave.

10

I left on foot. For the first time since I'd moved back to my parents' house, I allowed myself to walk the streets of Amherst, to see and be seen, to be recognized and shunned, or worse. I kept thinking of that one Birkenstock, the right one, that someone had thrown through my parents' window those many years earlier. It was in my head that the thrower had kept the left one in his arsenal all that time, waiting for my return. At every corner I flinched, thinking I would be recognized by some large-footed hippie and brained with that left sandal.

But I wasn't. It was strange. Block after block, I wasn't recognized, and so I began to actively court recognition. I'd stop at houses I knew — here, the house where my childhood friend Rob Burnip lived; there, the Shumachers', where my parents would play cribbage every Thursday — and linger on the sidewalk, waiting for someone to emerge from the house and say, *Hey, it's Sam Pulsifer. I haven't seen you since . . .* And so on. And people did come out of the houses, but they didn't recognize me and I didn't recognize them. They were simply younger versions of the people who used to live there: assistant professors, or young dot-com near-millionaires with new families who'd moved out from Boston or New York to Amherst because of the good schools and clean air and overabundance of coffee shops, or enviro trust-funders who might still have lived in Berkeley, as their parents did, if the insurance on their Volvos hadn't been so ruinously expensive out there. The town was still old — each house and each church probably knew someone who knew Cotton Mather — but the people who lived in it were not.

Even the farmers had changed. This was Sunday, the day the farmers traditionally sold their wares. I could see the banner — AMHERST FARM-ERS' MARKET — stretched over the parking lot next to the town green, and memory pulled me toward it, the way only memory can. When I was a child, the Sunday farmers' market was run by the farmers after whom it was named, dour men who wore overalls and had chapped hands and faces and who sold their goods out of the backs of their pickup trucks. They sold butter-and-sugar corn and tomatoes mostly, but also some green beans and garlic and cucumbers and summer squash in the sum-mer, and hard, crisp McIntosh apples in the fall and even broadleaf tobacco, big, flat boxes full of the stuff, which seemed right because the farmers smoked while they sold their goods, smoked constantly while they put the produce in paper sacks and miscounted my parents' change. Sometimes, when my parents weren't looking, the farmers gave me cubes of sugar probably meant for their nags, and I ate them and had some unhappy dealings with my dentist later on because of it. But even so, those were good days. Those were very, very good days, and by the time I actually reached the market I was feeling nostalgic for that world and time and would have hugged the first farmer I saw. So maybe it was a good thing there weren't any there.

The farmers, apparently, were another part of the past that was gone. There wasn't a pickup truck or a cigarette to be seen. The produce was organic — signs told me so — and ugly from not having been grown with the fertilizers and insecticides that make fruits and vegetables look and taste so good. It made me sad to see the apples and green beans sitting there, gnarled and unhappy, sold out of the hatchback trunks of Volkswagens, and it also made me sad to see the men and women who sold them, the obviously rich but filthy men and women who could have been the bond analysts' kissing cousins, were their union suits and beards and fleece and flowing skirts and ratty but expensive sandals not largely in the way. My breath left me for a while when I realized how often and fast the world changes, something not even a career in a technologically advanced field like packaging science can prepare you for. It didn't take a genius to see that someday I, too, would be like the farmers, cast aside and obsolete and so completely lost without a world that needed me.

But here, too, no one recognized me; no one seemed to know who I was. As I left the farmers' market, I even walked up to one woman I thought I recognized from high school, a fit woman in expensive running shoes, walking her three children in their complicated, rickshaw-style stroller with its many mesh pockets and cup holders, and I said, "Hello, I'm Sam Pulsifer."

"That's fantastic," she said, and then veered around me on her fast-walking way through the farmers' market and around the town green.

"That *is* fantastic," I shouted after her. She didn't recognize me; *no one recognized me!* It was like Nero coming back to Rome years later and the few singed citizens who remained not knowing who he was.

There was one more thing to do to test my anonymity, one more bit of final accounting. I walked a couple of blocks to the east, to where the Emily Dickinson House used to be. They'd cleared away the charred wreckage, of course, the yellow emergency tape, too, but they hadn't built a new house to take the place of the old one. Instead they had planted trees, which were now decent-size eighteen-year-old birches and white pines and maples, and in the midst of this arbor there was a bronze plaque on a four-foot-high metal pole, probably explaining what had once been there and why it wasn't there anymore. I didn't read what was on the plaque, and if you didn't, you probably would have thought that there was nothing there before those trees except for other, older trees. You wouldn't have known about Emily Dickinson or her house, or about my accidentally burning it down and killing those poor Colemans.

And if you saw me standing there, chances are you wouldn't have recognized me as the boy who, some twenty years earlier, et cetera, even though, as mentioned, I'd once achieved a good deal of local celebrity. Was this so strange? After all, I no longer looked like the boy who had done what he had done: my face was redder even than it had been then, with more wrinkles and some flab and the beginning of jowls; my hair was both higher and curlier on my head and retreating backward; plus, I'd just started growing a beard, which promised one day soon to truly cover large parts of my face. I looked nothing like a boy anymore: I looked like someone else — a grown-ass man, maybe, who had a family he loved and had hurt, and who'd been exiled because of it and quit his job and moved back in with his parents and was now ready — no, *determined* — to make amends. Finally I really was a grown-ass man, and it was about time. I had waited so long to become one.

And what does one do when one finally becomes a grown-ass man? Why, one goes back to the people he's loved and lost and tells them, as the poet says, the whole truth and nothing but and then refuses to go anywhere until he is forgiven for lying in the first place. It was time. Hopefully it wasn't past time. I turned away from the Emily Dickinson House and began to walk back to my van, parked outside my parents' place. I was going back to Camelot, and in doing so, I had the idea that I was walking away from the past and heading toward the future and that I'd better hurry up and get there before I — like those poor farmers and their pesticided produce — was no longer needed and, if remembered at all, was remembered only as something that was bad for you.

Except then, finally, I was remembered; I was recognized and I learned some useful information when I was. I'd almost made it back through the farmers' market when I ran into Sandy Richards, a tenth-grade biology teacher at Pioneer Regional High School, which was where my mother taught eleventh-grade English. She walked right toward me, and I couldn't avoid her. I also couldn't avoid noticing Sandy had aged the way my mother had not: her face was a map of wrinkles and blotches; she had begun the once-a-week home-permanent routine in order to obscure her thinning hair; and most damning, she was wearing the sort of sweat clothes people wear, not when they exercise, but when they can't feel comfortable in anything else.

"Sam?" she said. "Sam Pulsifer?"

"That's me, Mrs. Richards," I admitted.

"I almost didn't recognize you," she said.

"Almost," I said.

"How have you been?"

"I've been OK," I told her. After that, there was a huge, oppressive silence surrounding us, a silence made up of all the past we couldn't speak of and all the present and future made unspeakable by the past. It was awkward. And in order to break that awkward silence, Sandy Richards said something that ended up being an important fact I learned that day.

"We've missed your mother," she said.

"You have?"

"I wish she was still at school," Sandy said. "We miss her" — and here her background in biology betrayed her and she searched long and hard for just the right word to describe what about my mother she missed — "spirit," she finally said.

"I bet," I said. "Now, I can't remember. How long have you missed it?"

"It must be about six years now," Sandy said.

"That's right," I said. "It must be." And then, "You know, my mother has always been a little foggy on the details of her retirement."

"Retirement . . . ," Sandy said, clearly unnerved by the conversation's turn. Her blotches and liver spots seemed to grow and throb with her unease. "Well, I suppose she was asked to retire, sort of."

"Oh."

"Because of her drinking," she said.

"Right," I said. "Her drinking."

"It's a disease," Sandy said. "Treatment, not punishment, that's my motto."

"That's a very good motto to have," I told her.

After that, we were surrounded by another silence — a more reward-ing one for me, although I can't speak for Sandy. My mother had been forcibly retired from her job six years ago but hadn't told me, had lied to me about going to work, and not just on a Saturday, either. Why? Had she told my father? Where did my mother go every day? And how could I find out?

"Sam?" Sandy said. "Hello?" She had clearly been talking to me while I'd been having these thoughts, and I heard her voice from far away, then followed it until I left my world and returned to hers.

"Hello," I said. "I'm back."

"Yes, well, I have to go," Sandy said, and then she shook her canvas tote bag full of organic vegetables, as though the vegetables were late for an appointment. "Please give my best to your mother."

"I will," I said. "I most definitely will."

11

It was a triumphant walk from the farmers' market to my parents' house that afternoon. I had learned something, something large, but it wasn't the learning something, in itself, that was so satisfying: it was that I would get to go home, tell my mother that I knew the truth about her "work," and then say, *Aha!* It was the *Aha!* I was so looking forward to, so much so that I momentarily forgot my plan to go back to Camelot, to force myself and my apologies and confessions and further apologies upon Anne Marie and the kids until they took me back. The prospect of saying, *Aha!* to my mother had that effect on me, like amnesia. I bet I wasn't the only one for whom this was the case. I bet it was also the triumphant *Aha!* and not the truth itself that had fueled all those famous literary detectives I knew not much about except their names — Philip Marlowe, Sherlock Holmes, Joe and Frank Hardy. I felt like yelling something celebratory on my way home, something like, *Yeah!* or *Fuck, yeah!* just like Marlowe would have yelled, just like the Hardys would have yelled, and maybe Holmes, too, although maybe that's why he kept Watson around: to tell Holmes to simmer down and not get too far ahead of himself.

Because maybe there is no true *Aha!* moment for a detective, or for anybody else, either. There sure wasn't one for me that night. I walked into my parents' house and found them sitting next to each other on the couch, talking to — I discovered in a few seconds — a cop. He was sitting in a chair with his back to me: he was wearing a gray hooded sweatshirt, the hood bunched and folded and looking like the rolls of an elephant's skin. My parents were drinking coffee, not beer, and so I knew that something was up and they were in a bad way.

"There . . . he . . . is," my father said. His hand shook a little as he spoke, coffee dribbling over the cup's lip. The cop stood up and turned around. He looked exactly like the guards I remembered from prison, who were overweight and overwhelmed and, if not for their guns, exactly like the junior varsity high school football coaches they might have been. Except this one was even younger looking than the guards. He was in his midtwenties, tops. His cheeks were bright red, as if he were cold or ashamed, and he was exactly my height, too, and all in all he looked as though he might have been my much younger brother if my parents had decided to have one and then dress him in entirely neutral colors: in addition to his gray sweatshirt, he wore khaki pants and tan work boots and a tan barn jacket. "Here I am," I said, echoing my father, my face flaring up almost automatically to match the cop's, as though his shame were a challenge to mine.

"I'm Detective Wilson," he said in a surprisingly high voice for such a big guy. He took my hand and shook it vigorously, making up for not ever having shaken it before. His hands were large and soft, as if made of something once hard that had melted. "I was just asking your folks a few questions."

"About what?"

"There was a fire last night, Sam," my mother said. Her voice was calm, perfectly calm, and her coffee-cup-holding hand was steady, but I could see that her other hand, her right one, was gripping the couch arm tight, as though the couch were a seat on an amusement ride. "Someone tried to burn down the Edward Bellamy House."

"OK," I said, trying to act as though I were hearing this for the first time. This was difficult, though, in part because I knew all about it, but also because Detective Wilson wouldn't let go of my hand. He wasn't shaking it anymore, just holding it gently, as though trying to help me through an especially difficult time. Or maybe it was me helping him; he was young enough that this could have been his first case. Maybe that's why he'd given us his title — *detective* — and not his first name, because he couldn't believe he actually had one. A title, that is.

"Edward Bellamy was a writer," the detective said. "He wrote books." He smiled at me broadly, as if this were good news and he was pleased to be the one to spread it.

"Oh," I said flatly, and then, as if just realizing the import of this news, I said, "Oh!" again. My intent was to make this "Oh!" sound panicked, concerned, and maybe even a little indignant, but not at all guilty. But it didn't sound quite right, a little weak and insincere to my ears, and so I was going to let out a third "Oh!" — this one with a little more passion, a little more oomph. But my mother shot me a look that told me, more or less, to stop saying "Oh!" So I stopped.

"This happened last night," my mother said, repeating herself, talking slowly, helping me through this. "We told the detective that you were here all night, with us, in this house."

"That's true," I said, and it was.

"OK," Detective Wilson said, only now letting go of my hand. I put it in my pocket before he could decide to take it back. He turned to my father. "So why don't you show me that letter."

"Letter," my father said, and nodded. This was clearly something they'd spoken of before I'd arrived: all three seemed at ease with the fact of this letter's existence and with the prospect of Detective Wilson's taking a look at it. It was clearly something they'd already agreed upon. My father got up from the couch and lurched in the direction of his bedroom, and Detective Wilson followed him. From inside the bedroom, I could hear Detective Wilson ask my father, "Do you always keep the letters in this box? In this drawer?" I could hear my father mutter something affirmative. My mother remained on the couch and stared glumly into her coffee cup. "I could use a drink," she said. "A real drink."

"So," I said, again attempting to sound casual and unconcerned, but no doubt failing, as I picked up a napkin off the coffee table and began strangling it out of nervousness, "what letter is this Detective Wilson looking for?"

"You remember that box of letters your father has, from all those people wanting you to burn down those houses?" my mother said, still looking in dismay at her coffee cup. "There's one in there from some man wanting you to burn down the Edward Bellamy House. That's the letter he's looking for."

"So you know about those letters?"

"Oh, yes," she said.

"And Detective Wilson knows about those letters?"

"Oh, yes," my mother said again.

"How does he know about them?" I asked.

"Your father told him."

"He did?" There had been a little too much something in my voice — if I'd known exactly what it was, then maybe I'd have been able to keep it out of there in the first place. But whatever it was, my mother heard it. She raised her eyes from her cup, looked at me first with incredulity, then with pity.

"You thought it was just the two of you, didn't you?" she asked. "That the letters were your little secret." Before I could confirm this, my mother shook her head violently, as if to get me out of her head, as if I were one more unwelcome thought she did not want to get lost in.

But then again, I had plenty of new, unwelcome thoughts to get lost in myself. Someone besides me and my father and the letter writers knew about the letters — that was news enough. But what would Detective Wilson say when he found out that Mr. Frazier's letter was missing? What would my father say, and my mother? Would I tell them the truth about Mr. Frazier and how he'd taken the letter? What if the truth sounded like a lie to them, as it surely would? What lie could I tell that would sound less like a lie than the truth?

"Well," Detective Wilson said, emerging from my father's bedroom. My father was right behind him: his eyes darted to me, then to my mother, then to me again, and then back to his bedroom, before he closed them, his eyes exhausted from all that exercise. Detective Wilson paused to let my father resume his place by my mother on the couch; he then looked at each of us in turn — first wide eyed and then squinty, which I think was supposed to convey suspicion but instead made him look as though he were having contact-lens problems. Detective Wilson seemed to be waiting for one of us to say something, just as I was waiting for him to say, *The letter is missing.* Which after some further eye contortions, he finally did.

My father didn't say anything: he had been in the room, of course, and so already knew that the letter was missing. His eyes were still closed and I wondered if he'd fallen asleep. My mother and I didn't say anything, either. We looked straight forward, at the detective, maybe to avoid looking at each other.

"It certainly is," Detective Wilson said, perhaps responding to something he'd hoped one of us would say. "Do any of you know where the letter is?"

"No," my father said. His eyes were still closed, but he said this word clearly, although with some agony. He opened his eyes and looked toward his bedroom longingly, then made a clogged whistling noise through his nose. He sounded like a congested train passing in the night.

"No," my mother said.

"No," I said, and then added, unnecessarily, "I have no idea where it is, either."

After that, none of us Pulsifers said anything else. Detective Wilson tugged at his coat sleeves, then fiddled with his hood; for some reason he kept looking toward the door, as though he were onstage and his director was in the wings, about to feed the detective his cues. "OK, that's all I need for right now," he finally said, visibly drooping in the shoulders. "I'll be in touch." Then, without shaking anyone's hand or even giving anyone his card, he practically sprinted out the door and into the night. My father disappeared into his bedroom to double-check, no doubt, the status of his precious shoe box and its missing letter. But my mind was still on Detective Wilson, who'd come looking for an answer and left behind all these questions. Why hadn't he kept on questioning us until he'd gotten some answers? Was he a bumbler, too? Did anyone know what the hell they were doing around here? What sort of detective *was* he, anyway?

"What police department was Detective Wilson from?" I asked.

"You know, I don't think he said," my mother told me. I could hear my father in his bedroom moaning loudly and deeply, like a wounded cow. But my mother didn't seem to notice. She was staring at me, her eyes full of questions, those questions orbiting the stationary suns of her pupils. *Did you do something, Sam?* she wanted to know. *You just moved home: did you do something bad already? Oh, Sam, what have you done now? How have you disappointed me this time?* She had these questions, all right, but she didn't have to ask them. Because my mother, thank God, was a drunk, and this was another good thing about being a drunk: you always had a question that would trump all other questions.

"Who wants a drink?" my mother asked, then got off the couch and walked to the kitchen before finding out who besides her wanted one.

I WAS SO OVERFULL with questions that it wasn't until five in the morning that I woke up and remembered what had earlier seemed like some of the most pressing ones. Why hadn't my mother told me she'd been fired from her job? And what did she do every day when she was supposed to be at work? I could have waited until a decent hour to ask my mother these questions, but who knew, once I woke up, what other questions might need to be asked and answered? Who knew what other mysteries might yet pop up and obscure the old ones?

I got out of bed and made my shuffling, groggy way down to my mother's room, the room my parents' used to share. There is something creepy and illicit about sneaking into your parents' bedroom when you are young, and this is no less true when you're an adult. The door was closed. I stood there for a moment, steeling myself to be stealthy, then carefully turned the knob and opened the door. Even in the dark, I could see that the room was as I remembered it. There was a wooden dresser to the right of the door, where my father kept, or used to keep, his clothes; kitty-corner to that was the mirrored walk-in closet where my mother kept her dresses and skirts. Kitty-corner to *that* was an end table with a phone and a digital clock and various framed pictures of her and me. And in between the table and me was the bed, my parents' big queen-size bed, which was empty. No one was in it. I ran my hand over the bedspread and then sat on the bed itself to make sure. Not only was nobody in it, but nobody had been in it, either. The bed was made, the bedspread taut except for where I'd sat on it. There were two pillows at the head of the bed, and no heads had touched them, not that night, maybe not the night before or the night before that or . . .

So, despite my best efforts, here was another question, and first thing in the morning, too: Where the hell was my mother? There were so many questions that I began to wonder if I'd ever find any of the answers, if I even knew what an answer looked like anymore. And then I heard a thud downstairs. It was clearly the thud of the morning paper hitting the front door, and I realized that no matter what it looks like, an answer always sounds like a thud. That was my very thought, standing there in my boxer shorts. I walked downstairs, opened the door, brought in the newspaper, and began flipping through it in that half-zombie way you do in the too-early morning, looking for something that might wake you up.

I found it, right there in the local news section. In the early evening, someone had set fire to the Mark Twain House, in Hartford, Connecticut, forty-five minutes or so down the highway. The article said that the fire was "suspicious," although I knew this to be the case without their having to tell me so.

Part Three

12

If I were to write the bond analysts' memoir, *An Arsonist's Guide to Writers' Homes in New England,* my first piece of advice would be this:

Practice. For God's sake, practice.

Whoever had tried to burn down the Edward Bellamy House hadn't practiced, that was obvious, and that was also true of whoever tried to burn down the Mark Twain House. But before I went to the Twain House that morning, and before I go there in memory here, I first had to sneak into my father's room, open his shoe box of letters, and find out who wanted the Mark Twain House torched in the first place. Unlike my mother, my father was home: I could hear him in his room, snoring adenoidally and loudly enough to shake the house's shake shingles. I opened the door to his room — it caught and then creaked a little, as doors in old houses do, but not loudly enough to be heard over the snoring — and then crept in the direction of the end table. There was a streetlight right outside my father's window, illuminating the room until it was slightly on the bright side of pitch black, and I could just make out my father's blanketed shape on the bed. During waking hours, he looked small, diminished, but on that bed, in that filtered light and under the blankets, my father looked oddly huge and mysterious, much more of a man than he actually was. I remember thinking how sad that was, that my father — and maybe all of us — was more impressive asleep than awake.

In any case, I located the end table in the mostly dark, opened the drawer as quietly as I could, and removed the shoe box from the drawer and then myself from the room. I walked to the kitchen; there was a half pot of coffee from the day before, and so I heated and drank it while I flipped through the letters. They weren't in any particular order — Wharton was before Alcott, who was after Melville — but finally I found the Twain House letter. I carried the letter with me upstairs and put it in the pocket of the coat I'd wear that day, then showered, shaved, dressed, and generally made myself presentable to the world I wanted to investigate. Then I walked downstairs. About halfway down the stairs, I stopped: there was my father, walking back from the kitchen. He was wearing boxer shorts, and only boxer shorts, and looked oddly virile for the stroked-out sixty-year-old I knew he was: his arms and chest had some definition, and the skin under his arms wasn't loose and didn't sag earthward the way old-man underarm skin can; his stride was more hop than shuffle, and I almost yelled out something like, *Hey, looking good,* until I saw what he was carrying. In one hand, of course, was a big can of Knickerbocker. But in the other was the box of letters. My father was looking curiously at the box as he walked, as if the box were a stranger and my father was waiting for it to introduce itself. My father was still looking at the box as he disappeared into his room and shut the door behind him. What was my father thinking in there? Did he wonder who had taken the box out of his room and into the kitchen? Did he suspect it was me who had taken the box? After all, who else was there to suspect? Or did he assume maybe that he had done it himself while he was drunk the night before — the night before had been full of our normal familial drinking — and simply didn't remember? This was yet another good thing about drinking, of course: not that drinking made you forget things, but that it made it possible for you to plausibly *pretend* you'd forgotten things. In any case, there wasn't much use wondering about it: my father was back in his room with his box, and I had the letter, which told me exactly where to go and who wanted me to go there.

THE DAY ITSELF WAS MUCH different from the day I'd visited Mr. Frazier and the Bellamy House. This day, it felt like fall, real fall: the air was sharp in your throat, the wind was cold and looking for a scarf to blow around, and the sky was so blue it looked as if it had been chemically enhanced for maximum blueness. It was the kind of day where you would have smelled leaves burning somewhere if leaf burning hadn't been outlawed. I felt nervous, much more nervous than I'd been while driving to the Edward Bellamy House, maybe because I'd read so much of Twain at my mother's behest — he was my mother's favorite, and I'd known this and wanted to please her, and so I had made sure to laugh at the things she'd told me were funny, and to shake my head admiringly at the things she'd told me were wicked. Or maybe I was nervous because the drive was longer than the drive to the Bellamy House and gave me more time to be nervous, and this would be another thing I'd put in my arsonist's guide: for an arsonist just starting out, it's perhaps easier to burn down a nearby home of an obscure writer rather than burn down a more famous writer's house in a more distant city.

Once I got there, though, I saw that no one had really burned anything and that the Mark Twain House was going to be just fine. Again, there was yellow tape around the perimeter of the house; you could see some singe marks up near and around the first-floor windows, but nothing had really been permanently damaged except for some bushes that had caught fire and then been doused and were in a very bad way. The house itself was absurdly thick and tall — a normal Victorian house on growth hormones — and was surrounded by three other slightly less massive houses, and the whole compound reminded me of the houses in my dream of a few nights earlier, my dream featuring the many houses and the naked woman and the burning books, and maybe that's why I found the whole place especially spooky and sad and uninhabitable. Maybe that's what Twain had felt, too: he had built the place, the house of his dreams, and the whole thing was so impressive and dreamlike, finally, that he didn't want to live there. There were no lights on in any of the main house's windows, and the only humans on the property, besides me, were reporters: three or four television reporters in their sharp suits, followed by their cameramen with their high-tech gear, each one dressed in those many-pocketed khaki vests that would have looked good on safari. The reporters and the cameramen made me nervous, too, not because I thought they'd recognize me, but because they seemed so much better prepared, organized, and equipped than I was. But they were paying attention to the house and not to me. Besides, I'd seen what I'd come to see and knew the two things I now thought I knew: someone with access to my father's shoe box had memorized or copied the letters asking me to burn down the Bellamy and Twain houses; and the Mark Twain House had been burned, or not burned, by the same person who also hadn't managed to burn the Edward Bellamy House. It didn't occur to me that different people might fail at burning down different writers' homes in New England in the same way. Always count on a bumbler to think that he is unique in his bumbling, to believe his bumbling is like a fingerprint, specific to him. The truth is that the world is full of bumblers exactly like you, and to think that you're special is just one more thing you've bumbled.

AT LEAST I DIDN'T bumble the letter. I read it several times, and thoroughly, too. It was from an English professor at Heiden College, in Hartford, asking me to burn down the Mark Twain House as a present for his "lady friend," who was also a professor at the college. His name was Wesley Mincher and hers was Lees Ardor. The letter was extremely learned — there were *whom*s and *one*s everywhere, and lots of complicated punctuation — but it was difficult to tell why he wanted to give her this present. And why would she want it? Why not a necklace, a cruise, or a car? Mincher couldn't say, or at least I couldn't understand what he *was* saying: professorial hemming and hawing is much denser than a layperson's hemming and hawing, and I needed one of those big dictionaries that you can't read without a magnifying glass to help me get to the center of his meaning. At the end of the letter, though, he finally got to it himself: "In summary, then, I wish for you to burn down the Mark Twain House because Professor Ardor believes Mr. Twain to be something of a [and here you could sense the ashamed pause, lurking between the lines] female pudendum."

I had no idea whether the two professors were still together (the letter had been written eleven years ago) or if she still believed Twain was a female pudendum. I had a good idea what a female pudendum was, though, and I also had a good idea where I could find Professor Mincher: he'd included his office phone number on the letter. I called the number, but Mincher wasn't there, and I didn't leave a message. Instead I called the English Department number (Mincher had written his letter on English Department letterhead, as though his was a query letter and I were a journal). The woman who answered the phone said that Professor Mincher wouldn't be in; but then I asked about Professor Ardor, who, as it turned out, had office hours that very morning.

LEES ARDOR WAS AN associate professor of American literature—it said so on the plaque on her office door—but she didn't like literature, didn't *believe* in it. I found this out after I knocked on her door, she opened it, and I stood there for too many seconds, staring at her hair. It was long, red, and straight: it was the sort of hair that demanded to be brushed religiously, two hundred times a day. Her hair was as shiny as a newly waxed kitchen floor, as mesmerizing as a hypnotist's swinging gold watch, and it was the only physical characteristic of Lees Ardor's that stuck with me. I'm sure she had others—she had a body, for instance, and it was wearing clothes; she had a voice and it was somewhere in the range of normal human voices—but it was her hair I remembered. Lees Ardor's hair stood for the rest of her, the way Ahab's peg leg had stood for him.

Anyway, I must have been staring at her hair for too long, because Lees Ardor put her fingers right under my nose and snapped them twice. The snapping brought me out of my trance. I stuck out my hand and asked, double-checking the accuracy of the door plaque, "Professor Ardor?" Without sticking out her hand to meet mine, she asked back, "And what, exactly, am I supposed to profess?"

This threw me some, I'll admit, and because of that, I forgot to introduce myself and stammered for a moment or so before finally saying, "You profess literature," and then I pointed at the door plaque, where it said so.

"I don't *believe* in literature," she said. "I don't *like* literature, either."

"But you're a literature professor."

"That's correct."

"I don't understand," I said. I knew from experience that it is exactly this response teachers most desire, because it makes them feel necessary. While at Our Lady of the Lake, I had understood so few things that I became something of a teacher's pet.

"It makes perfect sense," she said. "Does it not?" Without waiting for an answer, she turned her back to me, walked around her desk, and sat in her chair, the comfortable rolling sort of desk chair that you can lean back in until you're nearly horizontal. The only other chair in the office was one of those ancient hard-backed wooden chairs that my stern Yankee ancestors probably made to be so uncomfortable that the Puritan sitting in it became miserable enough that he'd go back to work. I sat in it, across the desk from Lees Ardor. The desk between us, and the hierarchy of our chairs, made me feel diminished, like a lower life-form.

"Name a book that I should like," Lees Ardor said. "Name a book that's so great I should like it."

I thought hard about all the books my mother had made me read, about certain books that everyone knew were great, and of course I came up with *Huckleberry Finn*. It was my mother's favorite book: when, as a boy, I'd asked her why, she always said she saw herself in it, although

I never knew whether she saw herself in Huck, or Jim, or Tom, or the Duke, or maybe one of the minor characters. Plus, I was here because Lees Ardor's man, Mincher, wanted the Mark Twain House burned to the ground, and so I thought maybe I'd learn something important about her *and* the case if I said, "What about *Huckleberry Finn?*"

"*Huckleberry Finn* my ass," Lees Ardor replied. She smiled at me ingratiatingly, as if we had reached a kind of understanding, even though I didn't understand what "*Huckleberry Finn* my ass" meant, and I don't think Lees Ardor did, either.

I didn't get a chance to ask her to clarify, though. Lees Ardor went into a fury of book and legal pad gathering, then stood up, walked past her desk and me, and said over her shoulder, "We're late for class."

Of course, I hadn't introduced myself yet and so she must have thought I was her student, a student whom she didn't recognize and whose name she didn't know, even though the semester must have been more than half over by then. In any case, I got up out of that uncomfortable chair and followed her down the hall. The hall was beautiful, the most beautiful institutional hall I'd ever seen, and nothing at all like the halls at Our Lady of the Lake. There were no drop ceilings or water stains in the plaster, and it was all dark wood and marble, with even a few ceiling-tile mosaics here and there. Looking at the ceilings at Heiden College made you want to learn, whereas looking at the ceilings at my alma mater made you not want to look at the ceilings.

The students in Lees Ardor's class, though, probably looked much the same as the students at Our Lady of the Lake. The boys wore backward baseball caps, and the girls wore low-slung jeans and cropped shirts that left a strip of white, white skin between the shirt and the pants. Besides me, there were only two other aberrant-looking characters in that classroom: a Richard Nixon kook wearing a gray three-piece suit and red paisley tie, and a kook who looked like a female Chairman Mao, with that famous bowl haircut and matching workingman's denim ensemble, plus many facial piercings, including a hoop through her septum by which she could, I supposed, be led around. Those two were sitting in the back row, and I sat between them. They didn't acknowledge me when I asked the girl, and then the boy, "Hey, what class is this, anyway?" But still I felt an unspoken kinship with them, the way the untouchables in the back row always do.

Lees Ardor had positioned herself at the front of the classroom and was staring at the class, her hair flowing behind her as though it were her head's own academic gown. She stared for at least three minutes. At first I thought she was taking a silent form of attendance. But there were only fourteen people in the class—I counted—and it wouldn't have taken her that long to figure out who was there and who wasn't. Besides, she wasn't really looking at us but rather at some spot on the wall at the back of the room, as if trying to bore a hole through it. Finally, still looking at the wall, she said, "Willa Cather is a cunt."

"Whoa," I said, apparently out loud, since several of the real students turned and looked at me before assuming their previous face-forward positions. They seemed unimpressed, bored even, by Lees Ardor's pronouncement, but it threw me, that most forbidden of forbidden words, even though I'd read Wesley Mincher's letter and should have been expecting it or something like it. I turned to the Chairman Mao kook and whispered, "Did she really say"—and here I paused, not daring to say that word myself, the most off-limits of all the off-limits terms for the female pudendum—"that *word*?"

"Yes," she said. There was a strong, wet sibilance to the word, which made me suspect that she had a tongue ring, in addition to her many other piercings. She would have been in high demand as a model for *Face and Metal,* assuming there was such a magazine.

"Why?"

"We're reading *My Ántonia,*" the Chairman Mao kook said. My face must have looked as baffled as I, its owner, felt, because she clarified: "That's a book. By Willa Cather."

"I know that," I said. *My Ántonia* was another book my mother had made me read, and I remembered it well: the sweeping Nebraska prairie, the waist-high snow, the transplanted Scandinavians and Slavs and their work ethic, the strong women in calico always drinking strong coffee. And then there was Ántonia herself, who, as I remembered, was plucky, among her other notable qualities. "But why did she call Willa Cather" — and here I summoned all my courage and finally got it out — "a cunt?"

The Chairman Mao kook didn't flinch when I said the word. "Professor Ardor thinks all writers are cunts."

I turned to the Richard Nixon kook to get his take on the matter, but he wasn't paying any attention to us at all. His eyes were fixed on Lees Ardor; he had this aroused, glazed look on his face and kept smoothing and stroking his tie, and you didn't have to be an English major or a reader to know what *that* symbolized.

Meanwhile there was a discussion going on in front of us. One of the normal, scantily clad college girls had said about *My Ántonia*, "I liked it."

"What do you mean by *like*?" Lees Ardor asked, in the same tone she'd used when she asked me what she was supposed to *profess*. There followed a long debate about what it meant to *like* something. I didn't pay much attention to this at all, not so much because I didn't understand the discussion, but because it flew so far below the radar of my interest. Finally they exhausted that topic, I mean really exhausted the hell out of it: even the air in the classroom seemed weary.

"I'm sorry about your mother," one of the other normal, scantily clad girls said.

"What is she talking about?" I asked the Chairman Mao kook.

"Professor Ardor's mother died," she whispered back. "She canceled classes last week so that she could go to the funeral. It was in Nebraska." She paused again, fingered her nose ring like a thoughtful bull, and then added, "That's also where *My Ántonia* is set, by the way."

"I knew that, too," I said. "I've *read the book*, you know."

"Her mother died of cancer," she said. "The really bad kind."

I could hear something shift in the Chairman Mao kook's voice, could hear the boredom and knowingness seep out and the empathy flow in. I could see the change in her female classmates, too. They sat up in their chairs and leaned toward their teacher, and you could almost feel them waver in their dislike for Lees Ardor. The men did not care — they were slumped down in their chairs, as usual, their baseball caps pulled down over their faces in an attempt to either hide or call further attention to their apathy — but the women in the class *cared* about Lees Ardor: her mother had died, after all, and they had just read *My Ántonia,* and no doubt they were thinking what I was thinking. No doubt they had visions of Lees Ardor's melancholy return to the great sweeping North American prairie. On the prairie, the students probably imagined, there were self-strong women in calico showing off their self-strength during Lees Ardor's mother's funeral and drinking strong coffee afterward. And then there was Lees Ardor's mother herself, who (so we imagined, speaking for the female members of the class, whom I considered myself one of at that moment) was as strong and as stoic as any woman in Nebraska — strong when her husband had died ten years earlier of a heart attack and she'd had to sell their farm, strong during the six months she was dying of leukemia. Lees Ardor's mother was so admired by everyone who knew her that they felt no need to say so over and over again, and there were no teary toasts in her honor because, it was agreed, Mrs. Ardor would have hated such a gesture. Lees Ardor, I imagined, had been so moved by this stoic show of respect that she cried at the funeral, cried out loud for the first time she could remember. She put her hands over her face when she wept, and her crying sounded oddly far away, as if she were a princess holed up in some distant castle. Lees Ardor's mother was gone from the world and there would be no one else like her, and now there was just Lees Ardor herself. Lees Ardor could never carry on her mother's legacy, she knew that. How could she emulate her mother when she could barely stop crying long enough to accept the strong coffee from her mother's cronies, who would soon also die stoically? I'd imagined all of that, sitting there in my desk chair, and I bet the women in the class had, too, and in doing so we'd imagined our way into empathy for Lees Ardor. Someone even sucked back a sob, which Lees Ardor did not appreciate. I know this because she stared furiously at the class — her hair glinted like armor in the buzzing overhead lights — and said, "My mother was a cunt."

This was too much: there was a collective gasp, and then all the women in the class left en masse, even the Chairman Mao pierced-tongue kook. Almost all of the men left, too, not because they were offended by the word "cunt," I'm pretty sure, but because they hadn't been paying attention and saw the women leaving and probably assumed class was dismissed early. Then it was just mc and Lees Ardor and the Richard Nixon kook, who was looking at her as though in the throes of both fear and love. He was probably one of those buttoned-down guys who couldn't love anyone unless he was terrified of them. Lees Ardor's repeated use of the word "cunt" had no doubt made him fall for her hard.

"Get the hell out of here," Lees Ardor told him. The Richard Nixon kook went pleasurably limp in his desk chair and then got up, wobbly legged, and left the room. Lees Ardor crossed the room and closed the door behind him, then sat in one of the student desk chairs and started crying with such force that I was afraid that her eyes were going to fall out of her head and onto the desk, smearing the graffiti. And then, as if the weeping wasn't enough for her, Lees Ardor began banging her head, softly at first and then harder and harder, like a woodpecker determined to serve its purpose without its beak. I was afraid she was going to do some real damage, to herself and her forehead and to the desk.

"Please don't cry," I told her. I had said the same thing to Mr. Frazier just two days earlier. Was this what a detective did, after all? Did a detective try to get his suspects to stop crying long enough to ask them the things he needed to know? "Please don't."

"I loved her, so much," Lees Ardor said.

"Your mother?" I guessed.

"Yes," she said. "Why did I call her that?"

"You don't really think she's a cunt, do you?"

"No," she said. "I *loved* her."

"Then why did you call her that?"

"I don't know."

"Oh yes, you do," I said. Because I'd often given this answer — "I don't know" — to my mother when I was a boy and confronted with an especially difficult question, and I'd also tried it with my packaging-science professors, and none of them had accepted "I don't know." I bet Lees Ardor didn't take that sort of answer from her students, either, and now I wasn't going to take it from her. "Tell me why you called your mother a cunt."

"Because," Lees Ardor said. Her head was down on the table, her hands locked behind her head as though she were being arrested, and so the words came out muffled but with force, probably because she'd been wanting to say them for so long. "Because I didn't want to be a character in the book my students had been reading."

"You didn't want to be Ántonia," I said, although I wasn't really thinking about that book, or even about Lees Ardor: I was thinking more about my mother and how she had given up her books and whether it had done her any good. Which character did my mother not want to be anymore? I wondered. Were there so many characters in her that the moment she stopped being one, she immediately became another?

"That's right," Lees Ardor said. She picked her head up and looked at me urgently, as though she was saying something important for the first time ever. "I didn't want to be the hard-bitten character who had endured tragedy and come out a better, more sympathetic person."

"Why not?"

"You don't understand," she said, and started wailing again. "I want to be a *real* person."

"I do understand," I said. Because I was pretty sure I did, and I was also pretty sure I knew why she didn't believe in literature or like it very much, either. She didn't believe in or like books because she feared being a character in them and thus not a real person, whatever that was, and not knowing what a real person was made her hate the books even more, the books and the words within them, too, and then that hatred extended to all words everywhere, like "cunt," which was a word she loathed but could not stop using and which, like all words, was lousy and inadequate. Maybe it was words, all of them, all of them that could gesture feebly toward your anger but not do justice to the complexity of it, that made her — or her Wesley Mincher — go out and contact a complete stranger and ask him to burn down the Mark Twain House. This theory came out of my head, fully formed, like that Greek god's daughter, who leaped out of his skull and into the ancient world, fully formed.

Then I made a mistake. Empathy makes us do things we shouldn't, which makes you wonder why it's one of our most respected emotions. Empathy made me touch Lees Ardor, gently on her back, just to let her know that I understood what she was going through and that I was there, as her detective, to comfort her. But it seemed as though she didn't want a detective *or* a comforter. At my touch, she leaped out of her chair and turned to face me. Her tears disappeared almost immediately, as though made of an especially fast-drying sort of salt. "Who the hell are you, anyway?" she asked.

"I'm Sam Pulsifer. Your" — and here I paused, as anyone would have — "*manfriend*, Professor Mincher, wrote me a letter a long time ago, asking me to burn down the Mark Twain House."

Her face changed dramatically then. Outrage and suspicion took the place of sadness, as so often happens. "So you're fucking Sam Pulsifer."

"I am," I said, although the way she said it made me wish I weren't. Lees Ardor looked at me in such disbelief that I thought it might move the discussion along if I gave her some form of identification. So I took my driver's license out of my wallet and handed it to her. She looked at it, looked at me, looked at it again, and then said in a low, hissing voice, "You owe us three thousand dollars."

"I do?" I said.

"You do," she said. "Don't pretend you don't know what I'm talking about."

"I'm not pretending," I said.

"You are," she said.

"I'm not," I said, and we went around like this for a while, like enemies without weapons and armed with only a very limited vocabulary. Finally I decided just to ask the question that might end the fight: "Why do I owe you three thousand dollars?"

"Fine," she said. Then she adopted a theatrically bored tone, to let me know she was playing along but not at all happy to do so: "You owe us three thousand dollars because that's what we paid you to burn down the Mark Twain House. Which you did not do."

"Did you pay me in person?" I asked, playing along myself.

"No," she said. "You sent Wesley a letter saying you would be willing to burn down the house for three thousand dollars. Wesley agreed. He left the money in an envelope inside a dumpster next to the Cumberland Farms, right down the street from the Mark Twain House. That was yesterday at noon. You were very specific in your instructions."

"I guess I was," I said. "Except that wasn't me." And before she could respond, I said, "If that was me, then why would I show up right now, after I hadn't successfully set the fire you paid me to set, so that you could then demand your money back? Now that I had your money, why wouldn't I just disappear?"

She thought for a while, her forehead wrinkled, as if I were an especially difficult passage in a novel and she were trying to unpack me. Who knows, maybe she was trying to figure out whether I was a character, too, and if so, which one or ones.

"Shit," Lees Ardor finally said. "We'd better go see Wesley."

WESLEY MINCHER AND LEES ARDOR lived in West Hartford, in a home much like my parents': an old, musty colonial home full of rooms that all looked like studies and not the living and dining and parlor rooms they had probably been designed to be. Each room had towering, overflowing bookcases, and dim lighting, and the shabby look of neglect and intellectual wear and tear. We found Wesley Mincher sitting in the biggest of all these rooms: he had his legs propped up on a settee, and he immediately struck me as someone who probably didn't get enough exercise and had diabetes. His face was yellow, although that might have been from the lighting. He was reading a book, an ancient-looking, clothbound book whose pages were probably as yellowed as Mincher's skin.

"Wesley," Lees Ardor said, "there is someone here to see you." He didn't answer her, even though they were only a body length apart. "Wesley," she said again, but with more sweetness in her voice, as though she loved the way he didn't answer her. She said his name five more times, her voice sounding as if she were saying not, "Wesley, Wesley," but rather, "Love, Love." Still no response. It wasn't that Mincher was deaf; no, he was one of those distracted academics who are so lost in their own heads that it takes them a long time to realize that they might be needed in the world outside their skulls. But finally he did hear: he looked up and saw her and gave her a big, fond smile. He even put down his book, or rather he slid it into a protective plastic sleeve, the way Anne Marie might have slid a sandwich for Katherine's lunch into a plastic sandwich bag. I had designed both kinds of bags, by the way, or at the very least worked with someone who had.

"Wesley," Lees Ardor said, "this is Sam Pulsifer."

"I am a fourth-generation Mincher from the North Carolina foothills of the Great Smoky Mountains," Wesley Mincher said, apropos of nothing. He had a southern accent, the gentle, lilting kind. My father had edited many books by southern historians about southern history for the university press, and I'd met a few of what he called "his authors," had heard him talk about those authors, and so I immediately pegged Wesley Mincher for what he was: he was a character, too, the sort of southern character who believed that being a southern character had something to do with misdirectional doublespeak, and losing the Civil War and not wanting others to talk about it but not being able to stop talking about it yourself, and having wise, lugubrious old folks and front porches for them to sit on, and black people, always black people, about whom you knew everything and about whom no one else knew shit, and the idea that self-criticism is art but criticism from outside is hypocrisy, and wise, folksy sheriffs and God and farm animals and good food that wouldn't be good if you ate it in a restaurant and not in your mama's kitchen, and a set of whitewall tires leaning up against the barn that would look good on the 1957 Buick that you had a funny story to tell about.

"Mr. Pulsifer has something to tell us regarding the Mark Twain House, Wesley," Lees Ardor said gently, so gently. You could feel the fondness pouring out of her the way those tears had an hour earlier.

"The so-called hillbilly of the Appalachians speaks an English closer to true proper English than any Yankee who went to Harvard."

"He says he wasn't the one who burned down the house, or tried to."

"My mother could make a poultice out of the sap of a piney tree that could take away your toothache before you even knew you had one, buddy-ro."

"He says he wasn't the one we paid three thousand dollars."

"Our Bobby Lee kept a lock of his daughter's hair in his saddlebag. It was magic, that lock of hair. It protected him from the minié balls."

I just stood there, feeling sleepy in that dim light, enjoying the show. The two of them could have talked like this for hours, I bet, their meanings barely intersecting, until they arrived, always, at the end of the evening, at the necessary common ground.

"I believe him, Wesley," Lees Ardor said. "I think he's telling us the truth."

"Then I believe him, too, my love," Mincher said. He reached over and held out his hand, and she took it. They held hands for the rest of my time there, as though I weren't there at all, or as though I were there only to bear witness to their hand-holding.

I got exactly one piece of evidence that day, but it took hours and hours to get it. Mostly, Mincher told me the story of how they first met. They had been on the faculty at Heiden together for eight years, but they had never really noticed each other because they had each been walled up in their own ghetto of resentment, unable to see anything outside the walls. Lees Ardor was the only woman in the department, which was perhaps (she admitted) what made her say "cunt" so often. As for Wesley Mincher, he was the only southerner on the faculty — the only one who had a bachelor's degree from Sewanee and a PhD from Vanderbilt as opposed to Amherst and Harvard — and it was difficult for Wesley Mincher to see anyone else in the department over the high ramparts of his defensiveness. That was his phrase — "the high ramparts of my defensiveness" — and I remembered it in case I ever decide to build and then describe my own ramparts.

Anyway, it was Mincher who noticed Lees Ardor first, at a faculty meeting, the subject of which was a conference to be held at Heiden dedicated to the topic "Mark Twain: The Problem of Greatness." At the faculty meeting there'd been a long discussion on plenary and breakout sessions and keynote speakers, and at the end of all this, Lees Ardor had said, loudly, "Mark Twain is a cunt."

Her colleagues, of course, had heard Lees Ardor say this kind of thing many times before, and her ability to shock them, as with her students, was close to nil. They ignored her, but Mincher did not. There was something lovely, fragile, and mysterious about the way she said, "Mark Twain is a cunt," and after the department meeting was over, Wesley Mincher chased down Lees Ardor in the hallway and asked, "Do you have any interest in drinking red wine with me and talking about Confederate currency and maybe looking over my rare lithograph of the

Confederate mint in Richmond, Virginia?" To her own great surprise, Lees Ardor said, "Yes" (she did not remember, she admitted to me, the last time she had said yes to anything). Over the course of the next six months, Lees Ardor said yes many more times to Wesley Mincher (she blushed when he said this, but she wasn't displeased, you could tell), until finally he asked her why she'd said what she said about Mark Twain.

"I'm afraid of becoming Aunt Polly," Lees Ardor had confessed. She was talking, of course, about the shrewish spinster in *The Adventures of Huckleberry Finn* and *The Adventures of Tom Sawyer*. I had read those books, could easily see what she was afraid of, and realized that she was probably right to be afraid. "I don't want to be Aunt Polly," she'd told Mincher.

"I don't want that, either," Mincher had said to her, way back then, and also to me, in his house years later. "So I turned to chivalry, as men in my family always have." Thus he began to tell a long story about the many chivalric Minchers through the ages, leading, finally, to himself, Wesley Mincher, who decided to have the Mark Twain House torched as proof of his love for Lees Ardor. He had remembered reading about a young man who had destroyed the Emily Dickinson House in Amherst, Massachusetts (it had apparently reduced one of their colleagues — an expert in lyric poetry — to tears). So he wrote the arsonist a letter at his home address. Then he waited. Months and years passed; he fell deeper and deeper in love with Lees Ardor, and she with him. But there was that Mark Twain House: they passed it every day on their way to school (she'd moved in with him a year after they first fell in love), and it served as a reminder of his failures as a man, of how Lees Ardor still wasn't totally rid of her Aunt Polly nightmares.

"Wait a minute," I interrupted at this point in the story. "Why didn't you just ask her to marry you? She wouldn't have been Aunt Polly if you'd married her."

"I wanted to prove I was worthy of her first," Mincher said. "The destruction of the Mark Twain House would have proved my worthiness." This struck me as the most ridiculous sentiment I'd ever heard, the sort of absurd romantic hooey that Lees Ardor would have scoffed at if her students had expressed it or if she'd read it in a book. But when Mincher said this, Lees Ardor didn't scoff. She reached over and gently put her hand on his yellow neck and left it there; he shivered noticeably, as though her touch were the best kind of ice.

"But why did you wait so long for me?" I asked. "Why didn't you just try to burn down the house yourself?"

Mincher didn't answer; he just stared at me with disdain. I knew why, too: in Mincher's world, people were either experts or they weren't. He wouldn't have presumed to burn down the house, any more than he would have let me presume to know anything about the Lost Cause.

All of which brought us — and you — up to speed, to the day before I heard this story, when the letter from whoever was pretending to be me arrived at Mincher's campus mailbox. Wesley drove to the dumpster, deposited the three thousand dollars, and then went home and told Lees Ardor what he had just done, all for her. She had begun to cry, as tough-seeming people often do as a self-reward for appearing so tough.

"What's wrong?" Mincher had asked.

"That's so sweet," she'd said. "But that's not what I want."

"What do you want?"

"I want you to ask me to marry you."

This he did. "I've never been so happy," Lees Ardor said. Here, she flashed me a diamond engagement ring that was the only thing I'd seen thus far to rival the brightness of her hair. They — her ring and her hair — were like two guiding stars in the sick, murky light of the living room. "The only thing I'm not happy about is that you threw away all that money."

"Mincher women have always been . . . how shall I put it . . . *frugal*,"

Mincher said. He smiled at Lees Ardor, and I don't blame him: she looked beautiful, more beautiful even than the sum of her ring and her hair. She couldn't have been further away from the woman in the classroom, the Professor Ardor who called her dead mother a cunt.

"Do you still have the letter?" I asked them.

"What?" Mincher asked. He was back inside his head again, that was clear, except I bet that Lees Ardor was in there, too, leaving even less room for me and my questions.

"The letter I supposedly sent you, asking you for money. Do you still have it?"

"Yes," Mincher said. He got up and walked toward a desk in the corner of the room, withdrew a letter from one of the desk's drawers, came back from the desk, handed me the letter, sat back in his chair, and took Lees Ardor's hand again, all without taking his eyes off her, as if she were his compass, his north star. I took the letter out of the envelope. It was typed, and said, more or less, what Mincher and Ardor had told me it had said. The envelope was blank. There was no postmark on it, no name or return address, no sense of where it had come from or who had delivered it. It was basically the least helpful piece of evidence ever. I put the letter back in the envelope, then put it in my pocket, right next to the other letter, the letter that had led me to Wesley Mincher and Lees Ardor in the first place.

"Good-bye," I said to them, but they didn't seem to hear me, and why would they have wanted to? Why would they have wanted anything else to do with the world outside each other? Outside each other, they were mean little human beings like the rest of us, the kind of people you both loathed and pitied. Separately, they were characters, and not in a good way. But together they were something to wonder at and maybe even envy. I had this unoriginal thought as I walked out the door and toward my van: love changes us, makes us into people whom others then want to love. That's why, to those of us without it, love is the voice asking, *What else? What else?* And to those of us who have had love and lost it or thrown it away, then love is the voice that leads us back to love, to see if it might still be ours or if we've lost it for good. For those of us who've lost it, love is also the thing that makes us speak in aphorisms about love, which is why we try to get love back, so we can stop speaking that way. Aphoristically, that is.

13

No one parks on the street in Camelot. It's not illegal; there are no signs saying you must not park there between such and such a time on such and such a day for such and such a reason. But no one does, maybe because the driveways themselves are wide and deep enough to park a fleet of SUVs and minivans, the preferred family-friendly chariots of our tribe. Or maybe because there is something aberrant and lonely and sinister about a car parked on the street by itself, the way Thomas Coleman's black Jeep was that late afternoon when I pulled up to my house.

Was I surprised to see his Jeep there? I was not. Or at least I had been surprised too many times over the past few days to be truly surprised by anything. Surprise felt almost like its opposite, something familiar, like home itself. I parked my van in the driveway, next to Anne Marie's, in an attempt to distinguish myself (husband and father) from him (menacing stranger) in case someone was watching me from the front picture window. Which, it turns out, no one was.

I watched them, though, from the safety of my parked van. Not the kids — they were nowhere to be seen — but Thomas and Anne Marie. He was sitting on a stool at the breakfast bar. His right hand was on the counter, palm down. Anne Marie was standing over him, bent at the waist; she was putting what looked like a piece of gauze on the back of his hand, as though protecting a new tattoo, or perhaps dressing some kind of wound. Perhaps a burn wound. Of course. A burn wound. I was starting to see things clearly, and from my perspective inside the van, it looked as though Thomas had done more damage to his hand than to the Mark Twain House itself. Anne Marie smoothed and patted the gauze so gently and so many times that I began to get jealous of the gauze, and then the hand it was stuck to, and then the person whose hand it was.

Fear and love might leave a man complacent, but jealousy will always get him out of the van. I got out of the van, strode purposefully to the front door. I could really do it this time: I would tell Anne Marie the truth, starting with how much I loved her and how I'd never, ever cheated on her, no matter what I'd told her and what Thomas Coleman had told her, and how I knew where Thomas Coleman had gotten that burn on his hand. Then I'd go from there.

Except I didn't go anywhere. The front door was locked. I tried my key, but it didn't work: Anne Marie had changed the lock. It was bad enough that she was inside, touching the arm of Thomas Coleman, whom I'd begun to think of as less my victim and more my archnemesis. That was bad enough. But did she have to *change the lock on our front door*? I could think of no bigger betrayal than a wife's changing the locks on her husband, just as long as I didn't think about my burning and killing and then lying about it. And what does a husband do when he's been betrayed the way I'd been betrayed? He rages. Therefore I raged, which is to say, I pounded and pounded on the door. There is something humiliating about a man pounding on his own front door, though, and by the time Anne Marie finally opened it, the front door felt less like mine than ever.

"What?" Anne Marie said. She was wearing a long black skirt and those black boots I loved, and a white, nearly transparent top that bulged in all the right places.

"I love you so much," I said.

"Good for you," she said, arms crossed over her chest now. She looked like a Mediterranean General MacArthur with hair extensions and

without the corncob pipe. She had a military bearing, is what I'm saying. "What else?"

"Thomas," I said, feeling strangely breathless, and nearly panting the
word out of my mouth. "He isn't telling you the truth."

"He told me," she said, "that you didn't sleep with his wife after all. He
also told me that he doesn't even *have* a wife. Is that the truth, Sam?"

"Jesus," I said. "It is." I suddenly felt so tired I had to sit down, right on
the front slab. The truth makes you tired, not free; that's another thing
I'll put in my arsonist's guide — wherever it's relevant to burning down
writers' homes in New England, that is.

"OK, then," she said, and then turned to go back inside.

"Wait," I said, scrambling to my feet. "Can I come home now?"

"No," Anne Marie said, her back to me. Her hand was on the open
door, preparing to put it between her and me once again.

"Why not?" I asked.

"Because you lied to me," she said, turning around to face me. "I don't
know why you lied to me, but you did, and I don't trust you anymore."
Fatigue had replaced ferocity in Anne Marie's voice; maybe the truth
made her feel tired, too.

"Do you think you can trust *him*?" I asked, not needing to specify
who "him" was.

"I don't know *what* I think about him," Anne Marie admitted, which
was her way of saying that she knew me all too well, but that Thomas
was still mysterious and that mystery is sometimes closer to love than fa-
miliarity is — depending, of course, on whom you're so familiar with.

"Please, let me explain," I said, but she held up her hand to block my
explanation.

"Thomas hurt himself," she said. "I'm taking care of him."

"So why don't you ask him how he hurt himself!" I said, my voice getting high pitched and hysterical. "Why don't you ask him right now!"

Anne Marie looked at me curiously, her eyebrows and nose moving toward each other, making the face's own unique question mark. "OK, I'll do that," she said, and then closed and locked the door behind her.

I took this to mean, *I'll ask him and then come back out and tell you what he said.* So I waited there on the slab, for a long time. Night arrived and the streetlights came on. Neighbors came home from work, and since this was Camelot, they did their very best to ignore Thomas's car parked curbside and me sitting on the front slab. Finally I got tired of waiting. I rose from my slab and knocked on the door, and then I knocked and knocked and knocked and knocked. I was making such a racket that I wondered if even my fellow Camelotians could ignore me for much longer. But I didn't care. Let them look at me from their bay windows; let them watch me knock. I felt strong; I could have knocked all night.

I could have knocked all night, that is, if I hadn't heard a car pull into the driveway behind me. I stopped knocking, turned, and saw a dark green Lincoln Continental back in behind Anne Marie's minivan. It was my father-in-law's car; I recognized it right off because he'd always driven Lincoln Continentals and also because my father-in-law was a man of principle, and one of his most cherished principles was that you should always back into a parking space.

But it wasn't my father-in-law who first emerged from the car: it was Katherine, my daughter. She was strapped into a backpack so large that it rose almost to the top of her head. She walked up the driveway very carefully, maybe so the backpack wouldn't capsize her. It was like watching a young, overburdened female gringo Sherpa walking toward you, a Sherpa you loved and missed so much. "I love you," I told her when she was close enough to hear. "I've missed you so much." I gave Katherine and her backpack a hug, and they returned it, with feeling, for which I was grateful.

"Are you coming inside, Daddy?" Katherine asked. She was already adult enough to ask questions to which she already knew the answers and then to pretend not to recognize the lies those answers were.

"I'll be in in a second," I told her.

"OK," she said. Katherine walked up to the door, turned and pushed on the handle, and discovered, of course, that the door was locked. She turned to give me a quick look of assessment — *You are my father,* the look seemed to say, *and your front door is locked and you cannot open it* — then reached behind her, unzipped one of the backpack's many pockets, pulled out a set of keys, and expertly unlocked the front door. This was the most heartbreaking thing she'd done thus far — there is nothing sadder than a child with her own set of keys — and I would have cried right there, if Christian hadn't suddenly been around my legs, tugging on them and me as though we'd fallen right into our old game, in which I was the marauding giant and he the pint-size villager determined to topple me.

"Hey, bud," I said, holding him close to me. "Hey, guy." I was speaking in that awkward, bluff way fathers speak to their young sons, knowing that it won't be too long before their sons will grow up enough to tell their fathers to stop being so bluff and awkward.

"That damn car seat," my father-in-law said. He was right in front of me; his breath smelled of coffee and the Styrofoam cup it came in. "I couldn't get Christian out of that damn thing." His voice had a transportational effect on Christian: he disappeared from my legs and a moment later he materialized on the slab with his sister. Both of them waved at me and then vanished into the house.

About my father-in-law: He was shorter than me and slim, wore — and as far as I know still wears — pressed khaki pants and comfortable, broken-in loafers bought in the closeout section of the L.L. Bean catalog. You'd never see him wear a shirt without a collar and he was wearing a collared shirt now, with broad red stripes and the sleeves buttoned. I'd never seen him wear jewelry except for his wedding band. His wife, Louisa, only briefly enters this story, but she figured largely in her husband's: at extended family dinners, I often caught him looking at her, his eyes wet and grateful — grateful, I guess, to have her as his wife, and maybe to have the eyes with which to see her, too. He looked at

Anne Marie, his only daughter, in much the same way. He was a good husband and father, is what I'm saying. Of course, he was a racist, too, as I mentioned earlier; it probably does no good to say that he wasn't a racist unless the subject of race was raised, and then only some of the time. This is not to say that he wasn't a racist, but that when I see him now, I see his racism competing with his other, better qualities. I mostly liked him, and I wanted him to like me, and he had, too, mostly, I think, until now.

"Please leave Anne Marie alone," he said. The disappointment was heavy in his voice, pulling it down to its lowest levels. His eyes were baggy and resentful, and I felt sorry for dragging him into all this. My father-in-law had just retired after thirty-odd years of being an insurance claims investigator. He had finally paid off the mortgage on his house. His daughter had a marriage that had seemed to work; she had two kids, her own house, her own life. And now this. What a terrible thing it must be to be an aging father and grandfather and have to take on a second load of familial trouble just when you'd gotten rid of the first.

"I can't leave her alone," I said. "I just can't."

"You have to," he said.

"You don't want me to leave her with that" — and here I had trouble finding the right word to do justice to the specific feeling I had about this specific person — "*guy*, do you?"

"I know," he admitted, and this gave me some hope. "He worries me. But still, Anne Marie wants you to leave her alone."

"I can't," I repeated. "I love her."

"I know you do, Sam," he said, and I got that terrible shivery feeling you get when things are serious enough for people to use your name in conversation. "But I don't know if she loves you anymore."

With that, he, too, disappeared inside the house — he'd given a short knock on the door, which must have been the knuckled code, because the door opened enough to let him inside and then closed authoritatively behind him — and once again I was by myself in the driveway. I suppose if I'd been a better estranged husband and father, I would have resumed and persisted in my knocking until I'd gotten some answers, right then and there. But I wasn't any better an estranged husband and father than I'd been a normal, complacent one. And then there was my sadness, which was huge. If sadness were a competitive event, I'd have broken the subdivisional record. Sometimes when you're sad — as I'll write in my arsonist's guide — you have to sit around and wait for your sadness to turn into something else, which it surely will, sadness in this way being like coal or most sorts of larvae.

But in the meantime, at least I had these new mysteries to add to the old ones. Why had Thomas told Anne Marie the truth about my not cheating on her? What had he told her about that burn on his hand? And why didn't these things make her get rid of Thomas and take me back? I had hopes of finding out, as a detective if not as a husband. Because maybe this is yet another thing that defines you as a detective: not that you're especially good at *being* a detective, but that you're so bad at everything else.

14

It was after seven o'clock by the time I got to my parents' house, November dark, and darker still because a fog had settled in. It was the thick sort of fog that announces some major weather shift, the spooky sort of fog that makes you think you hear the mournful sound of hounds somewhere off in the distance. It was also the sort of fog where you don't see your parents' house until you're almost on top of it, and where you almost hit your mother sprinting across the street, away from the house and toward her car. My mother must have heard the squeal of my brakes, though, because she gestured obscenely in my direction without actually looking in my direction, and then jumped in her car. Her car was parked the wrong way on the street and not in our driveway because there were already several cars in the driveway, several lining the street, too; every light seemed to be on in our house, as if it were a three-story beacon in the fog, beckoning to who knew what kind of lost sailor. I wanted to see what was going on in the house, but I also wanted to know where my mother was going in such an awful hurry, on top of wanting to know why she'd lied to me about still being an English teacher, and where she'd disappeared to the night before. And so when she peeled out of her parking spot in her green Lumina, I followed her.

I followed her closely because of the fog. I mean, I was right on top of her, my headlights much too intimate with her tail. It was probably the

least inconspicuous surveillance in the history of surveilling; if I'd had
a license for surveillance, it would surely have already been revoked.
My mother didn't exactly make it easy on me, either: she was driving
angry, and following her in the fog was a lesson in rev and brake, rev
and brake. Luckily my mother didn't seem to notice me, and she didn't
travel far, either, just to downtown Belchertown, five miles away from
our house, where she pulled up in front of one of those old, monolithic
Masonic lodges that—because there are apparently a diminishing number of Masons to lodge there—now house offices, studios, community
theaters, apartments. My mother hopped out of her car, clearly still
worked up about something; she sprinted across the street and into the
front door. My mother had a long, graceful stride, too, making her the
sort of fleeting figure you might admire as she disappeared out of the fog
and into an old Masonic lodge.

I followed her, but since my stride is neither long nor graceful, I was
more than a few steps behind. By the time I was through the front door
and into the ceramic-tiled entryway, she was nowhere to be seen. There
was one door to the left of the lobby, and one to the right. Mr. Robert
Frost (whose house had less than one more day left on this earth as a
viable structure, as you'll soon learn) said that taking the road less traveled made all the difference, but this was only useful if you knew which
road was the one less traveled in the first place. I took the right door for
no particular reason.

What I found through that door was not my mother but a large, echoing hall that no doubt had once been where the Masons inducted their
young members and practiced their white magic. The hall was as big
as a high school gymnasium and was sheathed entirely in dark wood:
the floors were made of wide, dark-stained planks, and the walls were
paneled with that same dark-stained wood, and the high, high ceilings
were tongue and groove, acres of it. There were large vertical boxes the
size and shape of a confessional off to the side, too, the sort of containers in which you might cast your vote or confess your sins. The only

things not made of wood were a pipe organ and the elevated marble dais on which it sat. At the foot of the dais was a group of people, sitting on folding chairs arranged in a circle. They hadn't heard me enter the room, and so I crept up to them, hoping to see whether my mother was among them.

She wasn't, I saw that as I got closer, and I also saw that the group was composed of both men and women — maybe fifteen total — who were dressed as wizards and witches, with pointy hats and black cloaks decorated with pictures of harvest moons and magic wands and boiling cauldrons and other half-assed symbols of the occult. This frightened me for a moment, and I wondered if the Masons had reinvented themselves and gone coed and Wiccan. But then I looked more closely and noticed that each man and woman was holding a book. I recognized the book immediately. My kids each had a copy of it, even Christian, who couldn't exactly read yet. It was one of those children's books out of England that are so popular that somehow they aren't considered children's books anymore and that have, in any case, so frenzied their readers that they dress as the characters in the books dress and stand in line at midnight for the release of the latest in the series and use the word "jumper" instead of "sweater." In fact, both Katherine and Christian for a time had, like diabetics with their insulin, refused to travel anywhere without their book; they dressed up as characters from the book for Halloween, and for the day after Halloween, too. This seemed right to me. This was the way children were supposed to act: children became obsessed, children wore costumes. But adults were another matter, were they not? Was this what love for a book did to you? Did love for a book make you act like a child again? Or was this what love did to you, period, book or no book?

Possibly. But that's not why these men and women — my age and peers in parenting — were dressed as they were dressed, gathered as they were gathered, clutching the book they clutched. They weren't there for the book itself (I was eavesdropping now) but to better understand their kids, to become a bigger part of their lives, the way you might listen to your kids' hard-rock music or become addicted to their hard drugs.

"We need to support our kids," one wizard said. He had large, elongated glasses that were in danger of becoming goggles, and a salt-and-pepper beard, which he scratched earnestly as he spoke. "If they're reading and loving the book, then we need to read and love it, too."

"But what if the book isn't any good?" a witch in Tevas asked. "I have to say, I read the first chapter and didn't much care for it." When the witch in Tevas said this, she didn't look anyone else in the face; she looked at her feet, which were wide and fleshy and oozing out of the sides and tops of her sandals like melted processed cheese.

"It doesn't matter whether the book is good or not, in a sense," the wizard said sternly. "And besides, in a sense, the book has to be good. It's part of the *culture*."

There was a loud hum and murmur of assent from the group, and I used it as cover for my own noise as I pivoted and walked back on the road less or more traveled, whichever one was supposed to be the wrong road, and into the hallway, where I tried the left door, which was locked. What was I supposed to do with another locked door? I knew from very recent experience that knocking on a locked door would do no good. But what else could I do? Where was the poet to tell me what to do when the door to the road less traveled was locked? Where was the poet to tell me that?

He was in New Hampshire, or at least his house was, for the time being, and so I did the thing I knew to do, the thing at which I was getting expert: I walked outside and, through the fog, spied on my mother through the building's front windows, which were, like the rest of the building, massive. There she was, on the second floor. Hers was the only window lit, and my mother was sitting in front of it, at a table, with her chin in her hands, staring into space. The only thing lonelier than being by yourself in a room with nothing to look at or do or hold except your chin is watching someone else be that person. I wanted to run back inside the old Masonic lodge and snatch a copy of that famous book out of one of the faux witches' or wizards' hands and throw it up to my mother through her window, which I'd have to get her to open first, the way Juliet opened hers for Romeo, and Rapunzel for the guy who so desperately wanted her to let down her hair. If only my mother had a book to hold, she wouldn't have looked so lonely. And maybe this was another reason why people read: not so that they would *feel* less lonely, but so that other people would think they *looked* less lonely with a book in their hands and therefore not pity them and leave them alone. Did this not occur to the wizards and witches: that their kids read books so that their parents would think them not lonely and leave them alone? Maybe I'd tell them so while I was snatching a copy of their book to give to my mom.

"Sam Pulsifer," said a voice behind me. I turned and faced the voice and the person it belonged to: Detective Wilson.

He looked more like a detective this time: he still was wearing khaki pants and work boots but had ditched the hooded sweatshirt in favor of a blue button-down shirt and a blue sport coat that had probably been his father's or maybe an older detective's. The sport coat would have fit Detective Wilson if he hadn't tried to button it. But he had tried to button it, inflicting unnecessary punishment on his stomach and the coat and its buttons. Plus, someone had obviously told him that he couldn't be a detective without drinking way too much coffee. He was holding a large Styrofoam coffee cup, and he was blowing at the smoke drifting out of its vented top.

"What were you doing in there for so long?" he asked. "Visiting your mother?"

"Eavesdropping on the wizards," I said. "Witches, too."

"What?"

"I think I took the road less traveled," I told him.

"Speaking of the road," he said, trying to get the conversation back to a place where he could understand and control it, "I was behind you on the drive over here. You're a terrible driver."

"I was following my mother."

"You can't follow worth *shit*."

"I know that."

"I could have given you a ticket," he said.

"I'm glad you didn't," I said, especially since if he'd given me a ticket, then he would have asked to see my driver's license and I wouldn't have been able to show it to him. Because I'd never gotten my driver's license back from Lees Ardor — I had just realized that. I could see her in the classroom holding it and then not giving it back to me, and, like not getting the letter back from Mr. Frazier, this was another mistake I'd regret. But then again, I was pretty certain I'd make more mistakes, so I didn't dwell on the one I'd just made for too long. This is another thing I'll put in my arsonist's guide: if you make a mistake, don't dwell on it for too long, because you'll make more of them.

"If you'd tried to give me a ticket," I said, "I would have asked to see your badge." I was remembering a few things about Detective Wilson, and one of them was that he hadn't told my parents what police department he was from, if he was from any department at all. "Do you even *have* a badge?"

"Here you go," he said, and then handed me his badge, which was embedded in a slim wallet. The badge was gold and had some sort of raised seal or crest, and on the crest was some writing that was unreadable in the light and fog. Still, I pretended to examine it closely, as if I knew the difference between a real badge and a fake one. On the wallet flap opposite his badge was an ID with his picture, and his name, Robert Wilson, and his title: detective, Arson Unit, State of Massachusetts Fire Division. The ID looked real enough: I held it up to the streetlight and saw official-looking watermarks and holograms.

"You're a fireman," I said.

"I'm a *cop*," he said with a little too much force, letting me know exactly what nerve was exposed and how much it didn't like to be hit.

"OK," I said, and handed him back the badge. Detective Wilson took it and tucked it inside his jacket pocket. When he did so, his jacket popped open and came away from his torso and I could see his shoulder holster and the butt of his gun sticking out of it. So even if he wasn't a cop, he was a fireman with a gun, which I figured was pretty close to the same thing.

"Did you know that someone tried to burn down the Mark Twain House last night?" he asked.

"It wasn't me," I said.

"I didn't think it was," he said, although the knowing smile on his face said that he did in fact think I'd set the fire, which made me add, "It wasn't me who set fire to the Edward Bellamy House, either," for unnecessary good measure.

"I didn't think it was," he said again, this time with even less sincerity. He put his left hand in his sport coat pockets and tapped a happy beat through the lining and on his thigh.

"Sure you didn't," I said. "That's why you were following me here."

"Maybe I wasn't following only you," he said. "Maybe I was following your mother, too."

"Why would you do that?"

"Maybe I have my reasons," he said, and then waited for me to ask the obvious question, which I did.

"What are your reasons?" I asked. "Why are you following my mother?"

"The night someone tried to set fire to the Edward Bellamy House," he said, "you were at your parents' house, right?"

"That's right."

"Were they there, too?" he asked, hooking his thumb in the direction of my mother sitting in her illuminated window. "Was your mother there that night?"

"Of course she was," I said. But was she? Had my mother been home, after all? "Where else would she have been?" I said this to myself more than to anyone else, but of course I also said it out loud, thereby losing my sole rights to it.

"Maybe she was here," Detective Wilson said. "Maybe she was some-where else. Either way, I'll find out." He sounded confident, which scared me. There is nothing scarier to those who lack confidence than those who are full of it. And so I said something right then, something that in the end, and once again, I probably shouldn't have and would end up regretting.

"I know who tried to set fire to the Mark Twain House," I said.

"You do?" Detective Wilson said. His confidence didn't disappear en-tirely right then, but it did seem as though I'd diluted it some.

"Yes," I said. "His name is Thomas Coleman. He probably set fire to the Edward Bellamy House, too. I don't know where he lives, but you can probably find him at my house in Camelot."

"Your house in Camelot," he repeated.

"One thirteen Hyannisport Way," I said.

"Why would this guy be at your house?"

"He's sleeping with my wife," I said, admitting this to myself and to someone else for the first time. "Or trying to."

What was Detective Wilson's response to this news? It was unex-pected. He didn't ask me any questions, didn't wonder who this Thomas Coleman was or why he would want to burn down these houses or how I knew he had tried to do so. Detective Wilson didn't ask me any ques-tions at all. He simply turned away from me, walked over to his car, opened the driver's side door, and climbed in.

"Wait," I said, walking around to his side of the car. Detective Wilson's face looked as confused as it had appeared confident a few moments earlier; his face looked younger, too, which is to say that confidence ages you, but confusion keeps you young, the way a positive outlook and Swedish facial creams are supposed to but never do. "Where are you going?"

"I'm going to your house," he said, "to talk to your wife and this Thomas Coleman."

"Just because I said so?" I asked. Was being a stool pigeon this easy?

Who knew that all you had to do was give voice to your suspicions and blame someone else to get such quick results? "Just like that?"

"Yes, Sam," he said. "Just like that. But you'd better not be lying. You better not be jerking me around."

"I'm not," I assured him, even though I was the person who really needed reassuring. Thomas Coleman had been my number one suspect, my sole suspect, really. I had known with all my heart that he was the one who'd set the fires; I had known he was the guilty one. And then I had gone ahead and said so, to Detective Wilson, and then immediately afterward I had doubts, big ones. I'd said *guilty,* and immediately Thomas Coleman had seemed as if he might be innocent. I wondered whether, if I said *innocent,* he might seem guilty again. But it was too late to say that, so instead I asked, "But aren't you going to ask my mother where she was last night before you go? Aren't you going to ask her where she was the night of the Bellamy House fire, too?" I said this not because I wanted him to ask her that, but because Detective Wilson — with his badge and ID and gun and coffee — was seeming more and more like a real detective, and I wanted to know what a real detective might ask, and when, and of whom.

"Not now," he said. "Besides, I know where I can find her." With that, Detective Wilson rolled up his window and peeled out into the foggy night, leaving behind the squeal of his tires and the smell of his exhaust and this lesson: being a real detective meant knowing where you could find people. I knew now where I could find my mother. But why was she there? Was this her apartment? Was she staying with someone else? Was this her *home*? Was she in the apartment and not in our house the night of the Edward Bellamy House fire, and last night, too? Was she somewhere *besides* the apartment? I patted my coat pocket and felt the two letters: the one from Mincher asking me to burn down the Mark Twain House, and the other, anonymous and typed, asking Mincher for three thousand dollars to do the burning. The letter had no postmark, so that meant that someone had driven there, probably from close by. But why a letter in the first place? Why not just call Mincher and pretend to be me on the phone? The only answer was that whoever had typed and delivered the letter couldn't pretend to be me on the telephone. Any man could pretend to be me on the telephone, but a woman could not. And what woman would want to pretend to be me? I really only knew two women in this world: one of them was in Camelot, and the other was right in front of me, seeming less like the mother I thought I knew, and more and more like someone I didn't know at all.

"Oh, Mom," I said, softly. My mother was still sitting at her window, not reading, not looking out the window at me, either: as far as I could tell, she was simply staring into space.

At that moment, the book-group wizards and witches emerged from the building, each of them holding their copy of the book away from their body, as though it were a divining rod leading them directly to their children's heart of hearts. They looked so happy, overjoyed, the way people are when they think they've found the answer to a particularly difficult question. Each of them felt compelled to say their hearty "Hello's" and "Good evening's" to me and then commenced to talk about the fog and how it was a very English fog, and then there was a long, sincere discussion about how very magical fog was and how they'd be sure to wake up their kids when they got home to show them the fog and then find a passage in the book featuring fog, and then they'd compare the literary fog and the meteorological fog, and in the middle of all this I saw, peripherally, a flicker of light. I turned away from the witches and wizards and toward my mother's apartment window; it was now completely dark, and I couldn't see my mother anywhere. I must have stared at the window for five, ten, fifteen minutes. The witches and wizards got into their vehicles and drove away into the night, and still I stood there, waiting for my mother to turn her light back on, waiting for her to emerge from the building, waiting for *something*. But this is another thing I'll put in my arsonist's guide (which, as you've figured out by now, is also a detective's guide, a son's guide, a guide that is as specific or generic as you and I need it to be): you can wait only so long for a blackened window to be illuminated. And when you start to wonder whether the window will ever be illuminated again, and whether you were seeing what and who you thought you were seeing when it *was* lit, then you've waited too long, and the best thing is just to go home. So I just went home.

15

It should be said at this point that I knew all along that my father was a drunk and hadn't had a stroke at all. I must have known that; how could I not have known that? Of course I knew that. I was just *pretending* to believe that my father had had a stroke. Because we all know that to be a son is to lie to yourself about your father. But once you start telling yourself the truth, does that mean you are no longer a son, and he is no longer your father? And then what are you? And what is he?

The truth was that my father was a drunk, and there had been a party at my parents' house. It must have ended not long before I got home for the second time that night. The place was an even bigger wreck than before. There were ashtrays everywhere and they were full to overflowing, and so, rather than empty the ashtrays, the smokers had used every available surface — flat and concave, highly flammable and less highly flammable — to deposit their ashes. The living room looked postvolcanic. On the coffee table was a line of juice glasses, and inside each glass were the watery remnants of something dark and evil, something you were no doubt supposed to drink all at once or not at all. On the couch, someone had left behind the sort of visor you might see a card dealer or a cub reporter wearing in an old movie. On the floor between the couch and the coffee table, there was a translucent gasoline funnel. I picked it up and saw a long piece of white hose or tubing dangling suggestively from the bottom, and I put it down again. The exercise bike had been

thrown in the corner of the room, on its side; one pedal was pointed
ceilingward and still spinning. The television was on, but the sound was
not; it was a program devoted to heart surgery, and they kept showing
close-up shots of open and then closed chest wounds. There was music
playing loudly, so loudly I couldn't tell what it was or where it was coming from, especially since my parents, to my knowledge, didn't own a
stereo. I followed the noise through the living room and into my father's
bedroom. The bed was as big a disaster as the rest of the house: sheets
were draped over the chair, the end table, the headboard, everywhere
but the bed itself. There was a boom box on the floor, vibrating from
its own noise. Over the crash of guitar and bass, I could hear the singer
ask obscurely, "Does anyone have a cannon?" I turned off the boom box
and heard normal human voices coming from the kitchen. I followed
them. My father was sitting at the kitchen table, and across from him
was another man, someone I'd never seen before. In between them, on
the table, was the shoe box, and scattered around the table were the letters. I missed my mother right then, badly, the way you miss one parent
when the other one isn't doing what he's supposed to.

"I know where Mom is," I said to my father, but he didn't hear me,
or pretended not to. The other man did hear me, though; he looked
up and smiled at me in the vacant, unperturbed fashion of the truly
punchy. He was approximately my father's age, maybe a little older, was
wearing a beat-up gray corduroy blazer, and had a nose that might have
been Rudolph's had Rudolph been a boxer — a bad one. There were two
forty-ounce Knickerbockers on the table in front of them, and empties
scattered around the kitchen.

"Now, this," my father was saying, "this is one of my favorites. It's
from a man in Leominster who wanted my son to burn down the
Ralph Waldo Emerson House because he had been named Waldo, after
Emerson, and no one had ever let him forget what a stupid name he had."
I, too, remembered the letter: the letter writer had said that he probably
should have wanted me to burn down his parents' house, too, for naming

him Waldo in the first place, except they were dead and he was now living in their house and the mortgage was paid, free and clear, and if I burned it down, he'd have to pay rent somewhere else. My father handed the letter to the man across the table, and the man looked at it blankly, as if it were a picture of people he didn't know; then he put it on the table. "And this letter," my father went on, "is from a woman who wanted my son to burn down Herman Melville's house in Pittsfield . . ."

And so on. What matters here was not only what my father said, but how he said it. He slurred slightly when he spoke, but there was nothing halting or stroke damaged about his speech. I heard and saw and understood this clearly now. I was seeing my father, not by himself or with my mother, but in his element, and this is another thing I'll put in my arsonist's guide: seeing your father in his element will make you feel sad. I had been sad when I thought my father had had a stroke and was partially paralyzed, but at least then he could be considered heroic. This was a different kind of sadness, a deeper one, a sadness you feel when you discover that the person you love is not the person you thought you were loving. Would I wake up the next morning and find my father sad in a totally different way? How many different kinds of sadness were there in the world, anyway?

"But this is odd," my father was saying, although the man across the table from him wasn't exactly listening anymore: his hand was curled around the beer can, but his eyes were closed and his neck was fighting a losing battle to keep his head from crashing to the table. "There seem to be some letters missing." My father gathered all the letters, stacked them, and then began flipping through them, his lips moving as he took inventory. He finished the inventory, then took another one. The man's head fell to the table with a dull *thunk*, but my father didn't notice. Perhaps not wanting to be further ignored, the man got up from the table, a lump already formed on his forehead, and left the room and then the house: I could hear the front door open and then shut. My father didn't notice any of that, either. "I just don't understand," he said.

"Which letters are missing?" I asked him gently, because as far as I could tell, he wasn't aware of me standing there, and I didn't want to scare him. Except he didn't seem surprised at all to hear my voice. Maybe he'd known I was there the whole time, or maybe he didn't care.

"The Edward Bellamy House letter, of course," he said. "But there are six other letters missing, too."

"What are they?" I asked. I knew full well that the Mark Twain House letter was missing, since it was in my pocket. Sure enough, my father named it, and then added, "But then there are five others that are missing, too. I just can't figure out which ones."

"How do you know that many are missing, then?"

He looked at me with pity. "You were sent one hundred and thirty-seven letters. There are only one hundred and thirty letters here." He knocked himself on the head, as though to dislodge the forgotten names.

"Did you know that someone tried to burn down the Mark Twain House last night?" I asked.

"Yes," my father said. He turned to look at me for the first time, although his face was empty of anything except worry and bafflement. "That's how I can remember the Mark Twain House letter, because I knew someone had tried to burn it down. Your mother told me. She also told me that whoever did it didn't do a very thorough job."

"How did she know that?" I asked him.

"I suppose she read it in the paper," he said. "How did *you* know it?"

"I read it in the newspaper, too," I said, which was the truth, or part of it. And then: "Dad, I saw Mom leave the house earlier."

"Yes, she was here," my father said, starting to count the letters again.

"And then she left."

"She didn't look happy," I said.

"There was a bit of a mix-up," my father said. "I have one of these parties every Tuesday. Your mother tolerates the parties as long as she knows when they are so she won't be around. That's why they're every Tuesday."

"Today is Monday," I said.

"That was the mix-up," he admitted. "I thought it was Tuesday. So I called everyone and said, 'Where are you? Get over here.'"

"Tell me about the parties, Dad," I said, although I could picture them pretty well already. They would be populated by men like the old, red-nosed guy who'd earlier bounced his head off the kitchen table, men whose natural and sole habitat was the college town: failed or failing graduate students, drunk professors or book editors like my father, all of them wearing corduroy jackets in various stages of disrepair. These guys had once had their *fields* — Victorian literature, tropical botany, the cultural import of the manual typewriter — but one day they discovered that they didn't *like* their fields anymore, not as much as they liked to drink, anyway. And the only thing they liked as much as drinking was *oddity*, which made sense, since they were both odd and drunks themselves. My father and his free booze and his son the arsonist and murderer and all those letters fit both those bills. I could picture all of them, every Tuesday, showing up at my parents' house and drinking their booze and listening to my father read those letters until they'd exhausted most of the liquor and my father had exhausted most of their curiosity and they drifted away, until there was only one red-nosed guy left, always the drunkest one, the one with nobody to see and nowhere to go and nothing to do except sit at the kitchen table and drink the last Knickerbocker and listen to my father drone on and on and on about the letters, the letters, the letters, the way he'd talked to so many drunks before. I knew this without my father telling me, even though he did, in so many words.

"So Mom doesn't like these parties," I said. I could see why, but something didn't quite make sense to me. After all, my mother didn't seem to have a problem with drunks in general, being one herself, plus being married to one, plus being mother to a son who was well on his way to becoming a drunk, too. So why would a few dozen more drunks in corduroy blazers bother her so much? "How come she doesn't like these parties?" I asked my father.

"I have no idea," he said, and that's another thing I'll put in my arsonist's guide: be wary of a man who says, "I have no idea," when asked why his wife doesn't like something he's done, which of course is just another way of saying be wary of men in general. "Maybe she doesn't like what my guests do to the house," he said.

"Speaking of the house—," I said, "Dad, how long ago did Mom move out?"

"Move out?" my father repeated. "I wouldn't exactly say she has. Her clothes are here, after all, or at least most of them. She comes back here to drink most every night."

"Dad," I said, "I saw her apartment tonight. I saw her in her apartment in Belchertown, in the Masonic temple. I know all about that."

"Oh," he said. His face fell a little and began to look more like the face of the stroked-out father I believed and wanted him to be and he perhaps wanted to be, too. "I'm sorry you have to know all about that."

"Are you still even married?"

"It's complicated," he said.

"What is?" I said.

"Marriage," he said.

"Do you still love her?"

"I love her very much," my father said automatically. Did this mean he did, or he didn't? If he had asked me the same question about Anne Marie, I would have given him the same answer, and I would have given it automatically. "I wish your mother weren't in that apartment," he said. "I wish she were here, with us."

"So why isn't she?"

"It's complicated," my father said again. I could see that "complicated" was the word he used to describe that which he didn't understand, the way I used "accident." My father dropped his eyes and then returned them to the letters. He picked one up and I could see his hand shake. He seemed more and more feeble and distracted with each passing second, and I thought I'd better finish asking questions before he fully reverted to the stroked-out father I'd been thinking he was.

"Dad, how many people have seen these letters?"

"Too many to count," he said, and this seemed to please him. He rallied a little bit and started walking around the kitchen, waggling beer cans to see if they had any beer left in them, drinking out of the ones that did.

"Does anyone know where you keep the letters?"

"Of course," he said. He sat down at the table and started flipping through the letters again. "Lots of people do."

"Does anyone suspicious know where you keep the letters?" I asked. This was a weak question, and my father gave me a look as if to say, *They all were,* and so I thought about how to be more specific. *What would a suspicious person look like, exactly?* I asked myself, and immediately Thomas Coleman came to mind, especially since he'd seemed to know my father, knew where his bedroom was, and had been in this same home only the day before. Plus, I'd already fingered him as guilty to Detective Wilson, so I had some stake in his guilt. Plus, I didn't think I had anyone else to name except my mother, and I didn't want to name her, not unless I had to.

"Do you know someone named Thomas Coleman?" I asked him.

"I know lots of people," my father said.

"He has blond hair," I said. "He's thin, has blue eyes." I thought about it some more, wished there were more ways to physically describe the people who are ruining our lives. "Really thin," I said again. "Does that sound like someone who has seen the letters?"

"Lots of thin people have seen the letters," my father said, talking more to the letters than to me.

"Dad, pay attention!" I barked, the way a parent does to a child, and the way every child eventually does to his parent, too, taking revenge for being barked at so many years earlier, revenge being yet another one of the many kinds of sadness. My father's head jerked up and he held it there, at attention. "Thomas Coleman's parents died in the Emily Dickinson House fire," I told him.

"They did," he said.

"Yes," I said. "I killed them." It felt good to admit this finally, although every good feeling exists only long enough for you to ruin it, and I ruined this one by adding, "By accident."

"By accident," my father said.

"Do you know Thomas Coleman?" I asked. "Has he seen the letters? I'm pretty sure someone who has seen the letters tried to set fire to both the Bellamy House and the Twain House. They probably have the five other letters, too. Dad, please, think hard. Do you know a Thomas Coleman? This is *important*."

My father thought hard; I could tell by the way the worry lines on his forehead deepened and multiplied. He even brought his index finger to his lips and left it there. Finally he said, "I have no idea. I'm sorry, Sam, but I don't."

"OK," I said, and I believed him, and that will also go in my arsonist's guide: don't trust a man who says, "I have no idea," but also don't underestimate his capacity not to have one. "Dad," I said, "you don't think it could be Mom who tried to burn those houses, do you?"

"No," he said. "Why would you ask something like that?"

"Because I'm pretty sure it's a woman," I said. "If it's not this guy Thomas Coleman, then I'm pretty sure it's a woman."

"Why do you say that?"

"It's complicated," I said, throwing his favorite word back at him. "But trust me, I'm pretty sure it's a woman."

"Why would it be your mother?" my father said. He was really lucid now, his eyes suddenly clear of the booze and the letters and who knows what else that had been fogging them.

"I don't know," I said. "Maybe she's not happy I came back. Maybe it's because of me."

"Don't you ever say that!" my father yelled. I mean, he really yelled this, and then banged on the table, giving his fist the opportunity to yell, too. I don't think he ever banged or yelled once when I was a child; usually he moped and then fled. I'm not sure which was worse, or better. Were these my only choices? Shouldn't you get more than two choices? "Your mother would never do something like that to you," he told me. "Don't be ridiculous."

"OK," I said.

"She *loves* you, you idiot," he said. "You have no idea how much."

"OK, OK," I said. "But I'm still pretty sure it's a woman, though."

"Then it's another woman," my father said. "Go find another woman." Of course he said this, and of course I listened, *finding another woman* being both the hope that keeps most men going and the hope that eventually does them in.

That was the end of that. After he told me to go find another woman, my father seemed to stroke out again. He put the letters back in the shoe box, tucked the shoe box under his arm, got up from his chair, and shuffled toward his bedroom. Before he left the kitchen, though, he reached with his free hand and picked up a book on the counter. "By the way," he said. He held up Morgan Taylor's memoir, then tossed it at me. I didn't react quickly enough, and it hit me right in the gut, which, co-incidentally, is exactly where the book jacket promised the book would hit me. "I read this. Am I supposed to be in here?"

"Well, not you exactly," I said. "But the things you did, the places you went after you left Mom and me. Those are *your* stories."

"If you say so," my father said. He shrugged and then shuffled off to bed.

LIKE THE MANY SAD-SACK young male narrators of the books my mother made me read when I was a sad-sack young male, I went to bed that night without my supper, and for that matter without my lunch, too. My stomach was rumbling angrily, keeping pace with the rumbling in my head. There were so many things to think about that I couldn't properly think about any of them. When this happens, the only thing you can do is to locate one thought, the simplest one, the one nearest to you, and do your very best to eliminate it and then go on to thinking about the next thought you want to eliminate.

The thought closest to me that night was this: Morgan Taylor had stolen my father's stories for his memoir. My father had read the memoir and said he wasn't in it, even though those postcards he'd sent me said otherwise. When I was a child, I kept the postcards my father had sent in my closet, on the top shelf, in a manila envelope. I got out of bed, dragged a desk chair over to the closet, climbed up on the chair, reached up to the top shelf, and found the envelope. The postcards were inside: I read them like that, standing on the chair. They were exactly as I remembered, in my father's handwriting, the handwriting I recognized from the "Drink Me" notes he left in the morning beside my hangover potion. I'd remembered the handwriting so clearly, in part, because it was the only time I'd ever really seen either of my parents write *anything* except for the illegible marginal comments they made on student papers and manuscripts, and even that writing wasn't writing at all but rather symbols telling the writer to indent or not to. The way I figured it, my parents scribbled so much at work that they couldn't bring themselves to write anything at home — not even a grocery list or a birthday card. Except for my father's postcards. My father might not have remembered the postcards clearly, but here they were, written proof that something important had happened as I remembered it happening. Each postcard was signed, "Love, Your Dad."

"I love you, too," I said to the postcards, putting them back in the envelope and then putting the envelope back on its high shelf. The father downstairs was strange to me and unlikable, but the one I knew from the postcards was still here, with me, in my heart and on my high closet shelf. With one thing less to think about, I got back into bed and tried to go to sleep. I did, too, for three hours, until the phone woke me up.

It rang and rang and rang — my parents didn't have an answering machine, which seemed about right, because I don't think the phone had rung once since I'd moved home — until it finally pulled me out of bed and downstairs, where the phone was. I picked it up and gave the usual greeting, and in response I heard a man whose voice I didn't recognize say, "The Robert Frost Place, Sam. At midnight," and then hang up. I put the phone back into its cradle, then walked into my father's room. I was prepared to wake him, but he was already awake. The lamp on the end table was on. There was a box of wine on the end table next to the lamp, red wine dripping from its spigot onto the floor. My father was sitting in his chair, a glass of wine in one hand, the open box of letters in his lap. He was staying up late, drinking box wine, worrying about the missing letters, the way another father might stay up late, drinking coffee, worrying about his missing son or wife.

"Dad," I said, "did you hear the phone ring?"

"Yes," he said, then drained his glass. He placed the glass under the spigot, filled his glass only halfway, and then gave the box a disappointed glance that let me know it was empty.

"That was someone telling me that he was going to burn down the Robert Frost Place. In so many words."

"Peter Le Clair," he said automatically. "Ten State Route Eighteen, Franconia, New Hampshire." He looked at me sheepishly and nodded. "I should have remembered that one."

Part Four

16

New Hampshire was pretty. For one thing, it started snowing immediately after I crossed the state border, which gave me the feeling that it never stopped snowing in New Hampshire and that if I turned around and looked back at Massachusetts, I'd see a solid line of weather — on one side blizzard, on the other side nothing but palm trees and warm breezes. But I didn't look back to check. I kept my eyes straight ahead, on the road, because it really was snowing hard and you could hardly see a thing with all the trucks barreling northward, the snow whooshing and blowing in their wake and into my windshield. It was like driving behind a fierce and terrible tsunami with Quebec plates. Then one of the trucks got caught in a rut of snow, veered to the left, through traffic and off the highway, and jackknifed into a ditch, after which all the cars panicked and started skidding here and there, and it was like bumper cars that had lost their poles while going seventy, in the snow, with some horrible visibility. It was a real mess, and I knew if I stayed on the highway much longer, I'd soon be in a ditch myself or worse, so I took the next exit.

It was magical off the highway, still snowing hard but no semis and no high speeds and so more heavenly and not nearly as blinding and hazardous; all in all, it was a much better-looking New Hampshire. I went through about twelve towns, lovely towns full of white clapboard houses and snow-covered town greens and sensible white boxy Congregational churches and covered wooden bridges, and even a gristmill or two paddling their way through icy streams, not getting much done for all their paddling, but still plucky and hopeful. I wished that I wasn't just driving through and also that I'd learned to paint so I could be an artist and live in New Hanpshire and paint pictures of the towns. They were that handsome. I drove by an inn in Red Bell, and there were a half-dozen cars parked out front, all of them with out-of-state plates, people obviously on vacation. I'd never been on vacation myself, not really, and now I knew why people did it. People went on vacation not to get a break from their home but to imagine getting a new home, a better home, in which they'd live a better life. I knew this because as I drove, the hole that was me and my life was getting smaller and smaller and was being filled up with New Hampshire, or maybe it was only the idea of New Hampshire, but who cares, as long as it was filling up the hole. So maybe that's what a vacation was for: to fill up the hole that was you not on vacation.

Because that's what Red Bell was doing: it was filling me up and making me reflective, too. Now that I had seen the real deal, New England town – wise, I could see Camelot as Anne Marie had at first: cheap, sterile, and so lonely and, as far as homes go, no shelter at all from the cruel, cruel world. But if we could have moved here, near a gristmill, things would have been different. Was it too late? Maybe it wasn't too late. Maybe Anne Marie and I could work things out in New Hampshire; maybe the boxy churches would help her forget my lying and would also help me to finally tell the truth; maybe my bumbling wouldn't be so severe here, in Red Bell, or in one of its neighbors. After all, the place was so very old and had been through a lot, so you probably couldn't do much to it that hadn't been done to it already. The ancient, meandering stone walls, for instance: they were everywhere, and if the Indians and the British and generations of livestock hadn't wrecked them, I didn't see how I could do the walls much damage, either. They looked tough and permanent, those walls, but with the snow on them they looked soft, too, which was how I was starting to think of myself — or rather, was how I was starting to think of my future, New Hampshire self. Yes, New Hampshire was already doing strange things to me. After only an hour in the state, I had fully imagined life here with Anne Marie and the kids; it was easy to do so, easy to forget that Anne Marie was with Thomas Coleman now and wanted nothing more to do with me. I wondered if this was how my father had felt during his three-year exile — if he'd felt hopeful and dreamy about the prospect of a new life with his wife and boy in Duluth, Yuma, et cetera. It hadn't worked out that way for him, exactly, but it would work out better for me and mine — of that I was convinced. Because everyone knows that the one constant in the human story is progress, and my father's Duluth was not my New Hampshire, his familial disaster not mine, and so I pledged to look into local real estate prices and employment opportunities immediately after I found out who had called me, asking me to meet him at the Robert Frost Place at midnight.

But then I kept driving north, up into the White Mountains and toward Franconia, and it got so awfully poor and depressing that even the snow couldn't disguise it. First the clapboard houses lost their clapboards and took on some aluminum siding, still white but somehow dirty against the legitimately and naturally white snow. I felt bad for the houses, having to be compared to the white snow and failing so completely. It would probably have been better for the houses and the people in them to move south, where there was no snow to have to live up to.

Anyway, accelerating through time (because this trip took hours and hours — you could see why people in a hurry and with no eye for local detail are so completely devoted to the interstate), I drove farther north, and the trailers started popping up here and there, until there were only trailers and I started to miss the aluminum siding. Oh, those trailers were sad and made Mr. Frazier's neighborhood in Chicopee seem like Shangri-la. They looked cold, too, sitting there on the open ground with no trees to protect them from the wind and the drifting snow. Some of the trailers had plywood entrances tacked onto their fronts or sides, and

I could see the plywood jittering in the wind. Every trailer had a stove-pipe coming out of its roof, sticking out of the tar paper like a lonely digit. The smoke came furiously out of these pipes, the wood burning double time so as not to spend any extra minutes in the trailers. There were wrecked cars in every yard, taking the place of the trees, and they, too, were covered with snow, the way the stone walls had been farther south. But whereas the snow had softened the boulders, the wrecks looked cruel as the rusted and warped fenders punched through the snow, making harsh holes in the drifts. I was in Franconia now, with the White Mountains everywhere, and it should have been beautiful, but it wasn't. The mountains themselves seemed impossibly far away, as if they didn't want to get too close to the trailers. It was awful, all right, so depressing, so poor, and by now the hole inside me — the hole where Anne Marie and the kids were, the hole that pretty Red Bell had started to fill — was as large as ever, and I'd forgotten about Red Bell entirely, couldn't remember what made it so beautiful, couldn't even conjure up a gristmill. This is what poverty does, I guess: it ruins your memory of more beautiful things, which is just another reason why we should try as hard as we can to get rid of it.

Peter Le Clair's address: 10 State Route 18. I found his place because of the hand-painted number 10 on the mailbox, which was bent face down-ward, almost off its pole, as if ashamed of its address. His trailer was the same as the others except for one thing: Peter himself was standing at the trailer's one front window, watching as I pulled into his driveway. His face disappeared from the window, and seconds later the tan ply-wood door to the black plywood addition swung open and there stood Peter, five-day beard and flannel shirt and no coat, holding a gun. Ex-cept it wasn't a gun — my eyes and assumptions were playing tricks on me — it was a plunger (Peter had real plumbing problems, in addition to his other problems). Still, Peter looked mighty threatening. He was big, much taller than six feet, with a chest that was full barreled to my half. There was a doghouse in front of the trailer, right next to my minivan, and a dog howled from inside it but didn't come out. I wished I were in the doghouse with the dog, who knew Peter better than I did and could probably give me a few pointers about how to please its master. Or maybe the dog was trying to do just that, through its howling, which was loud and echoing from inside the doghouse. *Go away,* it might have been howling. *Go away, go away.*

But I couldn't go away. For one thing, it was only six o'clock, and I had to stick around until at least midnight to find out who had made that phone call and why. And for another, I had nowhere else to go, nothing left to do. Perhaps Peter's trailer in Franconia was as close to home as I was going to get. Perhaps, for a man like me, there was no longer any such thing as a true home and so I couldn't be picky, couldn't just sit in the van and refuse to come out because the homes were depressing and their inhabitants were large and menacing. Yes, I needed to get out of the van. Now that I knew that, the dog's howling took on a different meaning, and instead of *Go away, go away,* it was *Get out of the van, get out of the van.* I got out of the van.

Boy, it was cold. The sort of heart-clutching cold where after being out in it for a second, you can't bear another one. Even Peter and his plunger were less frightening than the cold. Plus, it was still snowing hard and I didn't have a hat, and if I stayed out there much longer, I'd be buried like the wrecked vehicles in the yard. There were three of them, to the left of the doghouse; I could see their antennas sticking out of the snow.

"Mr. Le Clair, I'm Sam Pulsifer," I said, walking up to him. And then — not reminding him of who I was or of the letter he'd sent me who knows how many years ago or even waiting for a response — I said, "Let's go inside, what do you say? My teeth are chattering right out of my gums, they're so cold." And with that, I kept walking, right past him and into the trailer, not because I was brave but because the fear had frozen inside me. It was that cold.

It was warmer in the trailer. There were boots everywhere, and coats, lined flannel shirts, and hooded sweatshirts hung on hooks and off the backs of chairs and even off the back of the TV, keeping it warm. It was an enormous, old TV. No remote control ever had or ever would control it. There were heavy tattered rugs everywhere, too — there was even one nailed to the living room wall, like an animal's hide — rugs with not much color in them (mostly brown and dark red), and you knew someone's grandmother had labored over them for a year and a day. Then there were the books: the living room — its furniture, its floor — was covered with a layer of books, like dust. The books were all from some library — I could see the telltale laminated tag on the spines. I looked down, lifted my left foot, and saw I'd been standing on a copy of *Ethan Frome,* a book every eighth grader in Massachusetts since Edith Wharton had written it had been required to read and then wonder why. I kicked the novel away from me, something I'd been wanting to do for twenty-six years, and in doing so I imagined I was striking a blow on behalf of its many unwilling, barely pubescent readers. There were so many library books that I wondered if Peter had put the local public library out of business and whether his living room hadn't become the real library instead. I say the living room, but in addition to being the library and the living room, it was also the TV room and the dining room. There was a separate kitchen, which was only a little bigger than the TV, and between the two rooms was the most important appliance in the house: the woodstove. The stove was really going, high and hot, and it was so dry in there that your sinuses couldn't help but go screwy. My face, which was still raging from the cold outside, was no less red now that I was inside, and the effect of the extreme heat wasn't much different from that of the extreme cold.

The door slammed and rattled nervously in its frame. I turned around. Peter was right behind me, standing at the mouth of the room. He was still holding the plunger — he really seemed attached to it — and still hadn't said anything. My face felt even redder, just looking at how his wasn't. Boy, he was white, like the snow, but much paler and not

so pure. Peter had tapped into some primordial whiteness, like a pre-
historic fish in a cave, except wearing flannel and well over six feet tall.
I was scared of him, always had been. There were guys like him in my
high school, country guys with big scarred hands, brooding hulks who
didn't say much and didn't need to. They seemed older, more serious
than me, more manlike, and they also seemed to have properties and
qualities and things that I did not, even when they didn't have much,
which Peter obviously didn't. I could see rolled-up newspapers and towels shoved into the holes at the bottom of the trailer, where the elements
had rusted through the metal.

"That's much better," I said, rubbing my hands together to indicate
the improvement of my blood circulation. "Whew." Peter still didn't say
anything, and now that I was warmer, I was feeling even more afraid,
and so to calm my nerves and butter up my host, I said, "That's a good
fire. I mean it. Really wonderful heat."

Still no response. I suddenly remembered this one time in high
school, when I'd finished an apple and thrown it in the trash can from a
great distance, or tried to. Instead I'd hit this dairy farmer's son named
Kevin. I was thirteen and Kevin was thirteen, but it seemed as if we
were from different planets, his the bigger one populated by a warrior
race, and he charged in my direction when he realized who had thrown
the apple. Once he got to me, he stared the way Peter was staring now,
and I babbled how sorry I was and that it was an accident and what a
poor shot I was in general (you could ask the gym coach), and so on and
on out of nervousness and terror until Kevin punched me in the right
cheek and knocked me down. I assumed he punched me because I'd hit
him with the apple, but I found out later, from reliable sources, that he
punched me because I just wouldn't stop talking. I couldn't stop talking
with Peter, either, which just shows that history repeats itself whether
you know it or not.

"Le Clair," I said. "Is that French? I mean French Canadian? From
Quebec?"

Nothing. If it were possible to slip out of silence into deeper silence, then Peter did so. His eyes, which were pale blue and already set back, receded even further into his face. His forehead and chin jutted out at me like weapons.

"Because I went there on my honeymoon," I said, "with my wife, Anne Marie. We're having some troubles, but I hope we can work them out, but it's too complicated to go into right now. I lied to her, but she thinks I lied to her about something I didn't, but I can't tell her that, because the actual lie is worse than the lie she thinks I told. Although she might be thinking I'm lying about something else entirely now. See, complicated. To Quebec, though, that's where we went on our honeymoon, even though I didn't speak French. Still don't. I've kind of always regretted not learning another language, although I have all these other regrets, too, to keep it company. I bet you do, though. Speak French, that is. Although maybe not. Did you ever learn it in school? I hear it helps to live in the actual country. Did you ever live in the actual country? Although maybe your parents taught it to you."

Still nothing. I could hear the dog howling outside, and again I wished I were with the dog in the doghouse and not in the trailer with Peter, because at least the dog wasn't mute and had something to say.

"What's your dog's name?" I asked him. "How old is he? Or she? I've never had a dog. Or a cat. No pets at all. Is your dog neutered? Spayed?" And so on, until I began to get sick of myself and my babbling. Then I changed my mind and got sick of him, Peter, and it, his silence, and then I got sick of stoic men in general. Did they not have anything to say, these stoic men? Did they have plenty to say but not the right things, or not even the ability to say those wrong things the right way? Well, so what. Had that ever stopped me? Did people not know that talking was good for you, like medicine or juice? Had someone told Peter that you had to be silent and gloomy to be a man? Was that what reading about mopey, inarticulate Ethan Frome had taught him? (I'd already kicked the book out of my kicking range, but I kicked it again, in my mind, for good measure.) I was so sick of these silent men, it seemed as if I'd been around them my entire life: not enjoying the silence, and not wanting it, either. Their silence was like an ugly hat someone had told them they had to wear, and so they did, but bitterly. I almost missed Thomas Coleman, who could at least *talk* and wasn't shy about doing so, even if the stuff he said was hurtful and sinister and some of it out-and-out deceitful. And of course he was saying this stuff to my wife, and — now that I thought about it — maybe he was with her *right now.* Suddenly I was sick of Thomas, too, and maybe it wasn't just that I was sick of silent men but of all men, which was troubling, since I counted myself one of them.

"Listen," I said. "Like I told you earlier, I'm Sam Pulsifer. I need to know now. Are you Peter Le Clair? Are you the Peter Le Clair who wrote me years ago, asking me to burn down the Robert Frost Place?"

Peter didn't put down his plunger at this news, and he didn't smile or say anything. But he did shrug. It was, as I learned over the next several hours, Peter's favorite gesture, one probably used to communicate knowingness, confusion, sleepiness, hunger, loyalty, drunkenness, impatience, empathy, sexual longing. It was an economical gesture, and I admired it so much that I thought about doing it myself right back at him. But then I remembered that time in prison when I said, "I'm a grown-ass man," after playing basketball, and Terrell beat me; there were no prison guards to protect me this time. So I didn't shrug. But I wanted to, and I bet, if given a chance, the mimicry would have done our relationship a lot of good. Because it seems to me that the world would be a nicer, more empathetic place in which to live if we were only allowed to mimic each other without the one being mimicked taking offense and threatening violence.

"You shrugged," I said. "Does that mean yes?"

"Yes," he said, his voice rough but a little higher than I expected, like a rugged Tweety Bird. "I am Peter Le Clair."

Well, now we were having a regular conversation — we both sat down, as if settling into something — and I certainly didn't want to lose its thread. So I kept the questions simple so that we could both follow them.

"Do you know why I'm here?"

"Yes," Peter replied, and then, before I could respond, he said, "I want you to burn down that house. But I can't pay you anything." When he said this, his eyes dropped to his boots and then rose up to my eyes, as if his shame were having an internal struggle with his pride. I felt for Peter and wanted to tell him that the struggle wasn't just part of his personal condition; it was the human condition, and it was my condition, too. Maybe that's why my face was so red. I wanted to tell him all this, but I also didn't want to get off the topic, which is my weakness, the way not speaking was his.

"Can't pay me anything," I said, just to buy myself some time to think and catch up. "Did you get a phone call saying something about burning down the Robert Frost Place?" I was also thinking about the phone call I'd gotten back in Amherst. It wasn't Peter's voice, I knew that now, but maybe Peter had received a phone call, too.

Except he hadn't. "No phone call," he said. "No phone." Then he shrugged again. It was a definitive shrug, one that told me there wasn't anything else to say about the phone call. So I didn't say anything and instead silently took stock of what I now knew or thought I knew. Peter hadn't gotten a phone call; I had, but the caller hadn't asked anyone for money to burn down the Robert Frost Place, assuming that's what he planned on doing. The person who'd tried to burn down the Mark Twain House *had* asked for money but had done so in a letter, not over the phone, and most likely wasn't a man and so most likely had nothing to do with whomever I was supposed to meet at midnight at the Robert Frost Place. And none of these people seemed to have *anything*, necessarily, to do with whoever had tried to burn down the Edward Bellamy House. I felt panicked, taking account of all the things I didn't know, the same kind of panic a schoolchild feels when picking up a pencil to take a test for which he is unprepared. And as every schoolchild knows, panic is to the bladder what love or hate or exercise is to the heart.

"I'll be right back," I told Peter, and then wandered to the left, down the trailer's only visible hall. The bathroom was the first door to the left and was interesting. There were appliances and fixtures everywhere — pipes and tubes of joint compound and fractured tile and shower rods and curtains and a medicine cabinet with no door. And as on Noah's boat, there were two of each of the most necessary items: two sinks (one fixed into the wall and one on the floor) and two ashtrays and two towels and two towel racks and two toilets, a blue one and a yellow one. *Now* Peter's plunger made a little more sense. But in my hurry I couldn't stop to tell which toilet I was supposed to use, so I used the blue one in honor of the boy I'd once been and still was, essentially. When I was done, I left the bathroom in a hurry and without checking to see whether it was the right, working toilet. Because if it was, great, and if it wasn't, well, I didn't really want to know.

"Can't pay you," Peter repeated as soon as I returned to the living room. I empathized: his lack of money weighed heavily on him and he needed relief from it, his poverty being to his vessel what my pee had just been to mine.

"Don't worry about the money," I said. "What do you say we drive over to the Robert Frost Place and see what we're dealing with."

"The truck's busted," he said.

"Which one?"

"All of them," he said. "We'll take your van. Let's go."

With that, he started shoving clothes at me — a once-white thermal shirt, now dirty to the point of being yellow; a lined flannel shirt; a big, bulging, blue parka that might have looked good on the Michelin Man; a black Ski-Doo ski hat with an optimistic yellow tassel that smelled as though a month earlier the dog had put on the hat before taking a dip in kerosene. Peter had a point. If we were going outside, then I'd better dress for it. It was dark by now and probably even colder than it had been, and all I had on was what I always wore: khaki pants with too many pleats, which bunched up unattractively when I sat, a pair of running sneakers, and a gray fleece pullover, and they weren't warm enough, even, for tropical Massachusetts. So I put on the clothes Peter gave me, right over my own. It was like adding another layer of skin, and then another. Even Peter was putting on a few extra layers of flannel and then a big hooded parka over the extra layers, and at one point, after all the piling on of clothes was finished, we turned to each other as if to say, *Ta-da!* There we were, in our beards and flannel, like a couple of girls dressing side by side for our big night out. It was unlikely and sweet, the way only unlikely things can be.

"Ready?" he asked. I was and said so. Peter threw the plunger into the corner of the room and then leaned over the couch. There was a dog curled up there, among the blankets; I assumed it was the same dog that had been howling from its doghouse earlier. Peter had obviously let him inside while I was in the bathroom. You could barely see the dog — it was, like everything else in the trailer, somewhere between brown and deep red — but you could hear it sigh happily when Peter placed his hand on its head and left it there for a moment, and this sound filled me with sadness of the worst, self-pitying kind. How was it that this mottled pooch had these most precious things — the love and affectionate touch of another, a couch to lie on, a place (two places) to call home — and I did not? Was this what it had come to? Was I lower and less fortunate than a dog? Was there a sadder person in New England, in the *history* of New England? Would even sad-sack Ethan Frome look at me and feel lucky to at least have his piss-poor land, his failing farm, his drafty house, his shrewish wife, his impossible true love, his barely functional vocabulary? Would even Ethan Frome be glad he wasn't me? Yes, the self-pity was thick in the air; the room was full of it, the way I had been full of pee a few minutes earlier. Maybe that's what the other toilet had been for. It was an interesting idea — having a place in which to deposit your self-pity — and it made me feel better, for a second, for having thought it.

Then *whoosh*, we went out through the cold and the snow and into the van. I can't remember anything about it except that at first it wasn't any warmer inside the van than out. Oh, was it cold! I can't emphasize that enough. It was the kind of cold that makes you insane and single minded, thinking only about how to get warmer, warmer, warmer. The heater was so slow in its heating, and to keep myself from thinking about how cold I was, I concentrated on Peter's directions to turn this way and that, and on the snow in the headlights, swirling and bouncing like molecules, and outside the snow the deep, deep darkness. Remembering it now, I realize it was nice: the world felt small and homey, just me and Peter and the snow and the darkness and the truck and the heat — because here it finally came, really blasting at us, just in time for me to pull up in front of the Robert Frost Place. The house was your standard old white farmhouse — the sort where you wouldn't be able to keep the hornets out during the summer, or the heat in during the winter — and the only things truly notable about it were that it hadn't been burned down yet, it was ringed by parked cars, and it was lit up like Christmas. Every light in the house must have been on, and even Mr. Frost must have been able to see it from his new and more permanent home in the Great Beyond.

"What's going on here?" I asked.

Peter shrugged, which I took to mean, *I don't know.*

"Let's go see," I said. Peter shrugged again, which I took to mean, *No.*

"Why not?" I asked, and you already know what his answer was, or at least how he gave it, and so I won't bother to interpret it for you.

But no matter what, I was going in that house: already that week I had been locked out of my house and my mother's apartment, and I was not going to be kept out of this place, too. I got out of the van, walked up to and inside the house, and guess what? Peter followed me. This is yet another piece of necessary advice that'll go in my arsonist's guide: if you lead, they will follow, especially if it's painfully cold outside and your followers don't want to be left in the unheated van. If you lead, under exactly these kinds of circumstances, then they will follow.

17

Let me say now that between the *then* when this was happening and the *now* from which I'm writing, I've become something of a reader. Back then I hadn't heard of the author who was inside the Robert Frost Place, about to read from his most recent book, but I've heard of him now and have read all his novels, too. Each of his novels is populated by taciturn northern New Hampshire countrymen with violent tendencies, doing violent things to their countrywomen and children, then brooding over the violence within them and how the harsh northern New Hampshire landscape is part and parcel of that violence. Recently the author moved to Wyoming to get away from the city folk who are moving to New Hampshire, and he's now setting his books in Wyoming, where the men are also taciturn and violent, et cetera. And the books have won a few awards, and they've been made into major motion pictures — I should say that, too.

It was a good thing Peter and I arrived when we did, because we got two of the last available seats. I did a quick scan of the crowd for arsonists or potential arsonists, but I recognized no one, no one at all. There were a few women scattered around, but mostly the audience was composed of men. Some of the men were dressed like Peter and wore red plaid hunting jackets or bulky tan Carhartt jackets or lined flannel shirts, and all of those men were wearing jeans and work boots. Some of the men wore ski jackets and hiking boots and the sort of many-pocketed army green pants that made you want to get out of your seat and rappel. Some of the men wore wide-wale corduroy pants and duck boots and cable-knit sweaters and scarves. It was a regular United Nations of white American manhood. But all the men, no matter what they were wearing, were slouching in their chairs, with their legs so wide open that it seemed as though there must be something severely wrong with their testicles.

In front of all of us was a podium with a microphone sticking out of it. On the front of the podium — and all over the walls, too — were posters announcing the reading, and also announcing the reader's position as the current Robert Frost Place's Writer-in-Residence. There was a picture of the Writer-in-Residence on the poster, and from the picture I recognized him in person, sitting off to the right of the podium. He, too, was wearing a red plaid hunting jacket and had a big red beard and a pile of graying red curly hair. Sitting next to him was a thin, bald man wearing wire-rimmed glasses and a yellow corduroy shirt so new that it looked as though it had just come out of the box. The thin, bald man got out of his chair, walked to the podium, and introduced himself as the Director of the Robert Frost Place. He talked about the history of the Robert Frost Place Writers-in-Residence, and how each Writer-in-Residence was chosen for the way he and his work embodied the true spirit of Robert Frost and of New England itself. The Director then talked for a while about what, exactly, the true spirit of New England was. I can't say I listened to all, or any, of what he said, the way you don't really listen to those car commercials when they tell you how their vehicle embodies the true spirit of America.

Anyway, this went on for a while, and at some point he must actually have introduced the Writer-in-Residence, because the Director suddenly sat down, there was some applause, and the Writer-in-Residence took his place at the podium. He took a bottle of Jim Beam the size and shape of a hip flask out of his jacket pocket and took a pull from it, and without saying a word of thanks to us for coming, he began to read. The story was about a woodpile and the snow falling on the woodpile and the old man who owned the woodpile and who wasn't actually that old but who had been so beaten down by life that he looked old. The old man was sitting at his kitchen window drinking bourbon straight from the bottle and watching the snow wet the wood that he and his family needed for their heat and that needed to be chopped, pronto. His son was supposed to chop the wood, the son had promised, but he was off somewhere getting into trouble with a girl the old man didn't much care for because she was a slut (she was a slut, it seemed, not because she'd actually had sex with someone or someones, but because who else but a slut would date the old man's son?). The old man hated the girl and he hated the son and he hated the snow and he hated the un-chopped wood, which clearly was some sort of symbol of how the man's life hadn't worked out the way he'd planned, and the old man hated the bourbon, too, which he kept drinking anyway. I couldn't understand why the old man didn't just get off his ass and chop the wood himself, and I also couldn't understand why the author didn't use metaphors or similes in his story, but he didn't; the story was more or less an un-adorned grocery list of the things the old man hated. And speaking of grocery lists, the old man's wife entered the kitchen with *her* grocery list and told the old man that she was going to the store, and as an aside she looked at the dead woodstove and said, "Pa." The old man didn't answer her, maybe because he didn't like to be called "Pa," or maybe because he liked to be called "Pa" so much that he wanted his wife to call him that again, or maybe because men like him are only called "Pa" in books and he didn't realize he was in one. In any case, his wife said it again — "Pa" — and then: "It's cold in here. Why don't you go out and chop some wood?"

The old man didn't look at his wife when she said this; instead he looked at the ax resting in the corner, and he looked at it in such a re-signed, meaningful way that it was clear that he wouldn't chop wood with it but would instead use the ax to commit some horrible violent act against his wife or his son or both and that the violence was inevitable.

The story ended with him staring at the ax, and then the Writer-in-Residence left the podium and reclaimed his seat next to the Director.

There were several minutes of big, thunderous applause. It was like the time I spoke to Katherine's first-grade class for career day. I'd brought in the ziplock plastic bag I'd invented for show-and-tell, and I showed the kids how it zipped and locked, zipped and locked, and then told them how I'd made the bag that way and why. Afterward the kids gave me a sustained, raucous ovation, not because they were so impressed by the bag, but because they were competing with one another to see who could clap the loudest and the longest. The ovation in the Robert Frost Place was like that. Even I slapped my hands together, in the spirit of the thing and to be agreeable. The only person in the audience *not* clapping was Peter. At first I thought it was just that he clapped the way he talked. But then I noticed he was staring at the Writer-in-Residence, really staring at him, squint eyed and furious, as if the Writer-in-Residence were an especially hateful eye exam. Instead of clapping, Peter was grinding his right fist into his left palm in such a way that it made me feel very sorry for the palm.

"What's wrong?" I whispered.

"I hate him," he growled.

"Why?" I asked, but he didn't answer me, not even a shrug. That's how angry he was.

And after thinking about it a few moments — the applause continued, which was good because I think better with the help of white noise, the way some people sleep better with the help of a fan — I was pretty sure I knew why he hated the Writer-in-Residence. I had a clear picture of Peter sitting at home — the stove blazing away, his plunger and dog close by — and reading book after book after book. Maybe he'd read the Writer-in-Residence's books, too, and they — with the help of *Ethan Frome* — were telling him not what sort of person he *could* be but what sort of person he *was* and always would be: grim, beaten down, violent, inarticulate. Maybe this was what the Director meant by the true spirit of New England, *spirit* being not that thing that helps you rise above, but that which weighs you down. Maybe this was why Peter wanted me to burn down the Robert Frost Place: because they kept bringing in Writers-in-Residence like this Writer-in-Residence, kept bringing in men who told Peter who he was and who he wasn't, and not who he might yet be, and Peter was sick of it. This I knew for certain, as though I had Peter's letter in front of me and had read it many times and knew his reasons by heart, which of course I hadn't and didn't.

Because if I had, if I knew then what I know now (I recovered Peter's letter, a story I'll get to soon), I'd have known that Peter wanted me to burn down the Robert Frost Place because of the Director, who, of course, was sitting right next to the Writer-in-Residence. Six years earlier (Peter had written me the letter after I'd been released from prison), the Director had hired Peter to fix a leak in the roof. A week after Peter had fixed it and been paid for the fixing, the roof had started to leak again, and Peter refused to fix it again unless he was paid again. The Director not only didn't pay him again but also made it known that Peter was unreliable and shouldn't be hired, and now Peter couldn't get work. Even six years later, he apparently couldn't get work. And so he wanted me to burn down the Frost Place because he wanted revenge on the Director. The letter didn't say why Peter couldn't just burn the house down himself, but the humbled condition of his bathroom gave me a pretty good idea. In any case, his wanting me to burn down the Frost Place had nothing to do with the Writer-in-Residence, just as the Writer-in-Residence had nothing to do with Frost himself, even though he was there under Frost's name. I wonder if this is why writers die: so they don't have to sit around and have people misconstrue what sort of writer they are. I wonder if this is why *people* do it, too. Die, that is.

As for why Peter read so much and had so many books scattered around his house, his letter didn't say. Maybe because he couldn't get any work, he had so much time to kill, and reading helped him do that. Maybe he was bored. Maybe he *liked* to read. Maybe because the books were from the library and free, the way so few things are. Or maybe his reasons were private, if *private* means not that someone else wouldn't understand our reasons, but that we don't entirely understand them ourselves.

In any case, I thought I knew who Peter hated and why he hated him, and I felt for Peter and wanted to do something to help him, something besides what he wanted me to do. Meanwhile, the applause kept going on and on and the Writer-in-Residence sat there looking more and more severe and drinking more and more bourbon, and the Director was looking more and more pleased, and Peter's face was getting redder and redder, and you could tell his resentment was getting hotter and hotter, and let's just say I felt I had to do something. If that's not good enough, let's just say that if the spirit of New England was in the Writer-in-Residence, then the spirit of my mother — book reader and storyteller — was in me.

"I have a question," I said, standing up as I said it. I don't know if anyone heard me over the applause, but sooner or later a group of people sitting will take notice of one man standing. When this group noticed me a few minutes later, they stopped clapping. "I have a question," I repeated.

"No questions, no questions," the Director said, standing up. When he did that, Peter growled audibly, which I appreciated, and kept growling until the Director sat down. The Writer-in-Residence didn't seem to care one way or the other. He looked weary and dulled out, as though he knew exactly who I was, as though he'd played his Mercutio to my Tybalt too many times before. Even his drinking from the Jim Beam seemed to come at planned, regular intervals, as though part of the stage directions.

"Why does your character have to be such a" — and here I paused for just the right words, and not able to find them, I chose from the many inadequate words at my disposal — "mopey jerk?"

The Writer-in-Residence took another pull off his bottle of Jim Beam and said that he didn't feel it was his business to say why his characters were the way they were.

"Whose business is it?"

"It's nobody's business, and I mean nobody's," the author said.

This must have been a line from one of his books, because everyone around him cheered and hooted. This is the most terrifying thing about speaking in front of a crowd: not that you've lost them, but that you never had them in the first place and never will. My face felt so hot, so red, and I bet that if I'd touched my cheek to the floor, the whole house would have gone up in smoke, and Peter would have gotten what he wanted that way. But I didn't do that: I stood there and waited for the crowd's noise to finally subside, and then said, "But it *is* your business. You made him that way."

"I didn't make him that way," the Writer-in-Residence said. "That's the way he is."

"The way he is," I repeated. I borrowed this tactic from my mother. When I was a child and I would say something stupid, she would repeat it back to me so I could hear for myself how stupid it was.

"The way he is," the Writer-in-Residence repeated back to me. Maybe that was his tactic, too.

"But suppose that's *not* the way he is," I said, and before the Writer-in-Residence or his crowd could say anything else, I continued: "Suppose he's not an old man. Suppose he's a young man." The Writer-in-Residence nodded, as though that seemed a viable alternative, which only encouraged me. "Suppose he wasn't angry at all. Suppose he had a job. Suppose he was a farmer . . . " And here I paused. I remembered the bond analysts' memoir-brainstorming sessions; I remembered that they always urged one another, when trying to hurdle an especially big writer's block, to "write what you know." And in a sense, the bond analysts *did* write what they knew — they knew my father's postcards, knew where he had been and what he had done — and so it seemed like useful advice. But I didn't know anything about being a farmer, so I tried something else. "Or suppose he was a lumberjack." But again, same problem: I knew nothing about being a lumberjack, not even what sort of saw to use in killing which sort of tree. The only job I knew anything about was being a packaging scientist. But I remembered my father's initial reaction to my job — "No greatness in tennis ball cans" — and I suspected the Writer-in-Residence's reaction would be the same or worse. And so out of panic and with nothing else to say, I said, "Or suppose this young man was a bumbler and he accidentally . . . , " and then I basically told the story I've been telling you. It was a much shorter version, but it included most of the major events and characters: my mother's stories and the burning houses and the dead Colemans and their vengeful son and my beautiful wife and children and my drunk parents and their mysterious living situation and the letters and the bond analysts. It's true the story didn't have a proper ending — I only told the story up to the Mark Twain House fire and then said, "To be continued" — but I tried to keep things close to the facts. In fact, the only thing I made up about the young man was that he played a mean twelve-string guitar, because I'd always wanted to play guitar and because twelve strings seemed better than six, since there were more of them.

"What do you think?" I asked after I was done. In truth I was very pleased with myself and with my story and all that had happened in it. Because you can't help being impressed with your own story. Because if you're not impressed with your own story, then who will be? "What would you say about *that* guy?" I asked.

"I'd say he doesn't sound like a real person," the Writer-in-Residence said.

"He doesn't?" I asked. Oh, that hurt! Just the day before, Lees Ardor had told me she wanted to be a real person, and now I knew exactly what she meant. I would have given anything, right then, not to have told my story. I would have given anything to go back in time, before I'd told my story, and get Lees Ardor and bring her here so we could have sat there together and listened to the Writer-in-Residence tell us what a real person was.

"He doesn't sound like a real person at all," the Writer-in-Residence said. "He sounds like a cheap trick. No cheap tricks."

"No cheap tricks," I repeated. I fell back into my chair, hard, and I bet the folding chair would have folded with the impact except it had heard what had happened and felt pity.

"No tricks at all," the Writer-in-Residence said, and then he took another swig of his bourbon.

At that moment the Director stood up, walked toward the podium, and started waving his hands and arms over his head, as though he were shipwrecked and trying to get the attention of a plane flying overhead. "I believe that's all the time we have," he said, and then he announced that the Writer-in-Residence would be happy to sign books. This announcement caused a mad rush toward the front of the room. I sat in my seat, with my head hanging between my knees, in the crash position. Except I had already crashed and the position was taken too late. Peter was sitting next to me — I could hear the angry in-and-out of his breathing — but other than him, I felt completely alone. Even my mother's spirit had left me, as though it had, like the Connecticut Yankee, time-warped out of my body and this place and back into its own.

I don't know how long we sat there like that: it could have been a minute, it could have been an hour. Finally Peter grabbed the back of my (his) jacket and pulled me backward. I refused to look at him, so he had to grab my chin and turn my head and attention in his direction. Peter was angry, that was clear. I assumed he was angry at me: not only had I made a fool of myself, but by telling my story I'd probably drawn some unwanted attention to myself, and to him and his letter, and to what he wanted me to do. I hung my head again, in shame; and again he put his hand to my chin and raised it up, but gently, surprisingly gently.

"You understand now why I hate that guy?"

"I do," I said. Because I thought I did.

"OK?" Peter asked, then shrugged. I knew he was asking me if I'd burn the house down for him, for free; I knew that. I had no intention of doing what he wanted, but — and this is just one of the many things of which I'm ashamed — I was so grateful that he wasn't angry that I decided to play along, *playing along* being the thing we do when it's too difficult to do its opposite and just tell the truth.

"OK," I said.

"Good," he said. "Let's go."

"Where to?"

"The bar," Peter said.

"Good idea," I said. We got up and left the house, but before I did, I glanced back at the Writer-in-Residence. He was still sitting in his chair, still drinking his Beam. There was still a long line of people holding books for him to sign. The Director was still hovering over him for God knows what reason. But the Writer-in-Residence wasn't looking at the Director or his audience or their copies of his books. No, he was looking at us, longingly, as we walked out the door, and who knows: maybe he was thinking that we were real people after all.

18

The bar was a gray cinder block rancher with a black plywood entrance on the front and not to the side as on Peter's trailer. But they were from the same lowborn family of buildings. There were neon beer lights in the windows, and around the windows were flickering Christmas lights, but the lights were fighting a losing battle; half of them were out and dead. They'd probably been left up all year. There was no sign naming the place as this bar or that tavern, as if no name were sufficiently bad. The parking lot was full, the trucks — they were almost all trucks — parked at angry, confrontational angles, as if preparing themselves for a demolition derby or having just finished one. It was the sort of bar that gave one pause, especially if the *one* was someone like me, who'd never been in a bar like this before. True, I'd been to plenty of "bar and grille's": there were dozens of them near our house in Camelot. But they were the sort of places that provided crayons for the kids, and special place mats for them to deface, and stern warnings on the menu not to let the kids draw on anything but the place mats, and they were also the kind of places that issued even sterner warnings — on the place mats, on the walls, on the waitresses' and waiters' uniforms, *everywhere* — forbidding you to smoke or else, and in these ways the "bar and grille" seemed exactly like the world outside the "bar and grille" except with more rules and fewer ways to break them.

This place was different, and after entering it I understood immediately why bars exist and why people like to drink in them: if a "bar and grille" reminded you of all the things you shouldn't do, then a real bar gave you the idea that there was nothing you couldn't do, and no consequences to face if you did do it. My first impression of the place was wrong; it wasn't depressing at all. For one thing, it was better-looking inside than out. The bar floor was pine, with a bowling-alley slickness to it. Overhead there was a low drop ceiling with flaking acoustical tiles that I could touch and did, which gave me a nice sense of accomplishment. For another, there was Peter, standing next to the men's room, selling drugs—dime bags, he called them, ten-dollar plastic bags of marijuana—to guys who looked a lot like him but happier, more talkative. For that matter, Peter in the bar seemed a happier and more talkative version of Peter, too, and that's why I say the bar wasn't depressing. Being in it seemed to free Peter. Or maybe it was the pot, much of which he seemed to deal to himself. Or maybe it was that I'd agreed to do what I in fact had no intention of doing. Right when we first got to the bar, Peter pointed at me, said, "That's him," and made introductions all around. There was Barry, Mick, Shoe, and Lyle. Of course, I didn't get their names straight at the time, but they didn't seem to mind and made me feel right at home. At one point, Peter even put his arm around me and said, "We *need* you, bud," which nearly made me cry and made me feel as though I needed them as much as they needed me.

But then again, it might have been the booze making me feel that way. Peter bought me shot after shot of bourbon, and soon I started calling *myself* by the wrong name, and this got all of them laughing good and hard, which made me glad, so glad that I drank some more. I must have done at least a good baker's dozen of shots. After a point, I have no memory of any real conversation or of time passing, although it must have, because I found myself sitting on a stool at the horseshoe bar, the guys were nowhere to be seen, and there was a band playing.

There was no stage in the bar, but in one corner there was a band playing anyway, four guys — two guitarists, a bassist, a drummer — with long, stringy hair peeking out from under their ski hats, nodding their heads violently in time to a song that seemed to have no time. The bass was so loud it wasn't just a sound but also a feeling coming up through the floor, up into me, through my groin, my heart, my throat. The sound pulled me toward the band, although first I got another shot of bourbon from the bartender.

I took my drink and went and stood in front of the band. I didn't recognize the song they were playing, but when it ended, someone yelled out, "Creedence!" This seemed to encourage the guys in the band, because they launched into another song, a favorite apparently, and the dance floor got crowded — women dancing with men, women with women, men without partners stomping their feet and singing into their beer bottles — and before I knew it, I was dancing, too.

Yes, I was dancing, and immediately I remembered why I hadn't danced in a long time. Because when I dance, I dream, or at least I remember, which for me is exactly the same as dreaming. So the band launched into Creedence, if that's what it was, and I started stomping my feet and swinging my arms a little, and just like that, I started dreaming about the last time I'd danced, at my wedding, with Anne Marie. It was our wedding song, and I don't remember what it was — another thing of which I'm ashamed — but I had the impression it had been many other people's wedding song as well. I noticed many of the older married guests go soft in the eyes and clasp hands. It felt good to be in the company of so many similarly and successfully betrothed, and for that matter it felt good to have my beautiful girl in my arms, my beautiful, tall girl, who'd worn low-heeled shoes so that she wouldn't be too much taller than I was, my beautiful, tall, thoughtful girl, who smelled like the cake we'd just cut. All was well except that we were dancing, and I started remembering and dreaming *that* time, too, remembering and dreaming about my parents, who weren't at the wedding, of course, because I hadn't told them about it.

Specifically I was remembering the time when I spied on my mother and father dancing. This was a year after my father had returned from his exile, and it was certainly the first time I'd seen them dance. It might have been the first time I'd seen them even *touch* since he'd returned. They were dancing in the front entryway. I was watching from the staircase (I was supposed to have been in bed, but I'd heard the music — it was Benny Goodman, plus his big band, I remember that — and was spying). It was some highly conflicted dancing, at least on my mother's part. One moment, her eyes were closed, her head on my father's shoulder as if asleep and at peace; the next, her eyes were sprung open and angry, her palms against my father's chest and pushing him away, and the only thing holding her to my father was my father. He wouldn't let go, and she kept saying, "I don't know, I just don't know," and he kept saying, "I'm sorry, I'm sorry, oh God, I'm so sorry." Then she'd relax for a while, only to tense up again eventually, and so on. I felt so sad for these confused parents of mine and had the distinct impression that love and marriage and dancing were like being at war with your better judgment. Watching my parents dance made loneliness look happy and relaxing by comparison, and so I went up to my room and went to bed. When I was dancing with Anne Marie at our wedding, I was remembering all this, and at the moment when I remembered going to bed and being alone, happily so, I let go of Anne Marie and took a step to the side as if making a break for it. The guests gasped, Anne Marie grabbed me, I came to my senses, saw my beautiful girl and bride, and finished the dance, and we never spoke about it afterward. She'd grabbed me hard, too. Later on I noticed two large pincher bruises on my upper biceps, as if a lobster and not the human Anne Marie had prevented me from leaving the dance floor and ruining our marriage right off the bat and not waiting eight years to do it.

And I was remembering and dreaming all this in the bar, too. I was so deep in my dream that the song ended with a crash of drums and a shudder of bass and a screech of guitar, and still I danced in the middle of the crowd. People were staring at me. I didn't blame them one bit and would have stared, too. I drank down my shot of bourbon, as though that would make them stop staring. It didn't. I looked around for help, to see if there was someone around who could come to my rescue.

There was: a woman to my right, holding a lit joint. I hadn't noticed her before that moment, and I've never seen her since. She was exactly my height. Her eyes were dark brown and they were squinting at me in bemusement, or maybe from the joint's smoke. She wasn't wearing earrings and for that matter had no holes in her lobes in which to put them. Her hair was straight and black and about ready to come out of her ponytail, although you could tell she would be as beautiful with her hair down as up, and that hair didn't matter much to her and was just something that happened to be on top of her head. Other than these details, I know nothing about her, not even her name, although I think about her all the time, the way you do about people and things that change your life forever — although I doubt she thinks about me, which is the way life works, which is why I'm sure Noah couldn't ever stop thinking about his Flood, but once the water receded, I'm sure it didn't once think about him.

"You look like you could use this," she said, and then put the joint up to my mouth. I took a drag: it was my first drag ever, tasted like dirt, and made me cough but otherwise had no effect on me that the bourbon hadn't already had. Then the band started another song, one I recognized from high school: it was Skynyrd, the band doing its best to replicate the famous three-guitar attack with only two guitars. I didn't dance this time, though, so I didn't dream or remember — not about my parents or Anne Marie or the kids, everyone whom I loved and for whom I was put on this planet. How does this happen? Why don't we always have someone on hand to say, *Don't! Cut it out! Run out into the snow and throw yourself into a drift until your capacity to hurt and be bad is frozen out of you!* Why don't we have *that* kind of voice, a voice that tells us not, *What else? What else?* but *Stop! Desist! You are about to do harm!* But even if we had this voice, would we listen to it? What is it that makes us deaf to all the warnings? Is it need? Is it need that makes us so deaf, that fills us up to our ears so that we can't listen to our better impulses? Is it that we are so full of need, or so full of ourselves?

I wasn't thinking of any of this at the time. I wasn't even thinking about Anne Marie and Thomas, wasn't even lying to myself about being a victim with rights rather than a victimizer with no rights at all. All I was thinking was that there was a beautiful woman standing next to me, smiling at me even, her smile making the bad band sound not so awfully bad, and she had two cheeks and I wanted to kiss the one nearest to me. I leaned over and kissed her cheek, and then she turned her lips toward mine, and so I kissed them, too, with feeling, and when the kissing didn't seem to be enough anymore, we groped, enthusiastically and without regard to anyone else in the bar, as though our hands were made invisible on contact. All of this went on for a long time. I know this because eventually my lips began to get tired and there was considerable hooting and clapping that didn't seem intended for the band. I glanced up to see who was making all this noise and saw my father-in-law, Mr. Mirabelli, standing directly behind the woman. And a few feet behind him, I saw my mother. Neither of them was hooting or clapping. Both of them were looking directly at me in huge disappointment, as though the bar were a museum and I were a famous painting that they'd paid too much to see.

"Mom!" I yelled, breaking the lip-lock. "Mr. Mirabelli!" This surprised the woman almost as much as my mother and father-in-law had surprised me.

"What did you just call me?" the woman asked. She backed up a little and also turned my body, so that my back was to my mother and father-in-law, although the woman still held on to my biceps. She had quite a grip, too, a grip that reminded me of Anne Marie's at our wedding those many years ago, which makes me wonder if all women have this grip, this grip being the thing that keeps a woman steady while she's deciding whether to hold on to or let go of the man she's hitched to.

"Wait," I said. I tried to break her grip and simultaneously twirl us around so that I could face my mother and father-in-law again, and the resulting motion no doubt came off as something violent, because the woman said, "What the *hell* do you think you're doing?" She asked this question loudly, several times — the band had finished the song and were watching us, as we'd become the real attraction — and then she disappeared and several guys took her place, guys who I think were either related to the woman or wanted to be, all of them wanting to know if I had a *problem*. Peter and his friends had noticed what was going on, and they came over and asked these guys if *they* had a problem. All this took a while to straighten out, since each of us had so many problems, and by the time it was, my mother and Mr. Mirabelli were nowhere to be seen. I ran out into the parking lot; they weren't there, either, and there was no sign of her Lumina or his Continental. But as I walked through the parking lot, I passed by my van, and there, on the windshield underneath one of the wipers, was a bar napkin. On it were the words "I think I know you." I took this to be my mother's note (the handwriting was familiar in its loops and slants), although what the words meant exactly, I didn't know. There was so much I didn't know. How had my mother and father-in-law known where I was? Who had told them I was driving to New Hampshire? Was it my father? Had one or both of them been involved with the phone call? Did they know each other? *How* did they know each other? Had they driven there separately, or together? Did my mother know I'd told my wife, my in-laws, too, that she and my father were dead? Did Mr. Mirabelli know now that they weren't? Were she and Mr. Mirabelli talking right now about the woman I'd kissed and the wife I'd betrayed? Why would they follow me to the bar and then leave before saying anything to me? And what was that note supposed to mean? Why did my mother *think* she knew me? I was her son, was I not? Why would she need to *think* about *that*?

These were all questions I couldn't answer or at least didn't want to, and as a detective you learn, sooner or later, to stop asking yourself these sorts of questions and start asking questions that you actually *can* answer. So I asked myself: *What time is it?* Then I looked at my watch: it was twenty minutes after midnight, and that meant I was already late.

19

I was late but not entirely stupid. I didn't drive all the way to the Robert Frost Place, didn't park in the parking lot as I'd done earlier. Like a real detective might do, I pulled off the road about a quarter of a mile from the house, into a slot in the snowbank that the snowplows must have used as a turnaround, parked my van there, and sneaked up to the house. This cost me some more time, of course, and by the time I got there, the bond analysts had already set fire to the Robert Frost Place and were standing in the parking lot watching the house burn. Their Saab was next to them with its engine on. The parking lot was ringed by white pines, and I hid behind one of them, close enough to hear what the bond analysts were saying.

"He's not going to show up, is he?" one of the Ryans said, referring, I was pretty sure, to me. It was the first time I'd heard him speak. "What good is this if he doesn't show up?"

"He's missing one hell of a fire," Morgan said, and then I knew why they'd called me: to show me that they could set fire to a writer's home in New England without my help. They wanted me to be a witness. The bond analysts had always been like this: during their memoir-writing sessions in prison, they were always so eager to show one another how beautifully they'd written about the bad things they'd done. "One hell of a fire," Morgan repeated.

"Who cares how good the fire is if he's not here to see it?" the other

Ryan said. Tigue and G-off were leaning against the Saab, staring silently at the fire, as though it had taken their voices and given those voices to the Ryans.

"Shut up," Morgan said. "Trust me. He'll be sorry." He held up an envelope and then placed it in the middle of the parking lot, which had been plowed and was mostly clear of snow. With that, they piled into their Saab and drove away from the fire. As they pulled out of the parking lot, the Robert Frost Place's second story collapsed onto the first. I wondered momentarily if the Writer-in-Residence was still inside the house, drinking bourbon, but there were no cars in the parking lot, and I heard no screams. I found out later on that the Writer-in-Residence was not in residence at all but was staying at a nearby bed-and-breakfast. The Writer-in-Residence had gotten lucky, the way Thomas Coleman's poor parents had not.

I got a little lucky myself that night, or thought I did. I walked over to where Morgan had placed the envelope in the snow. Sure enough, it was Peter's letter to me, written those six years earlier, asking me to do what the bond analysts themselves had just done. I read the letter right there, in the light of the fire, learned exactly why Peter had wanted me to do what the bond analysts had done themselves. Morgan had no doubt left the letter there to be found by the police or fire department and thereby to incriminate me, whereas he could have saved himself the trouble and just trusted that I would eventually incriminate myself. I put the letter in my pocket.

That accomplished, I stood there for a while, watching the fire. It was beautiful — huge and crackling, and with more sparks and explosions than the Fourth of July, which is further proof that fire is the most impressive of the four elements — much more beautiful than the house itself had been. Although the house and the fire had a lot in common: a fire was a thing you created and admired, the way the person who'd built the house must have admired it, too. But no matter how beautiful the fire was, it wasn't particularly helpful and that saddened me: I knew now that the bond analysts had called me (or at least one of them had), and I also knew that they had burned the Robert Frost Place, and so those questions were answered. But those answers didn't bring me any closer to knowing who had tried to burn down the Edward Bellamy House or the Mark Twain House. What good was answering one question when you couldn't answer the others?

I heard the crunch of tires on snow, and so I turned away from the fire and crept back to my van. Before I got too close to it, I could hear an engine running, could see headlights boring through the night and bouncing off the snow, and so I slipped behind another white pine, white pines being as plentiful in New Hampshire as Volvos were in Amherst. It was another Lumina, and at first I thought it was my mother, but as it passed by, I could see Detective Wilson, hunched over the steering wheel, hauling ass in the direction of the burning Robert Frost Place, no doubt in search of his own answers to his own questions. When he was out of sight, I ran to my van and then headed back to Amherst. Because sometimes a detective shouldn't try to answer the tough questions, being not so tough himself. Sometimes it's better to let someone else answer them for you.

20

I remember the day my father left us. It was a Saturday. I remember this because I didn't have to go to school that day and so was witness to the aftermath. My mother and I watched, side by side, from our living room's bay window as my father backed out of the driveway in his Chevy Monte Carlo. It was October, late, and the trees were missing their leaves, their bony branches waving good-bye to my father and his car. The trees knew he was leaving, too, and when he did, it was as though he pulled my mother's face with him. The face of the pretty, modest woman I'd known as "Mother" stretched out as she watched my father pull away from the curb, and when he was out of sight, it snapped back. Now the face was harder, the blue eyes sharper, the mouth tighter, with a little smirk at the corners. This new mother of mine was less pretty but more beautiful than my old mother, which is to say, I guess, that prettiness is something to like and beauty is something to be scared of, and I was scared of it, and her. My mother walked around the house, picking up magazines, records, coasters, couch cushions, and framed family pictures, staring at them as if not believing they were actually hers, and then tossing them aside. That scared me, too.

"You're hungry," she finally said, turning suddenly toward me, as if just then remembering that though my father was gone, I was not. She was right: it was lunchtime, and I was hungry. "I'll cook something," she said, then retreated to the kitchen. I remained in the living room, picking up the things she'd scattered and in general staying out of her way, until I smelled something burning in the kitchen and went to see what it was.

The smell came from open-faced broiled cheese and tomato sandwiches, my favorite thing to eat for lunch. My mother had burned them to something resembling bread-shaped coal. She had rescued the sandwiches from the broiler, but too late, and was waving a towel over the charred mess and laughing, too loud and hysterically, and that also was scary. She was singing over and over, "She loved to cook, but not like this," as if it were a lyric to a song, a popular one I should have known but didn't. I said to my mother, "I don't know that song." Then, for some reason, thinking I'd let her down by not knowing the song, I said, "I'm sorry," and started crying.

This calmed my mother down, other people's hysteria being a well-known cure for your own. She stopped singing, made me another broiled cheese and tomato sandwich, and paid attention and didn't burn it this time. While I ate, my mother told me the first of her stories about the Emily Dickinson House, which, as everyone knows, I accidentally burned, just like my mother accidentally burned that sandwich.

Speaking of that sandwich, by the time I finally got back to Amherst from New Hampshire, it was nine in the morning, and I hadn't eaten anything in almost twenty-four hours. I was so hungry I would even have eaten my mother's by now thirty-year-old burned broiled cheese and tomato sandwich. So I stopped off at my parents' house to have a little breakfast before heading on to my mother's apartment in Belchertown. My father's car was parked in the driveway, and I figured while I was getting something to eat I'd ask him a few questions. The bond analysts had obviously stolen the Robert Frost Place letter from my father, and probably the four letters he couldn't remember, too. But how had they known where to find the letters, or even that they existed? Did my father know the bond analysts? And then there was my mother. How had my mother known that I was going to the Robert Frost Place? Had my father told her? Why had he done that? Had he told my father-in-law, too? And why had they followed me?

I opened the door and could immediately hear the ping and splash of the shower, meaning, of course, that my father was taking one. I went to the kitchen, intent on eating whatever I found in there, and fast. There were Knickerbocker beer cans scattered around, as usual; on the kitchen table, there was what appeared to be a shopping list that read, "Milk, cereal, beer, wine, flowers, cheese, bread," and so on. There was nothing unusual about that, necessarily, and in my hunger I nearly forgot about it until I considered the handwriting itself: it was absolutely unfamiliar, absolutely nothing like the other notes, nothing like the notes that said, "Drink me," or the note that said, "I think I know you," and, it now occurred to me, also nothing like my father's postcards. I took the note from the night before — the note my mother had left on my windshield up in New Hampshire — out of my pocket. The shopping list and the note were clearly written by two different people: one who dotted the i's, the other who didn't; one whose writing was cramped, one whose writing was expansive. These were two different writers. The writer who had written the notes had not written the grocery list. I knew my mother had written the note on my windshield, which meant my father had written the grocery list. But the postcards? Who had written those?

I dropped the grocery list, ran upstairs to my bedroom, pulled a chair over to the closet. I stood up on the chair, and for the second time in two days I took the envelope down from the top shelf, took the postcards out of the envelope, and read them. I read them for the handwriting and not the content and then compared the handwriting on the postcards to the handwriting on my mother's note. They had been written by the same person. Then I compared them to the grocery list. And then I looked at the postcards themselves. From Florida there were two large, barely bikinied breasts with the familiar coconut joke underneath; from Wyoming there was a bucking bronc, its back legs kicked upward toward the postcard's northern border — but the postmarks on the postcards read not Boca Raton and Cheyenne, but rather Amherst, Massachusetts. This, of course, made perfect sense: my father hadn't sent them at all (which is why he hadn't seen himself in Morgan Taylor's memoir). But my mother had, and my mother had sent them from Amherst, because that's where she lived, with me. But why had she done that? Why had she pretended to be my father sending me postcards from places he'd never actually visited or lived in? And if my father hadn't been doing all these things in far-off places, then where had he been? On that October day when he left us, and my mother sang her mysterious lyric and burned my sandwich and made me cry, where had my father gone? And what had he pretended to be once he got there?

"Dad!" I yelled out, charging down the stairs and armed with the postcards. "Dad!" Just after I yelled, I heard the shower kick off and so I positioned myself outside the downstairs bathroom door, my head filled with questions and waiting for my father to give me the answers.

"Sam?" I heard the voice coming from behind me, from the kitchen and not the bathroom. I knew it was my father's voice without having to turn around, the same way I knew the notes and postcards were written by one person, the grocery list by another. If I were a real detective, I might have had a voice and handwriting expert to tell me these things for sure. But this is another thing I'll put in my arsonist's guide: sometimes you have to be your own expert, and then after you acquire this expertise, you sometimes wish you hadn't.

"Sam, look at me," my father said. This wasn't the stroked-out father, not the drunk one, either, but rather the insistent, scared father, the father wanting to spare his son from seeing that which no son should see. "Sam, turn around right now."

I didn't turn around. I kept my eyes fixed on the bathroom door, which opened slowly, creaking the way doors in movies and old houses do, and my father's voice creaked a little bit too as he yelled, "Deirdre, don't open the door!"

But it was too late. Deirdre already had. She'd opened the door and stood there in front of me, a towel wrapped around her important parts, a blond woman vaguely my father's age, and for that matter my mother's age, too, and for that matter wrapped in a towel my mother had probably bought, long ago, back in the age when my mother bought nice things for the house and actually lived in it, too.

"Hello, Sam," Deirdre said, then extended her right hand, holding the towel in place the way women do, through some complicated arrangement between inner arm and armpit and rib cage and breast. And not knowing what else to do, I took it. The hand, that is.

"HOW LONG?" I ASKED my father. We were sitting in the dining room, at the table, drinking beer. Deirdre had disappeared into my father's room. I could hear a hair dryer in there, the steady hum and blast of its hot white noise.

"How long what?" my father repeated. His face was a mask of nonchalance, although I could feel his legs bouncing jackhammer-like underneath the table.

"How long have you been with Deirdre?"

"Off and on," he said, "maybe thirty years."

"Thirty years," I repeated, doing the math. It wasn't difficult to do. Thirty years. I was thirty-eight years old. That meant my father had been with this Deirdre since I was eight, which was, not coincidentally, the year my father left us for . . .

"Dad," I said, "when you left us, where did you go?"

"I went to Deirdre's." I looked at him for a while, and my face must have continued to ask him, not *what* or *why* or *when*, but *where*, because he then said, "Northampton," which is a town not far from Amherst. Maybe twenty minutes away. My father had lived twenty minutes away for three years.

"For three years?"

"Yes," he said. "Where did you think I went?"

Instead of answering him, I handed him the postcards. What a relief it was to do that: what a pleasure it is to use someone else's solid, reliable written words instead of your own less-than-reliable ones.

"I didn't write these," he said when he was through looking at the postcards. He put them back in the manila envelope and slid them half-way across the table, so that they rested between him and me like a fence between neighbors. My father still wore the mask of nonchalance, but now I thought I could see its little seams and stitches and all the things that were supposed to hold it together.

"No kidding," I told him.

"That's your mother's handwriting," he said.

"No kidding."

"Why did she do that?" he asked, presumably rhetorically, except then he looked at me for the answer, which unfortunately I was able to give him.

"Because she didn't want me to hate you," I said. "Because she wanted me to think you were out *finding yourself* instead of living in Northampton with Deirdre."

"She's a good woman," my father said.

"I know she is."

"How do you know that?" my father asked.

"Because she's my mother," I told him, knowing now that the "good woman" to whom he was referring was Deirdre and not my mother at all. I took a long slug of my beer, then took a silent inventory of all the things I wanted to say.

"Oh," my father said, and then the nonchalance cracked and fell off completely, and shame and regret took its place. His head dipped and seemed to be pulled toward the table, as if the table were one of the poles and my father's head something newly magnetized. "Your mother is a good woman, too," he said.

"You know" — my teeth were gritted, but the words made their way through and around them anyway, as the words you shouldn't say always do — "it worked for a long, long time."

"What worked?"

"Mom sent me the postcards because she didn't want me to hate you. And it worked: I didn't hate you. I never hated you until right now."

My words had their intended effect: my father's eyes got watery and then the rest of him seemed to get watery, too, his whole body sagging and turning to liquid except for his right hand, which kept its firm hold on the beer can. Then there was me, his son, across the table from him: the minute I said this mean, hateful thing, I, too, turned to liquid except for *my* right hand, with its firm hold on the beer can. Imagine if my mother had walked into the house right then and seen her two Pulsifer men, only thirty years separating their mirror images. Imagine what she would have thought if she'd seen us right then, just as the night before she'd seen me dancing with and kissing and groping the woman who was not my wife, and suddenly I understood exactly why my mother had thought she'd known me — I'd cheated on my wife just as my father had cheated on his — and I also understood that we hate our fathers only as practice for hating ourselves. If my mother had been there in the kitchen, I would have apologized to her, and then I might have apologized to my father, too, for being like him.

"Dad," I said, "did you tell Mom I was going to New Hampshire?"

"I did," he said. He was looking down at the table, refusing to meet my eyes. His voice was like a child's, watery and high. "I told her yesterday morning when she came by the house. She asked where you were and I told her. And then she went after you."

"Why?"

"Because she was worried about you. Because she didn't want you to do anything stupid."

"Too late," I said.

"It usually is," my father admitted.

"Did you tell anyone else?" I asked.

"I did," he said. He raised his head slowly, looking stricken but also hopeful, as though by giving me one thing I wanted, he might be able to give me more than just that.

"Let me guess," I said. "He was tall, thin, blond."

My father nodded. "He's one of my regulars. For maybe fifteen years now, week in, week out, except for this last week. He came by yesterday, right after your mother left. She almost hit him pulling out of the driveway. He asked me where she was going in such a big hurry . . ."

"And you told him."

"I did," he said. "That's the guy you were asking me about?"

"Thomas Coleman," I said. "You didn't know his name?"

"He probably told me once, but I forgot it," my father said, shaking his head. "I never thought it was important."

I could picture Thomas telling my father, *I'm Thomas Coleman,* and then waiting for my father to recognize the name and say, *I'm so sorry for what my son did. I'm so sorry about your parents, so sorry for everything.* Finally, though, Thomas realized that he wasn't going to get satisfaction from my father, so he tried to get it from me. I wondered if things would have been different if my father had recognized Thomas's name and apologized, if one apology really could have made all that much difference.

"How about the bond analysts?" I asked. "Do you know them, too?"

"The who?" my father asked, and I described all five of them. When I was done, my father nodded, and said, "That sounds like the writer and his assistants."

"The writer and his assistants," I repeated.

"Five guys came around a couple of days ago, but only one of them talked. He said he was writing a book about you; he asked if I could tell him anything about you that he might not already know."

"So you showed them the letters," I said, already knowing he had. "I can't believe you showed them the letters."

"He said he was going to portray you sympathetically," my father told me. "He said he was on your side."

"Didn't you think it was suspicious that there were five of them and not just one?" I asked.

"It takes a lot of people to publish a book," he said. "Trust me, I know."

"Dad," I said, "do you still work at the press?"

"No," he confessed. "I'm retired." This could have been the same kind of retirement as my mother's, but I didn't care enough to ask, and I didn't have to ask where he went during the day, either, every day, even on a Saturday. My father had been at Deirdre's for three years, and I guessed he still went there.

"Does Mom know about Deirdre?"

"She does and she doesn't," my father said. "It's hard to explain."

"Try," I told him.

"Bradley, we need to go." This was Deirdre, right behind me. She might have been there the entire time, listening to us. I didn't turn to face her, though. I didn't look at my father, either. I kept my eyes fixed on the kitchen table as he hauled himself out of his chair and out of the kitchen. As he passed by me, my father put his hand on my shoulder and left it there for a couple of beats. When he did that, I didn't hate him anymore, I really didn't, and maybe this is why people do so many hateful things to the people who love them: because it's so easy to stop hating someone if you've already started loving them.

Then my father lifted his hand and made his shuffling way out of the dining room. His hand was replaced by Deirdre's face: she leaned over me, with her chin practically on my left shoulder. She was too close to actually see, to focus on, and I wondered if anthropologists and people from other planets knew this: that it's better to look at alien cultures and worlds from afar, because if you're too close, you don't see anything but pores and the makeup that people use to try to cover them, and you don't smell anything but warm hair and toothpaste, which was what

Deirdre was to me that morning as she whispered, "Your father and I have been happy for a long time. And then you came back. You should never have come back. Don't you dare judge us."

Then she was gone, too. I heard her slam the front door on her way out of the house. I waited several minutes so that I wouldn't have to see my father and Deirdre outside, in my father's car, arguing or commiserating or consoling. I drank my beer slowly, then walked into the kitchen and put the can on top of the refrigerator, where my father put his beer cans when he was conscientious enough to put them somewhere other than where he'd finished drinking them. Then I opened another beer. There was an ugly gnawing in my stomach, which I pretended was still hunger. The only thing to eat in the house was one lonely piece of white bread: I slipped it out of its plastic sleeve and chewed it slowly and thoughtfully, like an especially contemplative cow. Then, after I was through with the bread, after I'd given my father and Deirdre more than enough time to get away, I put my open beer into a paper bag and grabbed the last six-pack out of the fridge. I was going to need whatever courage the beer might give me, plus some. Because now that I'd seen my father with his Deirdre, I was going to have to go talk to the people who'd seen me with my own.

21

It was snowing in Camelot when I arrived. This snow was different from the snow in New Hampshire: it was less intense and deadly and beautiful, just scattered big flakes floating earthward, like confetti separated from the rest of the parade. There was no wind at all; it was cold, not painfully cold but rather the kind of brisk, bright, invigorating cold that made you think cold might not be such a bad thing after all. The sun kept peeking out from behind the clouds, making the clouds and the snow seem more brilliant than they would have been on their own. There were no cars in any of the driveways, no children playing on their pressure-treated wood play sets, no one shoveling their front steps. It was lunchtime on a weekday. There is no quieter time and place than weekday lunchtime in Camelot, but this seemed even quieter than normal. I felt as if it were years in the future and I were pulling into some sort of subdivisional preserve, not a place where people currently lived, but a place designed to show busloads of field-tripping schoolchildren how and where people had *once* lived before they moved somewhere else.

I say there were no cars, but this wasn't entirely true. There was mine, of course, and in my driveway, there was my father-in-law's car and Anne Marie's minivan. Thomas Coleman's Jeep wasn't in sight. Katherine would be at school; Christian would be eating lunch. He was the sort of boy who ate intensely, and so he wouldn't be able to pay attention to anything except the sandwiches and milk he must finish. This would be my time: if Mr. Mirabelli had told Anne Marie what he'd seen, then I'd explain myself, I'd explain everything; if he hadn't told her, then I'd tell her myself. I drank the rest of my beer, threw the can toward the back of the van, got out, and marched to the front door. This was my last chance: I knew this was my last chance because my face didn't flame up but instead was ice cold, as though it were preparing itself to be another kind of face for another kind of life.

I knocked on the door and waited. The snow stopped falling for a moment, as though in anticipation; the sun shone on me the way the sun never had before, just like in the Bible, when the weather is there to emphasize human drama and not just to grow and kill crops.

Then the door opened. Thomas Coleman stood in the doorway. He was wearing leather sandals and a pair of black-and-white-checked baggy pants that weight lifters might wear over their spandex singlets during the Mr. Universe competition in San Diego. He was bare chested, his chest bony and flat and basically just a higher version of his stomach. His nipples were surprisingly large and choked with impressive, dark brown thatches of hair. He was wearing a white towel on his head, a thick piece of rope holding the towel tight to his skull. Thomas smiled and took a step toward me, and I hit him in the jaw as hard as I could, which admittedly wasn't very hard: my fist hit his jaw with a *thud* instead of a *crack*. Thomas fell back into the doorway and onto his ass; he sat there rubbing his jaw but still smiling at me. It was the first time I'd ever punched anyone, and it was the most unsatisfying feeling in the world, and I knew immediately it is better to be wounded than to wound, which is yet another truth I'll put in my arsonist's guide. Gandhi knew this, too, until someone wounded him to death, which goes to show that there is always an exception to the rule, which makes you wonder why we have rules at all.

Thomas scrambled to his feet, then stood there, still smiling, his arms crossed over his bare chest, and I finally considered his strange getup.

"Why are you dressed like that?" I asked him.

"Boola, boola, boola," he said.

"Oh no," I said.

"Boola, boola, boola," he said again, as though he were a Muslim calling other Muslims to prayer.

Which was exactly what he was supposed to be, I should say that now, and I knew exactly what was going on. The Mirabellis are a sentimental, rearward-looking brood, which is not only to say that they find comfort in the past, but that they re-create those comforts whenever they might most need them in the present. For instance, Anne Marie had a considerable stretch in her childhood when she went everywhere in her tutu, to which she was greatly attached. When we first moved to Camelot, and Anne Marie was having such a hard time with the thinness of the walls, her parents showed up one night wearing tutus, and this somehow made Anne Marie feel better, as though the thinness of the walls could be redeemed by the thickness of the past. As though it wasn't enough simply to remember the past; as though one had to re-create it in order for it to do any good. Then there was the time, right before Katherine was born, when Anne Marie had some complications in the pregnancy, some hiccup in our girl-to-be's heartbeat, and Anne Marie had to be hospitalized for a few days. To buck her up, and because Ben Franklin had always been by far Anne Marie's favorite founding father in grade school, Mr. Mirabelli had visited her dressed as Ben Franklin, complete with the spectacles and knickers and kite and almanac, and Mrs. Mirabelli had dressed, on alternating days, as Mrs. Franklin or a bawdy French dame. There were too many of these childhood moments to count, and one of them was the Mirabellis' only trip abroad, to Morocco, where they had heard Muslims calling to Muslims, which brings us to this lunchtime in Camelot. I'd always been included in these reenactments — had worn a tutu and dressed up as either Sam or John Adams, the stouter one — until now.

"Out of my way," I said, then charged past Thomas and into my house, through the empty living room and into the dining room. The table there was much lower than normal and was balanced on four of Christian's building blocks, its legs removed and stashed in the corner of the room, like kindling ready for the fire. The normal tablecloth — white, lace — had been replaced with a tablecloth with some complicated pattern meant to seem Middle Eastern. There were covered serving dishes filled with something I guessed would be almost edible (the Mirabellis weren't known for their skill around the kitchen). Mrs. Mirabelli was the only person in the room besides me; she was, despite her arthritis, sitting crossed-legged on the floor and was wearing a white homemade burka, which was clearly just a bedsheet with a hole cut in it in such a way that it covered her hair and ears and then extended southward. She had unstitched and then restitched a lace napkin or handkerchief for a veil; when she heard me come in, she lifted her homemade veil, looked at me in the way you might expect a mother-in-law to look at her wayward son-in-law — a look that was somewhere between pity and poison — and then dropped the veil again.

"Well, look who's here," my father-in-law said as he walked into the room. Mr. Mirabelli was dressed like the underground leader of a radical Islamic faction: he was wearing a green army jacket, a long white gown he might have stolen from a hospital, and a red-and-white-checked scarf wrapped around his head and flowing down his back. All he lacked was the Russian-made machine gun, for which, considering the circumstances, I was grateful. My father-in-law had his left hand on Christian's shoulder. Christian was dressed like Thomas — sweatpants and no shirt — except that the towel was in his left hand and not on his head, as though he refused to commit fully to the costume. Or maybe it was just that he'd spilled something, as he was inclined to do, and had used the towel to wipe it up.

"Hey, bud," I said to him. Christian smiled at me uncertainly; he raised his hand to his hip, gave me a shy, surreptitious wave, then took his seat next to his grandmother.

"Hello, Mr. Mirabelli," I said to my father-in-law, as though I were introducing myself for the first time. And as far as my father-in-law was concerned, I was.

"Coleslaw!" Mr. Mirabelli said, then sat next to Christian. Christian gave me a sudden look of blank panic, the way children do when they don't know whether something is supposed to be funny or frightening.

"Who?" I said. "What?"

"Please join us, Coleslaw," my father-in-law said. "It's dinnertime."

"Boola, boola, boola," Thomas said as he entered the room and sat at the end of the table, where I normally sat. It was hard to miss the symbolism, and I didn't; but I couldn't focus my full attention or outrage on it just then, either.

"Did you just call me Coleslaw?" I asked my father-in-law. If this was my nickname, I'd never heard it before. The Mirabellis had never been much for nicknames, not even shortened versions of their own names, maybe because Anne sounded all wrong without the Marie, and because Mrs. Mirabelli's name — Louisa — would be a man's if you shortened it, and because Mr. Mirabelli's name was Christian, and if you shortened *that*, it might be seen as disrespectful to his Savior.

"What else would I call you besides Coleslaw, Coleslaw?" Mr. Mirabelli said. He gave me a big, mirthless smile and then gestured toward a place at the table, opposite them, complete with plate and fork and napkin. I guessed the place setting had been intended for Anne Marie and not for me.

"Where's Anne Marie?" I asked, dropping to the floor with a creak of knees and a crash of ass. As I did, the gas fireplace in the room suddenly flared to life, as though my sitting down were Moses and it was the bush. Mr. Mirabelli held up the remote control that worked the fireplace, tucked it inside his green army jacket as though it were his sidearm, and then said, "Pass the couscous, please, Coleslaw." The couscous — which was actually rice, Uncle Ben's, the five-minute kind — was closer to Thomas than to me, but I did what I was told: I got on my knees, put my left hand on the table for balance, and then reached across with my right. But my weight was too much for the quadruple amputee the table had become: before I'd reached the couscous, my corner of the table slipped off its supporting building block and onto the wood floor, causing the plates, serving dishes, glasses, everything *except* the couscous, to come rushing at me as though I were the castle and the table settings the siege.

"I'm so sorry," I said, fumbling around until I found the building block, stuck it under that corner of the table, and then pushed the dishes, glasses, et al. back from where they'd been displaced.

"No problem," Mr. Mirabelli said. "That's life in the Casbah!"

At this, Thomas said a few more "boola, boola's" and Mrs. Mirabelli rang her finger cymbals and then fondly recalled the time in Morocco when Mr. Mirabelli had paid too much money for each family member, one by one, to ride on what had been advertised as a camel but apparently wasn't.

"I'm so sorry for *everything*," I said, once the hilarity had died down a little. I said this to Mr. Mirabelli, but loud enough for everyone to hear, in case Mr. Mirabelli had told them what he'd seen me do in New Hampshire. And in apologizing for everything, I was also apologizing to everyone except Thomas, who was sitting at his end of the table, spooning the rice into his mouth, a pleased look on his face. I was wishing now that I'd asked him a few questions — about what he'd told the Mirabellis, about what they knew and didn't know about my past and present — before I'd rushed into the house.

"I have no idea what you're talking about, Coleslaw," Mr. Mirabelli said pleasantly.

"About what happened in New Hampshire," I said. Because I figured that this was part of his plan: he'd get me to admit to the bad things I'd done rather than have him say them for me. This was a parental tactic: whenever Katherine or Christian did something wrong, we always made them identify their crime themselves, which then served as the appetizer to the main course of their punishment.

"New Hampshire," Mr. Mirabelli said. "It's funny you should say that, Coleslaw. I once followed a guy to New Hampshire."

"Thomas told you where I was going," I said, then shot what I hoped was an angry look at Thomas. Thomas didn't seem to care what was going on around him, though. He maintained a look of perfect contentment, obviously so happy to be allowed just to sit there at the head of the table and say, "Boola, boola, boola," at the appropriate moment and to act as though he belonged.

"I don't need anyone to tell me how to follow a guy," Mr. Mirabelli said. I remembered now that my father-in-law had been a claims investigator for thirty-plus years and had followed people for a living. No, Mr. Mirabelli wouldn't have needed Thomas's help to follow me up to New Hampshire, but I bet Detective Wilson would have needed the help. And I bet Thomas had given it to him.

"It was cold in New Hampshire," Mr. Mirabelli said. "I didn't like it much."

"I know," I said.

"You know?" he said. "How do you know, Coleslaw?"

"I know that's where you saw me kiss that woman."

"You kissed a *woman*, Coleslaw?"

"I don't even know her name," I admitted.

"Doesn't matter to me who you kiss, Coleslaw." Mr. Mirabelli said this in a way that sounded so nonchalant that it couldn't possibly have been nonchalant, as though Mr. Mirabelli had practiced saying it in the mirror before I'd arrived. "Does it matter to anyone else who Coleslaw kisses?"

Everyone, even Christian, shook their heads to indicate they didn't care who I kissed, which, under other circumstances, might have been nice of them, might have felt liberating. Thomas helped himself to another heaping spoonful of rice. Mrs. Mirabelli lifted her veil, reached out for a platter of what appeared to be wet garbanzo beans, scooped up three beans, and then, maybe thinking of her figure, put two of them back on the platter and one in her mouth, which she gently sucked on as if it were a delicate gum ball. Christian sat there, slack jawed, towel in his hand as though ready to wipe the drool that might come from his slack jaw.

"As far as we're concerned," Mr. Mirabelli said, "you can kiss whoever you want, Coleslaw."

"Except us," Mrs. Mirabelli said.

"You can kiss anyone but us, Coleslaw," Mr. Mirabelli said. "There are apparently *some* limits to who you can kiss, Coleslaw."

"*Why* do you keep calling me *that name*?" I asked him. I glanced again at Christian: his towel was now somewhere out of sight, and he was still wearing that slightly bewildered look, as though things were happening in a place where he could see and hear them but not understand them.

"I don't know what else I'm supposed to call you, Coleslaw," Mr. Mirabelli said.

"My name," I said. "Sam!"

"Who?" Mr. Mirabelli asked, and then looked one by one at Thomas and his wife and his grandson, and each of them in turn asked, "Who? Who? Who?" like inquisitive owls, even Christian, although I couldn't and didn't blame him, because what kid *doesn't* like to make animal noises? By the time the table was through asking who "Sam" was, I was starting to wonder myself. Which, I was now understanding, was the point — that I was no longer a son-in-law to them but was only a stranger with a strange name — and as with all points, I found myself thinking fondly of the time, a few moments earlier, when I didn't understand it.

"Where is Anne Marie?" I asked. "I need to talk to Anne Marie."

"We were just talking about her before you got here, Coleslaw," my father-in-law said.

"What were you saying about her?"

"That she's tough," Mr. Mirabelli said.

"She is," I said, agreeing with what he'd said, but not at all liking the sound of it.

"She got some bad news today, Coleslaw," he said, and of course I knew exactly what the bad news was and who was the one who'd given it to her. "She got some very bad news. But she's tough. She'll get over it. She'll move on. She already has."

"I'll be right back," I said. I walked into the kitchen, yelling, "Anne Marie! Anne Marie!" but there was nothing in there but the adobe tile and casement windows and restaurant-quality galley stove and titanium refrigerator-freezer. I walked back through the dining room and headed toward the stairs. "Anne Marie!" I yelled as I walked up the stairs, and then I yelled it again as I wandered through our bedroom, the kids' bedrooms, the hallway bathroom, the guest room in which no guest had ever stayed, the bathroom in the hallway, back into our bedroom again. I even pulled down the ceiling door to the attic crawl space and yelled, "Anne Marie!" into that and was answered by a shower of pink insulation dust, which I guess was the house's way of telling me, *She's not here. Your wife is not here.*

"Where is she?" I demanded of my in-laws as I charged down the stairs and into the dining room. "She has to be here. Her van is out front. Where is she?"

"Where is who?" my father-in-law asked. Then before I could clarify, his nonchalance disappeared for a second, and he said, "It's none of your *goddamn* business anymore." Then he recovered, made a slight adjustment to his head wrap, and added, "Coleslaw."

"Where is she, Thomas?" I asked, turning toward him. Thomas was no longer smiling, no longer "boola, boola'ing." He didn't look content, either, but nervous, as though his place at the table were in peril. Thomas shook his head gravely, lips locked, making it known that one of the big differences between him and me was that I was speaking and he was smart enough not to.

"Mrs. Mirabelli, please," I said. She was a volunteer for most of the

Catholic charitable organizations in the area, and so I hoped she would take pity and add me to her body of good works. Mrs. Mirabelli inhaled and exhaled loudly, her veil fluttering with each breath, but no words followed.

So I turned to Christian. He was all I had left in the room, in the house. The towel was on his head now, pouring down his neck and over his ears. He looked so nervous and scared and small, sitting there between his grandparents, not knowing whether to look at me or not, not knowing why he didn't know whether to look at me or not, but knowing all along where his mother was.

"She went to see my grandma," he told me.

"Grandma is right here," I said.

"My other grandma," he said. "I have another grandma?"

How to describe the way Christian said this? How to describe a five-year-old boy who finds out that he has two sets of grandparents and not just one? How to describe a boy who discovers that his father has for years and years lied about his own parents' being dead? And how to describe a father who doesn't once think that, in killing off his parents, he has killed his children's grandparents in the bargain?

"Oh, Christian," I said, "I'm sorry, bud." And then, because as we all know, sorry isn't good enough, I started crying just to show how sorry I really was, crying and crying and crying, all the while patting myself for a handkerchief, which I didn't have. So Christian took the towel off his head and gave it to me, and I wiped my face with it.

"Thank you," I told him.

"May I go watch TV?" he asked me, using the manners his grandparents or maybe TV itself had taught him, because I never had.

"You may," I said, and then he left the room with just the towel for me to remember him by, which made me cry even harder. All this crying must have softened the Mirabellis' hearts just a little bit, although maybe it would have been better if it hadn't: it would be easier for me to remember them now only as the hard-hearted, costumed lunatics they appeared to be, and not as my in-laws who allowed their hard hearts to be softened by the man who had hardened them in the first place and who would soon be just another part of the past, except I'd be a part of the past they *wouldn't* want to relive.

"Coleslaw, why don't you sit down and eat," my father-in-law said softly. "Things always seem a little better on a full stomach."

"Maybe you're right," I said. I began to take my place at the opposite side of the table, but Mr. Mirabelli said, "You're so far away down there. Why don't you sit here," and he patted the place where Christian had just been. Both elder Mirabellis moved over to make room for me.

"Are you sure?" I said.

"Yes," Mr. Mirabelli said. "But put your son's towel on your head."

I put my son's towel on my head and sat down between my in-laws, and we all ate slowly, in silence, as befitting a last supper. I wanted to ask so many questions. Why, if they were dressed this way for Anne Marie's benefit, was she not here? What exactly had Thomas told them, and when had he told it? Had he told them about my parents, or was this another thing Mr. Mirabelli found out on his own? But it was the sort of silence that was much preferable to the words that would break it. Besides, I had the feeling that once the silence was broken, the meal would be over and I'd be asked to leave. It was my house, and once again I'd be asked to leave it, and once again I would. Some men would refuse to leave their own homes, but I wasn't one of them. I'd given up my right to refuse, the way some criminals give up their right to remain silent.

But still, no matter how silent we were, the food eventually was eaten and the meal was over. Mrs. Mirabelli got up to clear the dishes, and Thomas helped her, leaving me and Mr. Mirabelli alone in the room.

"Mr. Mirabelli, may I ask you one question?"

"You may, Coleslaw."

"Why are you all dressed up like this if Anne Marie isn't even here?"

"She was here," he said, "but then before we even sat down to eat, she said she was going over to your mother's house. That all this" — and here he swept his hands over his costume in demonstration — "was ridiculous."

"She said that?"

" 'I'm not a *child* anymore' — those were her very words." I could tell that this was the saddest thing that had happened yet, as far as Mr. Mirabelli was concerned. His eyes went cloudy and wet; he closed them, took off his glasses, and rubbed the bridge of his nose for a few seconds. When he put his glasses back on and opened his eyes, they were clear again. "I'm sorry you have to go, Coleslaw," he said. "It feels like we barely got to know you, and here it is, time for you to go already."

"I'm sorry, too," I said.

"Everyone is sorry," he said, putting his hand on my shoulder. "You should say good-bye to your son."

"I should," I said. I got up without saying another word, walked to the TV room. Christian was lying on the couch in front of the squawking set. He was asleep, his head halfway hidden by the crook of his arm, and I could hear his sweet breath fluttering past his lips. I loved him. I loved him so much, and I was afraid to say good-bye. You should never say good-bye to your children, not because of what it will do to them, but because of what it will do to you. So I didn't say good-bye. Instead I took the towel off my head, spread it over him as a blanket, then kissed him softly on the forehead. He shifted and moaned in his sleep, and I turned and crept out of the room before he woke up. On my way out of the house, I passed by the dining room. Thomas wasn't there, but Mr. and Mrs. Mirabelli were sitting at the table, drinking coffee and talking about the time in Morocco when their tour guide asked them if they'd ever tried a hookah, and they thought he'd said "hooker." More hilarity, the sort that is years and years in the making. Mr. Mirabelli even took off his towel to hide his face, he was laughing so hard, and I took advantage of his momentary blindness to open the door and leave the Mirabellis and my house in Camelot behind.

. . .

THOMAS WAS OUTSIDE, waiting for me, leaning against my van, arms crossed over his bare chest. He must have been cold: it was snowing harder now, and the runtish maples lining Hyannisport Way were bending and swaying in the howling wind. Inside, dressed the way he was, Thomas looked as though he belonged; outside, though, he looked like a man who didn't have enough sense to wear a shirt in a snowstorm. Inside, he was mostly mute; outside, I hoped, he might answer some questions.

"Did you set fire to the Mark Twain House?" I asked him.

"No," he said.

"I don't believe you," I said. "What about that burn on your hand?"

Thomas removed his hands from his armpits and showed them to me. There, on his right hand, was the burn mark: it was about the size of a quarter, red around the edges, and already starting to scab over. "I got this from the burner on your stove," he said. "You really ought to fix that thing."

"I already did," I said. I knew what he was talking about. A year or two earlier, our stove's front left burner wasn't getting as hot as its three siblings. Anne Marie told me it didn't matter and to leave it alone. This I did not do. I figured it would be easy to fix. I figured it was a loose wire, and so I went inside the stove and loosened and then reconnected the wire to its port, or thought I did. In fact I'd managed to rewire the stove in such a way that the rear left burner didn't work at all, and in fact, when you turned that knob, it managed to heat the *front* left burner instead. A person who didn't know this about the stove could easily burn himself on it. It could easily happen. I'd promised Anne Marie I would fix it, again, but I never did. I'd never gotten around to it. "So you really didn't try to burn down the Mark Twain House?" I asked.

"No. That's what I told your Detective Wilson, too."

"This was before you told him I was going to New Hampshire, correct?"

"Correct," Thomas said, his teeth starting to chatter a little. He returned his hands to the caves of his armpits, where they'd been hibernating.

"Detective Wilson believed you?"

"I had an alibi," Thomas said, and pointed to my house. "I was here that night."

"All night?" I asked, not really wanting the answer. My heart was about to beat its way out of my chest. I almost took my own shirt off, thinking that maybe the cold would numb the pain and persuade my heart to stay in its cavity, where it belonged.

"All night," Thomas said.

"I don't believe you," I said. "You told Anne Marie that you lied about my cheating on her and she *still* let you stay all night? Why would she do that? Didn't she want to know why you lied in the first place?"

"Of course she did," Thomas said. "She asked me why in the hell would I lie about you, of all people."

"Oh no," I said.

"It was an excellent question," Thomas admitted. "It deserved an excellent answer."

"Oh no," I repeated.

"So I told her I did it to get back at you for killing my parents."

"You told her the truth," I said.

"That I did," said Thomas. He looked so proud of himself, as though the truth was the thing he'd never thought he'd be able to tell. "But she didn't believe me, not at first. Even when I told her about it in detail, about the Emily Dickinson House and the fire and you going to prison, she didn't believe me."

"She didn't?"

"No, she was convinced you wouldn't have hidden those things from her. 'Sam wouldn't do that to me' — that's what she said." Here he paused, and I watched his pride turn to confusion, as it often does. "I don't get it. She seemed to have really loved you."

"She still does!" I said. "She still does!"

Thomas didn't pay any attention to this, wishful thinking being the easiest kind of thinking to ignore. "So then I told her that if she didn't believe me, she should go talk to your parents."

"Oh no," I said, because if our life is just one endless song about hope and regret, then "oh no" is apparently that song's chorus, the words we always return to.

"And that's when she told me what you'd told her: that your parents were killed in a house fire."

"Let me explain," I said. I could tell his low-grade anger was about to turn into pure hatred and rage, the way you can tell when rain is about to turn into one of the colder forms of precipitation.

"Your parents *were killed in a house fire*," he repeated. "Was that supposed to be funny?" Thomas asked. He took a step toward me, removed his right hand from his armpit, and clenched it, and for a second I thought he was going to hit me, but he didn't. Maybe Thomas had learned from my mistake earlier, when I'd hit him. When we hit someone, we want that to be the final word. But it never is. And if a blow to the face wasn't the final word, then what was? Are we wrong for wanting there to be any such thing as a final word? Was there any such thing as a final word? And where, oh, where could we find someone to speak it?

"Wasn't it enough that you killed my parents?" Thomas said. "Did you have to kill your own parents in the same way?"

"I didn't kill my parents at all," I said. "Thomas, it was just a *story*."

"Shut the fuck up," he said. "In the story you killed your parents *in the same way* you killed my parents in real life."

"OK, I get your point," I said, his point being that once something bad happens to you, once you become tragic, you have rights to that tragedy, you own it—not just the tragedy, but the story of that tragedy, too—and then you and only you can do what you want with it. You could write a memoir about it, for instance. Yes, I had plagiarized Thomas's grief, the way the bond analysts thought they'd plagiarized mine. "I'm sorry," I said.

"You're damn right you're sorry," he said. "You're always sorry."

That was so obviously true that I didn't feel the need to confirm it. "And then I'm guessing Anne Marie told her parents what you told me," I said. "And that's when Mr. Mirabelli started following me."

"And then you kissed a woman who wasn't your wife with your father-in-law watching," Thomas said. "I didn't really have to do any work at all."

"My mother saw me do it, too," I admitted.

"That poor woman," he said.

"I know you know my father," I said. "Do you know my mother, too?"

"I've known them both for a long time, Sam," he said. His anger had turned to sadness now, meaning not that anger is fleeting, but that when anger melts away, then sadness is always there in its middle.

"From my father's parties," I said.

"No," Thomas said. "Your mother has never been at the parties, not that I know of."

"My father said she didn't like his guests."

"Just one guest, really," Thomas said, and finally I was starting to understand. My parents had something like an agreement: every Tuesday my father would have a party at the house with Deirdre among the guests, and my mother would know to stay away. As long as my father remembered what day of the week it was, my mother wouldn't have to see Deirdre, and as long as she didn't see her, she didn't have to admit she existed. She would go to her apartment that night, and Deirdre would come over to the house; when my mother came back to the house the next day, Deirdre would be gone. She did and she didn't know about Deirdre; now I knew what my father meant when he said things were complicated.

"So you know that my father has a Deirdre."

Thomas nodded. "It's complicated," he said.

"My father has been cheating on my mother for thirty years," I said. "That's not complicated."

"They're not bad people, Sam, not any of them." I recognized immediately what he'd said and the way he said it: this was a rationalization a son might make about his parents. It occurred to me that my mother and father had become his parents as much as they'd stayed mine. Or

was it my father and Deirdre whom he considered his parents? How
many parents might a person have in this life? Was there an infinite supply? And supposing there was, did this infinite supply of parents mean
an infinite supply of comfort, or of heartbreak?

"How do you know my mother if she wasn't at the parties?"

"Your mother came and found me after my parents died," he said.
"She wanted to say how sorry she was. She's the only one in your family
to say that. I used to come around and see her in her apartment once in
a while, but I had a feeling she didn't want me there."

"Why?"

"I don't think she likes me very much," Thomas admitted. I knew
why: my mother probably pitied Thomas too much to like him. I remembered there were books she wouldn't read, and wouldn't let me
read, because they were so full of pity. For my eighth-grade English
class, I was assigned *Uncle Tom's Cabin* and *To Kill a Mockingbird*, and
my mother refused to let me bring them in the house. I had to read them
on the front porch, even though it was winter and uncomfortably cold
even if you were completely dressed, as I had been back in eighth grade
and Thomas wasn't now. Snow was starting to accumulate on his hair,
his shoulders. He was hopping from one foot to the other to keep warm.
He was so cold, even his sternum was turning blue. The only reason I
could figure he didn't go inside was that he enjoyed showing me how
much he knew about my family that I didn't.

"Tell me about my mother's apartment," I said. "How long has she
had it?"

"A long time. Almost ever since I've known her."

"But when I came home from prison, she was living in the house," I
said. "My father didn't have any parties then, either. I lived there a whole
month."

"They tried for a month, for your sake," Thomas said. "And then you
left."

"But they *wanted* me to leave."

"It's complicated," Thomas said again, world-wearily, sagely, as if only he could know what it felt like to know so much.

"You seem to know so much," I said. "If you didn't try to burn down the Mark Twain House, then who did?"

"I have no idea," Thomas said. This was exactly what my father had said when I asked him why my mother didn't like the parties. But he'd had an idea, all right. My father had known exactly why my mother didn't like the parties, even though he pretended he didn't.

"What about the Edward Bellamy House?" I asked Thomas, knowing what he would say.

"I have no idea," Thomas said. *Now* he looked longingly toward the house, a *house* being not just a shelter from the elements but also a place where you could try to hide from all the things you didn't know or didn't want to know.

"I think a woman did it," I said, testing him out. "That's my theory. Do you know a woman who might have tried to burn down those houses?"

"I have no idea," Thomas said.

"I think you do," I said. I remembered what Detective Wilson had said the day before, when he'd seemed so confident, and so I tried to mimic him. "I don't know who it is yet," I said, "but I bet you do. And I bet I'll find out." I patted Thomas on his frozen shoulder, then walked around to the driver's side of the van, and Thomas followed me.

"Where do you think you're going?" he asked.

"I'm going to my mother's apartment to talk to her and Anne Marie."

"Jesus, Sam," Thomas said, shaking his head. "It's too late."

But it wasn't too late. I had an idea that it wasn't too late. "Why did Anne Marie take your Jeep to my mother's house instead of her van?" I asked him. "I'm just curious."

"My Jeep was blocking her in," he said. "It was easier for her just to take the Jeep."

"Why didn't you go with her?"

"She said she wanted to go by herself," Thomas said, not able to keep the resentment out of his voice. I knew then that he had wanted to go with her, and she wouldn't let him, and that he felt a little lost and abandoned because of it, the relationship between man and woman being like that between man overboard and life raft.

"It's *not* too late," I said.

"It is," Thomas said. "You should just *give up*." He suddenly turned away from me and ran to the house, brushing the snow off his head and shoulders as he ran.

Thomas was right: I should just have given up, and that's another thing I'll put in my arsonist's guide. Unlike other guides — those guides that tell you not to give up on this or that, never to give up, good things will happen if you just don't give up — I'll tell you to just give up, immediately and without a struggle, surrender being our most underrated reaction to difficulty.

But I didn't know that then, and so I didn't listen to Thomas. I didn't give up.

22

As part of my arsonist's guide to writers' homes in New England, I might include a chapter on how it feels to see your mother standing in the street outside her apartment and talking with your wife, your wife who up until now and for years and years has believed your mother to be dead, dead and in the ground, in the ground and so unable to tell your wife all the things about you, her husband, that you didn't ever, ever want her to know.

It feels bad. Not very good at all. The sight of them together took my breath away, and so I had to stop the van a block away from where they were standing, just to get it back (my breath, that is). My mother and Anne Marie were standing next to my mother's car and saying good-bye, that was clear: they hugged several times in the minute I sat there, watching them. Anne Marie grabbed my mother's hand with both of hers, held it, and said something and then something else; then they both doubled over, laughing. When they were done laughing, they hugged again and held it. I counted to ten, and still they hugged. It was snowing heavily now, and the air was so thick with the stuff that the streetlights had kicked on, even though it was barely three o'clock. The street hadn't yet been plowed, and the snow was perfect in the way of unplowed snow. It was the kind of snow that made you wish you had a sled, an old one with metal runners, and it was also the kind of snow that made you forget that you were the kind of person who wouldn't ever take care of the runners and they would rust and soon the sled would be useless, which is another way of saying that it was the sort of snow that tricked you into thinking things were better than they actually were. Because just then, my mother and Anne Marie broke their clinch, and my mother noticed my van, idling just down the block. I waved to her through the windshield. She shook her head, said something to Anne Marie, and then hopped into her car and drove off in the other direction. Anne Marie turned around, saw my van, and walked toward me. I got out of my van and walked toward her. I was still wearing the clothes Peter Le Clair had given me a day earlier; Anne Marie was wearing one of those fleece vests that are really soft but somehow also water resistant, the sort of vest that's so comfortable it makes your torso sleepy and your arms jealous of your torso, and wide awake and angry because of it, which is by way of explaining that once Anne Marie was in range, she hit me, the way I'd hit Thomas a few hours earlier. She had gloves on, plus she had zero experience as a fighter, so the punch didn't have much force behind it and barely hurt, but still I fell to the ground, because that's surely where I belonged.

"It is better to be wounded than to wound," I told her.

"The hell it is," she said. "Get up."

I did as I was told. I had been in Peter's clothes for almost a day now, and in my own clothes for even longer: I smelled of woodsmoke and bar smoke and beer and human sweat and fear and the several layers of wet clothes that kept the smells close by.

"My father said you kissed a woman in New Hampshire," Anne Marie said, her voice even. Maybe she'd been practicing in the mirror, too. "Is that true?"

I admitted that it was and then told her the whole story. I didn't leave anything out, not one significant detail, not even the groping. And then I went further back and told her everything else I hadn't told her about my past, all the things she knew by now, although not from me. I'd left too many things out for too long. Anne Marie's facial expression didn't change once during the telling. She didn't frown, twitch, or grimace, even when I said that I loved her and that my kissing that woman was the first time it had ever happened and that it would never happen again. At the end of my story, I said, "That's it," and she nodded. That was all. It was the greatest feat of strength and control I'd ever witnessed, to listen to the story — the story of how I'd lied to her for ten years — and then do nothing but nod in response. If listening stoically to the story of how you'd been betrayed by your husband had been an Olympic event, Anne Marie would have gotten the gold. It occurred to me then that I wasn't worthy of her — I'm sure this thought had occurred to her as well — and that Thomas wasn't, either.

"Thomas said he spent the night at our house," I said. "Is that true?"

"Yes," Anne Marie said. "He's spent more than one night."

"On the couch?" I asked.

Anne Marie didn't answer. She reached inside her vest, pulled out her pack of cigarettes, took a cigarette and a lighter out of her pack, and lit the cigarette, all without taking her gloves off. I realized right then that Anne Marie was a capable woman. I'd never thought of her that way before. There were so many other questions I wanted to ask her — what had she and my mother talked about? for instance — but I didn't, because I now knew she was a capable woman, and capable women don't answer questions from people who have no right to ask them. This will go in my arsonist's guide, too.

"Where did my mother go just now?" I finally asked, picking what I hoped was an innocuous question that Anne Marie would be willing to answer. She did.

"She went to work."

"Work?" I said. "Where's that?"

Here something odd happened: the smoke poured out of Anne Marie's mouth and she smiled at me, like a softhearted dragon. "You'll never guess where she works," Anne Marie said.

"I probably won't," I admitted.

"She works at the Student Prince," Anne Marie said. The Student

Prince was the German restaurant in Springfield that Anne Marie and I had lived above when we were first married. I knew now why she was smiling at me: she was remembering that happy time, our first child, our first home, the early, best stages of our love. This is not to say that love endures, but that the memory of it does, even — or especially — if we don't want it to.

"What a coincidence," I said.

"It's not a coincidence," Anne Marie said, and then before I could ask her what she meant, she threw her spent cigarette in the snow and said, "You'll have to ask her yourself."

"OK."

"Your mother's a good woman, Sam," she told me. "She deserves better than your father."

"I know."

"She deserves better than you, too."

"I know that," I said. For the first time, I was thinking of what I'd done to my mother and not what I thought she'd done to me. She deserved a better son than me, a better *person* than me. This is another way you know you've become a grown-ass man, when you realize — too late, too late — that you're not worthy of the woman who made you one. Of the *women* who made you one.

"Your mother is afraid that you set fire to those writers' houses," Anne Marie said, and then she named them: the Bellamy and Twain houses. She didn't mention the Robert Frost Place. This probably meant my mother had stopped following me after she'd seen me kissing the woman in the bar, which was too bad: if she'd followed me to the Robert Frost Place, then she'd have known I didn't torch it, and she'd also have seen who did. "She's worried about you."

"I didn't set fire to any writer's house," I said.

"Except for the one," Anne Marie said.

"And that was an accident," I said.

"I don't want to hear it," she said.

"A woman set fire to the Bellamy and Twain houses," I went on.

"What woman?"

"I don't know yet," I said. "But I'm pretty sure Thomas has an idea."

"Sam . . . ," Anne Marie said. I could hear the exasperation in her voice, so beautiful and familiar, but sad, too, like hearing church bells right before your funeral. I should have stopped talking right then, but I didn't, and my words were like the snow, which kept falling and falling even though too much of it had fallen already.

"And then the bond analysts burned down the Robert Frost Place."

"The what? And *who*?" Anne Marie said, and then before I could answer, she said, "Forget it. I don't want to hear about any fucking *bond analysts*. I don't want to hear about anything anymore."

"But Anne Marie," I said, "it's true."

"Oh, Sam," Anne Marie said. "Why don't you take some responsibility for once?"

"For burning down those houses?"

"For *everything*," she said. Then she turned around and walked through the snow back to Thomas's Jeep. I didn't chase after her, didn't call out to her, didn't tell her to come back, come back. Talking had gotten me into nothing but trouble. Maybe the best way to get Anne Marie to come back was just to stand there in the snow and not say anything and wait for her. It worked, too. She spun her wheels in the snow, did a ragged three-point turn, and pointed the Jeep in my direction. *Come back to me*, I said in my head. *Come back to me.* And she did. Anne Marie pulled up right next to me, reached across the front seat, rolled down the passenger side window, and said, "You're going to go see your mother, aren't you?"

I admitted that I probably was.

"Then you should go home and change first," she said. "Shower, too. You look terrible, Sam. You don't smell so good, either." And then she rolled up the window and drove away.

23

As everyone knows, you can't go home again. That famous book told us so, even if it took way too many pages to do it. But what *that* book didn't tell us, and mine will, is that you can't go home again even to change your clothes and shower before meeting your mother at the Student Prince, because if you do, you'll find Detective Wilson sitting at your dining room table, waiting for you. He was baggy eyed and armed with another large coffee, the way I was baggy eyed and armed with another large beer, which is just further proof that all men are but slight variations on the very same theme.

"You don't seem surprised to see me," he said.

"I'm not," I said. Because I wasn't: after all, there had been so many non-Pulsifers showing up at my home the last few days that I'd have to expand the definition of *home* to include people who didn't actually live there, in addition to the people who were supposed to live there but didn't. "I'm not surprised at all," I told him. I raised my bagged beer in toast, then sat down across the table from him. Between us was a bulky manila envelope that I figured was mail for one of my parents.

"You've been busy, Sam," Detective Wilson said. He took several envelopes out of his jacket pocket, withdrew pieces of paper from each envelope, and then spread them on the dining room table, covering the manila envelope. The pieces of paper and the envelope looked dirty, torn, abused, and I was pretty sure I knew what they were without reading them, even though I did read them, if for no other reason than to

buy myself a little time. They were the rest of my father's missing letters, from people who wanted me to burn down these writers' houses:
Edith Wharton's, Henry Wadsworth Longfellow's, and Nathaniel Hawthorne's, as well as a replica log cabin at Henry David Thoreau's Walden
Pond. The letter writers had gotten what they wanted, too: someone
had burned down all those houses the night before, one after the other,
and someone had then left the pertinent letter near the place where
the house had just been. Detective Wilson told me this as I pretended
to read the letters. I knew the bond analysts had done the burning, of
course — I could picture their route south from New Hampshire and
east toward Boston as they burned, could hear Morgan saying, *He'll be
sorry,* as he produced and planted the letters. I should have told Detective
Wilson about the bond analysts; I should have produced Morgan's book
and the postcards and then explained their reasons for burning these
houses and framing me. Then I would have gone on and admitted to
Detective Wilson that I didn't know any of the bond analysts' last names
except for Morgan's, nor did I know exactly where in Boston they lived.
But Anne Marie hadn't wanted to hear about the bond analysts, and I
could imagine Detective Wilson reacting the same way, could imagine
him agreeing with the Writer-in-Residence: he would clearly think the
whole thing was a cheap trick, and that the bond analysts didn't sound
like real people. So instead of telling him the whole truth, I told the
simplest part of it — "It wasn't me" — and then slid the letters back toward him.

"Yes, it was," Detective Wilson said. He put the letters back in their envelopes and returned them to his coat pocket. I looked down at the table
where the letters had just been. There was that manila envelope. I looked
at it rather than at Detective Wilson and noticed what I hadn't before: in
the upper left-hand corner, in official letterhead style, it read: "Wesley
Mincher, English Department, Heiden College, Hartford, CT 06106."
There was no postmark on the envelope, no proper mailing address,
either, but there was, in the middle of the envelope, in big block letters

so you couldn't miss it, my name: "SAM." I looked back at Detective Wilson, and while I was doing so, I reached down and turned over the envelope so that my name was facing the table and not me or him.

"No," I said, "it wasn't."

"Of course it was, Sam," he said, and then patted his coat pocket where the envelopes were, the incriminating letters inside them.

"If it were me," I said, "then why would I leave the letters behind?"

It was clear that Detective Wilson hadn't thought about this, hadn't thought about the evidence except that it existed and that it proved what he wanted it to prove, evidence — as I'll put in my arsonist's guide — being just a more concrete form of wishful thinking. "Because you wanted to get caught," he said weakly. He hit his coat pocket, but harder this time, as though punishing the letters for letting him down.

"Why would I want to get caught?"

"Maybe you left the letters by accident," he said.

It made me feel so good to hear someone else say "accident" that I nearly forget about all of my own, which is why I then had another one. An accident, that is. "Come on. You can do better than that. I burned down five houses and then *accidentally* left letters at all of them?"

"I only named four houses," Detective Wilson, recouping quickly.

"Oh," I said.

"But you're right. There *was* a fifth house torched last night." I knew which one it was and so didn't bother to listen to him say it. I did, however, think of Peter Le Clair's letter in my pocket, could hear it calling to its siblings in Detective Wilson's pocket across the table. "I didn't find a letter there. But I know it was you who burned that house, too. Do you want to know how I know?"

"No," I said. After all, I knew everything Detective Wilson was going to tell me, knew what Thomas Coleman had told him, knew that he'd driven to New Hampshire to find me. What I didn't know was what was in the manila envelope, and how it got on my table in the first place, and whether Detective Wilson had already looked inside.

"Are you listening to me?" Detective Wilson asked.

"No," I said. "Should I have been?"

"Yes," Detective Wilson went on. "I was telling you how your Thomas Coleman called me and said you were about to burn down the Robert Frost Place in Franconia, New Hampshire."

"How did he know that?" I asked him.

"That's not important," he said, and when Detective Wilson said that, I was sure he didn't know the answer, "not important" being just one of the things we call that which we don't know. "What are you smiling at?"

"I'm not smiling," I said, although I was. Clearly Detective Wilson hadn't followed me to New Hampshire, which had been my big fear; clearly he hadn't seen me at the Robert Frost Place, at the bar, at the fire. And since he didn't have the letter, he clearly didn't know it was Peter who'd written to me, Peter being one of the other people who'd say with certainty that I'd burned down the Robert Frost Place. That was what I was smiling at, even though I said to Detective Wilson, "I'm not smiling."

"Ever since you came back to your parents' house," Detective Wilson said, "there's been trouble."

"That's true."

"You should never have come back," he said. Detective Wilson said other things after that, but once again I wasn't listening to them. I was thinking about what he'd just said— *You should never have come back*— and how Deirdre had said the very same thing earlier that day. As every detective knows, the rhetoric of crime and the rhetoric of crime solving are the very same, and if Detective Wilson were trying to solve the crimes, did that mean that Deirdre had committed one of them? Had she been the one who'd burned the Edward Bellamy House, or tried to, or the Mark Twain House, or tried to, or both? Was she the other woman my father told me I should be looking for? Was she the other woman, twice over? Suddenly I had a hunch— *hunch*, I discovered, being exactly the wrong word, because once I'd had the hunch, I suddenly found myself sitting ramrod straight, with perfect military bearing, not hunched at all.

"What?" Detective Wilson said. "Why are you sitting like that?"

"Don't worry about it," I said. "Is there anything else you need to say to me?"

"It would be better if you'd just confess right now, Sam," he said, consumed by a sigh that came from somewhere deep within him and drifted out his nostrils. "It just would be much, much better."

"For whom?" I asked.

"For *everyone*," he said, raising his voice now, raising your voice being the thing you do when you don't know what else to do with it. "Just tell the *truth*."

"It will make you feel better, dude," I said.

"What?"

"Nothing," I said. I was remembering, of course, the bond analysts and their theories about the memoirs they'd never written and how the one they *had* written hadn't made them feel better and wasn't their truth at all, or my father's, either, and how maybe the search for the truth was as pointless as looking for it to make you feel better. "I have to shower," I told him. "Are we about done?"

"So you're not going to confess," Detective Wilson said. "So you're going to make this difficult. What the *fuck* are you smiling at?" But then he got up and stormed out of the house before I could tell him that I was smiling about my mother. When I was a boy, she would make me read all those books and then ask me questions, these tough questions about what the book might or might not mean, and I'd always say, "You're making this difficult," and she'd always tell me what I would have told Detective Wilson if he'd still been in the house: "It *already* is difficult."

There was still the matter of the manila envelope. I turned it over and opened it. It was heavy and bulging, and I was pretty sure I'd find Wesley Mincher's three thousand dollars inside. I did — three rubber-banded groups of one-hundred-dollar bills. But there was also something else in the envelope: a handwritten note saying, "Meet me at the Emily Dickinson House at midnight." The handwriting wasn't familiar. It wasn't my father's from the grocery list, wasn't my mother's from the postcards, either. I looked at my watch: it was half past five o'clock. Plenty of time for me to shower, change, drive down to the Student Prince, and then meet someone — and I had that hunch as to who it was — at midnight at the Emily Dickinson House, or at least where it used to be. I put the money and the note back in the envelope, finished my beer, went up-stairs, and made myself a more presentable Sam Pulsifer. Then I went downstairs, grabbed another beer out of the fridge, walked out the front door, climbed into my van, and headed toward the Student Prince and my mother, not realizing I would see my parents' house only one more time, which would be the last time anyone ever saw it.

Part Five

24

One of the things it means to get older is that you start, in the overlong telling of your life's story, to introduce each scene like so: "Here I was, in ___ again, for the first time in ___ years." Which is just another reason you stay at home, or at least another reason the people listening to your story *wished* you had stayed at home.

But I hadn't, and here I was, in Springfield again for the first time in five years. It was much grimmer than I remembered. Main Street was absolutely deserted; the check-cashing places that had replaced the Italian restaurants and candy stores were boarded up. Maybe there were no checks left to cash in the city. Half the bulbs on the Paramount Theatre were burned out, which didn't matter because the marquee was blank and there was nothing playing there anyway. The gray concrete civic center — where I had seen this minor league hockey game and taken Anne Marie and the kids to see that Greatest Show on Earth — was closed for renovation, ringed by a ten-foot-high plywood fence, on which signs begged you to EXCUSE OUR MESS!! The grand old buildings lining Court Square — the courthouse, Symphony Hall, the Unitarian church — were still grand and illuminated by blindingly powerful spotlights, maybe to discourage looters. The barbershop next to the courthouse had clearly been closed for some time — its pole was stock still, its reds and blues faded — even though there was a sign in its window insisting it had been open since 1892. Kitty-corner to the barbershop, on the east side of Court Square, was an old storefront filled with dozens of discarded radiators, arranged in neat rows as though on display, as though to teach passersby something about the limitations of steam heat. I've never seen such a desolate place; there hadn't even been any snow to help cover it up. Clearly, even the snow had decided the place was beyond help.

The entrance to the Student Prince was in an alley, just off Court Square. The door was solid wood, so you couldn't see if there was light or darkness on the other side of it. There was no noise coming from inside, no music or human voices or clanging of dishes and glasses. I looked up, and there was Anne Marie's and my old apartment, where we'd rearranged our furniture and bred our children. The windows were dark, as were the windows in every other apartment in the building. The wind was up, and so cold, but it, too, was completely and eerily quiet, as though Springfield didn't deserve the wind's *whoosh* and *roar*. It was one of those moments when the whole world felt empty, as if you were the only one in it and you wished you weren't, wished you were in whatever world or antiworld all the people had fled to. It occurred to me that Anne Marie had lied to me about my mother's working there. Why she would lie to me about *that*, I had no idea, except that maybe I would open the door and see the Student Prince was empty, and that would be a metaphor for the rest of my life.

But the Student Prince wasn't empty. It was fire-code-violation full. Even though the Student Prince had three cavernous rooms with high shelves loaded down with German beer steins and coats of arms and Bavarian gewgaws from days gone by — even so, the place was full. Every table was taken and there was a line of people waiting to sit at them. It seemed as though every Springfieldian, past and present, was in the place, drinking a dark beer and waiting for their schnitzel. The roar of happy human voices was incredible and sounded like the wind personified, and for the first time, I knew what my mother had meant when she talked about it in the books she'd made me read.

My mother—I didn't see her at first. I walked through all three rooms: the barroom, to which I'll return in a moment; the largest dining room, filled with large families eating their large meals at large tables; and the newest of the three rooms, lined with mirrors and populated by men pretending to like the cigars they were smoking, and wearing Red Sox hats—that regional symbol of self-love and self-hate and male-pattern baldness—and talking loudly about how good their business was or was not, and half-watching something reality-based on TV. In each room, there were waitresses, squads of them, dressed in formless, sacklike white dresses. They'd worn these dresses five years earlier, too, and I couldn't tell then and I couldn't tell now whether they were authentic German barmaid gear or a new German immigrant's idea of what Americans might want to think of as authentic German barmaid gear. In any case, they were still wearing the dresses. But my mother wasn't among them, not that I could see, and so I retreated to the barroom, the room to which men looking for a woman always retreat. I found an empty seat at the bar, sat on it, and waited for the bartenders to notice me so I could order a beer, a big one, even though I'd had so many big beers already that day that they'd stopped having much effect except to make me want to keep drinking them. It was so crowded, though, that it was at least ten minutes until I was served, by a young guy—younger than me—with a shaved head and an old guy's waxed handlebar mustache. It had taken him so long to take my order that I ordered two large doppelbock beers to save him and me time.

"You with somebody, buddy?" he asked me, handing over the two large beers in two heavy glass steins.

"Nope," I said. The bartender looked at me, and then at the beers, and then at me again, as if to say, like my mother in her note, *I think I know you.* And who knows: maybe, like my mother, he did.

I sat there awhile and drank one beer fast, and the next one at regular speed. The bar noise and its makers advanced and retreated, advanced and retreated, but pleasantly, not like an army but like a tide coming in and going out, a tide coming in and going out that wouldn't make you wet as you listened to its dreamy tidal sounds. After a few minutes, or maybe it was an hour, I saw old Mr. Goerman, the owner, working the tables, shaking hands, and slapping backs. He was older, a little more raisined in the face, a little more pretzeled in the spine, but recognizably Mr. Goerman. Like the bartender, he also had a waxed handlebar mustache, and I figured maybe they were made to wear those mustaches, the way the waitresses were made to wear their white sacks. In any case, it was good to see him. I caught his eye, hoisted my nearly empty second stein in his direction. He waved back, and a warm feeling came over me, that sort of warm feeling you get when you've been recognized, remembered, and told in so many words that you belong. But then I watched Mr. Goerman wave to pretty much every other person in the Student Prince that night, and he couldn't have known everyone to whom he waved. So I kept drinking my beer, and that helped maintain my warm feeling long after it should have faded, which is of course yet another reason why people drink — in fact, the main one.

The bartender noticed that I'd finished the second of my two beers, and he must also have noticed that I hadn't done anything suspect while or after drinking them. He must have pegged me as the sort of guy who likes to peacefully order and drink his two big, strong beers at once, because he brought me two more.

"What do you say about something to eat?" he asked, gingerly twirling the sharp ends of his mustache.

"What a good idea," I said. No sooner had I said it — drunk time being drunk time — than there was in front of me a platter layered with five different kinds of Munich sausage with a dollop of hot mustard on the side, and on another platter a layer of creamed whitefish, surrounded by a border of hard crackers. Both of these platters appeared from behind me, one platter coming around me from the left, one from the right, the deliverer right up against my back. It was the way food wouldn't be served in a restaurant unless you were being served in a pleasant dream by a very attractive person who wanted you sexually, or unless the server knew you well.

The server knew me well. It was my mother. I turned to face her; she was wearing the white sack. I recognized it, too — not from the other waitresses, but from that night a week earlier, when I'd first come home and seen my mother and she'd looked like the Lady of the Lake. She wasn't; she was a waitress at the Student Prince. I silently handed her one of my beers and she took it and drank it quickly, then handed the empty stein back. Still, she didn't say anything. I didn't *want* her to say anything, because I was afraid that she, like the Mirabellis, would call me by a name that would not be Sam, but Coleslaw or some other name by which she could say she no longer knew me or no longer wanted to.

"Sam —," she finally began, but before she could get any further, I leaped off my stool and hugged her for using my right name. She let me hold her and hugged me back a little, too. My mother smelled like applesauce, which she must have served that night; when I was a child, she often smelled like applesauce, which she must have served me then, too.

"What are you doing here?" I asked, still holding her, talking into her hair.

"I work here," she said, pushing me away a little.

"I know that," I said. "But why here? Did you know Anne Marie and I used to live upstairs?"

"Yes," she said. "That's why I work here. And that's why I used to drink here before I worked here."

"I don't get it."

"I just wanted to be close to you, Sam, to know where you were."

"But why didn't you just come upstairs and let me know you were so close?"

"I don't know," she said. "I didn't want to be too far away, but I didn't want to be too close, either."

"Of course you didn't," I said. My father left us but moved only twenty minutes away; my mother wanted to be in the same building as me, but not in the same apartment. I moved back to Amherst, but not too close to my parents; and then I moved back into my parents' house, which was not too close to my family in Camelot. *Not too close* was our family curse, the way incest was for some royal families and hubris for others. "But wait," I said. "We moved to Camelot five years ago."

"I know."

"But you're still here. Why?"

"Hey," a waitress said to my mother as she careened by with her full tray of dishes and steins, "Beth, I could use some help. Table six."

"I'll be right back," my mother said to me, and then she walked off in the direction, I assumed, of table six.

"Beth!" I called after her. "I knew you seemed like a Beth now!"

"You know Beth?" the bartender said. I sat back on my stool and swiveled to face him. Two freshly poured steins of beer sat between us on the bar.

"I'm not sure," I told him.

"She's a sweetheart," he told me.

"She is?" Of all the many words I'd heard used to describe my mother, "sweetheart" had never been one of them. I'd never even heard my father call her that. I wondered if he ever called Deirdre that. I wondered if my mother wondered if he ever called Deirdre that. "Beth is a sweetheart?"

"Sure she is," the bartender said. "Just look at her."

I turned and did. My mother was standing at a table in the barroom, talking with a man and his son. The man was a genuine, prematurely white-haired Yankee Brahmin sheathed in dark corduroy and wool, and waterproof in his duck boots. His son wasn't even a little bit Yankee or Brahmin. He was a baggy-pants-and-expensive-sneakers kid wearing headphones who would have been the same kid if he'd grown up in New Jersey or California. He was the sort of kid who would get older and move to Phoenix and hustle insurance in a mean glass tower and water his grass in the desert. I could hear the father lecturing my mother about something or other, because he was that sort of Brahmin: the sort who felt compelled to give you a lesson on some important subject or other. No doubt that's why his kid was wearing headphones. My mother *Elizabeth* wouldn't have been lectured for ten seconds. She would have ripped the headphones off the kid's head and told the Brahmin where he could stick them. But not *Beth*. She stood there with a pleasant expression on her face and listened until the Brahmin was through with his lesson; then she tousled the kid's hair as she headed toward the kitchen. My mother was a Beth, all right, and Beth was obviously a sweetheart.

"You're right," I said. "Beth is a sweetheart." I must have said this in such a way as to give the impression that I was smitten, because the bartender grimaced empathetically, and said, "Sorry, bud, she's married."

"Married," I said, waving my hand, by which I meant to communicate, *Who isn't?*

"Yeah, but she's *really* married," the bartender said.

"Have you met the guy?" I asked.

"No," he said, "but she talks about him *a lot.*"

"What's she say about him?"

"He's got a big brain," the bartender said, and then, maybe sensing that I didn't have one, he tapped his forehead with his forefinger.

"I bet he reads books," I said.

"He gets *paid* to read books," the bartender said, shaking his head, as though wondering who would pay a person to do such a thing, which, after all, he'd probably do anyway. The bartender poured himself a free beer, then began drinking it, still shaking his head at the good fortune of some men. "*And* he's got a woman like Beth."

"Do they have any kids?" I asked.

"Just one. He's a scientist."

"Packaging scientist," I said.

"You know the guy?" the bartender said. "She talks about *him* a lot, too. Says he's brilliant. A good son, to boot. You've never seen a woman love two guys more than she loves her son and husband."

"Lucky guys," I said.

"They are," the bartender agreed, and then he moved to the other end of the bar. I knew now why my mother had stayed at the Student Prince after I'd moved to Camelot. At the Student Prince she could be Beth, a sweetheart with a terrific husband and son. But in Amherst, she was Elizabeth, a drunk ex-teacher who lived by herself in an apartment in Belchertown while her drunk husband was back in their house, where he'd been carrying on with another woman for thirty years, and her ex-con son was getting kicked out of his own house, quitting his job, kissing other women, and possibly (my mother thought) once again burning down writers' homes in New England. I understood everything now: if I were my mother, I'd want to be Beth at the Student Prince, too.

Just then, someone clipped me in the back of the head, hard, and then didn't apologize the way a complete stranger would have. I turned and my mother was there, holding her serving tray. There was an empty stool next to me, but my mother didn't take it, preferring, I guess, to face me and get the complete view of the whole man.

"So tell me," she said. "Who was that woman in New Hampshire?"

"I don't know," I admitted.

"Let me guess," my mother said. "You were drunk. It didn't mean anything."

"I *was* drunk," I said, not adding that it didn't mean anything, because of course it did. "You wrote on that napkin that you thought you knew me. What did you mean by that?" And then, before my mother did or did not answer the question, I answered it myself. "I know all about Dad. I know Dad didn't send those postcards from those places. I know you wrote and sent them from Amherst. I know you were fired from your teaching job for being a drunk. I *know* some things, Mom."

My mother sighed, then sat down on the stool next to me. All the sweetness seemed to have left her, all the smart meanness, too. She didn't seem like Beth or even Elizabeth anymore, just a sad, tired woman who hadn't found a name to fit her yet.

"What do you want from me, Sam?" she said, closing her eyes and leaning against the bar.

"I want you to tell me what happened with Dad thirty years ago."

She did. She was too exhausted *not* to tell me things anymore. So my mother told me about what had happened thirty-odd years ago. She'd been scheduled to stay in Boston overnight for a mandatory public school teacher's conference, but when the day's duties were finished early, my mother decided to come home that night and not the next morning. She thought my father would be pleasantly surprised — this was her exact thought when she walked into the kitchen and saw a woman sitting on her stove top, a pretty blond woman with her dress pushed way, way up her white, white legs, which were — as they said in some of my mother's books — akimbo. My father was standing between the woman's legs. His pants weren't down at his ankles yet, but they soon would have been. You didn't need to be a genius to know it was going to happen.

"She loves to cook, but not like this," my father said to the woman, and they laughed identical, low, gurgling laughs deep down in their throats. The "she" who loved to cook, but not like this, was my mother. You didn't need to be a genius to know that, either.

"Where was I when all this happened?" I asked.

"You were upstairs, sleeping. I remember that. I remember not wanting to wake you up. I remember telling the woman to get out of my house, but quietly, so I wouldn't wake you up. And she did."

"You said that same thing when I was a kid, the day Dad left us."

"I said what?"

"'She loved to cook, but not like this.' You said that."

"I did?" she said, opening her eyes for the first time since beginning the story.

"After you'd burned my sandwich."

"That's funny," she said. "I don't remember that. I remember so many things, but not that."

"What did Dad say?"

"He said that he was drunk and that it didn't mean anything and that he loved me and that this was the first time it had happened and that it would never happen again."

"He did," I said, recognizing most of his words as mine and feeling so ashamed—for the bad things I'd done and the borrowed words I'd used to excuse them. Why is it we can't find our own words for the bad things we do? Is that part of what makes them so bad? "What did you do next?"

"I kicked him out."

"I thought you kicked him out because he couldn't decide what he wanted to do for a living and he was pathetic and driving you nuts."

"That's just what I wanted you to think. I really kicked him out because he was cheating on me."

"Did you love him?"

"Yes," she said immediately, just as my father had when I asked him if he loved my mother. My parents were certain they loved each other, and yet look at how they'd turned out. Maybe it would be better not to be so certain. Maybe love, and marriage, and life, and maybe anything that matters, would work out better if we weren't so certain about them.

"Mom," I said, "why did Dad come back?"

"Because I let him," my mother said. "Because he said he'd made a terrible mistake. Because he missed us. Because he said he loved me and not that woman on the stove. Because he said he would never, ever see her again."

"And you believed him," I said.

"I did," she said, and I could hear the voice the bartender no doubt heard when my mother talked about my father, the voice that wanted the story she told about her husband to be the truth, and the truth to be just a story. "I still do."

"Mom," I said, as gently as I could, "you live in another apartment in another town. You come back to the house to drink, but then when it's time to go to bed, you drive to your apartment. On Tuesday nights you don't come home at all. There must be a good reason."

"There must be," she said, nodding.

"What is it?"

She closed her eyes again, as though trying to remember the lies she'd told herself for so many years and now wanted to tell me. She kept her eyes closed for so long this time that I thought she'd fallen asleep. Then suddenly she opened them and said, "The apartment is a place for me to get away, that's all."

"Get away from what?" I asked, because I wasn't going to let it go. Because like Socrates and his method, I wasn't going to let my mother get out of this conversation without her giving me the answer I wanted.

"From life," she said.

"So what was our house for?"

"A place to come back to," she said. "For you, too." She got up, tucked her tray under her arm, and said, "Time to get back to work."

"I know about Deirdre," I told her, because I wanted everything out in the open, where we could see it, where we couldn't ignore it anymore, and as I'll say in my arsonist's guide, once you get everything out in the open, you wonder why, oh, why would you ever want *that.*

"How do you know about her?" My mother was trying to remain calm, but it was a losing battle. She went fierce and far away in the eyes, as though she'd just spotted her enemy from a great distance. She raised her tray and held it in front of her chest like a shield. "How do you even know her name?"

"I met her at our house," I said.

"Our house," she repeated, trancelike. "When?"

"This morning," I said. "I know you think it was me who burned down those houses. But it wasn't. I think it was Deirdre." I'm not sure my mother even heard this last part, though, because this is the way the human mind works, or doesn't: when it understands that the worst thing has happened, it can't think about the second- or third- or fourth-worst thing until it takes care of the first-worst thing, either by making it better or by making it even worse.

"You weren't ever supposed to know about her," my mother said. "He promised."

"That's why you sent me off to college, isn't it?" I asked. "You knew Dad would go back to her, and you didn't want me to find out."

"He *promised*," my mother said.

"I don't understand why you didn't just divorce him," I told her. "Why didn't you just end it and move on?"

"Why didn't you just tell Anne Marie about the fire you set?" my mother wanted to know. "Why didn't you tell her about the Colemans, about me, and about your father?"

I didn't answer her; I didn't need to. Because we both knew that sometimes the lies you tell are less frightening than the loneliness you might feel if you stopped telling them. My mother was too scared to get a divorce, and I was too scared to tell Anne Marie the truth. It was that simple. Sometimes there *is* a simple answer. Sometimes things aren't complicated at all.

After a moment she placed the tray on the empty barstool, took off her apron, and put it on the tray. "Last week you asked me why I got rid of my books," she said, looking me in the eyes. She was Elizabeth again, the mother she used to be, except there was a look of wild desperation in her eyes, and that scared me more than ever. "Do you really want to know why?"

"Yes."

"Because," she said, "they were always full of people like me, and her, and him and you and it."

"It?" I asked.

"The house," she said. "*Our* fucking house." She said it the way Ahab might say to Ishmael, "*Our* fucking whale," and now I understood, for the first time, why Melville had him talk about the whale so many times, over so many pages, and why my mother had made me read the book, so many times, over so many years. To my mother, *our* house was more than just its roof and walls and the furniture inside them, just as Moby Dick was more than just its blubber to Ahab.

"Beth," the bartender said, "would you bring these drinks over to table twelve?"

"No," she said, and then she walked away from both of us, toward the door. There was a blue peacoat draped over an empty chair, and she grabbed it and put it on, even though I was pretty sure it wasn't hers. She opened the door and the wind whipped her hair around.

"Where are you going?" I yelled.

"To see your father," she yelled back, without turning around, before closing the door behind her.

"What did you do to Beth?" the bartender asked when she was gone, and then, before I could think of a concise answer, he said, "You've had enough," and he snatched my last, half-consumed beer away from me. He was right. I'd had enough; everyone had had enough, that was clear. Maybe that's why Deirdre wanted to meet me at the Emily Dickinson House: maybe she'd had enough, too.

25

It was twenty minutes before midnight when I got to where the Emily Dickinson House used to be. The place looked much different at night than it had in the daytime just a few days earlier. There was easily a half foot of snow on the ground, but it had stopped falling sometime earlier, and the sky had cleared, so that you could name the stars above, assuming you'd learned their names in the first place. It was windier than before, though, and the scattered clouds were racing across the sky, and the spindly birches were waving in the wind and sometimes knocking into their neighboring white pines and maples. One of the nearby streetlights sent its flickering glow through the trees, and I kept expecting to hear an organ and see Vincent Price emerge from the shadows. Plus, there was a bone-chilling *hoo, hoo* sound coming from somewhere nearby, the classic sound of a haunting, although it could just have been the sound fraternity brothers make while ritually beating their pledges. The sound was spooky, whoever was making it.

I made my way through the trees until I found Deirdre standing next to a wooden bench, a bench no doubt meant to commemorate the Emily Dickinson House. Deirdre was early, too. She was wearing a red jacket and a red scarf and red gloves and a red ski hat, all obviously part of a matching set. And this will also go in my arsonist's guide: if you want to appear menacing, then don't wear a matching set. Deirdre was the least spooky thing about the place.

"Sam," she said, "how does it feel to be back here?"

"It feels excellent," I said. "Terrific. Why am I here?"

Deirdre looked confused. Her face puckered, an expression you might find attractive if you were looking to be attracted. I could imagine my father finding it attractive. Her hair was long and blond, as my mother remembered it, almost down to her shoulders, and Deirdre stroked it nervously with one of her gloved hands. "You're here because I asked you to meet me here."

"I know that," I said, "but *why* did you ask me to meet you here in the first place?"

Right then the birch trees started creaking and swaying, double time, in an uptick of wind, making such a racket that Deirdre and I momentarily forgot what we were saying and looked at them. They were silvery white and so different from the trees around them. The pines and maples were all clumped together and sturdy, but the birches were thin and lonely, each of them far apart and like an only child among larger, happier broods. I knew from Mr. Frost that the birch was supposed to be the most New England of trees, and if that was so, then I couldn't help thinking that New England was a very bad idea.

Then the wind died down and the birches stopped making their noises and we returned to our conversation, which was, basically, why was I there?

"Because this was where the Emily Dickinson House was, Sam," Deirdre said very slowly, as if I were having trouble keeping up. "You burned her house down. It's *ironic*."

"You're right, it is ironic," I said, except I wasn't talking about the house: I was talking about Deirdre herself. She was clearly my double, my doppelganger in bumbling. She and I were our own matching set. I wondered if my father had fallen in love with her because she was like me, and fallen out of love with my mother because she wasn't, and if love itself wasn't something we, the products of love, then make impossible for our parents because we can truly be like only one of them. Maybe this is why people have more than one child: so that neither of the parents will feel jealous and lonely.

"Does my father know you've asked me to meet you here?"

"He doesn't know anything about anything," Deirdre said. "He doesn't want to see me anymore."

"Why not?"

"Because of you," Deirdre said. Her voice shifted when she said that, and I could tell Deirdre's hatred for me was the only thing preventing her from crying. "Because after what happened at the house, he felt ashamed. He said he couldn't do it anymore. He told me he couldn't ever see me again, and no matter how much we loved each other, it was over."

"Maybe you're not really in love."

"We were in love," Deirdre said. "Things were good."

"They weren't so good for my mother."

"Things were good," she insisted, "until you came home and messed everything up."

"Deirdre," I said, "did you try to burn down the Edward Bellamy House?"

As I said earlier, I've now become something of a reader and have read my fair share of detective novels and even a few essays on how to write detective novels, and so I now know that this shouldn't have worked: you can never ask a suspect if she's guilty, and you can never expect her to confess if she is; you must catch your suspect in the act, red handed. I know this now, and next time, if there is a next time, I'll do things differently and by the book. But remember, I was a bumbler and didn't know that I couldn't ask this sort of question, and Deirdre was a bumbler and didn't know that she couldn't answer it.

"I tried to," she said, dropping her face into her red-gloved hands.

"How about the Mark Twain House?"

"I tried to," she repeated, her voice muffled in her gloves. "I just can't do anything right."

"Why did you do it?"

"Because I knew this would happen," she said, lifting her head out of her hands and looking straight at me. "I knew when you came home, Bradley would feel guilty and get rid of me and go back to your mother. I had to do something."

"So you tried to set fire to those houses, thinking I'd get blamed for it," I guessed.

"I can't do anything right," she said, weeping. Deirdre was wrong here, of course; Detective Wilson was running around trying to blame me for the fires and prove exactly how wrong Deirdre was. I hated Deirdre right then for doing what she'd done to me and my mother and father and even those homes, too. But I also empathized, because she'd tried to do these things out of love, and because she had bumbled the attempt, and I suppose this — the ability to empathize with the people we hate — is exactly the quality that makes us human beings, which makes you wonder why anybody would want to be one.

"Sam," Deirdre said, and I could already hear the desperate pleading in the way she said my name, could hear the way her voice was sandwiched between too much hope and too much grief. I knew what Deirdre was going to ask, and I was glad, because I knew how I would respond, knew I would answer with that mean little hammer of a word, that word that gives its speaker a feeling of the purest satisfaction, always followed soon enough by a feeling of the purest regret.

"No," I said, for my mother.

"Your father is home right now."

"No," I said, for myself.

"I want you to go home and tell your father to take me back. You know he loves me. You can save us. He wouldn't have done this for all these years if he didn't love me so much, if I weren't the one he really loved."

"No," I said, for my father, even though — or because — I knew Deirdre was right.

"You can have the three thousand dollars, the money in the enve-lope," she said. I could hear the last gasp in her voice, the sad whine of it. "Please, Sam."

"No, no, no," I told her, by which I also meant, *Revenge, revenge, revenge.*

When I said my last no, Deirdre seemed to get tired, very tired. Her arms dropped to her sides and her shoulders slumped. "No," she repeated dully, then reached behind the bench, picked up a red plastic gasoline can, and held it up in front of her, neck high, as though it were some sort of offering. I immediately wanted to take back everything I'd just said, wanted to take back each and every no, wanted to turn each no into a yes, the way Jesus supposedly turned water into wine, a loaf of bread into food for a crowd. And why did he do that? Was it because he was worried about his people, or about himself? Was it because he didn't know if his people could live on only bread and water, or because he didn't know if he could live with himself if he let them?

"Deirdre," I said, trying to be very calm, "I didn't really mean all that."

"Maybe you did."

"Maybe I didn't," I said. "Please put down the gas can."

"I don't want to live without your father, Sam," Deirdre said. "I feel so dead without him."

"Maybe you'll meet someone else," I said.

"Maybe I don't want to meet someone else," she said, and then she raised the gas can over her head and tipped it, dumping the contents on her head, letting it run in streams down her back and front. This happened so suddenly that I didn't have time to do or say anything. Or at least this is what I tell myself. Because after all, I'd seen the gas can, and what did I think she was going to do with it? Was what happened next because of what Deirdre did, or because of what I didn't do? Are we defined by what we do, or by what we don't? Wouldn't it be better not to be defined at all?

"Good-bye, Sam," she said. "Please forgive your father. That poor man loves you so much." Then she pulled out a lighter, flicked it, and grabbed a clump of her hair. Deirdre was setting herself on fire, not starting at the feet the way the people at Salem did to their supposed witches, but starting with her hair. With her hair. Even now, seven years later, it's the memory of Deirdre clutching her hair and setting it on fire — the dry *snick* of the lighter; the way Deirdre tugged on her hair, as though she were a child whose hair was being pulled by an especially mean teacher or classmate; the way burning hair makes the smell of gasoline almost welcome, like perfume; the terrible, sad, patient look on Deirdre's face as she waited for the fire to creep up her hair toward her head, her face; the way her face screamed and then disappeared in the fire; the way I stood there, watching her do it — it's that memory that wakes me up from a deep sleep shouting and crying, or prevents me from falling into one in the first place. If I could pick one moment, one detail I wish I couldn't remember, it's this one, and that is another thing I'll put in my arsonist's guide: detail exists not only to make us remember the things we don't want to, but to remind us that there are some things we don't deserve to forget.

"Deirdre, don't!" I yelled, but who knows if she actually heard me. By then the flames had already crawled up the wick of her hair, and her hat burst into flames. And then her head was on fire, her head *was* fire, a ball of fire, and for a moment it was the only part of Deirdre on fire. The rest of her body was standing still, and her head, on fire, was cocked to the side as if she were listening to her own inner voice, except that her inner voice wasn't asking, *What else? What else?* but instead was telling her, *Nothing, nothing.*

"Sam, do something!" I heard a voice say, but it wasn't my voice, it wasn't that voice inside me, it was Detective Wilson's, who was all of a sudden right next to me. He, as I found out later, had read the note in the envelope after all and knew to show up at midnight. And he had. But I had shown up early, and so had Deirdre, and she was on fire because of it. Together, Detective Wilson and I ran toward her. Detective Wilson tackled her, and she landed with a hiss in the snow. "Give me your coat!" he yelled (he was only wearing his hooded sweatshirt). I did, and he started patting Deirdre down with it, saying soft, comforting things to her under his breath as he patted.

"This is your fucking fault, Sam," he said to me over his shoulder. I caught a glimpse of Deirdre lying there: her red jacket had turned black, and her face had turned black, too. The only thing of hers not black and scorched were her eyes: they were white and blank and staring skyward, at the birches, at the stars, or at nothing. I looked away and then at the gas can lying next to her body. I could tell, even in the darkness, that it was one I'd helped design back when I was still a person who designed things. And then I looked away from the gas can, too, and closed my eyes. They immediately started to tear up, tears being your eyes' way of forbidding you to look away, of forcing you to look at the world you've made or unmade.

"It wasn't me," I said, and started backing away, the way we do when we're not brave enough to do anything else. "She set herself on fire."

"Fuck you anyway," Detective Wilson said, still furiously patting her through my coat. "I *saw* her do it. So what? You didn't fucking stop her."

"She asked me to meet her here," I said. "She wanted me to save her and my father."

"You could have saved her," he said, and I realized that he had started crying, crying being that thing you do when you've done everything else, and then *I* started crying, crying also being that thing you do when you haven't done enough and you're afraid it's too late to start.

"Is she dead?" I asked.

"You could have saved her," Detective Wilson said, "and you didn't."

At that, I turned and broke into a sprint. Deirdre had wanted me to save her and I showed up too early and didn't. But Deirdre had also wanted me to save my father. My mother was only a few blocks away, at our house, with him. I ran as fast as I could, but even so, when I got there I was too late.

26

You wouldn't expect a burning house to look like a burning woman, and you'd be right: it doesn't. There is nothing beautiful about a woman on fire, but there is plenty that is beautiful about a house burning hot and high in the dark, cold night: the way flames shoot out of the chimney like a Roman candle; the way the asphalt roof shingles sizzle and pop; the way the smoke pours and pours and pours heavenward like a message to the house's great beyond. There is something celebratory about a house fire, which is why so many people always gather to watch it, just as there were so many people gathered to watch my parents' house burn that night. The crowd was three or four deep, and I had to push my way through, jostling and shoving until I got to the front row, next to my mother, who was standing there, holding a forty-ounce Knickerbocker, regarding the fire thoughtfully, as though it were an especially difficult question that she was *this* close to solving.

"There you are," she said. She offered me a sip of her beer and I took it, took more than a sip, then gave the can back to her. The wind shifted and the smoke blew toward us, and the crowd bent over, as one, until the wind shifted back and we all resumed our upright fire-watching position. There were firefighters everywhere now, looking puny and laughable with their axes and their floppy hoses. Even their helmets looked like a joke version of red next to the real red of the fire. The house was looking bigger and bigger, as though the flames were its fourth and fifth stories.

"Here I am," I told my mother. We were surrounded by people, at least ten people within earshot, but their hearing and all their other senses were fully devoted to the fire. Something exploded in the house — the furnace, maybe — and there was a terrible shriek of something metal becoming something not. The people in the crowd shrieked in response to the house, and the house shrieked back at them, the heat stoking the noise. I wasn't worried about anyone listening to us when they could be listening to the house. "Where's Dad?"

"It was so easy," my mother said. She was talking calmly, evenly, and I would have found this creepy and awful if I hadn't been listening calmly, evenly, myself. And how could I have been so calm? you might want to know. I don't have a good answer, not even now, seven years after the fact. Was it because of what had just happened to Deirdre? Was I think- ing that nothing could be worse than Deirdre's setting herself on fire? Was I thinking that no matter what happened to my father, it couldn't have been as bad as what happened to Deirdre? When the worst thing happens, does it then make us calm in expectation of better things, or does it just prepare us for the next worst thing? "I dumped gasoline on the couch and lit it," my mother said. "That's all I needed to do."

"Mom," I said, "where is Dad?"

"I lit some of the curtains, too, in the dining room, just in case. But I didn't need to. It was so easy. I didn't expect it to be so easy."

"Mom," I said, "where is my dad?"

"Why wasn't it more difficult?" my mother asked, still calm. "Shouldn't some things be difficult?"

This was the scariest thing my mother had said thus far. She'd set our house on fire; I knew that. That wasn't so scary. But it came so easily to her, as easily as reading a book or busing a table or drinking a beer or pretending she had a happy family — that was the scary part. My mother is the most capable person I have ever met, even more capable than Anne Marie. She could do anything she wanted, which was why she'd always scared me and still does.

"Mom," I said, very, very slowly so that she'd understand me, so that there would be no confusion. "Dad left Deirdre to be with us. To be with you. He loves Deirdre, but he's chosen you and me."

"I know," my mother said, turning away from the fire and toward me. The fire lit up the left side of her face, making it glow, while the right side looked so cold, so white in comparison. "He told me the very same thing. He said he wanted me to come home. He said he really meant it this time. He said I could believe him." Then she turned back to the fire, her whole face glowing with the heat and the light, and I was glad, because she looked beautiful. I wanted her to look beautiful, and maybe this is what all children want: for their parents to look beautiful. And in order for them to look beautiful, you have to find ways to ignore their ugliness. It is easier to be ugly yourself than to admit to the ugliness of the people who made you; it is easier to love the people who made you if you are ugly and they are not. And it is easier to live on this earth if you love the people who made you, even if that means risking the love of the people you yourself have made. Even if.

"Sam," said a familiar voice behind me. I didn't have to turn around to see who it was or to know what I had to tell him. Because I could also hear another voice, not my inner voice, not the voice that said, *What else?* and not Deirdre's voice, the one that told her, *Nothing*, but Anne Marie's voice, telling me that it was time to take responsibility for something, for *everything*.

"It was me," I said, not looking at Detective Wilson, still looking at my mother — who was looking at her house and her fire — still thinking about Deirdre's burning herself to death and my doing nothing to save her. "I did it." My mother didn't say anything; she kept staring at the fire, as if she knew that it was making her beautiful, as if fire were the best kind of makeup.

"You set fire to your parents' house before you went to meet Deirdre," Detective Wilson said, helping me out. "Before you watched Deirdre burn herself to death, you set fire to your home." I was still looking at my mother when he said this. She closed her eyes for one, two, three beats and then opened them again. For years, my mother must have hated Deirdre; for years she must have wished her dead. And now that Deirdre was dead, my mother looked no different than she had when she thought Deirdre was alive — not guilty, nor relieved, nor happy. How was this possible? How could my mother know Deirdre was dead and still look at the world as if it were the same world, at the fire as though it were the same fire? But maybe this is what happens when you hate someone for so long: the person you hate dies, but the hate stays with you, to keep you company. Maybe if I'd hated Deirdre for longer, I wouldn't have felt so bad about not saving her.

"That's right," I told Detective Wilson. "I burned my parents' house. It was me."

"You were the one who tried to burn down the Edward Bellamy House. And the next day, you left the letter with that old man."

"Mr. Frazier," I said. "That's right, I did."

"And then you tried to burn down the Mark Twain House. That's where all that money came from in the envelope. And you left your driver's license with the people who paid you to do it."

"Yes," I said, "I did."

"People saw you at the Robert Frost Place the day you burned it. You made quite a scene."

"I told my story," I said. "That's true. And I left the letters behind at the other four fires. I wanted to get caught. You were right about that."

"You set all the fires," Detective Wilson said. "This fire and all the other ones, too."

"All of them," I said.

"Sam," he said softly, "is your father inside that house?"

"He is," I said quickly, before I could give myself time to think about what I was admitting to, and this is another thing I'll put in my arsonist's guide: the mouth moves fast because the mind will not.

"I suppose you're going to tell me you didn't know he was in there when you set the fire. That it was an accident."

I took a deep breath. There was that word, my very favorite: I held it in my mouth for a second, savoring it, knowing that I would miss it so much when it was gone, miss it the way I would miss my father, the way I already did, the way I still do, the way I always will. "It wasn't an accident," I finally said.

"Thank you," Detective Wilson said, his voice full of relief. I was happy for him, happy to give him the illusion that he'd gotten something right and was no longer a bumbler. And for that matter, now that I'd taken some responsibility, I didn't feel like a bumbler anymore, either. It felt as though bumbling was a disease for which we'd found a cure.

"You're welcome," I said.

"You finally told the truth," he said.

"I really did."

"Doesn't it feel better to tell the truth?" Detective Wilson asked, but then he yanked my hands behind my back and cuffed them before I could decide whether it felt better or not.

27

So here I am again, in prison, a medium-security one this time. This time I'm not locked up with white-collar criminals, and not really blue-collar ones, either, since none of my fellow inmates seems to have had the sort of job on the outside that would require him to wear blue-collared shirts. But the story of the soft hero doing hard time is one you've heard before, so I won't bother to tell it to you here. Besides, I'm nearly a third of the way through my twenty years (the rest of the sentence says "to life," but who can think about that and still care about living it?), and my time hasn't been all that hard so far. The other inmates know I'm writing a book, that I'm telling my story, and they respect that and pretty much leave me alone. After all, they can't stop telling their own stories, either: to one another, the guards, their families, their lawyers, the parole board. Even if they've never actually read a story before, they can't bring themselves to stop telling their own. Who knows, maybe this lack of reading will help them the way all my reading and my mother's reading didn't exactly help us. I wish them well.

It's hard to write in here, though, harder than you'd think. For one thing, I get letters, lots and lots of them. Wesley and Lees Mincher (they're married now and she's taken his name) write me every month or so, always on English Department letterhead, and always demanding their three thousand dollars back. I write them back and tell them that

I appreciate their testifying against me in exchange for their immunity from prosecution, and that the three thousand dollars have gone the way of my parents' house and they're out of luck. They don't seem to believe me; they seem to think that, as in *The Adventures of Tom Sawyer*, I've hidden their treasure in some cave. At least that's what I think they think. It's hard to tell from their letters. When Wesley writes them, the letters are so thick with verbiage that you need an explanatory footnote just to understand his "Dear's" and "Sincerely's." And when Lees writes, she calls me a cunt so often I've started to think that's her nickname for me, the way Coleslaw was for the Mirabellis. Other than their missing three thousand dollars, however, they seem happy.

Once in a while, I get letters from Peter Le Clair. He, too, testified against me in exchange for immunity and feels guilty about that in the extreme. I know this because his letters say, "Sorry," and that's all they say. I send him long letters back about nothing in particular, just so he'll have something to read besides his library books, and then something to burn in his woodstove once he's through with them. Occasionally, after sending him one of these letters, I get one back that says, "Thanks," which I appreciate.

Mr. Frazier didn't testify at my trial — maybe because he hadn't done anything wrong and had no need for the immunity they offered him — but I've not heard from him, not once, and since he seemed like a guy who would take great pride in writing long, formal letters with his antique fountain pen, I have a feeling he is dead and his house in Chicopee already broken up into apartments. Maybe he's with his brother, in some happier place. Last year I finally read that book his brother loved so — Edward Bellamy's *Looking Backward* — and Mr. Frazier was right: it's about a utopia, a perfect, egalitarian Boston of the future, so perfect that I found it wide eyed and goofy and more than a little boring. But if that's where Mr. Frazier and his brother want to be, who am I to say they shouldn't?

That's not all: every day I get letters and more letters, not just from people who are angry about the houses I confessed to burning, but also about the houses I *didn't* burn. For instance, I keep getting letters from a woman who's furious that I tried to burn down the Mark Twain House but not the Harriet Beecher Stowe House, which was right next door. I didn't know that, as I've explained to her in my letters over and over again, but she won't listen. She insists that I didn't think enough of Stowe as a writer to burn down her house and how this is just *typical* and another slap in the face for Stowe and for women readers and writers everywhere, another example of how the world undervalues Stowe and her novel *Uncle Tom's Cabin* and overvalues Twain and his books. If there were any justice in the world, she writes, I would have torched Stowe's house and not Twain's. I agree with her, every time, but this doesn't stop her from writing her angry letters, each of which she signs "Professor Smiley," which I can only assume is a pseudonym.

So the letters keep me busy, as do my many visitors. The bond analysts visit me once a week because they feel so bad that I've taken the fall for them; they successfully blamed me for the fires they set, and this makes them feel guilty, not happy at all. They don't understand that I've taken the fall for them intentionally, willingly, that this is a sacrifice and not a mistake. They don't understand this because sacrifice is an alien concept to them, having made only one sacrifice themselves.

"Take our story," they tell me. "You've already taken the blame for our fires; go ahead and take credit for it now. Write a book about it. We owe you one, dude; you have our permission."

"But what about the truth?" I ask them. "'Just tell the truth, dude. You'll feel better afterward.' Remember that?"

They laugh at that one every time; the bond analysts found that telling the truth was as unsatisfying as burning down houses or writing a book, and they're now back to analyzing bonds, whatever that means. But once a week they take time out of their busy schedules to visit me and help me write my arsonist's guide. They tell me the best way to burn what sort of writer's house, when you should pour gas down the chimney and when you should just throw a Molotov cocktail through the window, and what sort of life lessons readers might learn from each method. They remind me, too, that my arsonist's guide is also a memoir and that one can't write a memoir without a troubled childhood. Except they don't think my childhood, as troubled as it was, was troubled enough. They want me to make one up. Mostly they want me to blame my father, who isn't around to defend himself or protect his story. I tell the bond analysts that I love my father and I miss him and I don't want to say anything about him that's untrue and hurtful. They think this is ridiculous and won't have any of it. So to get them off my back, I write sentences like this: "My father abused me as a child; no doubt that abuse contributed to my desire, in my later years, to burn." This pleases them, and it also pleases me: because if I were to tell the truth about my father, if I were to say, *My father did some bad things, but I still love him, I still miss him so much,* and if I were to tell the truth about Deirdre, if I were to say, *My father loved another woman and I hated her for it, and so I let her die,* I would start crying and never stop. If you tell the truth, you will start crying and never stop, and what good will that do you, or anyone else for that matter? Besides, would anyone want to read a true story that made you start crying and never stop? Would *you* want to read such a story? Would you read it because it was true, or because it made you cry? Or would it make you cry because you thought it was true? And what would you do, what would you feel, who would you blame, if you found out it wasn't?

Maybe one day I'll know the answers to these questions, but for now I tell lies about my father and pass them off as the truth, and this makes the bond analysts happy. But it also fills them with nostalgia: when I read to them from my arsonist's guide, I can see the bond analysts gaze longingly into the distance, as if my memoir is a ship at sea, and their bonds are the shore.

To be honest, though, I'm not just writing *one* book; I'm writing two of them. Both books begin with "I, Sam Pulsifer . . . ," and then one of them tells the story you know by now, and the other one is my arsonist's guide; one is the story of the one house I actually burned and the ones I didn't, and the other one is about how I *did* burn those houses and the details and lessons therein. I plan on calling the story you know a novel, and the arsonist's guide a memoir. Why write both books? Maybe I just want the best of both worlds, which is exactly what both worlds usually *don't* want you to have, and the bond analysts aren't entirely sure they want me to have it, either, which is why they insist I call the story that includes them a novel and the story that doesn't a memoir. They tell me, "You need to protect the innocent, dude," which is what the guilty always say when they need to be protected.

And then there is Thomas Coleman. He's living with Anne Marie and the kids now, but when he visits, he and I never talk about them. He comes by himself, every other week. Thomas has put on some weight: I can see the buttons on his shirt strain a little with his new gut, can see his shirt collar creep up and crowd his jowls, too. He always comes on Monday, always with a red face, always with that suburban man's week-end yard-work tan, and I can imagine him on my self-propelled mower; no doubt he keeps his shirt on, and no doubt the other Camelotians like him for that. But we don't talk about any of that stuff, either. We don't talk about whether he knew, or suspected, that Deirdre had set those fires. We don't really talk about anything at all when Thomas visits: we sit there in silence, just two ordinary men with fires and dead parents in their pasts, and a common family in their present, and who knows what in their future, and hearts with holes in them, holes that are in various stages of excavation and filling. I don't understand why he visits me; when he does, I am sorry to see him come, and then I'm sorry to see him go. I don't understand that, either.

Then there are Anne Marie and the kids. Sometimes Anne Marie brings the kids with her and sometimes she comes by herself. When all three of them are there, I talk to Katherine and Christian about their days and what goes on in them. Katherine is fifteen years old now, beautiful and tall and dark haired like her mother and something of a model citizen, too. Last week when they visited, I learned that she'd just been chosen to go to Girl's State.

"I'm so proud of you," I said.

"Thank you," she said.

"What's the difference between Girl's State and Boy's State?" I asked her.

"You must be kidding, right?" she asked back, and I said, "Yes," because I must have been.

Christian is twelve years old, smack in the middle of the age of balls and bats. It's not clear he can speak about anything else, and because we have so little time together, I don't ask him to. Recently he's become obsessed with athletic footwear and its latest innovations. For basketball, Christian told me last week, the soles of his shoes are filled with air; for baseball and soccer, his shoes have spikes that are made of something that isn't metal and isn't plastic, either.

"What are they made of, then?" I wanted to know.

Christian thought about this for a minute, hard. He has a head like mine, outsize for his body and a little blockish, and I could see it begin to corkscrew with the effort of his thinking. Finally he gave up and said, "Something *safe.*"

"I hope so," I told him, and then, because I could sense the guard behind me about to remind us of the time and how we were out of it, I told them both, as I always do, "I love you," and they both nodded, as *they* always do. A nod means, *Yes, we love you, too, Dad,* among children who are too shy to tell their father that they love him even though there are so many reasons not to. Everyone knows that the nod is the same as an "I love you, too." This is the most common kind of knowledge. Is it not?

When the kids are around, Anne Marie and I don't talk much. But when she comes by herself, as she did yesterday, we have plenty to say. They're things we've said already, many, many times, although the questions don't seem to lose their interest because of the repetition. I ask if she's OK, if she has enough money, and she tells me yes, yes, she's fine. I know they've promoted her to full-time manager at the home-supply superstore, and so I ask her about that, and she tells me about lumber that was supposed to be pressure treated and wasn't, or that wasn't supposed to be but was. I ask her if Thomas is still living at the house, and she tells me that he is, and I ask her why, and she tells me the truth: "Because we have a lot in common."

"Like what?"

"Like you've hurt both of us a lot." I don't say anything more to this, because I know there is nothing a victimized woman loves more than a victimized man, and because I also know that what she says is true. She doesn't ask me about the fires themselves or the people who died in them, about why I did what I did or why I did what she thinks I did — maybe out of kindness, maybe out of sadness, or maybe because she can't stand to think about them more than she already has and does. I will never tell her the truth about those fires, because that would mean I'd have to admit that I lied to her, again, again, and I know how much that would hurt her, and maybe this is what it means to take responsibility for something: not to tell the truth, but to make sure you pick a lie for a good reason and then stick to it. In any case, we don't talk about any of that. It's safer to talk about Thomas, and so that's what we do.

"He's really good to the kids, Sam," Anne Marie says.

"I'm glad."

"He's good to me, too."

"OK," I tell her.

"I'm sorry," she always says, and I always ask her what I asked my mother that first night I moved back home, seven years ago now: "What happens to love?" I asked her, my mother, and now I ask Anne Marie.

"I don't know," Anne Marie says, just telling the truth, that being just one of the many enduring qualities that makes me love her, still, still.

"I still love you," I tell her.

"Well, me, too," she says, by which she means, I think, that love endures, but that it isn't everything, and it isn't ever what we want it to be, which was probably what those books my mother made me read and then got rid of were trying to tell me, and us, which was just one of the reasons she got rid of them.

Speaking of my mother, she doesn't visit me much. The prison is two hours northeast of Springfield and hard to get to if you don't have a car, which my mother doesn't anymore. She doesn't have a license, either. My mother lost both in a drunk-driving accident, two weeks after I came here. She's moved out of her place in Belchertown and into my old apartment, the one above the Student Prince, so she can walk to work and not drive and still drink.

So my mother doesn't visit me much, but she does take the bus up at least once a year, for my birthday. I turned forty-five just last week, and she brought me a present: a worn, creased, used-up copy of Hawthorne's *The Blithedale Romance*.

"Happy birthday," she said.

"Thank you," I said. "How did this thing get so beat up?"

"I have no idea," she said, but she did have an idea, and so do I. My mother is reading again, the way you always return to something you've quit, like drinking, which my mother hasn't done. Quit, that is. I know that, too: I can always smell the Knickerbocker on her breath, her clothes, coming out of her pores. But I don't tell her what I know, and I don't tell her that I've already read and reread the book since I've been in prison. It's about a utopian community, about how a group of people in Massachusetts tried to become one big, happy family and failed completely.

"Thanks a lot," I told her. The guard came over and made sure I hadn't been given contraband, saw that it was only a book, and then left us alone. Once he was gone, I asked my mother, "Do I look forty-five?"

"Absolutely," she said. "Do I look sixty-six?"

I didn't answer. To be true, she looks older than sixty-six. She's still thin but looks stooped and wizened now, not fit at all. Her hair is mostly gray, and her face looks grayer, too, and lined with deep wrinkles, the sort no cream can make vanish. She looks like an old woman who was once beautiful. Maybe it's all the drinking that's aged her so. Or maybe it's my father; not necessarily that she killed him, but that she hoped once she'd killed him, things would change and she would stop loving him so much, stop hating him so much, stop missing him, stop feeling so lonely, and she hasn't. But my mother never talks about my father, and I don't ask her about him, either. And for that matter, my mother has never asked me about Deirdre. She knows that Deirdre killed herself. But she's never asked me for details, never asked me why I was with Deirdre that night in the first place. She's never asked how I feel about Deirdre's being dead, about my not saving her. You never ask your son how he feels about the suicide of his father's lover, just as you never ask your mother how she feels about killing your father, just as you never answer your mother when she asks whether she looks her age.

"You never answer your mother when she asks whether she looks her age," I told her.

"I suppose that's going in the arsonist's guide, too," she said.

Because my mother knows about the arsonist's guide, and the other book, too. I've told her all about them, let her read the rough drafts of some of my chapters, too, and already she's started giving me advice: about what in the books seems softhearted and softheaded; about whether I'm as big a bumbler as I say I am, or whether I'm an even bigger one. But mostly she doesn't seem to know *what* to say about the books. Maybe that's why she's started reading books in general again, so that she'll know what to say about mine.

"I have to go," she said, getting up from her chair. "My bus leaves in a half hour."

"OK."

"Are you behaving yourself?"

"I am."

"Please behave yourself, Sam," she said. "I want you to come home to me." Then my mother stood up, kissed me on the cheek, and left me sitting in the visiting room until, maybe, my next birthday.

Because this is what my mother seems to want, more than anything: she wants me to come home to her. My mother knows that if I behave myself I'll be out in a little more than thirteen years. And when I do, she wants me to move in with her, into her new and my old apartment. There is a job waiting for me at the Student Prince — she's already cleared it with Mr. Goerman and Mr. Goerman's son, who was the bald, mustachioed bartender, apparently. I have a job washing dishes and busing tables, if I want it. My mother tells me that I could drink for free, which I admit, after twenty years of not drinking, would be a plus. I've made my mother no promises, but who knows? I'll be finished writing my books by the time I get out of prison, and maybe then I will be done telling that story for all time. And after you're done telling your story for all time, then who knows what happens next? Maybe I'll do what my mother wants: maybe I'll move in with her and take that job at the Student Prince. Maybe then we'll be happy. Maybe we'll live our lives quietly, and maybe we won't ever need to talk about the past, about the loves we've lost or the people we've killed or the fires we've set. Maybe we'll be like normal people, people who, after a long day's work, want to do nothing else but have a drink and read a book. And maybe, then, I'll be able to tell that story.

ACKNOWLEDGMENTS

Thanks to the following people, places, and things:

The very helpful and superbly titled *A Guide to Writers' Homes in New England* by Miriam Levine.

The great Student Prince Restaurant on Fort Street in Springfield, Massachusetts.

The Giustinas of Springfield and the Clarkes of Mashapaug, wherever you happen to be and under whatever aliases you happen to be traveling.

The Taft Fund, the Ohio Arts Council, and the University of Cincinnati for their financial support.

The editors of and at *New England Review, Vermont Literary Review, failbetter,* and Sarabande Books, who first published sections of this novel, often in dramatically different form.

Rupert Chisholm, former bond analyst.

Chuck Adams, Brunson Hoole, Michael Taeckens, Craig Popelars, and the rest of the good people at Algonquin, and my agent, Elizabeth Sheinkman.

And finally, to all my usual aiders and abetters: you know who you are.

AN ARSONIST'S GUIDE TO WRITERS' HOMES IN NEW ENGLAND

A Conversation with the Author

Reading Group Questions and Topics for Discussion

A CONVERSATION WITH THE AUTHOR

Sam Pulsifer: First, thank you for giving me the last name Pulsifer. I like the way it has the word *fire* in it, because there are fires in the book, of course, and also *Lucifer,* or, at least, *Lusifer.* Very clever.

Brock Clarke: Huh? I didn't intend that at all. It never occurred to me until you mentioned it.

SP: Why did you name me Pulsifer, then?

BC: Because I've only met two families with that last name, and they're both from New England.

SP: That's your reason? That's a terrible reason.

BC: I know, I know, it's pathetic.

SP: And you say I'm a bumbler.

BC: Let's move on, OK? Ask me something else.

SP: Where do you get your ideas?

BC: From all over. From other books, from overheard bits of conversation, from road signs, from friends, from enemies. But actually, those aren't ideas: they're material. I get my ideas from the same place everyone gets them: we have a library full of the things we care about, passionately—in the case of *An Arsonist's Guide,* I care passionately about books, about family, about New England—and we borrow from the library, transform (or, to push the library metaphor too far, deface) what we've borrowed to fit the needs of our characters, our places, their stories, until that which we've borrowed looks and sounds and feels somewhat different than what we originally borrowed. And then we call that thing a book.

SP: Hey, I went on Amazon.com and read some of the reviews that readers have written about the book. A lot of them love it and say great things about you. Others, though, really, really hate it, but usually instead of attacking you, they say hateful things about me, about how I'm a loser and they can't "identify" with me. You were the writer here—why are they attacking me, and why did you make it so people would hate me?

BC: It's funny. I don't think you're an unlikable character at all. Sure, you do some questionable things, but I think, I hope, you're entertaining while you're doing these questionable things. And some of them, after all, you do out of love, just as some of them you do out of fear, jealousy, self-interest. These are exactly the qualities I like in literary characters, and in people, too. I like characters and people not because they're *good,* but because they're complicated, because they're conflicted. No, I wouldn't say you're unlikable. I'm actually quite fond of you.

SP: I think you like my mother and father better than me.

BC: I like you all the same, Sam. I like you in different ways, for different reasons, but I don't like any one of you better than the others.

SP: Why did you put me in prison, then . . . *twice*?

BC: It made sense, dramatically speaking. Plus, you had it coming. You seemed to realize that.

SP: My mom and dad have a pretty rough time of it in the story, yet both of them come across almost more sympathetically than I do—and my dad cheated on my mom, which set all the bad stuff into motion, and then my mom caused the big problem at the end of the story. It's because of her I had to go to prison again. Do you think that all children have to suffer for their parents' sins, or is it just me?

BC: I don't think it's just you. I think all children, in some ways, bear the burdens of their parents' pasts, of the secrets their parents keep from them—often for good reason. And in the same way, parents are constantly forced to watch—sometimes mutely, sometimes not—as their children do the same ridiculous, self-destructive things that they themselves have done. We—parents and children—are fortunate in this way. We make the same mistakes, and so it's difficult for any one of us to feel superior. This is why we end up loving our parents, and children, so much. If we're not allowed to feel superior to them, we might as well go ahead and love them.

SP: You say I'm not unlikable. But is it safe to say that I'm unreliable?

BC: That's safe to say, to a point. To a point, all first-person narrators are unreliable, and you go a bit beyond that point. But I don't think you're totally unreliable. I think you're trying to find the truth behind all the stories told in the novel: all the stories about you, about all the people whom you hurt, all the people who hurt you, all the people who want you to burn down all those writers' homes in New England. I think you're trying honestly to figure out why people tell stories, what they want to get out of them, even though you're not always willing to admit to what you've found. You're unreliable, but you're trying hard not to be.

SP: I'll tell you what I think. I think that everything that happened in the novel exists only in my head. It's all my fantasy. I think I'm in prison for burning down the Emily Dickinson House the entire time. The novel is me in prison, imagining what might happen once I get out of prison.

BC: What? No! What are you talking about? Everything that happened in the novel really happened.

SP: Really happened? I thought that's the whole point. That nothing really happens in books. That all books are fantasy, even memoir. That people who say otherwise are fooling themselves.

BC: I suppose. But real things happen in the context of a book that's made up. The book is fiction, but we can understand things as meant literally within the fiction. Does that make sense?

SP: No. It sounds like the kind of thing a memoirist would say to defend stuff he, or she, made up instead of telling the truth.

BC: Now you're just being mean.

SP: You must be pretty pleased with yourself now that all these memoirists are getting caught lying in their memoirs.

BC: It gives me no pleasure at all.

SP: Why are you smiling then?

BC: That's just the way my face is. Seriously, every time I read about one of these memoirists who write memoirs that aren't memoirish enough, I think, *That would have made a good novel. Why didn't you just write a novel?*

SP: Is it safe to say that you don't like memoirs?

BC: It's safe to say that memoir is not my favorite genre.

SP: Is it safe to say that you hate every single book that's ever been written? That you think the world would be a better place without books?

BC: What? No, it's not safe to say that at all. I love books. I love the writers whose houses get burned in my novel. I love Mark Twain, Emily Dickinson, Robert Frost. I love every Edith Wharton novel except for *Ethan Frome*. That's just for starters. I can't imagine a world without books. I wouldn't want to imagine one. Just because I poke gentle fun at the literary world doesn't mean I don't want there to be one. Just because I poke gentle fun at you doesn't mean I'm sorry I made you.

SP: I suppose you're going to tell me that criticism is a form of love?

BC: I couldn't have said it better myself.

SP: What genre do you think this book falls into? I heard that you got asked to speak on a mystery writers' panel. When you sat down to write this book, did you know that you were writing a mystery, and is that what it is?

BC: I do think this book is a mystery, although I think it's a bunch of other things, too. But no, I didn't know I was writing a mystery at first, and I had a rough time with the novel because of it. It had no direction, no sense of mystery to guide it. That is why I've come to love mysteries. They give the reader and writer a sense of purpose: this guy needs to solve this mystery or else. And I thought it especially relevant in writing this book because you, Sam, don't know the first thing about mysteries, mostly because your mother never allowed you to read them as a kid. And so you're as much a bumbler at being a detective as you are at everything else. That was important to me because the one thing I distrust about some mysteries, some literary detectives, is that they're implausibly good at it. You, thankfully, were not.

SP: Now that you've told my story, what's next?

BC: I'm writing a book called *Exley.* It's about, in one way or another, the writer Frederick Exley, who wrote the book *A Fan's Notes,* which he called a "fictional memoir."

SP: Again with the memoir. Again with the writers. What makes this book different than mine?

BC: Well, for one, you're not in it. And no one burns down anything in it, I don't think. And there are no bond analysts running around, making life more difficult for the narrator of the new book. It's a totally different book, except, of course, that I'm the one writing it.

SP: What is up with those bond analysts, anyway? What are they doing in the book? They speak as a group. They steal other people's stories and try to pass them off as their own. They're ridiculous.

BC: That's why they're there. I wanted them in the book so that you would look better by comparison. It's easier to love someone if you have someone around who is so obviously less worthy of love.

SP: You're speaking in aphorisms again, just like you had me speak in aphorisms in *An Arsonist's Guide*. Are you going to use aphorisms in *Exley*, too?

BC: No, that was the very last time.

READING GROUP QUESTIONS

AND TOPICS FOR DISCUSSION

1. The novel makes fun of reader's guides found in the backs of books, the kind of reader's guides that ask questions like, "How does this book make you feel about the Human Condition?" (page 85). What, if anything, is objectionable about those sorts of questions, those sorts of guides? What questions might we ask instead of those questions? And what is the "Human Condition," anyway?

2. The novel is interested in New England, in the way Sam sees it, the way other people see it, the way it's been portrayed in books, and the way Sam portrays it in the book(s) he's writing. What are the clichés associated with New England, its people, its landscape, its literature? Is the problem with these clichés that they have no foundation in reality or that they're so familiar that they prevent us from seeing what New England is, or might be, beyond the clichés? Does the novel help you see New England (and the literature about it) in ways that the Writer-in-Residence and his story (page 204) do not?

3. Why doesn't Sam just tell his wife and kids the truth about his past? He says, on this subject, "Because this is what you do when you're a liar: you tell a lie, and then another one, and after a while you hope that the lies end up being less painful than the truth, or at least that is the lie you tell yourself" (pages 40–41). Does this kind of claim make you sympathize? Do you believe that because Sam lies to his family, he doesn't really love them?

4. The novel explores stories, why we write them, why we read them, what we hope to get out of them, and whether we can (or should) get out of them what we want to get out of them. How would you describe the characters' (Lees Ardor, Peter Le Clair, Sam Pulsifer, Elizabeth Pulsifer, the bond analysts) feelings about books? What do they want, or not want, to get from reading and writing? Why do we read books? What do we want to get from our reading? And if we don't get what we want, does that mean the book is a failure?

5. Memoirs are everywhere in *An Arsonist's Guide to Writers' Homes in New England.* Are they as unavoidable in real life as they are in this book? What is the author saying about memoirs, about their place and role in our culture? When he satirizes memoirs, is he also satirizing the people who read them? If so, why? What might novels in general — and this novel in particular — do that memoirs cannot, or should not?

6. On page 249, Thomas Coleman says of Sam's parents, "They're not bad people." Do you feel the same way—not only about Sam's parents, but also about Sam, Thomas, and all the people who want Sam to burn down writers' homes? After all, these characters do, or want to do, awful things. If those things don't make them bad people, then why not? How does the novel help you see these people beyond some of the bad things they do?

7. Sam receives letters from hundreds of people asking him to burn down various writers' homes in New England. And yet (with the exception of Lees Ardor) the anger people express toward the writers' houses seem to have little to do with the writers' books. Why? Why do we care about writers' homes in the first place? Do we visit writers' homes because they intensify the feelings we have about their books or because they give us some insight the books do not?

8. Speaking of Lees Ardor: what's her problem? And why does she repeatedly use one particular bad word? And the bond analysts: why don't they stop worrying about writing their memoirs and go back to analyzing bonds? And Sam's mother: if she has to give up something, why not drinking instead of books? And then Peter Le Clair: why doesn't he just talk already? And then all of the other characters, with their ridiculous troubles, most of which they've brought on themselves and deserve: what's up with them? What is wrong with these people?

9. Sam says that "to be a son is to lie to yourself about your father" (page 176). What does he mean? Is it only true for the father and son in the book, or is it true of all fathers and sons? Is this the Human Condition we wondered about earlier?

10. Sam says, "All men are but slight variations on the very same theme" (page 258). Is that true, or is it just something Sam says to make himself feel better? And if it is true, then why do the "capable" women in the book care so much about these men?

A recipient of a 2008 National Endowment for the Arts fellowship, Brock Clarke has twice been a finalist for the National Magazine Award for fiction. His work has appeared in a number of publications, including the *Believer, OneStory, The Pushcart Prize* anthology, and on NPR's *Selected Shorts.* The author of three other works of fiction, he teaches creative writing at the University of Cincinnati.

Other Algonquin Readers Round Table Novels

Water for Elephants, a novel by Sara Gruen

As a young man, Jacob Jankowski is tossed by fate onto a rickety train, home to the Benzini Brothers Most Spectacular Show on Earth. Amid a world of freaks, grifters, and misfits, Jacob becomes involved with Marlena, the beautiful young equestrian star; her husband, a charismatic but twisted animal trainer; and Rosie, an untrainable elephant who is the great gray hope for this third-rate show. Now in his nineties, Jacob at long last reveals the story of their unlikely yet powerful bonds, ones that nearly shatter them all.

"[An] arresting new novel. . . . With a showman's expert timing, [Gruen] saves a terrific revelation for the final pages, transforming a glimpse of Americana into an enchanting escapist fairy tale." —*The New York Times Book Review*

"Gritty, sensual and charged with dark secrets involving love, murder and a majestic, mute heroine." —*Parade*

AN ALGONQUIN READERS ROUND TABLE EDITION WITH READING GROUP GUIDE AND OTHER SPECIAL FEATURES • FICTION • ISBN-13: 978-1-56512-560-5

Saving the World, a novel by Julia Alvarez

While Alma Huebner is researching a new novel, she discovers the true story of Isabel Sendales y Gómez, who embarked on a courageous sea voyage to rescue the New World from smallpox. The author of *How the García Girls Lost Their Accents* and *In the Time of the Butterflies*, Alvarez captures the worlds of two women living two centuries apart but with surprisingly parallel fates.

"Fresh and unusual, and thought-provokingly sensitive." —*The Boston Globe*

"Engrossing, expertly paced." —*People*

AN ALGONQUIN READERS ROUND TABLE EDITION WITH READING GROUP GUIDE AND OTHER SPECIAL FEATURES • FICTION • ISBN-13: 978-1-56512-558-2

Responsible Men, a novel by Edward Schwarzschild

When a divorced man from a family of mostly upstanding salesmen decides to change his less-than-honorable ways, things do not go exactly as planned. This is the story of three generations of men struggling to be good sons and good fathers in a world of big dreams and bigger temptations.

"Marvelous. . . . It's impossible to avoid falling for Max." —*Entertainment Weekly*

"A compassionately and deftly told story."
—William Kennedy, Pulitzer Prize–winning author of *Ironweed* and *Roscoe*

AN ALGONQUIN READERS ROUND TABLE EDITION WITH READING GROUP GUIDE AND OTHER SPECIAL FEATURES • FICTION • ISBN-13: 978-1-56512-543-8

The Ghost at the Table, a novel by Suzanne Berne

When Frances arranges to host Thanksgiving at her idyllic New England farmhouse, she envisions a happy family reunion, one that will include her sister, Cynthia. But tension mounts between them as each struggles with a different version of the mysterious circumstances surrounding their mother's death twenty-five years earlier.

"Wholly engaging, the perfect spark for launching a rich conversation around your own table." —*The Washington Post Book World*

"A crash course in sibling rivalry." —*O: The Oprah Magazine*

AN ALGONQUIN READERS ROUND TABLE EDITION WITH READING GROUP GUIDE AND OTHER SPECIAL FEATURES • FICTION • ISBN-13: 978-1-56512-579-7

Coal Black Horse, a novel by Robert Olmstead

When Robey Childs's mother has a premonition about her husband, who is away fighting in the Civil War, she sends her only son to find him and bring him home. At fourteen, Robey thinks he's off on a great adventure. But it takes the gift of a powerful and noble coal black horse to show him how to undertake the most important journey in his life.

"A remarkable creation." —*Chicago Tribune*

"Exciting. . . . A grueling adventure." —*The New York Times Book Review*

"Gripping. . . . Echoes the work of Cormac McCarthy." —*The Cleveland Plain Dealer*

AN ALGONQUIN READERS ROUND TABLE EDITION WITH READING GROUP GUIDE AND OTHER SPECIAL FEATURES • FICTION • ISBN-13: 978-1-56512-601-5